A Pretend Proposal

JACKIE BRAUN
ALLY BLAKE
ROBYN GRADY

D1809829

MILLS
BOON
&

First Published in Great Britain 2016
By Mills & Boon, an imprint of HarperCollins*Publishers*
1 London Bridge Street, London, SE1 9GF

A PRETEND PROPOSAL © 2016 Harlequin Books S. A.

The Fiancée Fiasco, *Faking It to Making It* and *The Wedding Must Go On*
were first published in Great Britain by Harlequin (UK) Limited.

The Fiancée Fiasco © 2012 Jackie Braun Fridline
Faking It to Making It © 2013 Ally Blake
The Wedding Must Go On © 2012 Robyn Grady

ISBN: 978-0-263-92080-2

05-0916

Our policy is to use papers that are natural, renewable and recyclable products and made from wood grown in sustainable forests. The logging and manufacturing processes conform to the legal environmental regulations of the country of origin.

Printed and bound in Spain
by CPI, Barcelona

THE FIANCÉE FIASCO

BY
JACKIE BRAUN

Jackie Braun is a three-time RITA® Award finalist, a four-time National Readers' Choice Awards finalist and the winner of the Rising Star Award for traditional romantic fiction. She can be reached through her website at www.jackiebraun.com

Good things come in threes.
Welcome to the world, Tedder triplets:
Mikenzie, Jameson and Savannah.

CHAPTER ONE

THOMAS Waverly needed a bride.

Time was of the essence, so he couldn't afford to be too picky. Even so, as he mentally thumbed through his little black book, he knew that none of the women he'd dated in the past would do. They would read *way* too much into the situation. They would expect it to be real. But the heirloom diamond engagement ring and all talk of a future wedding would be only for his grandmother's benefit.

Nana Jo was dying.

At least she claimed to be.

Her physician assured Thomas that Josephine O'Keefe was in good health for a woman who'd had a hip replacement the previous year, a brush with breast cancer two decades prior and was now closing in on eighty-one. Her heartbeat could be a bit irregular at times, but medication had been prescribed to take care of that and, according to the doctor, it was. Nana Jo, however, was of another opinion.

She was dying.

It was the dreams, she told Thomas. For the past year, each night as she slumbered, she'd dreamed of her late husband and daughter—Thomas's mother. Nana Jo was sure the dreams were an omen of her own impending death, and nothing Thomas said could convince her otherwise. It was downright unnerving.

The previous Christmas, when he'd made the drive to upstate Michigan to spend the holiday with Nana Jo in her small condo in Charlevoix, she'd told him that the only gift she wanted was to see her only grandchild happily settled before she passed on.

The woman had raised him after a car accident claimed his mother, after which his father had fallen into an alcoholic tailspin. Thomas had been eight, and he'd essentially lost both of his parents. Without hesitation, and despite her own grief, Nana Jo had stepped into the huge void. Instead of enjoying her retirement, she'd taken on full-time parenting. And she'd done an incredible job.

How could he deny her wish? How could he indulge it? It was a no-win situation. So, yes, he'd lied.

He wasn't proud of that. Thomas wasn't one to bend the truth, whether in personal dealings or professional ones, but he would do anything to erase the worry he saw in her eyes. Anything short of actual marriage, that was.

So, even though he was between relationships, he'd said, "I've been seeing someone…special. For several months now, in fact."

The distinction had buoyed Nana Jo's spirits considerably. And no wonder. He'd never dated a woman longer than three months. By that point they were usually expecting things, like an exchange of house keys, a toothbrush in his bathroom and maybe even a drawer of their own in the bureau in his bedroom.

By three months, they were getting clingy, needy. The *L* word, he knew, wouldn't be far behind.

Love. No thank you.

He'd seen firsthand what that four-letter word had done to his father. It had been twenty-seven years since Thomas's mother's death, but Hoyt Waverly still couldn't face life as a widower without a fifth of whiskey handy. Over the years, the brands had become cheaper as Hoyt's finances had deteriorated right along with his health. Today, he was a shell of a man, who only turned up occasionally on Thomas's doorstep and then only because he'd run out of money.

Thomas had no desire to end up like his old man. So, he made a point of ending relationships before three months passed, sometimes before then if the woman started to fall for him a little too hard or too fast.

It wasn't that Thomas was God's gift to women. His ego was healthy, but not overblown. He supposed he was good-looking. Enough of his dates had told him so. And he made a decent living. Not exactly a millionaire since he'd poured so much of his own money into starting his business, but he was plenty comfortable thanks to hard work and some sound investments. Still, the real attribute that seemed to clinch it for him with members of the opposite sex wasn't his looks, his bank account or even, to his chagrin, his skill as a lover. It was his manners.

Apparently, while growing up, he'd paid too close attention to Nana Jo's instructions. She'd insisted that he be polite, chivalrous, attentive and always act interested in other people's opinions and pastimes—even when he wasn't. As a result, over the years a number of women had expressed, covertly at least, their desire to become Mrs. Thomas Waverly. But he wasn't in the market for marriage. Not now. Not ever.

For the past several months, of course, Nana Jo had thought otherwise. To her, special implied altar-bound.

He should have corrected her. But she was so happy, so excited. It was all she talked about whenever they spoke on the telephone. He just didn't have the heart. So, he kept his answers brief and changed the subject at the earliest opportunity. Still, she was so certain that he was heading toward "I do" with the fictional woman he'd named Beth that, finally, he'd just agreed with her.

He wasn't sure where the name had come from. Only that it seemed a suitable moniker for the sensible and sweet woman his grandmother believed had snagged his heart.

His lie had succeeded in easing Nana Jo's mind; now his was in turmoil. She was insisting on meeting his fiancée, and she wouldn't take no for an answer any longer. If Thomas didn't bring the young woman to Nana Jo's home in Charlevoix for the upcoming Fourth of July weekend, she threatened to get in her car and make the long trip downstate to meet his Beth.

He didn't like the idea of his grandmother tooling around town in her vintage Cadillac DeVille, much less getting on an expressway where other vehicles would be whizzing by and no doubt honking their horns in irritation since she always drove at least ten miles per hour below the posted speed limit. But if he told her the truth, she would only go back to insisting that she had one foot in the grave. He couldn't stand the thought of that.

The only solution, as far as he could see, was to produce a fiancée now, and then later, after a reasonable length of time had passed, have that fiancée call things off. If he seemed heartbroken, perhaps Nana Jo would stop pushing so hard, forget about the "dreams" and go back to living her life to the fullest.

A tall order, to be sure. He sighed heavily and closed his eyes.

A tap sounded at his door. "Excuse me, Thomas."

He opened his eyes to find his secretary standing there with a look of concern pinching her features. Annette was two decades older than Thomas and, like his grandmother, she worried about him. She, too, thought he should be married or at least in a serious relationship at this point in his life. As his employee, however, Annette was much less vocal on the subject, thank goodness.

"Is everything all right?" she asked now.

"Headache," he murmured. It wasn't a complete lie. It was Monday and he had until Thursday to figure a way out of this mess. His temples had begun to throb. He pushed back his chair from his desk and started to rise. "I think I'll knock off a little early."

"Oh." Annette's lips pursed.

"Problem?"

"No. Not really. It's just that the head of Literacy Liaisons is here to see you."

"Right now?"

She nodded.

Reaching for his calendar, he said, "I don't recall an appointment being scheduled."

"That's because she doesn't have one. She dropped in unannounced hoping for a few minutes of your time." Annette shook her head. "It's all right. I'll tell her that she needs to make an appointment. Maybe one day next week?"

Thomas held up a hand. "No. That won't be necessary. I'll see her now. Might as well get this over with." He rubbed one temple. "I assume she's after a donation."

His secretary smiled. "I'm sure you're right."

Three things struck Thomas immediately when the young woman entered his office. First, how small she was, despite wearing a pair of three-inch-high pumps that were the same color as her conservative gray pantsuit. Even in them, he doubted she topped out at five-five.

Second, her mouth. It was wide with full lips that were curving into a smile that lit up a pair of surprisingly dark eyes for one so fair. Add in a slightly upturned, freckle-dusted nose and bobbed blond hair that fell even with a blunt chin, and the adjective *cute* was a far better description for her than beautiful.

Third—and perhaps this was only because he was feeling so desperate—she wasn't wearing a wedding ring. In fact, other than a pair of simple pearl earrings, she wasn't wearing any jewelry at all.

He eyed her speculatively, both ashamed and intrigued by the direction of his thoughts. What if…? Nah.

"Good afternoon, Mr. Waverly. I'm Elizabeth Morris." She extended her right hand. "Thank you for taking the time to see me on such short notice."

He shook her hand. Like the rest of her, it was small. And soft. Her grip, however, was not. It was firm and all business. He liked that about her. There was nothing worse than a limp handshake, even coming from a petite woman who barely looked old enough to order a drink.

"Have a seat," he said.

"I'm pretty sure you've guessed I've come here today to ask for money." Those full lips bowed again, making him appreciate her forthrightness all the more.

The headache he'd been nursing began to disappear. He steepled his fingers in front of him and, in his most businesslike tone, said, "Waverly Enterprises is always interested in helping worthy causes in our community. Why don't you tell me a little bit about yours?"

She exhaled discreetly, as if she hadn't been sure Thomas wouldn't show her the door.

"Literacy Liaisons specializes in helping adults in our community learn to read."

"Is illiteracy really an issue in Ann Arbor?"

She tilted her head to one side. "That surprises you?"

"A little." The city was home to the University of Michigan and one of the best medical facilities in North America.

"Despite the fact that we live in a college town with a lot of highly educated residents, there are people here and in the surrounding communities who are either illiterate or functionally illiterate. That means they may be able to read well enough to get by during, say, a trip to the grocery store, but they cannot read well enough to hold a decent job. Many of them wind up poor, sometimes even homeless."

She inched forward on her chair, warming to her subject. Her face lit with the kind of passion that went hand-in-hand with conviction.

"They aren't intellectually challenged, although many of them do have undiagnosed learning disabilities such as dyslexia. As children, they fell through the cracks in our educational system and now, as adults, they continue to fall through the cracks. Our goal is to change that."

Finished, she shifted back in her seat. Her demeanor remained confident; her expression, determined. The mouse who roared, Thomas thought, more impressed than amused by the description.

"But it takes money," he said.

"It does, even though we rely heavily on volunteers

for tutoring, we have to supply materials and, some-times, day care or even transportation to our offices if the client is indigent. We deal specifically with lower-income people who would not be able to afford such services otherwise."

Intrigued now by the cause as much as by the woman, he asked, "How long has Literacy Liaisons been in busi-ness?"

"Nearly ten years."

"And how long have you worked there?"

"I founded it, Mr. Waverly."

Before he could stop himself, he blurted out, "How old are you?" He apologized immediately. "I'm sorry. It's just that…"

"I look young. I know." She tugged at the lapels of her jacket and added, "My power suit notwithstanding."

Her self-deprecating sense of humor caught him off guard. He'd been sure he'd insulted her with his care-less remark. Not sure what else to say—a rarity for him when it came to conversing with a member of the op-posite sex—Thomas apologized a second time.

She accepted it with a gracious nod and went on. "I got the idea for Literacy Liaisons while I was in college studying to become a teacher."

"U of M?" he asked. It was his alma mater, which gave them something in common.

But she was shaking her head. "Sorry. I hope it won't have a bearing on your interest in Literacy Liaisons, but I'm a Spartan."

Michigan State? The rivalry between the two Big Ten schools was legendary. He lifted one shoulder. "Good school."

"Good comeback." She laughed. "I take it you're a Wolverine."

"I bleed maize and blue," he admitted, referring to the university's colors.

"Good school," she said, mimicking his earlier reply. They both laughed before she went on. "Long story short, instead of going into a classroom to teach after I earned my certification, I decided to open the center."

Gutsy and not exactly the career path most recent college graduates would have chosen.

"Why?" he asked.

She moistened her lips. "I…saw a need."

There was more to it than that, Thomas thought as he studied her expression. He saw determination there and something else. Sadness?

She was saying, "Our primary funding source has been federal grants and some state Department of Health and Human Services contracts, but money is tight everywhere right now. With tax revenues shrinking at every level of government, cuts have been made. Unfortunately, as vital as having a literate population is to economic prosperity, our funding has been reduced significantly during the past two fiscal years alone."

"So, you're seeking donations from the business community."

"Actually, I'm doing more than that. I want to create an endowment fund to ensure the center's viability both in good economic times and bad. It's not easy to go begging for money, no matter how worthy the cause. I would prefer not to have to do it on an annual basis."

Again, she smiled.

"Then an endowment makes sense."

The more she said, the more impressed he was with her resolve. He couldn't think of another woman in his acquaintance who would have started up a nonprofit right out of college and, a decade later, be pounding the pavement to ensure it remained viable.

Of course, the women he dated tended to be far more egocentric than philanthropic. A good number of them didn't hold a regular job thanks to access to a trust fund or their daddy's continuing indulgence. Physically, they were Elizabeth Morris's polar opposite as well. None had been under five-eight. Indeed, a couple had stood eye-level with him in their bare feet. He favored model types, tall and leggy. Arm candy was what Nana Jo called them. It was an apt description. Every last one of them had been flawlessly beautiful and ultrafashionable. None would be caught dead in Elizabeth Morris's self-described power suit or her nondescript pumps. Which made her somehow all the more perfect.

What if...?

No matter how many times he tried to quell that inappropriate question, it just kept begging to be answered.

She cleared her throat, and he realized he'd been staring. So much for his renowned manners. This made twice in their very short acquaintance that he'd been not only impolite, but also openly rude. Before he could apologize, however, she was rising to her feet.

"I can see that I've taken up enough of your time. I'll just leave you with some additional information about our organization as well as our fundraising campaign. My contact information is in the packet should you have any questions."

There was no hint of a smile on her face as she pulled a folder from her satchel and laid it on his desk. She didn't look angry, but rather disheartened and maybe even a little bit weary. Who could blame her? Thomas imagined she'd probably run into a lot of closed doors and closed wallets during her quest.

"Please. Have a seat. I'll take a look right now," he said, forestalling her departure.

Inside the folder, he wasn't surprised to find several pages of carefully ordered facts about Literacy Liaisons's mission, each one bulleted for easy reading. He'd already determined that she was meticulous and organized. He glanced through the numbers regarding the endowment fund. She was nearly two-thirds of the way to her goal.

Prefacing this, he said, "I see you've been very busy."

"I've been at it for nearly nine months. Unfortunately, it's been slow going lately." She shrugged then and said, "The economy."

Ah, yes. Two words that said it all these days. The economy had wreaked havoc on Waverly Enterprises's bottom line, too, causing Thomas and his department managers to scour the company's budget for savings. The office Christmas party had been scaled back to a luncheon, wages had been frozen and some low-level positions were going unfilled.

Still, he'd tried not to cut back too much on charitable contributions—not because his accountants were quick to remind him that such donations were a tax deduction, but because he genuinely believed in being socially responsible.

Teaching people to read was not just commendable, it was essential. As a businessman, he understood that perfectly. Hers was just the sort of endeavor he preferred to support, especially if the bulk of his donation would go to actual programs rather than overhead, which the paperwork in front of him assured that it would.

The subtle scent of apple blossoms floated his way, and that crazy idea he'd been entertaining since she'd first walked through his door became all the more pronounced.

What if...?

The question no longer seemed so outlandish. Nor did asking it seem totally self-serving. After all, a sizable donation would put her endowment campaign over the top and ensure the future viability of Literacy Liaisons. They could help each other out.

Besides, Elizabeth Morris seemed to be a practical woman, the sort who would see his proposal for what it was: a mutually beneficial business arrangement. *Quid pro quo.*

"So, do you have any questions?" she asked politely. Her smile was back in place and just this side of hopeful.

Did he ever, and it was a doozy, but the one Thomas went with was: "Does anyone ever call you Beth?"

CHAPTER TWO

ELIZABETH felt her mouth fall open. Of all the questions she'd anticipated Thomas Waverly asking, that one wasn't among them. Inquiries about her business or her background? Certainly. Her nickname? Not so much. But since it would be rude to question his questioning—almost as rude as calling on him at his office without an actual appointment—she did her best to wipe away her surprise and answered him honestly.

"No one's ever called me Beth."

Lizzie sometimes, since that had been her actual name. She'd changed it legally once she reached adulthood. She liked the formality of Elizabeth, the utter timelessness of it, not to mention the respect that it seemed to engender. Queens and Hollywood legends were named Elizabeth. Lizzie? Put the word *tin* before it and it referred to a jalopy.

He inhaled deeply, as if preparing to make an earth-shaking announcement. But all he said was, "You look like a Beth."

"Perhaps you have me confused with someone else," she suggested, unsure what else to say.

The conversation had taken an odd and definitely awkward turn, and, even though she hardly could claim to be an expert on men, the speculation brewing in this particular man's gaze was unnerving. Okay, it also was a bit flattering. Men as gorgeous and accomplished as Thomas Waverly rarely gave Elizabeth the time of day—whether or not she'd made an appointment. They certainly didn't look at her like he was looking at her—as if he were interested in something more personal than making a charitable donation.

"Perhaps," he said with a nod before glancing away.

It sounded as if he muttered the word *crazy* half under his breath. If so, the description fit the situation, she decided. More likely, though, she was just imagining things or blowing them out of proportion. It was best to leave before she said something foolish, especially since he seemed interested in her cause.

Elizabeth started to rise. "I'd better be going. Thank you again for your time." She nibbled her bottom lip before adding, "I hope we will be able to count Waverly Enterprises among our contributors."

He pulled her business card from the folder she'd given him and held it up. "I'll be in touch with you. I promise."

"Terrific." She should have been relieved, happy. Why, Elizabeth wondered, did she feel apprehensive? No, what she was feeling wasn't apprehension, but anticipation, an almost foreign sensation where a man was concerned. But then, Thomas Waverly wasn't a man; he was a potential donor with pockets deep enough to push her cause much closer to its goal.

Just as she made that determination, he rose from his seat—a little more than six feet worth of perfectly formed and proportioned male. The custom cut of his suit showcased a pair of broad shoulders and a body made up of lean muscle rather than the kind of soft bulk found on a lot of the desk-bound CEOs she'd called on.

Not a man? Those words, unuttered though they'd been, taunted her. Oh, he was a man, all right. And every last inch of him was steeped in testosterone.

The satchel slipped from Elizabeth's hand and landed on the carpeted floor with a thud. Her fingers had gone as slack as her mouth. She snapped her lips closed as he came around his desk. He was bending to retrieve her case even before she managed to move. And here she'd been hoping to make her exit before she could make herself look foolish.

"This thing is pretty heavy." His smile, thank goodness, wasn't awash in amusement.

"Thank you."

Their fingers brushed in the handoff, and she experienced an unprecedented urge to sigh. Oh, it was definitely time to go. During the past month, she had managed to wrest precious little in the way of donations from the local business community, not sizable ones at any rate. Money continued to trickle in—a little here, a little there—but the well of largesse appeared to have run dry. Literacy Liaisons's endowment fund campaign not only needed Waverly Enterprises's support, but it was also desperate for it.

So, without further hesitation, Elizabeth beat a retreat, mentally kicking herself all the way home.

Howie greeted her at the front door of her small bungalow with an enthusiastic kiss after nearly knocking her off her feet. Whether she was gone an hour or all day, her golden retriever-slash-Labrador-slash-a-few-other-kinds-of-canine was always happy to see her.

Ecstatic, in fact. If only every door she opened held such adoration on the other side, her life and her job would be just that much more enjoyable.

"I missed you, too, boy."

She removed his big paws from her chest and stooped to pick up the scattering of envelopes that had been pushed through the door's mail slot.

Bill, bill, bill, junk, junk and a reminder that one of her magazine subscriptions was about to run out. The internet made communicating with friends, loved ones and business associates quick and easy, but Elizabeth missed receiving actual letters, even if the only person she really hoped to hear from was the one person who would never write. A person who couldn't write. Or read.

Her brother. She hadn't seen him in more than a decade, though he occasionally called their parents. For all intents and purposes, though, Ross had disappeared.

Howie's whining pulled her from the past, reminding her that he needed to go outside and do his business.

When she opened the door, the dog was out in a flash, a bullet of peaches-and-cream-colored fur that pulled up short just before the sidewalk. Elizabeth had installed an electronic fence to keep him within the boundaries of the yard. As she watched him take off after a squirrel in what had become a ritual game of chase, her cell phone rang.

She retrieved it from her satchel. "Hello?"

"Miss Morris?" The deep voice was familiar, but she couldn't quite place it.

"Yes."

"It's Thomas Waverly."

This was a surprise, so much so that the cell phone nearly fell to the floor, much as her bag had in his office. She bobbled it before managing to return it to her ear. The man had a way of making her uncharacteristically clumsy.

"Are you there?" he was asking.

"Yes, sorry. I just wasn't expecting to hear from you." She gave her forehead a slap. "So soon that is."

Cool, collected and confident—that was what she needed to be. Unfortunately, she sounded flustered and slightly breathless—reactions that someone as handsome as Thomas Waverly probably experienced on a regular basis when it came to women.

He was saying, "I was wondering if we could meet to discuss…a donation."

Had she imagined that slight hesitation? Well, no matter. She would clear her calendar if need be to accommodate someone interested in helping her cause. "Certainly. Just name a time and I'll be there."

"I was thinking tonight. Over dinner."

"Dinner. Tonight," she repeated in surprise, and wanted to smack her forehead again.

Put together like that, it sounded as if she thought he was asking her out on a date, which, of course, was ridiculous. Thomas Waverly was a busy man. His time was at a premium. More likely he preferred to get this out of the way so that he didn't have to waste office hours on what, for him at least, amounted to an inconsequential matter. That explanation made sense until a little voice whispered in her head that he needn't be bothered at all. A man of his stature had plenty of subordinates to take care of such things, including the efficient older woman who'd so kindly asked him to see Elizabeth in the first place earlier that day.

As if he could read her mind, Thomas said, "I know it's a little unorthodox, meeting over dinner, but I have something I'd like to discuss with you. An opportunity that is…" He paused again, just long enough to have Elizabeth holding her breath. "Well, in itself, rather unorthodox."

"Oh?" Color her intrigued. Before she could respond further, however, her dog sent up a booming howl of protest as the squirrel he'd been chasing perched on the lowest branch of the front yard's big oak and chattered noisily down at him.

"Howie!" she yelled.

Even though she'd moved the phone away from her mouth, she heard Thomas say, "I apologize. You have company. I should have realized."

Elizabeth nearly laughed out loud at the statement. Did he think she was entertaining a man? More like man's best friend. Sadly, no males of the two-legged variety had darkened her door in several months.

"Not how you mean," she told him, even though she found her dog to be excellent company. She'd rescued Howie from the local pound nearly two years earlier. He'd been on death row, though the pound didn't actually call it that. Still, his fate had been determined, his date with a needle full of sleepy juice scheduled. His crime? Few people wanted a nearly three-year-old, seventy-five-pound pooch who could be every bit as stubborn as he was affectionate. "Howie's my dog. He's chasing a squirrel."

"A futile endeavor, I take it." There was a smile in Thomas's voice.

A fellow dog person? That made him even more appealing in her book.

"Very, which is why he's barking loud enough to wake the dead." She held the phone away from her and covered the mouthpiece long enough to holler the dog's name a second time.

Mrs. Hildabrand, her neighbor from across the street, would be on her front porch any minute to warn Elizabeth that the police would be on the way if

Howie didn't quiet down. The elderly woman already had called the authorities twice in the past month with noise complaints. The officers the department sent out had been kind and even understanding. But Elizabeth couldn't afford to press her luck. Thankfully, this time Howie obeyed her command to cease and desist. He trotted to the porch and then through the door she'd opened for him, tail held high and wagging madly, probably for the squirrel's benefit.

"So, about tonight, do you have any plans?" Thomas asked.

"No. Not a thing." Because the stark reply made her sound, well, pathetic, she amended quickly, "What I mean is, nothing that can't be rescheduled."

Or recorded on her DVR. Yes, her social life was that pathetic.

"Terrific."

The relief she heard in his voice left her as curious as what his "unorthodox proposal" might be. After all, Thomas Waverly struck her as the sort of man who was always in control and only asked questions whose answers he already knew. Yet, he was acting very much like he needed her rather than the other way around.

They made arrangements to meet at an Italian restaurant where the highly rated menu came with equally high prices. Elizabeth had eaten at Antonio's exactly once, and then, since she'd gone with a girlfriend, she'd ordered only a bowl of soup. Everything else was beyond her budget, especially once a glass of wine had been factored in.

After hanging up, she paced her living room, absently stopping to pick up the magazines that Howie had knocked off the coffee table with his tail. The dog paced alongside her, his tongue lolling out from his openmouthed grin.

"I've got an hour before we meet."

Howie panted, as much from his recent exercise as from the heat. The house had no air-conditioning and wouldn't for the foreseeable future. She didn't have the extra funds in her household budget for that kind of luxury. Everything she had, she poured into her work.

"An hour," she repeated. "That's not a lot of time. I need to make the most of it." She let out a laugh that was brittle with nerves. For her benefit as much as the dog's, she added, "I've worked my way through the alphabet when it comes to donors. Obviously, at *W*, I'm getting a little desperate."

Howie stared at her, as if he suspected there was more to those nerves than desperation on behalf of the nonprofit she'd started from scratch a decade before.

"I need to do something to make Thomas Waverly sit up and take notice."

When Elizabeth sat down in front of her laptop, the dog laid his head on her knee. She planned to print out a batch of success stories from Literacy Liaisons's client list. The testimonials were proof of how life-changing learning to read could be. But as she perched on a chair in front of the computer screen, she fiddled with the ends of her hair and became distracted. She was due for a trim.

"Maybe the next time I see my stylist I'll ask about a perm. What do you think, Howie?"

The dog lifted his head from her leg. She swore he looked confused, and no wonder. Why was she thinking about this now?

"Never mind."

Howie continued to stare at her.

"Look, I know this isn't a date." She patted his broad head. Again, for his benefit as well as her own, she said, "But it never hurts to look one's best. Dress for success and all that."

With that in mind, she snatched up the phone and dialed her best friend's number, sighing with relief when Melissa Sutton picked up just before the call would have gone to voice mail. It was hard to catch her very social friend, even on her cell.

The two women had been tight since college, even though they seemed to have little in common with the exception of their commitment to battling illiteracy, which was why after a stint as a packaging engineer, Melissa had showed up at Literacy Liaisons, willing to take a significant cut in pay for rewards of another kind.

The similarities ended there. Where Elizabeth was reserved and, admittedly, a bit of a wallflower, her friend, who was nearly as petite as Elizabeth, managed to stand out. It wasn't only her infectious laughter and bawdy sense of humor that caught men's attention. Mel was a bona fide head-turner. On more than one occasion, Elizabeth had witnessed her friend's effect on men. It was almost comical the way they fawned over her and catered to her every whim. If only that kind of charisma could be bottled up and sold.

"I have an emergency," she said in a rush.

"My God, Elizabeth, what's wrong?"

"I need some of your clothes."

"My clothes?"

"I have an important meeting in roughly an hour and nothing suitable to wear."

"You're having a fashion emergency?" Mel's laughter boomed. "I think I need to sit down."

"It's not funny."

"Sorry." Her friend's tone turned serious. "It's just I've never had you call to borrow clothes for a date let alone for work."

"This is important."

"So you've already said. Work shouldn't be more important than your love life. That's just sad, honey. Sad." Elizabeth thought she heard a *tsking* sound before Mel went on. "You need to get out more, kick up your heels. And the heels I'm referring to are not those dowdy pair of black pumps that would suit my great-aunt Geraldine."

Elizabeth pinched her eyes closed. "Can we have this conversation another time, please?"

"Fine. Another time. And don't think I won't hold you to it," Mel warned, then added, "So, am I coming to your place or are you coming to mine?"

They decided on Mel's since her two-story town house was closer to the restaurant Thomas had selected, and it wouldn't require her friend to pack up an assortment of outfits.

Once there, Mel wasn't satisfied with dressing Elizabeth in a ruffled shift that was surprisingly flattering on her less curvaceous form, and pairing the soft pink number with strappy silver sandals. She insisted on restyling her hair and applying additional makeup, too.

The effect was an improvement, and she hardly appeared overmade, but it still presented Elizabeth with a dilemma.

Studying her reflection in Mel's vanity mirror, she said, "He's going to think I'm interested in him."

"He who?" Mel asked, leaning over to dab a little more coral-colored gloss on Elizabeth's bottom lip.

"Thomas Waverly."

Her friend drew back, eyes wide with surprise. "Thomas Waverly? *GQ*-cover-worthy Thomas Waverly? That's who you're having dinner with?"

"Do you know him?" Her stomach pitched. Had Mel dated him? That question was followed rapidly by: Why would that matter?

"I know *of* him," Mel clarified. "I saw him at a celebrity golf outing that I played with Dominic last summer."

Dominic, right. Mel's beau of the month several months ago. A corporate highflyer of some sort. Yet for all the money he'd lavished on Mel, he'd been downright stingy when it came to contributing to Literacy Liaisons.

"So, what's Thomas like?"

"We didn't actually meet, but I saw him tee off on one of the par threes. Very nice swing. Fluid and strong. He nearly wound up with a hole in one. He settled for a birdie thanks to one very smooth putting stroke." Mel made a purring sound that kick-started Elizabeth's barely settled nerves.

"Do you ever *not* think of sex?"

Mel propped one hip on the edge of the bathroom counter. "I only think of it so often to take up the slack for you. You need to think of it more."

"I don't have the time." A pitiful excuse, and, of course, Mel called her on it.

"Yes, it would be a real shame to miss your evening line-up of cable television shows once in a while."

"You like to watch *White Collar*, too."

"I like to watch the hunky guy who plays the ex-con," Mel clarified while examining her manicure. "But I'm not faithful to him. When I have a better offer, I go out."

Elizabeth scowled. "I haven't had any better offers." Indeed, she hadn't had any offers in months.

"Because you make sure every guy around thinks you're only interested in your work," her friend said.

"It's important."

"That goes without saying, Elizabeth. And I understand why it's so important to you. But—"

She put a hand out, pushing away the pain even as she redirected the conversation. "Can we get back to the crisis at hand, please?"

Mel sighed heavily. "Fine, but just so you know, I don't see Thomas Waverly as a crisis. In fact, I find myself a little jealous of you. He's one very prime specimen."

"I hadn't noticed." Elizabeth managed a nonchalant tone.

Mel wasn't fooled. In fact, she nearly doubled over with laughter. Her mirth echoed off the bathroom tiles.

"Oh, please. You'd have to be dead not to notice, and even then I have a feeling that man could raise a woman's pulse rate. Are you really going to sit there and tell me you don't find him hot?"

"He's attractive," Elizabeth allowed.

Mel merely raised her brows at the bland assessment.

"Okay. He's gorgeous. Drop-dead so. But we're not going out on a date, Mel." Elizabeth glanced at her reflection again. She liked what she saw—the softer hairstyle, the somewhat smoky eyes, the flirty dress. But that was the problem. She looked like a woman who was ready for an evening out. "I don't want him to think that I think it's a date."

Mel pursed her lips. Unlike Elizabeth's, they were an inviting pink color without any added gloss. "Why would that be a problem?"

"This is business. I need his donation."

"I understand that, but I don't think that's the real answer."

Elizabeth sighed. "You know me too well."

"And don't forget it. So, answer the question." She crossed her arms in challenge.

"Come on. Look at me, Mel."

"I am looking. I see a beautiful woman, not to mention one who is exceedingly smart and interesting."

Elizabeth rolled her eyes. "Well, I am wearing your clothes."

"I'm not just talking about what you've got on or the way your hair is styled, though that little finger-fluffing trick is flattering and a little extra gloss does wonders for what is already a great set of lips. But clothes, a different hairdo and a little more makeup don't make you smart and interesting. That's all you, honey." She waited a beat before adding, "That dress does make you sexy, though."

Mel's perfectly arched brows bobbed twice for emphasis.

Her friend's words should have done wonders for Elizabeth's ego, but Elizabeth had never had much confidence in her looks. She chalked that up to the fact that from an early age her post-hippie parents had discouraged any sort of "enhancement" or improvement to one's appearance. Both her folks sported long hair. Her mother wore hers in an unflattering ponytail. Her father's was twisted into dreadlocks that streamed halfway to his waist. Skeet Morris didn't believe in shaving. Neither did Elizabeth's mother, Delphine. *Anywhere*. To this day her parents were mortified that Elizabeth wore her hair short and styled, dressed in conservative garb and had plucked the unibrow she'd sported throughout high school into two distinct arches.

"You're my friend," she reminded Mel.

"That doesn't mean I can't be objective. Your problem, Elizabeth, is that you've spent your entire life blending into the background, so it makes you uncomfortable when you stand out."

"That's not true." Not completely anyway. She was perfectly happy to stand out when it came to her job.

Mel crossed her arms over her chest again. "It's a fact."

"Okay, we're getting off track here. I'm not after the man. I'm after his money." When her friend's lips twitched, she added, "You know what I mean. This is about a donation to Literacy Liaisons, one that very well could be large enough that you and I can sit back and relax for a while…figuratively speaking."

But Mel wasn't buying it. "I've never understood the big deal with mixing business with pleasure. As long as both parties go into it with their eyes wide open, why not? You're both adults."

Nerves fluttered in Elizabeth's belly. "Maybe I should send you to meet with him. You're a lot better at this sort of thing than I am."

Mel manufactured an insulted expression and said, "Excuse me?"

"You know what I mean. Men swarm to you. Thomas Waverly would be putty in your hands. In fact, maybe I should have been sending you to call on potential donors all along. We'd already have our endowment."

"Oh, no. No thanks." Mel was shaking her head. "I'm good at flirting, honey, not finalizing deals. Besides, I prefer to remain behind the scenes."

"So you always say." Elizabeth reached for a tissue

and blotted off a little of the coral-colored gloss. "I just don't want to give Mr. Waverly the impression that I would be willing to sleep with him in order to ensure that he cuts the agency a sizable check."

Mel winked. "Does that mean you'd be willing to sleep with him for reasons more primal?"

"God, Mel!" Elizabeth's nerves kicked up again.

"Just askin'." Grinning, her friend pointed to her wristwatch. "You'd better get going, Cinderella. Your ball is about to begin."

CHAPTER THREE

THOMAS did a double take when Elizabeth walked through the door of Antonio's. He'd arrived at the restaurant a few minutes early, assuming that he would have plenty of time to gather his thoughts and plot out his pitch. All of the women he knew were notorious for being late, in part because they preferred to make grand entrances. He should have known Elizabeth would be different. That was, after all, part of her appeal for the role he was about to ask her to play.

Even arriving early, she managed to make an entrance. No mouths dropped opened in awe, and conversations continued as before. But something inside of Thomas shifted before going oddly still. He couldn't take his eyes off of her.

Who knew cute also could be so sexy?

Since their meeting a few hours earlier, she'd changed her clothes. No real surprise, since he had as well, trading in his business attire for a more casual pair of pants and a button-down shirt. He'd left off his tie, too, but he found himself tugging at his collar anyway.

Her transformation was far more dramatic. He wouldn't have expected the woman he'd met in the severely cut suit and serviceable pumps to own such a fashionable outfit and shoes. The lines of the dress and the heels gave her the illusion of greater height. As small as she was, she had a pair of killer legs.

Because he felt himself beginning to ogle them, he returned his gaze to her face. That wasn't the safer bet, he realized immediately. She'd done something different with her hair. It was no longer quite so straight and tidy. *Tousled* was the word that came to mind. He wondered if it would feel as soft as it appeared. As for that mobile mouth of hers, it was now twice as inviting thanks to a slick coat of tinted gloss. How would it taste?

Uh-oh.

He scrambled to put the brakes on the hormones that threatened to rev into hyperdrive. Given what he was about to propose, quite literally, he couldn't afford to let anything more than business transpire between them. He couldn't have her thinking he wanted more than what he was offering: a mutually beneficial business arrangement.

He stood when she reached the table. It was second nature, thanks to his grandmother, as was pulling out Elizabeth's chair. In fact, Thomas beat the maitre d' to it. The man smiled uncomfortably before withdrawing.

"Sorry I'm late," she said, as she settled in her seat.

Thomas glanced at his watch, even though it wasn't necessary. "Actually, you're early."

"But not as early as you are."

He shrugged and sat down. "It's a habit of mine."

A bad one according to the last four women he'd dated, those grand entrances and all. They didn't appreciate answering the doorbell before they were ready to wow him with what waited on the other side.

"A good one," Elizabeth said, as if reading his mind. "There's nothing worse than keeping people waiting, at least in my book."

Thomas agreed wholeheartedly, but that didn't change his plan to keep her waiting, at least until the entrée course, before he started his pitch. By that point, he was hoping she wouldn't stand up and walk out on him, though he wasn't ruling out the possibility.

He bided his time, relying on small talk as their drinks arrived. She went with a glass of plain water garnished with a wedge of lemon. Although he wanted to brace himself with a scotch, neat, he settled for red wine, which he intended to sip slowly. He needed to keep a clear head—especially since the woman seated opposite him was having a definite, if odd, effect on his equilibrium. Nerves, he told himself. After all, he had a lot riding on the outcome of the evening. But then, so did she.

By the time the waiter brought their salads and a basket of warm rolls, they had thoroughly dissected the extended weather forecast for the upcoming holiday weekend. It was amazing how much people could talk without really saying anything. Recalling the passion and conviction with which Elizabeth had described her agency's mission to him earlier, he had a feeling she would be an engaging conversationalist if they ever strayed from the standard polite topics. Because he wanted to, he didn't. Stay with the script. This wasn't a date.

Finally, their dinners arrived and the moment of truth was at hand. She'd just taken the first bite of her grilled salmon when he put down his fork and cleared his throat. She glanced over in question. Now or never, he decided.

"I mentioned on the phone that I had an unusual proposal for you."

She nodded, swallowed. "*Unorthodox* is how I believe you phrased it."

"Yes. It is. Very." He swallowed as well, even though he had not yet touched his steak or the sautéed baby portabella mushrooms in wine sauce that smothered it. "I want to assure you, this isn't something I make a habit of."

Thomas had hoped to sound reassuring, but her expression made it clear he was doing a lousy job of it. She appeared a little alarmed, and no wonder given the way he was acting. Better just to get right to it, he decided, except that he didn't. Rather, he went on in uncharacteristic bumbling fashion.

"It's just that I find myself in a tight spot. I told someone—someone very dear to me—that I am…that is, that I have been seeing…" He laughed uncomfortably. "This is awkward."

Across from him, Elizabeth smiled encouragingly, though he thought he saw her glance toward the exit.

"The long and the short of it is I need…I need a…" His gaze focused in on her mouth and he swore his own started to water. "I need a woman."

Elizabeth wasn't sure whether to be flattered that he'd singled her out or concerned for her safety given his intense stare. One thing she knew for certain, she was curious. Why on earth did he need a woman? Surely female companionship was not in short supply for a man as successful and handsome as he was. There had to be a rational explanation for what he'd just said.

So, in her most polished business tone, she inquired politely, "Exactly what do you need a woman for, Mr. Waverly?"

"To act as my fiancée."

He was exhaling in a gust, even as Elizabeth's breathing stopped. She hadn't seen this coming.

"Are you asking…? You want me to…? You want to get married?" Her voice rose on the last word. Some of the restaurant's other patrons glanced their way.

"No. Actually, I just need someone to pose as my fiancée for a while." He smiled weakly. "So, um, under the circumstances, I think you should call me Thomas."

She rubbed her right temple in lieu of a response. She'd fallen into an alternative universe. That was the only explanation that made sense. She was wearing Mel's dress and had somehow become, well, Mel. Except that in the big mirror on the wall behind Thomas, she could see her reflection. The dress was Mel's, but Elizabeth was definitely the woman wearing it. And looking gobsmacked. She snapped her mouth closed.

"I know. Crazy, right?" Thomas said on an uncomfortable laugh.

"Certifiable," she agreed.

Both of them were, because, Elizabeth now knew for sure that she was feeling flattered. Thomas Waverly, successful businessman and five-alarm hottie, wanted *her* to act as his fiancée? But…

"Why?" she managed to ask at last.

His expression sobered. "Before we get to that, I want to make it clear that I'm not expecting you to do me a favor. I was thinking more like, we could, uh, do each other a favor. You help me out by posing as my intended, and I personally match the donation I've already decided to make to Literacy Liaisons on Waverly Enterprises's behalf. Between those two contributions, your endowment will be realized."

Because her mouth threatened to fall open again, she took a sip of her water. This was more than she'd hoped for. It was everything she wanted, being handed to her on a silver platter. A silver platter held by one of the most eligible bachelors in the city. She checked the mirror a second time, giving that alternative universe theory another go. The same baffled-looking blonde as before gaped back at her. Again, Elizabeth asked, "Why?"

"Right." He reached for his wine and took a sip. Setting the glass back on the table, he said, "Here's the thing. I told my grandmother that I was involved in a serious relationship with a woman."

"Serious as in headed toward the altar."

"Right. The problem is I'm not, but she's expecting to meet, um, my significant other..." He coughed. Choked? Before spitting out, "This weekend."

The long holiday weekend was mere days away, and Elizabeth already had made plans to spend part of it with her parents at their annual soy burger-and-tofu barbecue, but that wasn't what bothered her. Flattery only went so far. As did business dealings.

Her tone took on an edge that she rarely used and had never allowed to seep into her professional life when she said, "You lied to your grandmother?"

Hot or not, the man dropped several points in her estimation. Make that numerous points, and still counting. She didn't care how handsome he was or how successful. Nor did it matter how desperate she was for his dual donation—and, *God*, she was desperate for that donation. But a man who would lie to a frail, helpless little old lady—and that was the image that came to Elizabeth's mind—was a jerk. End of story. She retrieved the napkin from her lap and set it on the table, fully intending to leave.

Thomas rose part way from his chair as she stood. "Please. Stay and hear me out."

"You lied to your grandmother," she repeated flatly.

"Yes. I did. It sounds horrible, I know." He dropped back into his seat.

"That's one word for it," Elizabeth replied crisply, unwilling to let him off the hook, no matter how appealing he looked wriggling from it. Still, he did look remorseful. Slowly, she returned to her seat and spread the napkin back over her lap. What would it hurt to hear him out?

"Let me give you a little background before you form a solid opinion of the situation." Thomas held out his hands in appeal. "She claimed to be dying and, well, seeing me happily settled is a priority for her. I was hoping to take her mind off her aches and pains."

"Your grandmother is dying?"

"Her doctor says no, but…" His shoulders lifted in a shrug. "She's sure she is. And she's not easily dissuaded once her mind is made up. I hate seeing her so troubled, especially when there's no need to be. I'm fine. Perfectly happy, in fact. I'm just not married and making great-grandbabies for her to spoil."

"So you're lying to her to protect her?"

"I don't want to lie at all, but yes. If she thinks I'm heading toward 'I do,' then she'll be able to enjoy her life again. She deserves that."

"That's…sweet." And it was.

At least his unorthodox offer was rooted in something other than blatant self-interest. Still, what he was suggesting was crazy, but no more so than the fact that Elizabeth was actually considering it.

"Do you really think your grandmother would buy that you and I are…" She made a winding motion with her index finger, unable to speak the actual words. "I can't believe I'm your usual type."

She wasn't angling for a compliment. She wasn't expecting him to tell her that she was beautiful or even that he found her attractive. Expecting? No. But part of her must have been hoping, she realized, when her heart pinched painfully at his reply.

"You're not my type in the least, which, in a way, makes you perfect. My grandmother knows the sort of women I prefer to date. Since I've never allowed something serious to begin with them, she assumes that's because I've been dating women who are all wrong for me."

"Have you been?" She immediately shook her head. "I'm sorry. That's really none of my business." Even if she was, at this very moment, considering becoming his bride-to-be, at least for appearances' sake.

"Possibly. Probably." He shrugged carelessly. "I'm not looking for a deep and committed relationship. That's not what I'm after."

Ah, one of those. Elizabeth had dated a couple such men just out of college, not that she'd known their preferences going in, of course. Nope. She'd found out the hard way and wound up with a dinged-up heart for her naiveté.

"Which reminds me," Thomas was saying. "I never thought to ask if you were seeing someone."

His complexion bleached a little as he awaited her reply. She wasn't trying to exploit that with her hesitation. She just wanted to find a way to relay her single status without making herself sound like a loser.

"I date here and there," she said at last. "But I'm not seeing anyone in particular."

"Terrific." He had the grace to grimace. "That came

out wrong. What I mean is if you agreed to act as my fiancée, I wouldn't want to put you in an awkward position."

She appreciated that, but… "Excuse me for saying so, Mr.…er…Thomas. The situation is already awkward. I barely know you. We met only today. And you're asking me to pose as your fiancée in an attempt to fool your elderly grandmother into believing you've found your soul mate."

He grimaced again. "It sounds even worse when you say it. In my defense, there's nothing for me to gain here. I'm doing this for the right reasons, even if I seem to be going about it the wrong way. I love my grandmother, Elizabeth. She's pretty much all the family I have. She basically raised me."

So many layers to the man, Elizabeth thought. She wanted him to be what he first appeared when he suggested the arrangement: shallow and callous. Then it would be much easier to tell him no, the sizable donations he was promising be damned. She had standards. She had principles. She also apparently had a soft spot for men who had soft spots for their aging grandmothers.

"Why don't you tell me a little bit about her," she suggested, folding her hands in her lap.

"Nana Jo?"

Nana Jo. Cute. He scored another point in his favor. Elizabeth smiled her encouragement.

"She's a pistol." His expression turned fond. "She has an opinion on everything and offers it freely, whether you want to hear it or not."

"My mother's that way, too." Elizabeth had little doubt her expression was one hundred and eighty degrees from fond. She shook off all thoughts of Delphine.

"And right now Nana Jo's opinion is that you should be married."

"Actually, that's been her opinion since I graduated from college." He shrugged.

"But you're not marriage-minded. Commitment's not your thing. You prefer to keep your options open and continue to play the field." She paraphrased his earlier comment.

His frown came as a surprise. She got the feeling he wasn't happy with her assessment, though he didn't try to correct her.

"About a year ago, my grandmother started telling me she didn't have long for this life and that the only way she could leave this world peacefully was to know I was settled and happy."

"That's because she loves you."

"And I love her. I'd do anything for her. As I said, she raised me."

Elizabeth tamped down the questions begging to be asked. Chief among them: Where were his parents when he was growing up? Was he, like Mel, the product of a broken home? She pitied him if that were true. Skeet and Delphine might not believe in the institution of marriage, so their exchange of vows was unrecognized by the state as legally binding, but they were committed to one another in their own way. As counterculture and plain old wacky as they could be, at least Elizabeth had the luxury of an intact family. Or she had until her brother decided to drop out of high school and then drop out of sight.

Thomas was saying, "I told her I was seeing someone special mostly to give her something positive to occupy her thoughts. It worked a little too well and spiraled out of control. From that simple statement she extrapolated my impending nuptials."

"And you didn't do anything to stop her?"

"I didn't have the heart. It made her so happy. She went from telling me which outfit she wanted to be buried in to what she planned to wear to my wedding. A pink organdy gown, by the way. She sent me a magazine clipping of it, as well as suggestions for my tuxedo. Black tails. Very formal and timeless, in her opinion."

One corner of his mouth lifted in a bemused smile that tugged at Elizabeth's heart. Oh, he'd dug himself a deep hole all right.

"Why not tell her the truth now? They say honesty is the best policy for a reason."

"I've thought about it. Believe me. But I'm afraid Nana Jo will just go back to fretting over her health and my future, and dropping brochures for headstones in the mail to me."

"But you actually don't plan to get married to me or anyone," she pointed out. "Eventually, your grandmother is going to figure that out."

"I know." He rubbed his chin. "Which is why I was thinking that, after a reasonable length of time, I would tell her that things between you and I had ended."

"My doing, of course."

He smiled guiltily. "She'd be upset. But I think she also would be a little relieved that I almost made it to the altar."

"Commitment phobia cured?"

With one eye closed, he squinted at her with the other. "You don't pull any punches," he said wryly. "I had you pegged as practical, but not quite so blunt."

"That's my professional persona," she reminded him.

"I can hardly afford to insult someone who is about to cut my agency a check."

"Present company excluded, of course."

"Your check—"

"Checks. One from my business. One from me."

"Whether one check or two, they are coming with a lot of strings," she reminded him.

"I want to make one thing clear. The check from Waverly Enterprises will be forthcoming regardless. I believe in your cause, and I respect what you're doing."

Slightly mollified, she said, "Thank you."

"As for the other check, the one from me personally, yes, it does have strings as you called them. But I prefer to think of them as conditions, in which case they would serve to keep what would go on between us a business transaction as well, just with the funds coming from my personal bank account rather than my company's."

That made some sense, but... "I'm not saying I agree, but let's discuss that business transaction. What exactly would it entail?"

"Some of your time, for starters. We would need to get up to speed on each other in short order. We're supposed to have been dating for several months. Beyond knowing that you have a dog named Howie and started your nonprofit just after college graduation, I don't know anything about you."

"I could write up some notes."

"Crib sheets, you mean?" His smile was engaging.

"I never had to resort to them myself." She regretted the chiding comment when his lips flattened into a thin line.

"For the record, I'm not a fan of cheating, or lying, although I can understand where you might find that hard to believe right now. See, this is exactly the reason we need to spend time together before this weekend."

"Assuming I agree."

"Assuming that. Yes."

"So, I would meet your grandmother and visit with her over the weekend?"

"That's right. She's incredibly easy to talk to and fun to be around. She plays a mean game of cribbage. Who knows, you might even enjoy yourself," he said.

"Assuming I agree to do this," she repeated.

"Assuming."

But they both seemed to know she was leaning in that direction.

"I won't lie to her, Thomas." This time, his given name slipped easily from Elizabeth's lips. It was important they were clear on this point. She might be willing to bend her principles, but she would not break them. "For her to assume is one thing, but if she flat-out asks me a question that requires me to lie, I won't do it."

"This is assuming you agree." He beat her to it this time.

"Let me make something else clear. The only reason I am even entertaining the possibility of doing this is because Literacy Liaisons means so much to me."

"I know that."

Of course he did. He was banking on it, she realized.

"So, is that a yes?"

She exhaled slowly, knowing her life was about to take a huge and unexpected turn. "Yes."

Once Elizabeth agreed, the rest of dinner passed in a blur for Thomas. When it came time for the check, he didn't remember eating, possibly because more than half of his steak remained untouched on his plate, as did the side of risotto and steamed vegetables.

He was relieved that she'd said yes, of course. Her agreement was what he'd hoped for. Still, he couldn't quite shake his apprehension. Now, he had a fiancée—a woman who was also a stranger. He needed to remedy their unfamiliarity and fast.

As he walked her to her car a little later, he said, "So, I'll see you tomorrow."

She stopped, blinked. "Tomorrow?"

"We only have a few days to get to know one another as well as two people who have been dating for several months would," he reminded her.

"Oh, is that all?" He appreciated her attempt at humor, even if her smile was forced. "So, where and what time?"

"Does nine o'clock work for you?"

Her brow crinkled. "It's a little late," she began. "I'm an early riser, which means I tend to turn in not long after the sun sets."

"In the morning," he clarified.

"Oh. Well, I have to work."

"Yes. I realize that. I was hoping maybe I could come by your offices, see what you do. You can tell anyone who asks that I'm a potential contributor, which is true," he added, in case she was going to remind him that she wasn't willing to lie outright about their relationship.

"Hmm." He watched as Elizabeth mentally flipped through her morning's schedule. "I think that will work."

"Terrific."

Their plans for the next day finalized, they stood in awkward silence beside her car. Though this wasn't an actual date, it had all the hallmarks of a first one thanks to the potent combination of anticipation and apprehension he was feeling. Thomas stuffed his hands into his front pockets and rocked back on his heels.

"So…"

"Thanks for dinner."

Since she'd already thanked him twice on the short walk to her car, he said, "You're welcome. Again."

"Well…" She held up her keys and gave them a shake.

This wouldn't do. Not in the least. Nana Jo was too canny to believe that he and Elizabeth were wildly attracted to one another, much less mildly smitten, given their stilted behavior. Thomas might not want to be in love, but he knew how people in love acted.

Before she could slide onto the driver's seat, he stopped her by saying, "I think we need to get something out of the way right now."

"What?"

"This."

He pulled his hands from his pockets, framed her face with them and leaned down, unable to resist the sweet temptation of those full lips. He thought he heard her sigh. He knew he wanted to moan, and that was before her lips parted. His hands moved from her face to her shoulders and then down to her waist, pulling her closer. It was the small hands lightly touching his back that unnerved him.

He didn't trust himself with her, he realized. He didn't trust himself not to become greedy and demanding. He drew back—but not too quickly; trust be damned, he wanted to savor her—and gazed into a pair of surprised dark eyes.

It must have been his libido-fueled imagination talking, but he swore she asked, "Why did you stop?"

"I…I…"

While he stammered, she took a step back, creating an acceptable amount of space between their bodies. This time, he heard her clearly when she said, "Why did you do that?"

"Sorry." The apology was second nature. It slipped out even before he could wonder if he meant it. She accepted it with a nod, but appeared to be waiting for an explanation. Did he have one?

He knew what his reason for the kiss had been before their mouths met: to put them both at ease about any upcoming shows of affection intended for his grandmother's benefit. And, okay, he'd been a little curious, too. What man wouldn't be when looking at that pair of perfect lips? But how to explain the latter to Elizabeth without damning himself, especially since he'd made it clear their supposed relationship was for show only? So, he went with the former. Sort of.

"I thought it might take the edge off."

Her eyebrows shot up, and no wonder. As explanations went, this one had a decidedly sexual overtone. It also was inaccurate, as he knew only too well. That kiss hadn't taken the edge off of anything. Not in the least. If anything, it had heightened his curiosity. What other secrets were hidden beneath the woman's prim exterior?

He tried again and said, "It's just that people who are engaged and presumably in love are expected to kiss and be affectionate with one another."

Hell, most people assumed engaged couples were doing a whole lot more than that. Just that fast, the image of he and Elizabeth embroiled in a heated encounter flashed through his brain. Scorched through it, more like. It was all he could do to keep a moan from escaping.

"I guess you're right," Elizabeth said. She looked about as off balance as he felt.

"My grandmother will expect to see us touch one another and be comfortable doing so."

He reached over and tucked some hair behind one of her ears, testing himself. It was every bit as soft as he'd assumed it would be.

"Okay." He watched her swallow.

"So, tomorrow. Around nine."

"At my office." She smiled uncertainly, probably wondering what she'd gotten herself into, he thought.

"At your office."

"See you then."

"Looking forward to it." A polite response that was also disturbingly honest in this case.

She slipped behind the wheel of her car. Thomas closed the door and stepped back, offering a wave once she started the engine and shifted into Drive.

Long after he lost sight of her taillights in the flow of traffic, he stood in the parking lot of Antonio's. He was going to have no problem convincing Nana Jo that he found Elizabeth Morris attractive. No problem at all. Which caused him to wonder: What had he just gotten himself into?

CHAPTER FOUR

"So, how did it go last night?" Mel asked the next morning as she and Elizabeth sat at the small round table tucked into the corner of Elizabeth's office at Literacy Liaisons. Her friend grinned broadly. "Did you seal the deal and get great gobs of money for our endowment fund?"

"Not exactly," Elizabeth hedged.

She sipped her coffee, her fourth cup so far, and tried to think of a less damning way to explain the "deal" that Thomas had proposed. She still couldn't quite wrap her mind around what he'd suggested…er…proposed. Much less the fact that she had agreed. She told herself it was the agency's needs that caused her to tell him she'd do it, but every time she recalled that kiss in the parking lot, she knew she was lying.

She replayed it now, remembering the feel of Thomas's mouth when it met hers. He'd watched her carefully—curiously?—not closing his eyes until the last moment. Elizabeth knew this because she'd kept both of hers wide open, afraid even to blink lest she find him and the entire evening a figment of her imagination.

But a figment didn't kiss like he did. No one she'd ever met had kissed like he did, evoking responses and tugging forward needs she didn't know she possessed. Thomas had ended the contact before things could progress too far. She'd wanted to think that he was being considerate, chivalrous even. The man was so courteous. His expression, however, said otherwise. He looked surprised, a reaction that could be taken a couple different ways, unfortunately, one of them not so flattering.

"Earth to Elizabeth. Earth to Elizabeth." Mel was snapping her fingers. Then she demanded, "What exactly does 'not exactly' mean?"

"Well, what it means is…um, it means—"

"That I haven't presented her with the check yet."

Thomas stood in the doorway, his expression infused with amusement and something else Elizabeth couldn't quite decipher. Was he embarrassed? Uncertain? Was he recalling that kiss that he'd said had been intended to put both of them at ease? And—God!—what if it actually *had* put him at ease?

"Mr. Waverly!" She shot to her feet. Her hip bumped the table's edge and her coffee spilled, spreading over the tabletop in a brown wave and threatening to drip into Mel's lap.

"I thought we agreed you would call me Thomas." His smile was engaging and just this side of intimate, no doubt for Mel's benefit. Before either woman could react, he walked over, took the handkerchief from his pocket and laid it over the puddle of java to prevent further damage.

Not that the coffee was what held Elizabeth's attention. No. It was the man and the ridiculous effect he was having on her. One simple smile—calculated for maximum impact, most likely, since everything between them was intended for show—and her insides were whipping around like the blades of a ceiling fan stuck on high. But who could blame her? Look at him. He was gorgeous. The lean cheeks and square jaw. The blue-green eyes set off by slashing dark brows. The tidy hair that was just this side of black. And that build. She couldn't help it. She sighed.

No matter what he wore, he wore it well. Already, she'd seen him in casual attire and a three-piece suit. Today, he'd paired a herringbone jacket with dark jeans, managing to look more put-together and sophisticated than men who were going for just that effect.

Meanwhile, she was back to wearing sackcloth. Well, not exactly. But she might as well have been. Her stint as Cinderella had ended, and Mel's borrowed clothes had been returned. In their place, Elizabeth had tucked a plain white blouse into a navy pencil skirt. The strand of imitation pearls around her neck added little in the way of embellishment to an otherwise boring outfit.

The sad thing was she'd picked it out with care that morning, hoping for simple sophistication. Now, she merely felt plain, especially sitting next to Mel, who wore a leopard-print wrap dress tamed by a black blazer.

"I wasn't expecting you yet. You're early," Elizabeth said. She glanced at her wrist before realizing no watch was strapped to it. She'd opted to leave it off today since it was a little clunky.

Mel cleared her throat, reminding Elizabeth of her manners.

"Oh. Mr....Thomas." She managed a smile. "This is my good friend Melissa Sutton. Mel's in charge of Literacy Liaisons's volunteers, both recruiting them and then training them to tutor our clients."

Elizabeth held her breath after the introduction, well

aware of the effect her best friend had on men. Not that it mattered in this instance. From a purely practical standpoint, however, it wouldn't do for him to be attracted to other women if he was trying to convince his grandmother he'd fallen head over heels for Elizabeth.

He smiled politely and pumped Mel's hand. A cadre of bangle bracelets jangled. Thomas, however, showed no outward sign of being interested.

Hmm. This was a first. Elizabeth had witnessed men of all ages—married, single and every status in between—come on to Mel in one form or another with no encouragement whatsoever. A young seminary student had opted not to pursue the priesthood after meeting her, such was her friend's natural allure. But Thomas's only interest in Mel apparently was to point out, "My handkerchief didn't cover everything, I'm afraid. You'll be wearing some of that coffee if you don't move."

"Oh!" Mel glanced down and managed to shift out of harm's way a second before coffee dribbled over the table's edge. She divided her gaze between Thomas and Elizabeth as she rose. "I'll just go get something to clean this with."

"It was nice meeting you," Thomas said.

"The same." Mel offered a cheerful smile. She waited till she was at the door and Thomas's back was to her before she mouthed to Elizabeth, "Oh, my God!"

"I hope I didn't catch you at a bad time," Thomas said. "I did say nine."

The clock on the wall read eight forty-five. He was early again, which she should have expected. But Elizabeth had been running uncharacteristically late all morning. She hadn't slept well. In fact, other than a couple of hours just before her alarm went off, she hadn't slept at all. Who could blame her? Forget

Thomas's "proposal," it was that kiss that had caused her insomnia.

She touched her lips now, remembering it, savoring it. Lost in recalling exactly how his mouth had felt pressed to hers, it took her a moment to realize that the man responsible for that kiss was smiling at her. She pulled her fingers away.

"Nine. Right. You said nine." She nodded, mortified at the way she was acting. "I remember that now."

He nodded, too. Then, when the silence threatened to become awkward, he spread his hands wide. "So, this is Literacy Liaisons."

Work. Good. Excellent. It was the center of her life, what she poured most of her time and effort into, which meant it would be easy to talk about. And that would help take her mind off how sexy Thomas looked in that herringbone blazer and crisp blue oxford shirt sans necktie.

"Let me show you around," she suggested.

She started in the main meeting room, which resembled a classroom, with the letters of the alphabet posted on the walls along with pictures that corresponded to the sounds those letters made. Instead of rows of desks, however, there was a large conference table. Elizabeth had found that adults responded better to that setting than the more traditional one. Some of them had had bad experiences with school. Others were embarrassed by their situation. A conference table made it seem more like a workplace. Even though they were students in the true sense of the word, her clients also felt more like respected adults here. She explained that to Thomas.

He glanced around, nodding in appreciation. "I guess I never thought of it that way."

"It's not an issue for some people, but when we re-

alized it was for a lot of our clients…" She shrugged.
"The goal is to make them as comfortable as possible
so they can focus all of their attention on learning to
read."

"How exactly do you do that? The teaching, I mean."

"There are a variety of different methods. For instance, the Barton Reading and Spelling System has
proved a good fit for a number of our clients. It focuses
on phonics and recognizing the sounds letters make."

Thomas's nod was perfunctory. He found her work
interesting, but the woman even more so. His gaze kept
straying to her mouth. He'd hoped to find he was wrong,
but the fact remained that last night's attempt to quell
any nerves over upcoming physical contact had backfired miserably. One kiss, and now he kept imagining a second and a third. His gaze strayed to her open
collar. With only the top button left undone, he could
only make out the hollow of her throat. Since when did
he find that part of a woman's body so arousing? He
watched her swallow and other sorts of intimate activities an engaged couple—or any consenting couple—
would enjoy popped into his mind. Activities that would
take place in a bedroom with the door closed and without the barrier of clothes or the bother of inhibitions.

Disturbed and aroused at the direction his thoughts
kept taking, he had to exhale slowly between his teeth.
Even then, a portion of his pent-up groan escaped.

"Am I boring you yet?" Elizabeth inquired.

"Sorry. Not at all. In fact, quite the opposite. I'm
fascinated," he admitted truthfully. He forced his gaze
from her lips again. "That is, with what you do here.
It's…fascinating."

If only he'd left it at that. But he lifted his hand to
her face, and brushed his fingers over the slope of her

cheek before tucking some hair behind her ear. He'd done something similar while they'd stood next to her car the previous evening. Though her hair was back to being stick-straight today, it was just as soft, and blessedly free of the sticky hairspray and comb teasing the women of his acquaintance tended to use in abundance.

"Thomas?"

He lowered his hand. "I was wondering…" He let the thought go unfinished since it was heading to boggy territory. He needed to keep their interaction professional, even if everything about their agreement was rooted in being personal. He cleared his throat. "Will it be possible to meet again this evening? We have a lot yet to learn about one another."

"I suppose so."

"Maybe I could come by your place, bring some Chinese food? Do you like Chinese?"

"M-my place?"

It sounded so much more damning when she said it, especially since her eyebrows were raised in alarm. So, he amended with an easy smile, "I'm eager to meet Howie."

The door had barely closed behind Thomas when Mel grabbed Elizabeth by the arm and began peppering her with questions.

"Okay, what exactly is going on? He looked like he was really into you. Not that I was spying or anything. I mean, the door to the main meeting room has a glass panel in it after all."

"Nothing is going on." Elizabeth wasn't trying to lie or be evasive with her friend. The truth was, she was having a hard time processing the events of the past twenty-four hours.

"He caressed your cheek."

A simple touch to which Elizabeth's entire body had overreacted foolishly. Indeed, just recalling it caused gooseflesh to prick her arms now.

For her benefit even more than Mel's she said flatly, "It's not what it seems. Nothing about it is."

"Really? It seemed pretty romantic to me." Mel crossed her arms. "Men don't touch women like that unless they're interested in more than making some sort of charitable contribution, worthy cause notwithstanding, sweetie. If you don't get that you've been off the dating circuit for far too long."

"They do in this instance," Elizabeth noted wryly. She glanced at her wrist again.

"Your watch still isn't there," Mel pointed out. "Now you've got me really curious. You're acting all airheaded. That's not like you at all."

"It's a long story, one you'll want to dissect, and we have clients coming in a few minutes." Besides, Elizabeth wanted to dissect it first.

"Fine." Mel sighed. "We'll talk about this at length over lunch, but for now, give me the abridged version."

Elizabeth sucked in a breath. "Thomas has agreed to make a personal donation to our campaign, a large one that will match the one coming from Waverly Enterprises."

Mel's expression barely flickered. "And?"

"You could at least act excited about that. We'll be meeting our goal."

"I am glad. Yay, us." Mel flashed a grin that was gone almost as fast as it appeared. Then she cocked her head to one side. "And?"

"He needs a favor. Yes, that's all it is. He needs a favor."

"You do realize that when I said to give me the abridged version, I didn't mean for you to speak in some sort of code," Mel replied dryly.

Elizabeth took another deep breath. "Okay, here's the long and the short of it. He needs a fiancée. More precisely, he needs a woman to act as his fiancée, just for this weekend when he goes to visit his grandmother."

Her friend's eyes widened. "Did you say *fiancée*?"

"*Act* is the key word here," Elizabeth stressed. "He's asked me to *act* as his fiancée. He's not interested in me in that way at all."

Despite that bit of clarification, her friend grabbed her wrist none too gently and pulled her toward the office. "Our clients can wait. I need you to start at the beginning and tell me everything."

The closer it came to the time to meet Elizabeth, the more unsettled Thomas became. It didn't make sense, yet it did. While he never was nervous before a date, when it came to an important business deal? Yes, occasionally. So that part fit. But he didn't slap on cologne before business meetings, no matter how vital they were. Nor did he change his clothes—twice—and even then worry about his appearance and what signals it might send to the other party. Too casual? Too formal? In the end, he wound up back in the same herringbone jacket, shirt and pants he'd worn to her office.

In the right front pocket, he'd tucked the box holding the engagement ring his father had given his mother more than three decades before. It was a pretty ring, more old-fashioned than timeless because of its carved white-gold setting. The diamond was a half-carat, round brilliant cut. It had come to be in Thomas's possession only after his father had pawned it to buy more liquor during one of his mad binges when Thomas was a child. He'd saved up his pennies and bought it back, able to afford it only because the shopkeeper's wife was sentimental. He'd kept it all these years, not to give to his own glowing bride-to-be someday, but as a reminder of the pain that kind of love and commitment carried.

On the way to her house he picked up the Chinese food he'd ordered ahead of time. Since he hadn't thought to ask Elizabeth her preference, he'd gone with a few options: one sweet and sour, a basic chicken stir-fry and, since he was fond of a little bite, something off the Szechwan side of the menu. Coming out of the restaurant, he spied the florist shop next door. A cart full of bundled fresh flowers was parked out front.

Women liked flowers. In Thomas's experience, they were especially fond of roses, attaching all sorts of meaning to them, especially when they were red and long-stemmed and came in a ribbon-tied box. With that in mind, he picked out a simple bouquet of white daisies in a cone of cellophane. They made a suitable hostess gift.

He drove slowly to Elizabeth's house, taking a mental inventory of all that he hoped to learn during the evening ahead. How her skin felt and what her hair smelled like were off the list. Instead, he needed to find out basic things, such as her date of birth and family background. Were her parents still alive? Were they together? Where did they live and was she on good terms with them? Did she have any siblings? If so, their names and ages, etc.

Should he ask about ex-boyfriends? He swallowed. Or…ex-husbands? No, he didn't want to go there. Her romantic history was of no importance to him, at least where Nana Jo was concerned, which made it difficult to explain the odd twist in his gut whenever he thought about Elizabeth sharing a bed with someone else.

He stopped for a traffic light, waited for it to turn green. When it did, he shifted more than the car's gears. His focus was now on the very safe topic of her education. The problem was, he already knew which university she'd attended, what discipline she'd studied while there and what she'd opted to do with her life upon graduation. Okay, that left her spare time. What did she do when she wasn't working? What were her hobbies and interests?

What were her vices?

On a groan, Thomas switched on the radio, flipped the station until he found some mind-emptying, bass-thumping rock and listened to music for the remainder of the drive.

Fifteen minutes later, he turned on Clement Avenue, going slow, not only out of deference to the children who were outside playing, but also so that he could read the address numbers.

Elizabeth lived in one of the city's older neighborhoods. As such, the street was lined with mature trees and with homes that, while generally well-kept, were in need of a little updating. Hers was no exception, Thomas thought, as he pulled his car to a stop in front of a small bungalow. The faded green aluminum awnings that covered the porch and front windows harkened back a good half century. They reminded him of the awnings that had graced his parents' house. The home he'd grown up in until the accident that had taken one life and irrevocably changed three others.

Nana Jo had moved into the house with Thomas during his father's first unsuccessful stint in rehab, appalled to discover that her son had removed every last trace of his late wife from the rooms. Gone were the photos, the mementos, even some of the furniture that Lynn had purchased. Indeed, gone in some places was the plaster, where Hoyt had smashed his fist through the wall as he'd raged against God and fate, and drank himself into oblivion while his young son watched, frightened and baffled.

Four more stints in rehab followed before Thomas started middle school. At first, Hoyt came home between his stays at Brighter Futures Addiction Recovery. Sober, he was full of apologies and promises, but also weighted down with guilt and the dooming grief that he was never able to shake. Eventually, he stopped going to rehab and he stopped coming home. Thomas would have wound up a ward of the state, the house lost to back taxes, had it not been for Nana Jo.

She had been, and in many ways remained, Thomas's rock.

Gradually, she'd brought more of her belongings over from her own house across town. Doilies appeared on the living room tables, knickknacks on the empty shelves that bracketed the kitchen window. A cheery, hand-crocheted afghan was draped over the back of the sofa, and new linens appeared on the beds. The walls were patched and repainted. The house became a home again and Thomas's busted-up life was put back together, too.

Nana Jo sold the house after he left to attend college and then purchased her condo in Charlevoix, which had no yard work or outside maintenance for her to do. He still missed that little house sometimes, but only because of the good memories that Nana Jo had taken such care to preserve and later create.

Dated or not, Elizabeth's house managed to be every

bit as inviting as his boyhood abode thanks to a vivid assortment of flowers that spilled from a pair of large pots on either side of the front walk. From one side of the porch, a fern dripped from a hanging basket. The word *Welcome* was printed on the mat, but it didn't need to be.

Home, he thought. And that word stayed in his mind, even after the woman appeared in the door.

CHAPTER FIVE

AT HOWIE'S barking, Elizabeth peeked out the window and spied Thomas standing on the sidewalk. He was gazing at the house, a far-off expression on his face. She could only imagine what he was thinking.

He was fifteen minutes early. Again. At least this time she was ready for him. She'd left work early so that she could let Howie out to work off the worst of a day's worth of pent-up energy, and so that she could tidy up her house. Of course, her small bungalow didn't need much tidying.

She liked order. Growing up with her freewheeling parents, who'd eschewed home ownership for a more nomadic lifestyle, Elizabeth now thrived on the stability of knowing where she would be sleeping each night and that the bed would be made with fresh linens. Small things like having a well-stocked refrigerator and the appliances necessary to make a hot meal added a sense of security that her childhood had lacked. She wasn't completely boring, but she had a clear plan for her future. Surprises were fine as long as she was prepared to deal with any consequences that came along with them. Her parents were no good at dealing with consequences.

She loved them dearly, but she didn't want to be anything like them, except where their relationship with one another was concerned. Skeet and Delphine were quirky, oblivious and downright irresponsible, but they loved one another without reservation or condition.

So, she'd been looking for a man who was nothing like her father; but, at his core, very much like her father. That is to say, capable of deep love and lifelong commitment. What she hadn't been looking for was a man like Thomas Waverly, but that was exactly who now stood on her doorstep holding a bag of Chinese food and a clutch of daisies, and wearing a forced smile as Howie growled menacingly at him from behind her.

"Howie!" she admonished. To Thomas, she said, "He's really nothing but a big baby."

Her "big baby" looked ready to jump through the screen door at her guest, which was odd. He'd never had this reaction to company in the past.

"I'm sorry. I don't know what's gotten into him. He's never acted like this before."

"Apparently, I bring out the worst in him." Thomas laughed tightly.

"It's probably just that not many men come to my door…lately."

Thomas eyed the dog and drew a different conclusion. "He's protective of you. It's a good quality in a dog."

"I guess so." She reached for Howie's collar, pulling him back. "I'll just go put him in my bedroom."

"I'd appreciate it," Thomas said.

When she came back down the hall, he was still standing on her porch. "All clear?"

"All clear."

She held open the door and then led him back to her small kitchen. Its harvest-gold appliances and battered Formica countertop were hopelessly out-of-date. As were the white cabinets that had been painted so many times that some of them refused to close properly. Renovation was on her to-do list, but she had neither the time nor the money to tackle any serious home improvement for the foreseeable future.

"It's very retro in here," Thomas commented.

"Retro. Yes. That's exactly the vibe I was going for."

"You have a good sense of humor," he accused on a smile as he set the cartons of food on the small, bar-height bistro set that was tucked into the corner of the tiny kitchen. "A dry one."

"I guess I do," she agreed. "Are those for me?"

He was still holding the flowers.

"Yes."

He all but thrust them into her hands. Elizabeth gave the bouquet a sniff. Daisies didn't emit the lush fragrance of, say, carnations or lilies, but she found their subtle earthiness refreshing. "Daisies are my favorite flower."

"They're a hostess gift," he blurted out with curious intensity.

"Well, they're lovely. Thank you." As she pulled a vase from a cupboard and put them in water, Elizabeth said, "Has anyone ever told you that you have wonderful manners?"

"All the time." He removed his jacket and placed it over the back of his chair before taking his seat. "It was my grandmother's doing."

"I like your grandmother."

"Just wait until you meet her."

Both of them grew serious then. That was the objective. For Elizabeth to meet his grandmother and pass muster as his supposed bride-to-be.

"Do you think she'll like me?" Elizabeth realized it was a silly question as soon as she asked it. She shook her head. "She already does, doesn't she? I mean, the fabricated version of me." It hit her then. "Beth. That's my name as far as she knows."

"It is." He tilted his head to one side. "Do you mind being called Beth?"

"It's only for a little while. I'll get used to it." She shrugged and went to get plates and utensils. She was quite proficient with chopsticks, but she grabbed a fork for Thomas just in case.

He didn't appear satisfied with her answer. "You know, the more I get to know you, the less you look like a Beth."

"Oh?" Curious, she asked, "What does a Beth look like?"

He flushed slightly. "It doesn't matter. I'll call you Elizabeth. It suits you better anyway."

"And how do you know that?" she challenged.

"I…I don't." His mouth snapped shut and he was silent a moment. Then he asked, "What kind of movies do you like?"

His quick switch in topics baffled her. "Movies?"

"We're getting to know one another, remember? That's the whole point of this evening."

Of course it was.

"Movies," she repeated. "I don't go to the theater often. To be perfectly honest, I'm not much for first-run films. I can't name any of the big stars currently walking the red carpet at premieres and award shows." In a teasing tone, she asked, "Does that make me a Beth or an Elizabeth?"

"It makes you a smart-ass," he shot back, after which he immediately apologized for cursing.

Ah, those impeccable manners of his. She didn't want to acknowledge what a turn-on she found them to be. She busied herself setting the table.

"So, you like old movies," he prodded.

"Mainly Alfred Hitchcock films, although I'm also a sucker for anything that stars Katharine Hepburn and Spencer Tracy."

"No way."

"What? You like Tracy and Hepburn?"

"No. Hitchcock. The man was a genius," Thomas replied solemnly. "*Dial M for Murder* is my favorite. You?"

"*North by Northwest,*" she replied without hesitation.

"Let me guess. Cary Grant has something to do with your preference?" He opened the containers and scooped out a clump of white rice onto each of their plates.

"Well, maybe just a little," she admitted on a grin as she levered herself onto the chair opposite his. "He's also the reason I love *To Catch a Thief.*"

"Grace Kelly." Thomas sighed. "She starred in that one with him."

"She starred in few Hitchcock movies, including your favorite." Elizabeth arched a brow. "Am I sensing the reason behind your preference?"

"Guilty. So, what about *Psycho*? Fan of that one?" He made a slashing-knife motion with the corresponding sound effect that had turned the simple act of showering into the stuff of nightmares.

She couldn't help it. She shuddered. "I saw it once, as an adult no less, and that was enough for me. I found it a little too intense."

"Twice here. Also as an adult. Both times while out

with women. Based on my dates' reactions, they also found it intense. I didn't mind." His smile, accompanied as it was by a pair of bobbing eyebrows, had her laughing.

Feeling the need to redeem herself, Elizabeth said, "I've watched *The Birds* again and again."

"A cult classic," Thomas agreed.

She helped herself to some Kung Pao chicken. "I will admit that, as a kid, it made me look at seagulls in a whole new light. Going to the beach was a traumatic experience for a time."

He went for the Kung Pao chicken as well once she set the carton back on the table.

"Definitely dry." At her blank expression, he added, "Your sense of humor." He motioned with the serving spoon. "Back to *The Birds*, how about that scene at the elementary school? All those crows perching on the monkey bars?"

"Creepy in the extreme."

"Wasn't it, though? I was nine the first time I saw that movie. It was on television one rainy Saturday afternoon, and I watched it while Nana Jo was hosting her bridge club. I was awake all night long."

"I was eleven. Slept on the floor in my parents' room for a week."

"I wouldn't admit this to just anyone, but seeing as how you and I are engaged…" He shrugged. "I slept on my grandmother's floor for two." They both laughed. "It came to a head when she tried to take me to the playground and I begged to stay home."

"What did she say?"

"Well, she was mystified."

"Understandable."

"But she didn't press." His smile turned nostalgic.

"That's her way. Or at least it was back then. She's run out of patience, apparently. As for *The Birds*, I eventually confessed all."

"And?" Elizabeth broke apart the wooden chopsticks that had come with their meal.

"Nana Jo took me to the local pet store and subjected me to an hour in the bird aisle. Even with every last one of those birds confined in cages, it was terrifying."

"Did she really do that?"

Thomas glanced at the fork she'd set out for him before picking up his pair of chopsticks and breaking them apart. "She felt it was the best way for me to confront my fear. In fact, she bought me a cockatiel."

"Did it work?"

"Yes. I was cured thereafter, but hopelessly hooked on Hitchcock." He attempted to pick up a bite of his meal. Chicken and rice slipped from between the chopsticks. His expression reflected his dismay.

"What did you name the bird?"

His frown of a moment before turned into a sly grin. "What do you think?"

"Hitchcock."

"Exactly. Confronting fear head on, remember?"

They both laughed. Then Elizabeth took a bite of the food. The hot peppers in the Kung Pao chicken made her eyes water, even as her tongue caught fire. She set her chopsticks aside and fanned her face.

"Oh, my God! I need a glass of water." She scooted off her chair. "I never thought to ask if you wanted something to drink. I have wine, Cabernet Sauvignon." It was a date-night staple, or so Mel always claimed. Elizabeth added, "Or some diet cola if you'd prefer."

"Water's fine."

"Tap?"

"With a couple ice cubes if you've got 'em."

When she returned to the table with their glasses, he was again struggling to pick up a piece of chicken with his chopsticks. This one wound up in his lap after leaving a trail of sauce and bits of rice down the front of his shirt. His smile was sheepish, and all the more appealing because of it, as he blotted the fabric with a napkin. "I'm not as good at this as you are, I'm afraid."

"But you just keep trying."

"That's me. Once I set my mind to doing something, I don't give up easily."

"I'm the same way. Determined." She laughed. "Mel calls it being stubborn."

"I guess we both are, then."

His smile was warm, yet she had to suppress a shiver. Elizabeth cleared her throat.

"You're holding them wrong." She picked up her pair again and demonstrated. Even though Thomas did better this time, his grip was still a little off.

"That's an improvement, but it's more like this." She reached over to adjust the placement of his middle finger between the two sticks. Just that little bit of contact sent a spark of heat zipping up her spine, every bit as potent as the previous evening's kiss. She snatched her hand back and glanced up to find him watching her. His dark eyes were narrowed and had grown hooded.

Was he recalling that kiss as well?

She was being foolish, she decided, when he made a couple of pinching motions in the air.

"I think I've got it," he declared before attempting to pick up another piece of chicken. This time he brought it to his mouth without incident. He raised his empty chopsticks in triumph afterward.

"Very good," she said.

"Well, you're a good teacher."

She wrinkled her nose at the compliment. "Nah. You're a smart man from what I've observed. You would have figured it out for yourself eventually."

"Still, you deserve a reward." He picked up a second piece of chicken and, after making sure it wasn't going to fall from the chopsticks, offered it to her.

Elizabeth must have lost her mind, because she leaned closer and opened her mouth. All the while, her gaze stayed on Thomas rather than the prize he offered. Even as her lips closed around the chopsticks and heat—both that inspired by the hot peppers in the recipe and that inspired by need—wound through her, she maintained eye contact.

"I wouldn't have taken you for the sort of woman who enjoyed Kung Pao chicken," he said slowly. "It's got a lot of kick, especially from the restaurant I patronize."

"Hence the sweet and sour pork and chicken stir-fry," she replied.

His smile was lightning quick and appealing. "I was hedging my bets with a good assortment."

"That was very thoughtful, but as it turns out there was no need. I like spice. Lots of it, in fact." She sipped her water, took her time swallowing. Regardless, the heat not only remained, but also burned even hotter.

That studious look was back on his face. "I have a feeling there's a lot more to you, Elizabeth Morris, than first meets the eye."

She held his gaze. "The same is true for most people, I think."

It was definitely true for Thomas. She'd had him pegged as a smooth operator based on his handsome face and admitted commitment-phobia. Add in that kiss and she'd known he was vastly experienced when it came to casual physical relationships, making him exactly the sort of man any woman who valued keeping her heart whole knew to avoid. But that opinion shifted once she figured in his manners and his deep love for his grandmother. Just as she had the night before, Elizabeth found herself marveling at all of his layers and almost wishing they were involved in the sort of relationship that allowed one to delve deeper, explore and, eventually, see more.

"What you're telling me is you can't judge a book by its cover," he said.

"Am I sensing some regrets? Perhaps I'm not the right woman for this…job after all."

"No. No regrets." But he was frowning when he said, "I have a feeling you're perfect."

CHAPTER SIX

THEY talked throughout their meal about the inconsequential things that ultimately helped people get to know one another. Little by little, more of the true Elizabeth Morris emerged. As Thomas already had surmised, there was far more to her than first met the eye. And he wasn't completely comfortable with the woman now seated across from him.

He'd meant it when he'd said earlier that he had the feeling she was perfect. Not just for the role he wanted her to play, either. She was funny, interesting and smart, definitely. And he knew from that kiss that, under different circumstances, he wouldn't mind pursuing a more intimate relationship with her. But that would have to wait, assuming she felt the same way. Right now it was business. Even if it also came with a few perks, he decided, as his gaze slid to her mouth. As long as they were on the same page, he might as well as enjoy them.

He rounded up the last morsel of chicken on his plate and grinned in satisfaction when it stayed between his chopsticks. After eating it, he motioned across the room. "Tell me about that picture on your refrigerator door."

She glanced over. Amusement was apparent in her eyes and her voice when she replied, "The one of Mel and me shrieking like a pair of loons?"

"Exactly."

"I'm a roller-coaster junkie," she admitted, reaching up to adjust the band that held her hair back from her face. "I'm guessing that comes as a surprise to you, too."

"Guilty." While he would have pictured her holding on for dear life as the car crested the summit and plunged over, he saw proof to the contrary affixed to the refrigerator. The photo of her and the young woman he'd met at Literacy Liaisons showed Elizabeth in the front seat of the first car, slim arms waving over her head, a delighted grin flashing over her face.

"Well, I am. The steeper, the faster, the more winding the better." She said it with pride and just a little defiance.

"When and where was that taken?"

"Last summer. Mel and I took some of our younger clients on a field trip to an amusement park in Ohio," she told him. "That particular coaster was new and billed as the highest and fastest one in the Midwest. Mel dared me to go on it and take that first plunge hands-free." Now her smile was every bit as smug as it was nostalgic.

"Can't turn down a dare?" His mouth began to water. He blamed it on the spices that were still making his tongue sting.

"Sure I can. But not one where I know I can do it."

"Dang." He snapped his fingers in mock dismay. "Another one of my misconceptions busted."

"Besides, there was an ice-cream cone riding on my saying yes."

"Ice cream. I like ice cream." His gaze was on her mouth and his own was watering again. This time, there was no denying the exact cause.

"Who doesn't?"

"What flavor do you prefer?"

"Vanilla." Elizabeth cocked her head to one side. "Before you condemn me for being boring—"

"Never." He meant it. He was finding her way too enchanting to be bored.

"Good." She offered a quick smile before continuing. "Vanilla is my favorite because it's the most versatile flavor of ice cream out there. As such, it offers one a chance to get creative."

"I guess I never thought of it that way before," he replied truthfully.

"Most people haven't, but they should. Buy a half gallon of vanilla ice cream and you can add whatever you want and create the exact flavor you're after."

"Practical," he agreed.

Her frown told him she didn't quite care for the description, even before she said, "I prefer to think of it as being flexible, maybe even a little imaginative. Add fresh strawberries, chocolate syrup, caramel, peanuts, what have you and you've crafted a new flavor."

"The possibilities are endless." Suddenly, he was seeing vanilla in a whole new light, just as he'd already begun to see Elizabeth differently.

They chatted about coasters and ice cream for the remainder of their meal. When they finished eating, he helped her carry their dishes to the sink. She tried to shoo him back to his seat.

"There's no need. Really. You're my guest."

"Actually, I'm your fiancé, remember?" He chose not to ponder how easily the word rolled off his tongue. "My grandmother was a stickler when it came to household chores. From the first day she came to live with us, she drilled into me the importance of cleaning up after myself."

"Smart woman."

He nodded. "That bit of instruction has served me well. I may be a bachelor, but my house isn't a pigsty."

Her brows rose. "Cleaning lady?"

"Well, yeah. But she only comes every other week."

Elizabeth grinned as she finished rinsing off their plates and stacking them on the counter next to the sink. Afterward, she turned toward him, her expression both innocent and beguiling when she asked, "So, now what?"

Now, there was a question. Usually after dinner with a woman one of two things happened. If it was early in a relationship, they engaged in prolonged foreplay. If they'd been dating awhile and were mutually agreeable, they skipped all pretense and headed to the nearest bedroom. Maybe it was just as well that Elizabeth's was currently occupied with one very large and not so friendly canine.

He glanced at his watch. It wasn't quite nine. The last time he'd ended an evening out with a member of the opposite sex this early, he'd been a teenager with a curfew. Besides, they had barely scratched the surface. He didn't know nearly enough about Elizabeth to satisfy either his grandmother's or his own curiosity.

"I'm eager to hear more revelations. What other dark secrets are you hiding?" He said it in jest, but for a second she looked…guilty?

He must have imagined it, he decided. Because a moment later she was grinning gamely when she announced, "Well, I like to play poker."

"Poker?"

"It's not like I'm a contender for one of those televised tournaments where the stakes are huge or anything, but I enjoy the game." She rinsed out their glasses. "More water?"

"After that revelation, I think I could use a glass of that wine you offered me earlier."

He uncorked the bottle while she got out a couple of what appeared to be handblown goblets.

"Fancy," he commented as he poured.

"They were a gift from a client, one of our first. Cassidy McClurg. She's on track now to earn her sommelier certification. Her dream is to work someday at a top New York restaurant. I think she's well on her way."

"To Literacy Liaisons and changing lives." He handed Elizabeth one of the glasses and then clinked his against it.

They adjourned to her small livingroom then. Since the windows were open, he could hear the crickets chirping outside and sundry other noises associated with nightfall in a neighborhood. He missed those sounds now that his windows were always closed with the central air-conditioning humming.

Like the kitchen, the room needed updating. The carpet, a nondescript brown color, was faded in places with well-worn paths from the postage-stamp-sized foyer to the kitchen and the hallway that led to the bedrooms. But the place was tidy. And homey thanks to all of the little touches that, quite frankly, were lacking in the sprawling house he'd lived in for more than half a decade.

He settled into the recliner after Elizabeth sat on the love seat. Their positions made for easier conversation. That's what he told himself anyway, since the empty cushion next to her looked way too inviting.

"Let's get back to you and poker."

It turned out she played mainly at charity fundraising events and had never been to any of Michigan's American Indian tribe-run casinos, let alone the huge gambling venues found in Las Vegas. But she knew the difference between a full house and a straight and, given that serene, guileless expression of hers, he'd bet she was a pro at bluffing.

Still, she threw him for a loop when she added, "Mel, a couple other friends and I have been getting together about once a month for the past couple years. We play for bragging rights mostly."

A bunch of women playing poker on a regular basis? "Please tell me you don't sit around smoking cigars and talking sports, too?"

Amusement shimmered in her eyes. "Sports, sometimes. If it's college football season, Mel and I usually have a side bet going. She went to State like me, but she's still a Wolverine fan. Family tradition."

"I'm surprised her family didn't toss her from the fold when she decided to attend State then," he teased.

"She had a full-ride scholarship. It was kind of hard for her parents to be upset with her choice in universities when they didn't have to pick up the tab for a Big Ten school's tuition." Elizabeth shrugged. "Not that my scholarship stopped *my* parents from being upset."

"You had a full-ride scholarship to State and they were unhappy about it?" he asked incredulously.

"Not exactly a full ride, but enough that I was able to afford my four years there when supplemented with student loans. My parents' objections were more... generalized." She shook her head. Before he could ask what she meant by that, Elizabeth said, "Back to Mel, she chose State because it has a strong program in her field of study."

"Which was?"

"Package engineering."

"So, she went from designing the packaging for products to vetting literacy volunteers?" He scratched his chin, not quite able to connect the dots. "I'm not seeing the correlation between the two professions."

"That's because there is none. Mel was great at her job and made a lot of money at it, but she didn't like what she was doing or where she was doing it." Before he could ask, Elizabeth supplied, "San Francisco."

"Yeah," he replied dryly. "I can see how living in the 'City by the Bay' would be a real downer, especially in the middle of winter when we're buried in snow here."

Elizabeth laughed. The sound was lyrical and the way her face lit was, well…he liked it. A lot.

"She didn't miss Michigan's weather, Mr. Smarty Pants. She missed the people here."

"Mr. Smarty Pants?" he repeated with brows raised.

Thomas couldn't recall a single woman who had ever referred to him as such. Well, except for his grandmother. The young women of his acquaintance had other, far more flattering pet names for him. Names that usually couldn't be repeated in polite company since they had to do with things that had occurred behind closed bedroom doors. Those names had helped stroke his ego. Yet he found himself more amused than offended by Elizabeth's assessment. Her engaging grin probably had something to do with it.

"You think you have all the answers." The charge was leveled too lightly to be an accusation.

"Do I now?"

"Just an observation." She shrugged and reached for the wineglass she'd set on the coffee table.

"My guess is you were one of the things your friend missed about Michigan."

"Well, we are BFFs." Elizabeth smiled fondly.

That had come through loud and clear when he'd been introduced. As had her friend's protectiveness. She might be as petite as Elizabeth, but Thomas got the feeling she would cheerfully scratch out his eyes if she thought he'd hurt Elizabeth.

Elizabeth was saying, "Long story short, she ditched a lucrative career in the corporate world for something she finds more personally satisfying."

"Now she uses her power for good," he teased.

"More like for the greater good."

"I'd say it worked out for both of you, then. Does she, um, know about our arrangement?"

"Yes. BFFs, remember?"

"Right."

Elizabeth nibbled her lower lip thoughtfully for a second. "Can I ask you something?"

"Of course." Thomas lifted his shoulders in a shrug. Because he felt the need to remind himself, he told her, "That's whole the point of this evening, Elizabeth. We're supposed to be getting to know one another. So, ask away."

"Do you…are you…? It's just that Mel is very…" She let out a bemused laugh and readjusted her headband. Before it was back in place, blond hair cascaded about her face. He liked it better that way. "This is really awkward."

Which made Thomas all the more intrigued. "Why don't you say it fast, like pulling off a bandage?"

"Okay." But she still took a moment during which she sucked in a deep breath. "It's just that, to me at least,

Mel seems more your type. Yet, when you met her earlier today, you didn't pay very much attention to her."

More his type? Hmm. Thomas supposed that, except for her petite stature, Mel Sutton was in league with the sort of women he tended to date. At least her physical appearance. She was sexy and beautiful. Oddly enough, he hadn't been attracted to her. And even if he had been, since he'd gone to Literacy Liaisons to see Elizabeth, his pseudo-fiancée, it would have been impolite to openly ogle her friend.

"I didn't mean to offend her," he began.

Elizabeth shook her head. The band loosened again. "You didn't offend her. I was just surprised that, well, that you didn't—"

She stopped abruptly. Thomas had a feeling he knew why. Now, he was a little offended. "That I didn't what, Elizabeth? Hit on her?"

"Well, no." She moistened her lips, readjusted her headband again.

He was tempted to pull it off completely. He didn't care for the prim look. He liked her hair better loose so that, if he wanted to, he could run his fingers through it.

"Then what?"

"Okay. I did think that maybe you would…hit on her, to use your term. And, quite frankly, I wouldn't have been surprised."

Oh, he was definitely offended. "Because I'm a lecherous pig."

She blinked at his bald statement. "No! It's just that Mel's gorgeous."

"So?"

On a frown, she asked, "Are you going to sit there and tell me you didn't notice?"

"No. I'm not blind, so, sure I noticed, just like I would notice a gorgeous sunset or a stunning piece of artwork. I appreciate beauty in all things. Everyone does. That's human nature. But I am capable of some restraint, you know," he finished dryly.

He thought that would be the end of it. Subject closed. It wasn't.

Chin notched up, Elizabeth declared, "Just so you know, Mel is every bit as pretty on the inside as she is on the outside. She's not merely an attractive package."

"Even if she is a packaging engineer."

His attempt at a joke fell miserably flat.

"Mel is smart and funny and generous, not that most men ever figure that out or even bother to try."

Her vehement defense of her best friend might have been touching if it hadn't also highlighted Elizabeth's own insecurities.

"So are you…every bit as pretty on the inside as you are on the outside, from what I can tell." Indeed, the more he saw, the more he liked. And the more attractive he found her to be.

That disturbed him a little. What was it his dad had said just prior to going on one of his drunken binges? That he'd fallen in love with Thomas's mother not in spite of her quirks and imperfections, but because of them.

Elizabeth was quick to disagree with his assessment. "I'm not pretty. I'm not ugly or anything, but…" She fiddled with the headband again. "I'm rather plain."

"Plain?" Did she really think so? With that lush mouth and those rich, dark eyes? Not a chance. He might be out of line, but he reached over and tugged the headband free, tossing it on the coffee table like a gauntlet. A cascade of satiny tresses fell forward, all but obscuring her face before he pushed them back. "From where I'm sitting you're very pretty," he challenged.

A blush stained her cheeks as she fiddled with the stem of her wineglass.

It had been a long time since Thomas had been around a woman who became flustered from a simple compliment. "By the way, Elizabeth…?"

"Yes?"

"I'm not most men."

CHAPTER SEVEN

As if she needed reminding on that score. Quite frankly, Thomas was unlike anyone she'd ever met—personally or professionally. And that was saying a lot given all of the doors upon which she'd knocked during the past several months to raise funds for the endowment.

She still wasn't quite sure how to act around him in part because their relationship was professional and personal at the same time. It didn't help that she found him so appealing. But that was superficial. It was based on sexual chemistry, she reminded herself. Beyond his good looks and his love for his grandmother, what did she truly know about him? If she was to pull off her part as his fiancée—and that was her only motive here— she needed to know more about him.

Much more than that she found him too handsome and charming for her peace of mind.

Besides, she'd rather he be the one in the hot seat.

"You know, I just realized that while I've been telling you a lot about myself, I don't know nearly enough about you except that you matriculated from Michigan and have the good sense to be a fan of Alfred Hitchcock."

"What else do you want to know?"

Where to start? Favorite color? Favorite dessert? Where he went on his last vacation? How old he was when he stopped believing in Santa Claus? Benign topics, all, and definitely the sorts of things a fiancée should or would be expected to know.

But the question she heard herself ask was "When did your last relationship end?" Followed quickly by "You're not involved with someone right now, are you?"

Last night, Thomas hadn't kissed like a man who was stepping out on his girlfriend, but then their situation was hardly normal. The kiss had been for effect. It was intended to put them both at ease, not that the objective had been achieved as far as Elizabeth was concerned.

"I'm not seeing anyone."

She let out a breath that she hadn't been aware she was holding. "Good. I mean, it would be awkward otherwise. For her. And, well, for me. I'd hate to be the 'other woman,' even if only in theory." She ordered herself to stop babbling and cleared her throat. "And as for my other question, what's the answer to that?"

Thomas's expression turned oddly introspective as he studied his wine. After taking a sip, he said, "I don't know that I'd necessarily call it a relationship, though it was exclusive for as long as it lasted." He looked up, his gaze locked with hers. "When I'm seeing someone, Elizabeth, I'm faithful."

"We're not really 'seeing each other,'" she said before she could wonder if he even meant to apply monogamy to their situation. Hoping to lighten the moment, she added, "I mean, could it even be considered cheating if said cheating involved a fictitious fiancée?"

At his lifted brow, she figured she'd made things clear as mud with her attempt at humor.

"Fictitious or not, I won't be dating during our... engagement."

That should have been reassuring, except that it

called to mind another question Elizabeth realized she hadn't yet gotten around to asking. "How long will that be? You never actually said."

He frowned. "I don't know the exact length of time, but I'll only need your, um, services—" He must have found that word as unsavory as she did. "That is, your cooperation for this weekend. Nana Jo just wants to meet my fiancée. And, given the distance between here and Charlevoix, it's not like she's going to be expecting us to drive up for Sunday dinner each week."

"Oh. Good." And that was good, she reminded herself, when she experienced a foolish twinge of disappointment.

"I won't withhold my personal donation to Literacy Liaisons until our 'breakup,' if that's what you're worried about. The check will be on your desk the first business day after the holiday weekend."

Waverly Enterprises's check had been received not long after he'd left her office earlier in the day. Already, it had been deposited into the agency's special bank account.

"I wasn't worried." She'd forgotten all about the check during the past couple of hours, but she would do well to remember that Thomas's generous donation was the reason she was doing this. Even so, she nibbled her bottom lip and asked, "So, how long did it last?"

"What?"

"Your last relationship."

"Oh." He appeared to do some quick mental calculations. "I guess it was nearly two months."

"Wow. A whole two months. And you managed to stay faithful the entire time."

"Sarcasm. Hmm." His expression turned bemused

and he wagged a finger in her direction. "I wouldn't have thought you capable of it."

Elizabeth rarely resorted to sarcasm or to sarcastic humor. In fact, she found it a bit of a turnoff, one of the main reasons she didn't watch many television sitcoms, which relied on it so heavily for their laughs.

"I apologize for the sarcasm."

"No need."

"There is," she insisted. "My comment was rude."

Thomas's smile was rueful. "But not completely unwarranted or off base. As I told you last night, I'm not interested in commitment. So, I tend to end relationships quickly with the women I date. I prefer for things not to get too…"

"Intimate?"

"Messy."

"I see. And when was it that you ended things this last time?" she asked.

"Three weeks ago."

"Three weeks ago." Elizabeth resisted the urge to whistle through her teeth. She didn't like the sound of that, though why it should matter she didn't know. Still, there was no denying that it did. It made her feel only marginally better that he'd been the one to end it. No pining going on, apparently. But three weeks? The scent of the woman's perfume was probably still lingering in his home. And on his linens.

"Is that a problem?" he asked.

"No. Why would it be?" Why, indeed?

"No hearts were broken, I can assure you," he said.

She slowly turned the stem of her wineglass. Gaze affixed to the deep red liquid, she asked quietly, "Have you ever had your heart broken?"

"No. Not once, which has been my objective." It was

a curious thing to admit. Before she could question him on it, though, he said, "What about you?"

She thought about the guys she'd dated in the past. She wasn't as prolific a dater as Thomas apparently was, but she'd enjoyed a couple of long-term relationships, including one that had lasted more than a year. Things had progressed at a normal pace, though they'd never gotten past the point of exchanging keys, much less making promises to spend a lifetime together. Her heart had been dinged up afterward, but broken? She'd thought so at the time, but now…

"No."

"So, you've never been in love, either?"

"I guess not." That came as a sad revelation. After all, Elizabeth was pushing thirty.

But Thomas looked pleased. "Good. It's not worth it, you know."

"How can you say that when you just admitted that you've never been in love yourself?"

"Let's just say I know. I saw firsthand what it can do to people." He shook his head. "No thanks. I don't want to be that—"

"Vulnerable?"

"Foolish," he clarified.

He saw love as foolish? Perhaps she should have expected that since here he was trying to pass off a woman he barely knew as his fiancée. Still, it seemed…sad.

Thinking back on her own relationships now, she said, "I think it would be nice to be deeply in love with someone."

"In love? Yes. But you can't stay there." His tone was matter-of-fact.

"Why not? You don't think love can last?" She had her parents' example to prove otherwise. No marriage certificate bound them together, but their commitment was real.

But Thomas wasn't disagreeing. Not exactly. "It lasts. Unfortunately, it lasts beyond the grave."

"Should it have a time limit, an expiration date?"

"No. No." He shook his head, looking both lost and resolute. "It shouldn't, and it doesn't end. It lasts forever. It's a chronic condition, not a terminal one."

"I'm not sure I understand your objection, then."

"My dad loved my mother. Deeply." His tone was barely above a whisper when he added, "Desperately."

"And that's bad?"

"Not when she was alive, it wasn't." Half of his mouth lifted briefly before his lips thinned into a straight line. "My parents and I were involved in an accident when I was eight. Our car skidded off the road in a rainstorm and wound up upside down in a water-filled ravine."

His tone was flat, but his expression was haunted. So much so that it made Elizabeth ache for him. Ache for them all.

"Your mother didn't make it," Elizabeth guessed. Pieces of the puzzle started to fall into place. She didn't like the picture that was emerging.

He shook his head slowly. "For my grandmother's benefit, my father claimed that she died instantly. But I was there."

Thomas said no more than that. He wasn't trying to be evasive. He simply wasn't capable of forcing the words past his lips and giving voice to a truth that had haunted him for more than two decades: Had the choice been left to his father, Hoyt would have saved his wife rather than his son.

But Thomas's mother hadn't given her husband the option. As murky water had gushed into the car through the broken windshield, and Hoyt had struggled to un-buckle her jammed seat belt, she'd batted his hands away and screamed, *Don't worry about me! Get Tommy out! Get Tommy out!*

"Oh, Thomas. I'm so sorry."

Elizabeth's sincere sympathy wasn't able to banish the hellish memories. Nothing was. He knew that from experience. But he couldn't deny that he found her concern soothing, settling.

"It's not something I like talking about it," he admitted. Even with Nana Jo, he preferred to steer clear of the subject. It was just too damned painful, for her as well, he figured, since she'd lost her only child.

"I understand. Ordinarily, I would consider this none of my business, but, given our unique set of circumstances…how did your grandmother come to raise you if your father is still alive?"

"My father's an alcoholic." Another admission he rarely shared. "He was what I'd call a social drinker before the accident. Afterward…" Thomas set the wine he'd barely touched on the coffee table. "He could down a fifth of whiskey in a day and then stumble to the store for more. He tried rehab, more than once. But I don't think his heart was in it. He was lost without my mother. He still is. And he's still drinking. Of that much I'm sure, even though I rarely see him."

Thomas glanced over, fully expecting to see pity in Elizabeth's eyes. It was there, along with something else, something that made him almost yearn for the comfort he knew she wanted to give him.

"It's hard when someone you love walks out of your life."

"I had no choice in the matter," Thomas heard himself say.

He swallowed thickly afterward. Even so, feelings welled up, helplessness chief among them. He'd had no say in his father's emotional and physical defection, just as he'd had no say in surviving the accident. *Get Tommy out!* How ironic that his mother's unconditional love had made him unlovable in his father's eyes. At least that was the way Thomas saw it.

Elizabeth said nothing. Instead, she came over and sat next to him on the love seat, angled toward him. Their knees bumped. She laid one of her small hands overtop of his, which were clenched tightly together in front of him. The gesture was one of comfort. Because that was what he knew he would find, he pulled away and stood.

"You know, it's getting late."

"Oh. I guess it is." She wasn't quite successful in hiding her bafflement.

"Thanks for dinner."

"You brought the Chinese," she pointed out.

"The company, then." He started for the door.

"You're welcome." But her smile was uncertain.

She followed him onto the porch. Outside, darkness was falling. Up and down the street, landscape lights were starting to click on. Elizabeth reached back into the house and flipped on the porch light, but it barely illuminated beyond the steps.

"Be careful getting to your car," she said as he started down her walk.

"I'm good." He waved and then made a liar of himself by tripping on the buckled pavement.

"Thomas—"

"I'm fine!"

"Good night," she called.

Rather than echo the sentiment, he halted midstep,

turned around and returned to her, stopping one crumbling cement step shy of the porch where she still stood.

"Did you forget something?"

In his haste to leave, he almost had.

"My jacket." The engagement ring was in its pocket still. He would hand her the box and go. That way he'd be gone before he had to listen to her ooh and aah over it. She could put it on her own finger.

"It's in the kitchen."

He followed her back inside the tidy little home that still felt too welcoming for his peace of mind. But his gaze wasn't drawn to the furnishings or kitschy bric-a-brac. It was on her back, sliding south even as he ordered it to return to a safe point between her shoulder blades. She might not have a lot in the way of curves, but what she had filled out the seat of her pants well enough to make his mouth water. A groan slipped out as need surged in. She turned. The view from the front was just as appealing.

"Did you say something?"

Tell her no, get your jacket and go, he ordered silently. But what came out was her name. He stepped closer, until a mere whisper of space separated them. Then his hands were in her hair and he was moving closer. The kiss started out light and gentle, just as it had the night before. With mouths meeting. Breath mingling. Passion still leashed, but straining to break free.

And no wonder. One taste of the woman wasn't enough. Not by a long shot. He angled his head, delving deeper and giving himself over to need. She didn't seem to mind. In fact, she kept up with him just fine. Her hands had gone from trapped safely between their bodies to his shoulders and now were fisted in his hair, letting him know he wasn't the only one being carried away.

Stop!

His silent command went unheeded. Thomas wanted more and, gauging from her response, so did Elizabeth. It was mutual, consensual. Briefly, he considered his options. Her bedroom was just down the hall, but occupied at the moment with one very large and overprotective dog that Thomas could hear whining for freedom even over the blood rushing in his ears. The love seat was closer anyway. He backed toward it and lowered himself onto the curved arm. They could work their way around to the cushions in a minute. Right now, he preferred Elizabeth right where she was, standing between the *V* of his legs with her small, perfect breasts nearly level with his mouth.

Her hair was mussed from his fingers. Her lips full and inviting. Her gaze was wide. Expectant? Eager?

Go slow.

This silent command was easier to follow than the last one. He brought his mouth to her neck, nipping softly with his teeth as he worked his way lower. Elizabeth tilted her head to the side and he continued down. At her collarbone, he stopped, savored, even as the buttons on her blouse beckoned.

As his eager fingers fumbled with the top one, her breath sighed out as if she were luxuriating in the moment. Meanwhile, his pulse had picked up speed and the breath sawed from his lungs, hot and urgent.

Thomas was two buttons in when she decided to return the favor. Her fingers were much more nimble than his and made fast work of the buttons holding his shirt together. When she finished, she pushed it back onto his shoulders. The corners of that sexy mouth curved up. There was no mistaking the desire in her dark eyes. No mistaking it at all.

Curiously, it helped stopped him from doing something foolish. He couldn't do this. *They* couldn't do this. Sex would complicate things. No doubt, Elizabeth would read too much into the act, especially given the current role-playing that was going on. Physical need would turn into emotional need. She would expect more than he was able to give. It was best to nip this in the bud before she got hurt, Thomas decided, refusing to consider that the heart he was hoping to protect from harm very well might be his own.

He pulled his shirt back over his shoulders.

"This got a little out of hand, I'm afraid. I only meant to kiss you like I did last night. Sorry."

Elizabeth stumbled back a couple steps, looking as if she'd been slapped. He regretted that, but it was better this way. For both of them. He needed her to *act* as if she loved him. Not to actually fall for him.

She reworked the buttons on her blouse, fastening them all the way to the throat. He hadn't gotten a chance to see what was beneath the fabric, except for a tantalizing glimpse of pink lace. That, along with her wounded expression, would keep him awake tonight.

"We need to get used to doing that," he managed to say in a matter-of-fact tone. It was a pitiful explanation for his behavior, but she nodded anyway.

He rose and buttoned his own shirt. Instead of tucking the tails into his trousers once again, he left them out as a cover for his arousal. He was nearly to the door when she stopped him with one quietly issued question.

"Do you think we will?"

He turned, studied her. The woman had him stirred up on so many levels. In the span of a couple dates that weren't really dates at all, she had him sharing things and remembering things and, worst of all, wanting things that he'd long ago decided were off the table when it came to negotiating the terms of his future happiness.

And so it was that, just before he rushed out her door, he said with great feeling, "God, I hope so."

CHAPTER EIGHT

ELIZABETH woke the following morning with a headache that throbbed long after she'd downed a couple of
painkillers with her first cup of coffee.

It didn't help that Howie and the pesky squirrel
started their game of chase as soon as she opened
the front door. Already, her neighbor from across the
street had come calling. Mrs. Hildabrand had stood
on Elizabeth's porch, decked out in curlers and a worn
plaid robe, complaining and threatening to make another nuisance report.

All that before seven o'clock and a second cup of
coffee.

Elizabeth was sipping that second cup now while
sitting in her quiet kitchen. Howie, suitably chastised,
sprawled on the rug in front of the sink. She swore he
was pouting. With the mug cupped in both hands, she
sat on the chair Thomas had occupied the evening before. His herringbone jacket remained draped over the
back of it. Though he'd returned for it, he'd still wound
up forgetting it.

But he hadn't forgotten to kiss her…and then some.

A sloppy mix of emotions churned inside of her at
the memory. Curiously, embarrassment over her enthusiastic response wasn't among them. Perhaps she

would be embarrassed the next time she saw him, but right now she was still tingling all over and regretting that he'd stopped.

She tilted her head to one side and, when she caught the scent of his cologne, inhaled deeply. Potent stuff, that. It suited him. Everything about the man packed a punch. Just as every time she thought she had him figured out, he threw her for a loop. He'd come on to her last night like a man who was very much interested in more than a business deal or friendship. Then he'd stopped. He'd *apologized*!

She was still struggling to make sense of his parting words in response to her foolishly uttered question about whether or not they would ever get used to kissing one another.

God, I hope so!

He'd said it so emphatically, but what exactly did he mean? And why did the possibilities leave her both excited and leery? A glance at the clock reminded her she didn't have time to figure it out now.

After showering, she stood clad in a towel and rummaged through her closet for something to wear to the office, dismissing one outfit after another until she'd worked her way through her entire wardrobe. Maybe Mel was right about her needing some new clothes. Eyeing the panorama of outfits, it struck Elizabeth that practically every article of clothing in her closet came in one of four colors: black, white, navy or tan. A bland and boring palate that also was abundantly safe. She didn't need to worry about drawing attention to herself, whether negative or positive, garbed in these things. No one really noticed her, and that had suited Elizabeth just fine after growing up with her "out-there" parents.

She certainly hadn't learned anything about fashion

from her mother, except what to avoid. Delphine sewed her own clothes and accessories from colorful scraps of old fabric. Sometimes she even tried to sell her creations at local craft shows. She didn't have many takers. The outfits were creative and economical, but hardly stylish. Even so, Delphine loved the attention her homemade clothes attracted—and they attracted plenty.

At first, holey blue jeans were patched in bold hues. Later, her mother recycled them into skirts, shorts and even purses. That wasn't so bad, but polka-dotted bed-sheets or mattress ticking turned up as tunics, bandanas and skirts. The winter Elizabeth turned thirteen her mother had turned green wool blankets from an army surplus store into long, shapeless coats for the entire family. It was impossible not to stand out while wearing pea-green bedding, which was why she'd started buying her own clothes as soon as she was able to squirrel away funds from a regular babysitting gig. That is, what the family didn't require to keep a roof over their heads.

Pushing wet hair back from her face now, Elizabeth eyed her reflection in the full-length mirror. She'd gone from one extreme to the other, from standing out to blending in, but there was no help for it now. Besides, why should it matter to her? It didn't matter to Thomas. Indeed, he'd picked her for the role of his make-believe fiancée based on her appearance alone. She looked like a "Beth," or she had. And she'd been in the right place at the right time.

She would do well to remember that, despite his later claims about no longer judging a book by its cover.

Chin lifted in annoyance with herself as much as defiance, Elizabeth reached back into the closet and chose her oldest, most conservative black suit—the one Mel had dubbed Abbey-wear, because she claimed Elizabeth looked as if she was headed for a nunnery whenever she wore it.

She was slipping into her most comfortable pair of shoes—a low-heeled design in scuffed black—when her cell phone jangled. She glanced at the small screen. Despite her best efforts, her pulse went all wonky upon seeing the caller's identity.

"Hello, Thomas."

"Hi. Good morning. I hope I'm not catching you at a bad time."

"Not at all. I'm just getting ready to leave for the office." She gave herself a mental high five for managing to sound perfectly nonchalant and normal despite the kicked-up cadence of her pulse.

"Same here."

"Are you calling about your jacket?" she asked. It was the reason they'd gone back inside her house last night.

"My...ah, right. My jacket. I left it in your kitchen, didn't I?"

"Yes. I saw it on the back of the chair this morning." And then she'd sat there sniffing his cologne like an idiot. "I'll return it when we see each other again, unless you think you'll need it sooner."

"No. But that's what I'm calling about. I realized after I left your place last night that we never decided when we would meet today."

Probably because they'd both had other things on their minds. *Business, business, business*, Elizabeth reminded herself now when her barely settled pulse got all wonky again. Forcing her focus to her schedule, she said in her most professional tone, "I've got a meeting at ten o'clock that I can't reschedule. After that, though,

I can shuffle a couple meetings around if you want to have lunch together."

Lunch was safe as long as it was in a populated place where public displays of affection would be inappropriate, assuming he had any such displays in mind.

"Unfortunately, I'm busy from eleven-thirty until nearly four going over the results of a marketing survey." He waited only a beat before saying, "How about dinner again?"

"Dinner?"

"Or we could meet up later in the evening if you've got something going on."

"No. Dinner's better. There's an Indian restaurant not far from the campus that I've been wanting to try. How does that sound?"

"Good. And spicy. Just like you like it." Had she imagined that strangled tone?

"I'll meet you there at—"

"No. I'll come by and pick you up."

"Oh, that's not necessary." Indeed, until she got her feelings under control, it bordered on cruel and usual punishment.

"If this is about last night—"

"It's not," she lied.

"Still, I feel I should apologize again for…what happened."

What did it say about her, Elizabeth wondered, that she would much rather he apologized for what *hadn't*?

"Don't! I mean, there's really no need. As you said last night, we both just got a little carried away." Not nearly far enough that she'd woken up feeling boneless and satisfied, but enough that his obvious regrets now were starting to make her feel like a first-class idiot.

"Yes. We did." He was quiet a moment. His tone was

oddly resolute when he said, "I'll pick you up. Just tell me what time."

"Does five-thirty sound okay?" Arguing would only make her seem more foolish, she decided. It would make it seem as if she didn't trust herself to be alone with him. In a car. For a short drive. To a restaurant. For spicy food.

"Sure. Five-thirty."

"At my office," she added hastily. "I'll be out front at five-fifteen."

She trusted herself, but still…

"What's with the Abbey-wear?" Mel wanted to know even before Elizabeth had a chance to boot up her computer. "I thought we agreed that you would burn that overly conservative getup and donate the shoes to an old folks home."

"It's comfortable." Elizabeth sniffed.

"Comfort can be attractive, hon."

Her friend should know. Mel looked perfectly at ease strutting around in a pair of stilettos. Today, the stilettos were a bright raspberry color and she'd paired them with a navy suit that might have been considered conservative if not for the high slit in the skirt and Mel's well-defined curves.

She looked gorgeous, of course. And stylish. Standing near her, Elizabeth felt especially frumpy. She was one hundred and eighty degrees the opposite of Delphine and her cacophony of colors all right. Unfortunately, that still didn't make Elizabeth's wardrobe choices any more fashionable.

Her irritation came out in the form of defiance.

"I'm not going to change my appearance and contort

myself to fit into someone else's ideal of beauty, especially when he probably wouldn't care anyway."

"Okaaaay." Mel pursed her lips. "I was going to ask how last night went, but I think I have my answer. I take it Thomas wants you to dress differently and you're rebelling by wearing your, um, least flattering attire."

Frowning, Elizabeth replied, "This suit isn't that bad. It's a high quality label, I'll have you know. It didn't come cheaply."

"Then in addition to committing a fashion crime, you were robbed," Mel remarked blandly.

Elizabeth let it drop since the price tag really was a moot point. Instead, she plucked at the jacket's prim mandarin collar, determined not to recall the way Thomas had fumbled with the buttons on her blouse the previous night, and said, "Actually, this is how his Beth would dress."

"*His* Beth?"

"You know what I mean, Mel. That's his fiancée's name as far as his grandmother is aware. I'm just the stand-in for the girl of his..."

"Dreams?"

"More like imagination."

"So, in order for you to be plausible as *his Beth*, he's encouraging you to play down your best assets."

"No. Thomas has never said anything one way or another about the way I dress." Elizabeth frowned again. "Although, last night after dinner, he did remove the headband I was wearing."

He'd seemed agitated at the time. Frustrated?

"Is that all he removed?" Mel bobbed her eyebrows twice.

Another time, Elizabeth would have laughed. Mel was good at that. Her knack for levity had served them both well over the years, and it never failed to put their clients at ease. But her words had Elizabeth recalling the shirt she'd been helping Thomas remove.

"Nothing happened."

"Nothing?" Mel crossed her arms.

Sighing, Elizabeth slumped down onto the seat of her chair. "Nothing *much*. He...kissed me again."

"And you liked it. Again," Mel surmised. "Face it. You like *him*."

Some of Elizabeth's annoyance with herself and Thomas leaked away. Frustration and a fresh dollop of confusion took its place.

"What's not to like?" She sighed in defeat.

Her friend levered a hip onto Elizabeth's desk. "Are we talking about the kiss in this case or the man responsible for it?"

"Either. Both."

"Uh-oh."

"There's no 'uh-oh,' Mel. There can be no 'uh-oh.' Thomas is a nice guy, and he's very likeable."

"Don't forget hot," Mel inserted on a wink.

"No need to remind me on that score." But now that she had, Elizabeth's internal thermostat was working its way into the red. "The man sure knows how to kiss. But we're *not* dating."

She said the last part a little too emphatically. Mel's eyes narrowed. "I gather you're having a bit of trouble remembering that."

"Guilty as charged. I wasn't expecting—"

"Fireworks," Mel finished.

Oh, yeah. And a dizzying display, no less. But since mention of their sexual chemistry was too damning to dwell on, Elizabeth said, "Actually, I wasn't expecting us to have much, if anything, in common."

"But you do."

"We both like Hitchcock movies and spicy Chinese." She chuckled at the memory of Thomas fumbling his food during dinner. "Even if he can't use chopsticks to save his life." Her grin was short-lived. "God, Mel. He's exactly the kind of man a smart woman steers clear of."

"But you have common interests, and I thought you just said he was nice and likeable and hot?"

"We do and he's nice and likeable and hot, all right. He's also smart and sexy, and…from what I can tell, the flattering adjectives are practically endless where Thomas is concerned." She grabbed Mel's arm. "Did I tell you about his manners? He pulls out chairs, opens doors. He even apologizes when he swears, not that he makes a habit of it."

"Apologizing?"

"Swearing." She let go of her friend's arm.

Mel shook her head. "I'm sorry, hon. I'm not seeing the problem here. You obviously like him. I *know* you like the way he kisses. And he likes you."

Elizabeth closed her eyes briefly and took a deep breath.

"No, Mel. Thomas *needs* me. That's one of the big red flags waving madly here. This is business."

The corners of Mel's mouth turned down in dismissal and she shook her head. "I'm not buying that. He *likes* you, and as more than a pal," her friend insisted again. "You've already agreed to spend some time with him *acting* like a happy couple. So what if a little pleasure is starting to slip into your business arrangement? What will it hurt? For that matter, who knows where it will lead?"

"I know where it will lead. Nowhere."

But Mel shook her head again. "You are one of the

smartest, most self-assured women I've ever met when you're dealing in a professional capacity. But you don't give yourself enough credit where men are concerned. He may just fall gorgeous head over pricey wing tips for you, for real."

No wonky pulse now. Instead, Elizabeth's stomach took a roller-coaster-worthy plunge. Is that what she wanted to happen? She wasn't sure. They didn't know one another well enough. Yet. Even if everything she knew about him so far, she liked. Except… "He's anti-commitment," she told Mel.

"Come on. Did he actually say that?"

"Yep." Elizabeth nodded. "He made it clear in no uncertain terms when we had dinner the first night that he has no plans to settle down. Ever."

"All men say that."

"No. He means it." Her heart squeezed as she relayed what Thomas had told her the previous night about his parents, the horrifying car accident that had claimed his mother and his father's subsequent alcoholism. "He thinks of love as a disease, a chronic one is how he phrased it."

Mel nibbled the inside of her cheek, uncharacteristically quiet. At last she said, "In his defense, he had a tough break. He was a kid when the accident happened and so it was easy for him to see love as the reason his father is the way he is. But that doesn't make it so. His father suffers from a disease all right. Alcoholism. That's why he basically abandoned his son. The accident might have been the trigger, but…" She lifted her shoulders. "The poor guy. It's no wonder he turned out so gun-shy."

"I know." Elizabeth sighed again. "I wish he could be just a jerk, though. You know?"

"Yeah. A garden variety misogynist would make your situation less complicated," Mel agreed. "You could always tell him that you've reconsidered your bargain and want out. We can find another way to make Literacy Liaisons's endowment a reality."

"I've thought about that, but I've committed myself." Ironic laughter followed her statement. "At least one of us is capable of doing so."

"Are you sure you want to go through with this?"

Elizabeth hesitated only a moment. "I'm sure. It's only for a matter of days. This time next week, Thomas and I will have gone our separate ways."

Yet that thought brought precious little in the way of comfort, a fact Elizabeth tried to ignore.

"Well, at least your eyes are wide open," Mel said.

"Yep. Wide open. There's no changing someone who doesn't want to change. You can push and prod and you just wind up shoving them further away."

"Are you okay?"

"Sure. I like Thomas, and I'm definitely attracted to him, but it's not as if I'm in love with him or anything," she hastened to assure them both. "Right now, I've got paperwork to catch up on." She swiveled in her seat and began typing her password as Mel started for the door.

"Elizabeth?"

"Hmm." She glanced up from her computer screen in time to catch Mel's worried frown.

"Your eyes, I know you said they're wide open, but prop them that way with toothpicks, 'kay?"

In lieu of toothpicks, Elizabeth got down to business. Personal business. There would be no meandering conversation during dinner tonight, she decided. That was too much like what occurred on real dates. Nope. She would treat this like a job interview even though, technically, she'd already been hired. She created a file and made a list of questions she needed answered. Then she spent the next fifteen minutes ruminating over what more to tell him about herself.

She decided to break the information down into likes and dislikes. Since he already knew her preferences when it came to movie genres, directors and actors, she started with music, moved on to authors and completed the entertainment category with board games, adding in the dislike category her disdain for the computer variety.

From there she moved on to her basic values, causes beyond literacy that she supported and a very brief sketch of her education, since he already knew she'd attended State. She considered attaching her high school and college transcripts, but that seemed overkill.

As for her childhood, Thomas had met Howie and she knew that as a child he'd owned a cockatiel named Hitchcock. She jotted down the names of the guinea pig, flop-eared rabbit and pair of very long-lived goldfish she'd had while growing up.

When it came to her parents, she filled in their vital stats, leaving out their lack of a marriage certificate and their other free-spirited oddities. As for her brother, she touched on Ross only briefly, in part because she knew so little about him these days, including his whereabouts.

She swallowed thickly and touched his name on the computer screen. She missed him. As always, she wondered if he ever would decide to come home. Unlike her parents, she did not view her brother's vagabond lifestyle as freedom even if it was a kind of escape. No, Ross had run away. It didn't matter that he'd been five months shy of eighteen years old at the time, close enough to adulthood, according to their parents, to make his own choices.

"He's happy," Delphine had claimed at the time. "You like school and you were smart enough to get a scholarship. But not everyone's cut out for book-learning and college, Lizzie."

Skeet had seconded the opinion. And why not? Their father had gotten by on charm and luck, working odd jobs to raise his family. More often than not he'd been paid under the table. If at times they'd had to live with relatives or crash in friends' apartments that was okay in his book.

It's all good. That was Skeet and Delphine's mantra.

But they weren't to blame for Ross's leaving. No that fell squarely on Elizabeth's shoulders. Where their folks hadn't been tough enough on Ross, Elizabeth had been unyielding in her nagging after he quit school.

"You're squandering your life," she'd raged during that final argument before he'd left home for good. "You're going to end up penniless, homeless."

"Mom and Dad have done just fine."

"That depends on your definition of fine, Ross. How many times would we have wound up in a shelter if not for friends or family opening their homes to us? In the meantime, the job market has only gotten more competitive."

"You're competitive enough for all of us." He hadn't intended it as a compliment. "When are you going to accept that I'm not smart like you?"

He was smart, every bit as bright as she was. Intelligence and literacy didn't go hand-in-hand. But she'd nicked his pride and had put him on the defensive, a mistake she never made these days with Literacy Liaisons's clients.

If she hadn't been so critical of Ross, so self-righteous and pushy, he would have been comfortable confiding in her what their parents had long known. Ross could barely read above a third-grade level. Instead, he'd bolted without speaking another word to her.

Thomas thought her cause noble. He thought she was so selfless in starting up her nonprofit and wanting to see it survive. Indeed, last night he'd told her she was perfect.

Elizabeth knew the truth. She was anything but.

After that steamy encounter in her living room, Thomas worried that he would have a hard time keeping his hands to himself the next time he saw Elizabeth.

He worried that once again he would be compelled to satisfy his curiosity where she was concerned. And that was all this was, he assured himself, a really severe case of curiosity.

What else could it be?

Of course he liked her. It was impossible not to. She was smart, ambitious, interesting and all of that. A little voice in the back of his mind kept reminding him that brains and spunk had never proved such a huge turn-on in the past. Nor had he ever found himself this wildly attracted to a woman he would describe as cute and petite.

And then there was that tantalizing glimpse of pink lace he'd spied beneath her blouse. The memory of it was eating away at his peace of mind. Like a rip in the paper wrapping on a Christmas present, it invited his imagination to fill in the blanks. And was it ever.

Even so, he would make sure everything between them returned to normal—or as normal as possible given the odd set of circumstances surrounding their relationship.

They didn't.

The first indication came that evening almost immediately after he picked her up for dinner.

"This is for you," she said. They were stopped at a red light when she presented him with what amounted to a resume that included her background and interests.

"Ah, this is…helpful." The light turned green and he pulled ahead, not sure what else to say.

"I thought it would be. Time being so tight and all." He barely had a chance to digest that when she told him, "I made a questionnaire for you to fill out."

"A questionnaire."

"You don't need to fill it out tonight. You can get it back to me later. By tomorrow afternoon, say. I included my fax number at the top of the first page."

"Fax," he repeated inanely.

"Yes. I thought this would be a time-saver. Of course, you can email it to me if you'd prefer. My office email address is on the business card I gave you."

He wanted to appreciate her professional approach to the matter, but he'd been enjoying the way they had been going about getting to know one another.

They arrived at the restaurant and Thomas handed the keys to the valet. Elizabeth was out of the car and almost to the door before he caught up with her. For a small woman, she moved fast and with just enough sway to her hips to make up for the severe cut of her suit.

Was she wearing anything pink and lacy underneath it today? That question, inappropriate though it might be, occupied his thoughts through the salad course, and had his gaze straying time and again to the prim mandarin collar. He imagined himself unfastening the top button, albeit with a bit more finesse than he'd exhibited the previous night, and then working his way down.

He reached for his ice water and downed half the glass before setting it back on the table.

"So, tell me about your day?" He worked up a smile. "Any success stories to share?"

He'd asked the question as much to break the silence as to redirect his thoughts. Whatever his motives, though, he was rewarded with a smile.

"One of our clients read *Mr. Brown Can Moo! Can You?* today. Aloud. Cover to cover. Dr. Seuss in case you're wondering."

"My mom used to read it to me. It was one of my favorites as a kid." He smiled, surprised by the happy memory. He'd locked away so much of his pre-accident childhood that the good had been banished along with the bad.

"Mine, too. Anyway, our client got through the entire story with no mistakes. And there wasn't a dry eye in the room afterward." Elizabeth's eyes grew bright now at the recollection. "He's thirty-four, has twin toddler daughters and when he first came to see us more than a year ago his goal was to be able to read them a bedtime story."

"Now he can. That's nice. For him and for you." He reached into his pocket, pulled out his handkerchief and handed it to her. "Your job must be very satisfying."

"It is." She sipped the diet cola she'd ordered. "What about you? What did you do today?"

"Nothing quite as rewarding as hearing someone read their first book." He shrugged. "Mostly I shuffled through paperwork with Waverly's chief financial officer. We had plans for an expansion, but they've had to be put on hold. Some of our financing fell through. Now, we're busy trying to line up some other investors."

"That can't be easy in this economy."

"About as easy as reaching your endowment fund's goal."

"You're making that possible."

Though she smiled after she said it, the warmth of a moment earlier was gone. She returned to business mode and, before long, had him hauling out the form she'd filled out. Before the waiter came to ask if they wanted dessert, Thomas had a bad case of indigestion, but he knew that Elizabeth had once owned a guinea pig named Ziggy, a floppy-eared bunny named Kip and a pair of goldfish she'd called Bonnie and Clyde.

How was it possible, Thomas wondered, that even though he knew a lot more about her, he found her more of a puzzle than before?

After they finished their meal, he drove her back to her car in Literacy Liaisons's parking lot. The ride had been nerve-gratingly quiet. Now, as he stood next to her car after opening the door for her, the mood progressed from strained to outright awkward.

"Good night." He leaned in to kiss her, intending a quick, chaste and perfunctory peck, but she stuck out her hand instead. It poked him just below his breastbone.

"Sorry." She coughed. "I know you said we should get used to kissing and pretending to be affectionate with one another, but I'm really not comfortable doing that."

This came as a surprise, and not necessarily a good one. Here he'd been steeling himself for physical contact, determined not to let a simple kiss boil out of control, and she was essentially telling him thanks, but no seconds for me. He'd never had a complaint when it came to his kissing and Elizabeth hadn't seemed to mind it the previous night. In fact, she'd participated rather enthusiastically, if memory served correctly. His ego had Thomas pointing that out.

"You seemed pretty comfortable last night."

"Yes, well, I think it blurs the lines a little too much given the true nature of our relationship."

"Uh-huh."

She swallowed and he needed to believe her expression held some regret before she added, "But don't worry, Thomas. When we're around your grandmother, I won't pull away if you put your arm around me or anything."

"Gee, that's good to know."

"As for the rest, if she asks, maybe you could just tell her that Beth isn't comfortable with public displays of affection."

He didn't remind her that he no longer thought she look like a Beth. The name was beside the point. She'd referred to herself in the third person. If that didn't imply distance, Thomas didn't know what did. What could he do but respect her wishes? He shook her hand, bid her good-night. Just before she slipped into the car, he told her, "I'll have that questionnaire filled out and faxed over first thing in the morning."

By the time Thomas arrived home twenty minutes later, he was feeling particularly cranky. The house, a large ranch-style on a cul-de-sac in a newer subdivision populated with professionals, was quiet. Though the evening air was hot and humid, he turned off the air-conditioning and opened the windows. The sound of crickets, however, did little to ease his agitation. Nor did filling out Elizabeth's questionnaire.

His inseam and sleeve length? Really? Thomas might have found her attention to detail amusing if not for the fact that he had dozens of questions when it came to the woman, and not one of them focused on her clothing sizes.

Two hours later, he was pacing his bedroom when the telephone on the nightstand rang.

"Tommy, hello," Nana Jo greeted him when he answered. "I wasn't sure I would catch you at home."

A glance at the clock showed it was after ten. Worry came instantly, as it always did where his grandmother was concerned. "Is everything okay?"

"Fine. Just getting excited about the weekend."

"I am, too." It was the truth, for the most part. He always looked forward to seeing his grandmother.

"I can't wait to meet Beth. You're both still coming, right?"

"On Friday, yes." He pushed aside his nerves. "In fact, she and I talked about the weekend over dinner tonight." He had to admit, it felt really good not to have to lie to his grandmother, even if he still wasn't being completely truthful.

He heard the smile in her voice when Nana Jo asked, "Did you take her to a fancy restaurant with candlelit tables and strolling violinists?"

"I don't know that they have those anyplace but in old movies," he replied. "We ate at an Indian restaurant. It was more comfortable than fancy, but our table did have a candle on it." He recalled the way the flame had reflected in Elizabeth's dark eyes. "It was nice."

"An Indian restaurant. I've never been to one. It sounds exotic and spicy."

Thomas smiled at Nana Jo's assessment. "Elizabeth has an adventurous palate."

"Is she with you now?"

"Nana Jo, she's not that kind of girl," he said on a laugh that only served to mock his libido. "Besides, we both have to work in the morning."

"I know how young people are now. I'm just pleased you decided to get married rather than move in together. That seems to be what everyone does nowadays. But when it's right and you're in love, why not make it legally binding?"

Because Thomas found what his grandmother was saying to make way too much sense, he decided to end the conversation.

Thomas figured he would see Elizabeth again before the weekend, but it didn't happen. They spoke by telephone a couple of times, and she'd emailed him once to let him know that she'd received his fax. Other than that, nothing.

He had to admit that he was disappointed, especially when she turned down his offer to see a Hitchcock film at the restored Michigan Theater on Thursday night. He'd been sure she would jump at the chance. Indeed, he'd thought of her the moment he'd spied the marquee announcing performance times for *Vertigo* while driving down East Liberty.

He'd been thinking of her a lot, regardless of—or perhaps because of—the way she'd insisted on shaking his hand when they parted on Wednesday night. But no more face-to-face meetings occurred, let alone sequels to that heated encounter in her living room that still ran through his mind in a never-ending loop.

If Elizabeth were another woman, he might think she was playing hard to get. He didn't like the fact that if she were another woman it wouldn't be working.

Thomas was eager to see her again, a fact that had him nervous as he packed his bag for the long weekend early Friday morning. His trepidation increased tenfold when he arrived at her home to collect her just after nine and she met him at the door with no suitcase in sight.

"I appreciate a woman who packs light, but don't you think you'll need a few things?" he asked.

She tucked her hands into the back pockets of a pair of khaki capris. "I was thinking we could just go for the day instead of for the entire weekend."

"The day? My grandmother lives in Charlevoix, Elizabeth." The city was located on the northwest side of the Lower Peninsula, a good four-hour drive from Ann Arbor even without the added holiday traffic they were likely to encounter despite getting a jump on the weekend.

"I realize that, but the less time we spend with her, the fewer questions she'll be able to ask. I'll share the driving," she offered, as if to sweeten the deal.

"Nana Jo is going to have questions either way and, believe me, she won't hesitate to ask them, whether in person or over the telephone." Of course, then answering them would be his problem to deal with rather than hers.

"Do you talk on the phone often?"

"Pretty much every day, but I haven't seen her in months. I miss her."

He hadn't intended to use the sentiment to score points, but Elizabeth softened. He saw it in her expression.

"Tell you what," he began. "We can come home on Sunday instead of Monday. You mentioned before that you'd canceled some of your plans to accompany me.

Maybe the weekend won't be a total bust for you if we leave a day early."

"I was just going to go to the beach with Mel and some other girlfriends." She shrugged. "It was no big deal."

"Don't you do anything with your family?"

"My parents have an annual barbecue on the Fourth."

She hadn't told him much about them, and even the written biography she'd given him the other evening contained precious little information beyond their names and dates of birth, so he was intrigued. "Good. Then you will be able to attend it. Will your brother be there? Ross, right?"

She shook her head. He'd said something wrong, something that made her sad, though he wasn't sure what. But then, he knew better than most people that sometimes innocent questions about family could be as wounding as daggers. Hoping to chase the shadows from her eyes, he said, "There's nothing like a good barbecue to celebrate Independence Day."

He was relieved when Elizabeth's smile reappeared. "You don't know my parents," she said wryly.

No. Thomas didn't. He'd always made it a point not to meet the parents of any of the women he spent time with. He didn't worry about passing parental inspection. Rather, he knew the signal it would send to the other party. Meeting the parents made even the most casual relationship seem serious, at least where the marriage-minded were concerned.

Oddly, he found himself wanting to meet Elizabeth's, even—or maybe especially—after she asked, "Have you ever had tofu shish kebabs?"

"I can't say that I have."

"It's an acquired taste, believe me. The same can be said for soy-and-kelp burgers on unleavened bread."

"Soy and kelp, huh?" He rubbed the back of his neck. "I hope you're not too bored with Nana Jo's tame cooking. I think the most exotic recipe in her repertoire is fried green tomatoes. She started making them after she saw the movie of the same name."

"I'm nothing like my parents," she replied hastily, giving Thomas the impression that, just as he was, she was eager to ensure that the apple fell far from the tree and then kept right on rolling.

Elizabeth invited him inside while she packed her bag. Howie wasn't there. Mel had taken him back to her town house. If the dog were there, Thomas had little doubt it would be growling menacingly. It was if the hound knew that something about his owner's relationship with Thomas wasn't all it seemed to be.

Thomas paced the living room. His gaze kept straying to the love seat, specifically to the arm where he'd sat the other evening while he and Elizabeth had eagerly started helping one another out of their clothes. Sanity had prevailed, but he'd been going crazy ever since. After fifteen of the longest minutes of his life, Elizabeth finally emerged with a small carry-on-sized suitcase in hand.

"You really do pack light."

She shrugged. "A couple pairs of walking shorts, two shirts and nightclothes don't take up much room. You didn't specify a dress code."

She sounded defiant.

"There isn't one. My grandmother is pretty laid-back." He pointed toward the bag. "A bathing suit might come in handy. There's a nice stretch of beach nearby."

Elizabeth shook her head. "I burn easily."

And blushed easily, too, he noted.

"Well, I brought mine, but suit yourself." He took her bag. "Ready?"

In answer, she started for the front door, which she carefully locked behind them. Then they were on their way, heading toward the interstate in his car as Bruce Springsteen belted out "Born in the U.S.A." on the radio.

For better or for worse, there was no turning back now.

CHAPTER NINE

ELIZABETH hadn't intended to fall asleep, but a little over
two hours into their trip she dozed off. Before then she
and Thomas hadn't spoken much, other than to comment on the good weather—forecasters were calling
for sunshine and warm temperatures through the early
part of the following week—and go over a few details
of the visit.

She missed their easy conversation, but keeping
things all business was for the best. The lines of their
relationship weren't likely to become too blurry that
way. So, she'd pulled out a magazine she'd brought with
her and made a point of reading it. Or, rather, pretending to read it. Now that she was awake, she couldn't
recall a single article.

She straightened in her seat and stretched before
sending a sheepish smile Thomas's way.

"Sorry about that. I guess I drifted off."

"That's all right. You only snored a little." He winked
after saying so. She could only hope he was kidding.

"Where are we?"

"About fifteen minutes south of Charlevoix. I thought
we'd visit with my grandmother a bit before checking
in at the bed-and-breakfast where we'll be staying."

In separate rooms. He'd made that clear after she'd

made a point of asking him about it via email. Still, they would be under the same roof and that was enough to have her nerves and newfound needs percolating on high.

Elizabeth had never been to Charlevoix. Though her family had moved around a lot during her childhood, they'd done so mainly in the much more populated southern part of the state. So, she stared out the window as they made their way down Bridge Street with its quaint assortment of shops and eateries, acting the part of the tourist. Thomas indulged her, pointing out a fudge shop and other sights of interest, and giving her some background. The vast expanse of Lake Michigan stretched to the west of the town. The much smaller Lake Charlevoix was to the east.

"It's pretty here."

"It is. Nana Jo likes it, even though the winters can be harsh."

"She stays here year-round?"

"Yes." He chuckled then. "She's quite adamant that she'll never become one of those snowbirds who flies to Florida before the first snowflake falls. She and my late grandfather had always planned to retire here. He died when I was six. Heart attack. She was still set on moving to Charlevoix eventually. She was already looking at places at the time of the accident. Then she put everything on hold."

For him.

"Sorry about your grandfather," Elizabeth murmured. Josephine O'Keefe had lost her husband and only child in the span of two years. It wasn't only pity Elizabeth felt for the other woman, but admiration. She'd rolled up her sleeves and put her own plans on hold to raise a young, equally grief-stricken boy. "Your grandmother sounds like an amazing woman."

Thomas glanced over. His hand left the steering wheel to give hers a gentle squeeze. "She is. You're going to like her."

Elizabeth didn't need his reassurance. She already did, and it was a realization that made her all the more uneasy.

Nana Jo lived in a condominium complex not far from downtown, but only a short distance from the lake.

"Well, this is it," Thomas said, pulling into the parking lot. He sounded every bit as nervous as Elizabeth felt when he asked, "Ready?"

"As I'm ever going to be," she murmured.

She opened the car door before he had a chance to come around and do it for her, earning a frown. The day was warm, a fact the automobile's air-conditioning had done a good job of camouflaging. The sun's heat would have been unbearable if not for the stiff breeze blowing in off the lakes. It snatched at her neatly ordered hair and sent it flying around her face.

It also brought with it the appealing scents of summer, including the smoke from someone's barbecue. Before she'd dozed off, Thomas had asked if she wanted to stop for a bite to eat. She'd told him no, that she wasn't hungry. At the time she hadn't been. Nerves had tied her stomach into knots and she had been eager to get to their final destination. Now, her stomach growled and she found herself wishing for the last-minute reprieve of a meal.

Before she could say so to Thomas, however, she heard a squeal of delight. She turned to see a stylish older woman with a short cap of silver hair bustling across the parking lot toward them with her smile stretching nearly as wide as her arms.

"Tommy!"

He hugged the woman back, picking her up off her feet in the process. Elizabeth smiled as she watched them and something inside of her shifted to boggy ground once again. What was it Mel always said? You can judge how a man will treat you by the way he treats his mother. Nana Jo wasn't Thomas's mother, but close enough that her friend's pearls of wisdom applied. God help her.

"It's good to see you, too," he managed to respond after a moment.

Raw emotion thickened his voice, leaving no doubt as to the deep love Thomas had for his grandmother, the deep love they had for one another. Tragedy had made their bond all the stronger. Elizabeth admired it. She admired them for the way they obviously cherished it.

Two expectant gazes focused on her then. Showtime, she thought, wishing wildly, before she could catch herself, that the moment could be real. That she could be the love of Thomas's life, brought home to meet the woman who'd raised him.

"And you're Tommy's Beth."

Even if Elizabeth had had time to stick out a hand in a gesture of greeting, it wouldn't have mattered. Nana Jo closed the distance between them in short order and pulled her into an embrace that, while not strong enough to break bones, thoroughly shattered Elizabeth's preconceptions of Josephine O'Keefe as a frail octogenarian nearing the end of her days.

"H-h-hi." The single syllable sputtered out along with Elizabeth's breath as the woman rocked her side to side.

"Nana Jo, stop. You'll crush her," Thomas chided lightly when the embrace lengthened.

His grandmother pulled back on a robust laugh. "I'm sorry, my dear. It's just that I'm so tickled to finally meet you. Tommy has told me so much about you."

She patted Elizabeth's cheek before grasping her lightly by the arms and taking a step back. Then she frowned.

"I have to admit, I pictured you a little differently."

"Different h-how?" Elizabeth cast a nervous glance toward Thomas. What sort of description had he given her?

"I don't know. Just…just thinking out loud and being insufferably rude," she apologized.

"That's not necessary. I can honestly say you're not quite how I pictured you, either." If Nana Jo's health was failing it sure didn't show.

"It's just that you're such a tiny thing," mused Nana Jo, who stood half a head taller and had a more substantial build. She smiled at Thomas. "The breeze coming off Lake Michigan will blow her away if you're not careful to keep a tight hold on her, Tommy."

"I plan to do just that."

His smile was as warm as the gaze he sent Elizabeth. Though the words were said for his grandmother's benefit, Elizabeth's breathing hitched and she smiled back.

Nana Jo grinned as well, before demanding of herself, "Goodness, where are my manners? You must think me a horrible hostess, Beth, waylaying you in the parking lot like this." She winked from behind a pair of red-rimmed bifocals. "I plead guilty to watching for your arrival from my windows and then hurrying down here the minute I spotted you, too eager to wait for you to ring the doorbell. Pop open the trunk of that fancy car of yours, Tommy. Let's get your bags and go inside where we can all sit down and have a proper visit. I just made a fresh pitcher of iced tea and some cookies."

Elizabeth could see where Thomas had learned his polite ways, but that wasn't what had her casting an urgent glance in his direction.

"I—I thought we were staying at a bed-and-breakfast in town, Thomas?"

"We are." Both his expression and tone were apologetic when he told his grandmother, "I've booked rooms for Elizabeth and I at the Daniels Cottage over on Edgewater, Nana."

"We didn't want to impose," Elizabeth explained.

Nana Jo made a *tsking* sound and waved one hand impatiently. "Impose? Nonsense! It's no imposition. Of course you'll stay here. I have plenty of space." To Thomas she said, "Beth will sleep in the guest room. I put fresh linens on the bed just this morning."

"Where will I be sleeping?" Thomas asked innocently. But Elizabeth thought she caught a dash of the devil in his otherwise angelic expression.

"On the couch," Nana Jo retorted. "I'm too old-fashioned to agree to let you sleep in the same room with Beth, whether she's your fiancée or not."

She winked again at Elizabeth, who felt her face catch fire.

"Really, that's very kind. But I…we couldn't put you out like that," Elizabeth began. "Besides, Thomas already made the reservations."

It was a weak argument that Nana Jo dismantled easily. "He can unmake them. If the owner gives you any trouble, Tommy, I'll talk to him. I know Ned and Estelle from church." Lowering her voice, she added, "Estelle is on the list to bring dessert for funeral lunches, but we never put her rum cake out. She's a little too liberal with the libations, if you know what I mean."

"But—"

"Not another word. I won't have it any other way. You're all but family now, my dear, and family is never a bother. Tell her, Tommy."

Before Elizabeth could object further, Thomas said, "Arguing won't do you any good, I'm afraid."

He put an arm around Elizabeth's shoulders. She jolted at his touch, but didn't pull away. She'd promised him that she wouldn't. She hadn't promised to snuggle closer, though. She did so automatically, reeled in by the scent of his cologne. When she felt him drop a light kiss on the top of her head, she came to her senses. It was all for show, she reminded herself, even if they were attracted to one another. Ultimately, nothing real and lasting would come of it.

"He comes by his stubborn streak honestly, Beth. He gets it from me," Nana Jo claimed proudly. "Now let's see to your bags."

Thomas shrugged helplessly and mouthed an apology to Elizabeth. Even though they had decided to leave a day early, the weekend had just gotten much, much longer.

Nana Jo's condo was on the top floor. Despite their protests, she insisted on carrying Elizabeth's suitcase the entire time, not even setting it down during the short elevator ride. Thomas would have to have another chat with her doctor, he decided, and find out exactly what she should and shouldn't be doing. He knew better than to think he would get a straight answer from her. Stubborn streak, indeed. Hers was a mile wide.

Still, he was relieved to see her looking so healthy, not to mention so damned happy. She hadn't stopped grinning since their arrival. Thomas pushed away the twinge of guilt he felt for deceiving her. So far, the result was worth it.

She waved Elizabeth inside the condo, though she left it to Thomas to hold open the door. She patted his cheek on the way inside. The place was every bit as welcoming as she was, with the multitude of homey touches he remembered. Even though he hadn't grown up here, he'd spent enough time in the condo that he never felt like a guest.

Today, it smelled like a bakery thanks to a batch of fresh-from-the-oven cookies that were warming on the kitchen counter—chocolate chip, his favorite. He'd never brought home a woman before, but this was pretty much what he'd expected the reception to be. Nana Jo had pulled out all of the stops in an effort to make Elizabeth feel welcomed and comfortable. He eyed the couch sourly. Oh, yes. She'd thought of everything all right.

"If you want to freshen up, Beth, the guest bath is just down the hallway," Nana Jo was saying. "I've put out towels and a washcloth for you. If you need anything else or can't find something, don't hesitate to ask."

The grand tour didn't take long. Nana Jo's condo wasn't very large, even if it felt that way thanks to its open floor plan. In addition to two bedrooms and two full baths, it boasted an eat-in kitchen that was separated from the living room by a large, granite island.

He reached for one of the cookies on his way past, only to have his hand swatted away by Nana Jo, who barely glanced in his direction and never broke stride. The woman still had eyes in the back of her head.

"This is where you'll stay, Beth. Tommy, you can leave your bag in here for now so that we're not tripping over it in the living room."

"Gee, how very generous of you," he grumbled good-naturedly.

"You haven't canceled your reservation at the bed-and-breakfast yet, if the accommodations here aren't to your liking," she reminded him tartly as one brow arched over the top rim of her bifocals. He could only chuckle, especially since Elizabeth was trying to tuck away a grin.

When they reached the guest room, he stopped at the door after the women continued inside. After setting his luggage in the corner, he leaned against the jamb and watched Elizabeth take in the inviting floral comforter that covered a queen-sized bed. Coordinating curtains flapped at the large, open window that let in a breeze that made air-conditioning obsolete even on a day as warm as this one.

"I'm sure I'll be very comfortable in here. The room is lovely, Mrs. O'Keefe."

"It's Nana Jo, dear. And thank you." His grandmother wagged a finger in his direction then. "Tommy complains that it's too feminine for his liking."

"I feel like I'm sleeping in a posey patch, but it suits you, Elizabeth." He managed to sound lighthearted, even though he was picturing her on the bed, surrounded by the comforter's fussy floral print and wearing nothing but a couple of scraps of pink lace. On a groan he spat out a mild oath.

"Tommy! Your language," Nana Jo admonished. "I raised you better than that. What on earth are you thinking?"

What was he thinking? He glanced at Elizabeth. Her

eyes were wide, alert and, unless he missed his guess, full of interest. She moistened her lips, exhaled slowly. God help them both, *she* knew exactly what was on his mind.

While Elizabeth took his grandmother's suggestion and freshened up, Thomas helped Nana Jo carry out a tray of refreshments to the balcony that opened up off the living room. Large pots in the corners overflowed with bright red geraniums. Beyond the white wooden railing, Lake Michigan stretched as far as the eye could see. It was the kind of view one never tired of seeing. Even in the winter, when parts of the big lake froze and huge rafts of ice, pushed ashore by wind and waves, bounded the coast, the view was mesmerizing.

"It's a gorgeous day," he said.

"And yours is a gorgeous girl. I like your Beth, Tommy." She poured three large glasses with iced tea and set a small plate of lemon wedges and a sugar bowl in the center of the scrolled iron table.

"I thought you would." He managed to purloin a cookie this time without getting his hand smacked.

"I still don't understand why it's taken you so long to finally bring her to see me." Her tone held reproach.

"I'm sorry I put you off for so long. Things were crazy at work and then, well, I just wanted to be sure." He'd told her similar things several times in the past. This time they seemed less like an excuse.

"And are you?"

The pat answer he planned never made it past his lips. Instead, he walked to the rail, his gaze trained on a couple of sailboats that were nothing but white dots on a cloudless blue horizon.

"I've never met anyone quite like Elizabeth," he said

slowly, honestly. "I like being around her, spending time with her. The more I learn, the more I *want* to learn."

"You almost sound surprised."

"More like amazed." He took a bite of the cookie, turned and worked up a grin for her benefit. "She likes Alfred Hitchcock movies."

Nana Jo chuckled. "I see now what clinched the deal for you. That genre of film isn't for everyone."

"Actually, we have quite a bit in common, more than I expected."

"Well, that's what happens when you stop dating women who are all wrong for you."

He smiled since it was expected and finished the cookie, nearly choking on the last bite when his grandmother added, "Love has a way of finding us, Tommy. Even if we never look for it. Maybe especially when we don't."

Elizabeth joined them just as his coughing fit was subsiding. As soon as she stepped out onto the balcony, the breeze made a mockery of the time she'd spent returning her hair to its sleek bob. While she tucked it behind both ears, he rose from his seat and pulled out her chair, earning a nod of satisfaction from his grandmother.

"I'm so glad to finally have a chance to meet you, dear," Nana Jo said.

Just as he had, Elizabeth bypassed the sugar bowl and selected a wedge of lemon, which she squeezed into her glass.

"I'm enjoying meeting you, too. Thomas has told me a lot about you." Elizabeth smiled. "All of it good."

"Tommy, what have I told you about fibbing?" Nana Jo scolded, albeit teasingly.

Elizabeth looked uncomfortable despite her smile,

but he had to hand it to her. She was managing to be completely honest with his grandmother despite the big white elephant of a lie sharing space with them on the small balcony.

"Tommy tells me you like Alfred Hitchcock."

"I do."

"And she plays poker, Nana Jo. She and some friends get together regularly." He sipped his tea. "No cigars but they sometimes talk sports."

"Really?" Nana Jo's eyes lit up. "I belong to a bridge club, but I always wanted to try my hand at five-card stud. Maybe you could teach me sometime?"

"Sure."

"You have to watch her, Elizabeth. My nana is a cardsharp."

They laughed and the conversation flowed freely until Nana Jo asked, "Why don't you tell me a little bit about your family? I haven't managed to get much out of Tommy on the subject. But then you know how men are. They're stingy when it comes to offering details."

"My family?" Elizabeth took her time sipping her tea. "There's not much to tell, really. I, um, I had a pretty typical childhood."

Interesting, Thomas got the feeling she was lying now. But after what she'd told him about tofu shish kebabs, he could see why she might want to shade the truth. Not that his grandmother would care one way or another what her parents' diet preferences were. He certainly didn't.

"You're in Ann Arbor now, I know, but where did you grow up?"

"Oh, here and there in southeast Michigan." The answer was as vague as the one she'd written on her "resume."

"It sounds like your family moved around lot," Nana Jo said. "Your father's job?"

Elizabeth sipped her tea. "More or less."

"And you have an older sister."

"A younger brother," Thomas and Elizabeth said at the same time.

"My goodness, I *am* getting old," Nana Jo said. "Somehow I managed to get that completely backward."

She sent Elizabeth a bemused smile that took a calculating turn when it reached Thomas. *Uh-oh.* He knew that look. Nana Jo sensed something was afloat.

"So, how old is your brother?" Nana Jo picked up the plate of cookies and held it out for Elizabeth.

She selected one. "Ross is twenty-six."

"Is he married or engaged?"

"No. I… We don't see one another often."

"Oh, that's too bad. You must miss him."

"I do. Terribly."

Nana Jo made a sympathetic noise and patted the back of Elizabeth's hand. "Does he live out of state?"

"Yes. He…travels a lot. He hasn't been back to Michigan in years."

"Then your wedding will be a reunion as well. Will he be standing up?" Nana Jo asked. Nodding in Thomas's direction, she complained, "That one there won't tell me anything about the ceremony preparations. He won't even give me the date."

"Because we haven't decided yet," Thomas inserted hastily. "With our work schedules and such, it's not as easy as throwing a dart at a calendar."

"Well, surely you have some inkling of the number of groomsmen you're planning."

He glanced helplessly at Elizabeth. "I could ask Ross to be a groomsman."

"No!" She looked stricken. "I'm sorry."

"Or not."

Elizabeth apologized a second time. Her face was flushed. Her expression miserable. "I haven't mentioned this before, Thomas, but I don't know where Ross is." Her gaze shifted to his grandmother. "My brother left— ran away from home, actually—when I was in college. He quit school and just…left."

"And you haven't heard from him since then?" Thomas asked.

"Personally, no."

"I'm sorry," Nana Jo said softly.

Thomas was more than sorry. He felt culpable in forcing the admission. He reached for her hand and knitted their fingers together before bringing it to rest against his heart. "Elizabeth, I had no idea."

She allowed the contact for a moment before pulling her hand free, ostensibly to push her breeze-blown hair back from her face. "I don't talk about it often."

"But I'm guessing you think about him and worry every day," Nana Jo said sympathetically.

"I do."

"That's the way Tommy is about his father."

He blinked in surprise. He hadn't seen the switch in subjects coming. Caught off guard. he retorted sharply, "I don't give a damn where he is or what he's doing as long as he isn't on my doorstep looking for more money so he can pay off his bar tab."

"Thomas Jonathon Waverly!"

The use of his full name pulled him up short, just as it always had when he was a child.

"I'm sorry." He expelled a breath and turned to Elizabeth and repeated his apology.

"It's forgotten," she said.

"Nothing is forgotten."

Their gazes held until a gust of wind sent paper napkins flying off the table. He and Elizabeth both rose to fetch them before they could be carried over the rail.

"I should have brought a headband," she remarked, shoving her wayward hair back from her face and settling into her seat once more.

"I'm glad you didn't." Reminding himself it was expected for him to touch her, he gave in to temptation and brushed a stray tendril off of her forehead. "I like it loose like this and a little disheveled."

"Why?" She glanced at his grandmother before laughing uncomfortably. "I mean, I look a mess."

"Hardly, my dear," Nana Jo said. "You're too pretty to look anything of the sort."

Recalling how Elizabeth had disagreed with him the one time he'd called her pretty, Thomas half expected her to do so now. He told himself he only was forestalling her argument when he leaned over and, in a voice barely above a whisper, said, "I like it this way because it reminds me of how it looked after I had my hands in it the other night."

He was close enough to hear her breath hitch. He was smug enough to like it. He decided to press his advantage—for Nana Jo's benefit, of course—and kissed the corner of Elizabeth's mouth. Both women sighed afterward.

Nana Jo, however, had a bone to pick.

"I would remind you that it's rude not to speak loud enough so that everyone at the table can hear you, Tommy."

"Sorry." But he flashed a cocky grin that had her pursing her lips.

Still, Nana Jo accepted the apology with a nod. Then

she was grinning as well. "Based on Beth's very becoming blush, I gather that whatever you whispered in her ear wasn't fit for mine anyway."

Elizabeth laughed weakly. "Still, he is being rude."

She tried to tame her hair again, even though the breeze had other plans for it. The blush staining her cheeks was, as his grandmother said, becoming. Pretty? No. At that very moment, he thought her beautiful. Inside of him, something shifted with all the subtlety of an earthquake. It was a good thing he was seated or he might have wound up losing his balance.

Especially when Nana Jo added, "Yes, but that's what happens when a man's in love. He forgets everything including his manners."

This made twice his grandmother had used the L-word. His breath caught in his throat. Hell, he could hardly drag enough of it into his lungs, until he reminded himself that he wanted his grandmother to think he was in love. The fact that she did simply meant he was playing his role superbly.

Kudos to me, he decided sourly. If his business ever folded maybe there was a career waiting for him in Hollywood.

"Are you all right?" Elizabeth asked, looking concerned as she laid a hand on his arm.

"Allergies." He coughed for effect. "Must be a lot of tree pollen in the air around here or something."

Something being the operative word.

Nana Jo frowned. "Tommy, you don't have—" She broke off abruptly then. "Goodness, Beth, where's your engagement ring?"

Thomas would have appreciated his reprieve more if his freedom from the frying pan hadn't landed him in the fire. He knew where the ring was. It was exactly where he'd left it, in the pocket of the herringbone jacket that was still in Elizabeth's possession. He cursed himself for the oversight. Meanwhile, Elizabeth looked stricken.

"I...I..." She sent him a panicked look.

"It's being sized." He reached for her left hand and caressed its knuckles with the pad of his thumb. Her fingers were so small and delicate that the lie was believable. His mother's ring never would have fit without a jeweler's adjustment.

"I see."

Nana Jo's gaze made him nervous. When he was a kid, Nana Jo always seemed to be one step ahead of him. But surely she didn't suspect...

She kept him guessing with her next question.

"I'll have to settle for a description, then. What does it look like, Beth?"

Elizabeth appeared to be the one suffering a bout of something now. The blush of a moment ago was gone along with most of her color.

"You've seen it, Nana Jo. It's Mom's ring."

He had both women's full attention now.

"You gave Beth your mother's ring? How...how lovely." But she was frowning.

Don't ask, he ordered himself. Just leave it be. But he heard himself say, "You don't seem very happy about that."

"I guess I'm just a little surprised." She sent an apologetic glance Elizabeth's way. "But in a good way, of course. In a good way. It's a lovely ring."

He recalled it now. Lovely, yes. But somehow not at all right for Elizabeth.

Still, when Nana Jo lifted her iced tea and said, "Let's have a toast, shall we?" he raised his glass as well.

"To your engagement and the start of a wonderful new life together."

Glasses clinked, smiles were exchanged. But Thomas kept thinking that as real as the moment seemed, nothing about it felt right.

CHAPTER TEN

Somehow, they managed to get through the rest of the first day without further incident. For dinner, Thomas cooked burgers on the balcony's small grill to go along with the coleslaw and potato salad Nana Jo had made. They ate indoors this time. The breeze was just too strong.

After dinner, even though Nana Jo insisted they could go out if they wanted, they opted to stay in. To Thomas's dismay and Elizabeth's delight, his grandmother pulled out a stack of old photo albums.

"Don't show her the one of—"

"Too late," Nana Jo crowed. "Here's Tommy at twelve, shaving."

"Shaving at twelve."

"He didn't have a hair on his face but, bless his heart, he insisted he needed to start shaving." Nana Jo's laughter filled the condominium.

Thomas groaned louder when the page was flipped to reveal a shot of him at about fourteen dressed in a suit, a girl of the same age at his side. Hannah something. She was as tall as he was, but towered over him thanks to her hair.

"I love her 'do."

"Come on, admit it. You styled your hair the same way. All the girls did."

"Not me."

He believed her.

"First date?" Elizabeth inquired.

"School dance. She was the granddaughter of a friend of Nana Jo's."

"He holds that first fix-up against me to this day, which is why I've never again meddled in his personal affairs." When they both glanced her way, Nana Jo amended, "Much."

They finished with that album and Elizabeth pulled another from the stack.

"Not that one..." Thomas fell silent as she opened it.

A lovely brunette stared back at Elizabeth. Her hair was feathered away from her face. Her blue-green eyes were fringed with dark lashes. Elizabeth knew those eyes.

"That's Tommy's mom, my Lynn." Nana Jo's expression wasn't sad so much as resigned. "That picture was taken not long before the accident. She was a beautiful young woman. When she walked in a room, she lit it up with her smile."

"I can see that." Elizabeth chanced a glance in Thomas's direction. She expected to find him frowning, but the corners of his mouth were starting to curve.

He tapped the photograph. "Right before this picture was taken she'd grounded me from television for a week."

"For what?" Nana Jo wanted to know.

"I broke a glass baking dish."

"That doesn't sound like Lynn."

His smile bloomed in full. "I was using it to start a worm farm and dropped it on the kitchen floor. Worms were everywhere when Mom came in, and company was due in less than an hour."

Elizabeth laughed. His grandmother joined in. Thomas shook his head on a smile. "She was something. The day my grounding officially ended, she got out an old shoebox, lined it with plastic and then the pair of us went out to the flower garden and hunted up more worms."

"Lynn did that?"

"She wore a pair of gloves, but, yeah. The only time I recall her freaking out was when a big daddy longlegs climbed up her arm."

"My girl hated spiders," Nana Jo said. "Can't say that I blame her. I loathe the things myself."

Lynn Waverly might have hated spiders, but she'd loved her child more. Elizabeth could picture them, mother and son, on their knees in the dirt, small spades in hand, turning over the earth and squealing in delight—whether real or manufactured—over their finds.

"She sounds like the kind of mother I hope to be someday. Very hands-on. Very involved." Not the passive parents her own had been.

"Then you will be, my dear," Nana Jo said with such certainty that Elizabeth had no option but to believe, even if in the past she'd worried that Delphine's hands-off style might be hard-wired into her genes.

They continued with the photo albums after that, working their way through the entire stack.

"I hope we're not boring you," Thomas said at one point.

"Hardly." And she meant it. She liked hearing the stories that went along with the pictures. She liked hearing his laughter mingled with his grandmother's as they reminisced over the past.

A little later, when he excused himself to use the bathroom, Nana Jo pulled Elizabeth aside.

"I want to thank you, Beth."

"For what?"

"For Tommy's laughter and easy smile. We haven't looked through those albums in years. Especially that particular album. He's avoided talking about Lynn. In fact, he's avoided all of the memories that came before the accident, whether good or bad. Any time I've brought up his mother, he's changed the subject or found a reason to cut the conversation short."

"I didn't realize."

"After the accident, when I went to live with Tommy and his father, I was appalled that Hoyt had gotten rid of every last picture of her. But later, when Hoyt was gone and it was just Tommy and me, I started noticing that the pictures that I'd put out disappeared, especially the ones of the three of them looking so happy. I took my cue from him and tucked most of them away. And I stopped talking about Lynn, especially with him. It seemed to make him so sad."

Elizabeth wondered if in addition to making Thomas sad, he was worried that it made his grandmother sad. It was his way of trying to protect her, even if it had done the opposite.

"I'm sorry." Elizabeth squeezed Nana Jo's hand.

"I've been, too. Sorry for both of us. I miss my daughter. All these years later, the ache doesn't go away. But tonight…" The older woman's eyes misted and she squeezed Elizabeth's hand in return. "It was like Lynn was here with us."

"She was. In both of you."

"You're good for him, Beth. So very good for him. I can see why he loves you."

Elizabeth's smile faltered. She wished she could agree.

Elizabeth woke early and stretched on the bed. She'd slept well, incredibly well, all things considered. She credited the fresh air and the little sachet of lavender that Nana Jo had tucked under the pillow. The woman thought of everything.

Dressed in a pair of navy blue shorts and a sleeveless white blouse, Elizabeth left the bedroom. Then she gathered up her toiletries, hoping to scoot into the bathroom before she was seen. The scent of freshly brewed coffee hit her as soon as she opened the bedroom door.

Someone else was an early riser. A glance at the couch confirmed that it wasn't Thomas. He was still asleep, both feet sticking over the armrest, arms above his head. The blanket Nana Jo had provided him with was still neatly folded on the coffee table. It had been too warm for that, even with the breeze. As for the sheet, he'd kicked it off and it lay in a heap on the floor. He wore pajamas…of a sort: a white T-shirt and a pair of lightweight athletic shorts. The shirt's hem was pulled up just enough that she caught a glimpse of toned abs.

She was openly ogling them when Nana Jo slipped up behind her and said, "He gets that lean build from the O'Keefe side. My husband was the same way."

Elizabeth started. The older woman moved like a cat. "I…I…was just going to wash my face."

Nana Jo chuckled. Elizabeth thought she heard the older woman say, "Use cold water."

* * *

Since it was Elizabeth's first visit to Charlevoix, Nana Jo and Thomas insisted on showing her around town that afternoon. Walking along sidewalks crowded with tourists kept conversation to a minimum, a fact for which Elizabeth was grateful. Given the roiling mix of emotions she was experiencing, she was happy to window-shop and ooh and aah over the sights.

She might even have enjoyed herself if not for the loose hold Thomas kept on her hand as they strolled along. The only time he let go was when they entered a store, and then only so he could open the door, after which his hand would find the small of her back, guiding her along inside. It was such simple contact, but it kept stirring up needs, not all of them physical, though those were the most obvious. With her hormones threatening to go from simmer to boil, the stark line she'd drawn between reality and make-believe was turning into a blurry mess.

She'd promised him that she wouldn't pull away from his touch, and she'd been keeping her word. She'd also promised herself that she wouldn't get *carried* away. Well, so much for that vow. She was. Even though she was doing her darnedest to keep her feet planted firmly on the ground, her imagination kept taking flight, threatening to pull her heart right along with it.

But who could blame her?

She'd found Thomas tempting even before he'd transformed himself into the besotted bridegroom-to-be for his grandmother's benefit. Now, with his charm kicked into hyperdrive, it was ever so easy to believe that his one major flaw was fixable.

Except that it wasn't.

He didn't want a long-term relationship with the possibility of a lifetime commitment, no matter what his pretty words and solicitous behavior indicated now. While she hadn't been actively seeking love when she walked into his office that day, she knew what she wanted for her future, and it was the whole shebang— a husband and a couple of kids to go with the dog she already had. She wanted permanence, continuity, the kind of peace of mind her vagabond childhood had lacked despite her parents' unwavering devotion to one another.

Thomas couldn't provide that. He might like Elizabeth. He might even be interested in her romantically beyond their arrangement, since he seemed genuinely attracted to her, a fact that, in and of itself, caused her pulse to quicken and need to pool. But whatever happened between them wouldn't last. It would come with an expiration date that he had predetermined.

He ended things before they became "messy." He'd told her that, had made it abundantly clear. She would be a fool to allow anything to transpire between them. Yet, strolling hand-in-hand down a sidewalk on a warm sunny day, she found herself wishing for the impossible, because take away that one flaw of his—major as it was—and the man was perfect and, when she was around him, he made Elizabeth feel that way, too.

"Here's the restaurant I was thinking we could eat dinner at this evening," Nana Jo said, stopping outside a pair of bright red doors. A framed menu hung to one side. Pointing at it, she said, "Why don't you both take a look and tell me what you think."

"I think I'm shocked that you're not going to cook for us yourself," Thomas teased. "After making the burgers on the grill last night, I've been looking forward to a home-cooked meal. It's been ages since I last had one."

Nana Jo frowned before turning to Elizabeth with a quizzical expression. "Don't you cook, Beth?"

Uh-oh. She felt Thomas squeeze her hand. In desperation or in reassurance?

"Actually, I do," she replied truthfully. Feeling a little bit rebellious, she added, "Quite well, in fact."

"Oh?"

"I took a six-week course on Italian cuisine offered through the public school district's community education program a few years ago. I was tired of eating stuff that came out of a box or from the freezer."

"Smart cookie." Nana Jo tapped an arthritic finger to one of her temples.

"Yes. But our work schedules," Thomas began, going for the save, "sometimes they conflict. Other times, well, Elizabeth is just too tired to whip up a big meal after a long day at the office."

"Office? I thought you told me that Beth worked at a bank, Tommy? And, I've got to ask, why are you calling her Elizabeth? I noticed that yesterday, too."

Oh, he had both feet in it now. Still, Elizabeth had no intention of lying to bail him out. She told his grandmother, "Perhaps he confused me with one of the many other women he dated in the past. There were dozens of them from what I understand."

Nana Jo chuckled at that. Thomas didn't, but then the joke was at his expense. Even so, he did appear grateful no longer to be in the hot seat.

"I can promise you both I haven't confused Elizabeth with anyone else." His gaze turned intense. "That would be impossible."

His pronouncement caused her heart to squeeze and that was before he went on. "As for why I call her by her full name of Elizabeth, well, that's how I've come to see her. Elizabeth is a strong name. It fits a woman of such indomitable will and determination perfectly. I won't make the mistake of judging a book by its cover ever again."

"Thomas." Whether or not the words were scripted for his grandmother's benefit, Elizabeth was touched by them.

He continued, "Right after graduating from Michigan State University with a teaching degree, she founded a nonprofit agency whose goal is to foster literacy in adults. It's been going strong for a decade and will for many years to come thanks to her efforts to raise funds for an endowment. As you can see, Nana Jo, my Elizabeth is quite remarkable."

It wasn't his possessive reference that caused emotions to clog her throat, though it certainly was having an effect on her heart rate. No, it was the admiration evident in his expression. He meant it. Every word.

"Thomas," she said again.

This time, he leaned over and kissed her soundly on the mouth.

When he pulled back, Nana Jo was beaming.

"What an accomplishment!" she exclaimed, pulling Elizabeth in for a hug. "And you're so young!" She slapped at Thomas's arm. "I can't believe you didn't tell me, especially when it's obvious that you're so proud of her."

"I am proud of her."

"And rightfully so." Nana Jo made a *tutting* sound. "Madeline Stevens thinks her grandson is marrying well simply because his fiancée's family can trace its roots back to the *Mayflower*. What kind of an accomplishment is that? A mere accident of birth is what that is. I can't wait till our next bridge night so I can exercise my bragging rights."

Elizabeth remained flattered and flummoxed and that was before Thomas kissed her a second time and said, "I'm a lucky man."

"And a smart man if you keep telling yourself that," his grandmother advised. Turning back to the restaurant, she said, "So, about dinner, does this place look good to you? I've had their herb-crusted trout and blackened whitefish before. Both were excellent. And I've heard positive things about their steaks, though I steer clear of red meat these days for obvious reasons."

Elizabeth turned her gaze to the menu, grateful to have something to occupy her mind rather than the way she'd felt pulled to Thomas's side. Three words caught her attention immediately: formal attire required.

"The cuisine sounds delicious, but I'm afraid all of the outfits I brought to wear are way too casual," she told Nana Jo.

"I didn't pack a jacket, either," Thomas said.

His grandmother wasn't dissuaded. "Your navy sports coat is still hanging in the bedroom closet, I believe. As for you, Elizabeth, even a simple dress will do. No need for ball gowns or the like. The owners just put that there to keep tourists from stopping in wearing swimsuits on their way back from a day at the beach."

"I didn't pack any dresses."

Thomas chuckled. His arm was still around her. "You saw her bag, Nana. My Elizabeth packs light."

She was still digesting his "My Elizabeth" comment when his grandmother said, "Let's go shopping, then. My treat. Consider it a gift to celebrate your engagement."

"Oh, that's not necessary." She should have known arguing was pointless.

"I'm an old woman and it would give me great pleasure. Besides, I insist."

And as Nana Jo had already made clear, once she made up her mind there was little else one could do but shut up and agree.

"There's a store just up the way that carries some lovely dresses. And shoes, too. Back before arthritis got the best of me, I loved to wear high heels. I must have had at least two dozen pairs. I would have had more, but my closet wouldn't hold any more. That was before I moved here with a big walk-in one that's larger than the kitchen was in my first house."

"Do I have to come along?" Thomas wanted to know. "Shopping is really more of a female thing."

"You may be excused if it's all right with Beth, *er*, Elizabeth."

She made a flicking gesture with her fingers. "By all means, go and do something manly."

Nana Jo rubbed her hands together and her eyes lit with excitement. "Oh, this is going to be so much fun."

Elizabeth had never been much of a shopper, although every so often when Mel went to the mall in Ann Arbor, she insisted on dragging her along. Even then, she found the vast array of color choices and styles overwhelming, which made staying in her safe set of hues all the more appealing.

But the store Nana Jo had in mind was small, its merchandise neatly arranged with coordinating accessories within handy reach, and its staff helpful and eager to please. They were met at the door with beaming smiles and promptly assigned a saleswoman, who clearly knew Thomas's grandmother well.

"Mrs. O'Keefe, how nice to see you today," the young woman named Kendra enthused. "We got in some new Pima cotton sweater sets last week. I put one in your size in red in the back. I know how you favor that color."

"Thanks, dear. That's lovely. I'll have a look at it in a minute. Right now I'm here with my grandson's fiancée to see about a dress for dinner tonight. We're going to Edward's."

"Thomas is getting married?" The question came not from the salesclerk but from an attractive woman with flowing blond hair who stood just to their right. She'd had her back to them when they arrived, working her way through a rack of sundresses.

"Oh, Cecelia. I didn't see you there. Hello."

"Mrs. O'Keefe."

They shook hands. No bone-crushing hug from Nana Jo for this one, Elizabeth thought smugly. But then since the lush-figured woman stood half a head taller than Nana Jo, the hug wouldn't have had the same effect anyway.

"This is Elizabeth Morris."

One corner of the woman's red-slicked mouth turned up. In a wry voice, she replied, "Better known as the woman who managed to get Thomas Waverly to forsake bachelorhood. I stand in awe."

Cecelia didn't look awed. She looked put out and slightly amused.

"It's nice to meet you," Elizabeth said, even though the jury was still out on that one.

"I didn't realize Thomas had been ill."

"Why, he's fine," Nana Jo replied on a frown.

"Healthy as a...stallion," Elizabeth added, raising both women's eyebrows and her own color. Stallion, horse—they were the same thing.

"I'm glad to hear it." Cecelia's tone suggested otherwise. "I just assumed he must have suffered a near-death experience to change his mind on the subject. He was quite adamant about it when we dated last summer."

And then she was dumped, no doubt. Elizabeth wanted to feel sorry for the woman, but sympathy was a difficult emotion to muster under Cecelia's condescending stare. Her expression made it clear she wasn't as hurt that Thomas was settling down as she was annoyed that he was settling down with someone like Elizabeth.

"I suspect his change of heart had to do with finding the right woman," Nana Jo remarked. Her innocent expression made the barb appear unintended, but Elizabeth wondered if that really were the case. She'd already figured out that Josephine O'Keefe was a clever woman. After all, she had her very bright grandson believing she was heading toward eternity.

Cecelia left abruptly after that.

"She's a viper, that one," Nana Jo said. "Her parents bought a condo in the next building over two summers ago. She had her cap set for Thomas the moment she saw his fancy car pull up. Status is everything to her. Her parents are the same way. It's got to be designer labels and the latest trends or they're not having any of it." Nana Jo's lips pursed. "I was quite disappointed when I heard Thomas was dating her. Heard, mind you. He never brought her to see me on his own initiative, although every time his car showed up in the parking lot she soon found her way to my door."

"She's very pretty." The comment slipped out.

"Yes. Some of the most poisonous creatures on the planet are." To Kendra, Nana Jo said, "I hope I didn't cost you a sale."

"Not likely." The young woman rolled her eyes. "Cecelia comes in regularly and tries on half of the store, only to leave after complaining about our pitiful lack of inventory." She lowered her voice and admitted, "The other salesgirls and I draw straws to see who will have to wait on her. She's a lot of work and very little commission."

"Then I'd say you're well rid of her, too. Now about Elizabeth's outfit for tonight…"

Thomas hadn't wanted to go shopping with the women, but after circling around the block twice and pretending to be absorbed in a storefront display of hand-tied fishing flies, he gave in to curiosity and headed to the store where Nana Jo had taken Elizabeth.

He had two concerns. First, that Nana Jo, who preferred nautical themes and colors, would talk Elizabeth into a sailoresque outfit.

And second, that Elizabeth would think she needed to go for something flashy. He recalled how she'd looked on their first "date," if the outing could be called such a thing. The short dress with its horizontal flounces was more along the lines of attire the women of his acquaintance wore, and it definitely had caught his attention. She'd looked downright amazing in it. But there was something to be said for her conservative outfits. His mouth curved thinking of them. Prim as they were, they left his imagination to wonder what she had on underneath. Pink lace came to mind again as it had with disturbing regularity since that evening in her living room.

With that image taunting his libido, he stopped for ice cream on his way to the store. Instead of ordering his usual chocolate in a cone, he ordered plain vanilla, which he had the girl behind the counter sprinkle with chocolate chips.

He still had half the cone to go when he reached the shop, so he waited outside while he finished it. It wasn't brain freeze he experienced but something more primal when, through the window, he saw her step out of one of the dressing rooms. The tailored cotton shirt dress hit right above her knees, and was cinched in at the waist with a wide fabric belt. It was the epitome of conservative when it came to the cut, but not the color: red.

Not the nautical red that his grandmother liked. This red was more like chili peppers and packed as much punch. He was reminded of the heat in that Szechwan dish they'd shared in her kitchen. His mouth had burned then. Something else was on fire now.

He felt like a voyeur. He should just go in and quit acting like a Peeping Tom, er, Thomas. But he remained on the sidewalk while tourists strolled past and his ice cream melted, and watched through the glass as the salesgirl presented Elizabeth with a pair of tan shoes. The heels weren't stiletto height, but he'd judge them to be nearly three inches, and despite the neutral color they were sexy thanks to an open toe. He was too far away to see if her nails were polished when she slipped out of her canvas flats and slid the heels on. For some reason he knew they would be. A woman who wore lacy pink undergarments would take the time to paint her toes. Why that thought should excite him so much, Thomas wasn't sure. He only knew that it did. And then some.

Elizabeth took a few steps and he lost sight of her behind a circular rack of bathing suits. Then she was back, grinning madly, and looking more relaxed than he'd seen her look since their arrival the day before.

His grandmother was grinning, too. He told himself it was worth it, the lies and the subterfuge, to see Nana Jo looking this carefree and fit. Eventually, she would be disappointed when the wedding she'd chattered about for months never happened. He ignored the stab of guilt. And it *was* guilt. What else could it be? Certainly not his own disappointment.

Nana Jo glanced over then and must have spied him. She pointed his way, said something, and then Elizabeth's gaze turned in his direction as well. Her smile didn't quite disappear, but her expression grew serious.

Busted, Thomas thought. He waved nonchalantly, hoping to cover his embarrassment, but wound up feeling like an even bigger fool when what was left of his melted ice cream slid off the cone and plopped on the top of his shoe.

For the remainder of the afternoon, Thomas felt self-conscious and it had nothing to do with the sticky smudge that remained on the top of his sneaker. He felt oddly vulnerable.

He knew why Elizabeth had agreed to pose as his fiancée. She needed the hefty donation he'd promised for her charity's endowment fund. But a question was now nagging at him. Would she be interested in him for real if the carrot of a hefty donation for her charity were no longer dangling in front of her nose?

She seemed to like him, and, given the way she'd responded to his kisses, the sexual attraction he felt wasn't all one-sided. But…

In a very short period of time, they'd gotten to know one another better than Thomas could recall getting to know any of the other women with whom he'd spent a couple months. He credited the fact that Elizabeth was easy to talk to. They had shared some laughs and traded enough basic information to play the role of an engaged couple for a weekend. Still, he knew he'd barely scratched the surface. He wanted to know more. Much more. Beyond Chinese takeout preferences and toenail polish and undergarment choices.

No wonder he was feeling self-conscious and vulnerable. He'd always preferred women to start out as mysteries and remain that way. All of the little discoveries that couples made about one another during a relationship resulted in intimacy. Thomas strove to keep things casual with no deep emotional ties to untangle when it came time to break things off.

But Elizabeth intrigued him. God help him, but ties, emotional and otherwise, were starting to seem mighty tempting where she was concerned.

CHAPTER ELEVEN

Nana Jo had made reservations at the restaurant for seven o'clock that evening, which gave them all plenty of time to relax and get ready when they returned to the condo.

His grandmother decided to lie down for a short nap. Thomas and Elizabeth decided to shower before getting dressed. Since they were sharing the guest bathroom, he told her to go first.

That was a mistake.

She didn't take long. In fact, she was in and out in record time.

"All yours," she said when they passed in the hallway afterward.

Her hair was wrapped turban style in a towel and she was wrapped in a short terry-cloth robe that offered a tantalizing view of her legs and not nearly enough of the rest of her. His imagination got busy filling in the blanks, doing the job a little too well while he shaved. He nicked his chin twice with the razor.

He decided to make the shower a long, cold one, but even the chilly spray couldn't keep his imagination in check. It was a little too easy to picture her under the same pulsating water, her skin slick and inviting, slim limbs wrapped around him much the same way her scent was.

Thomas inhaled deeply and groaned. He'd caught faint whiffs of her fragrance during the day when he'd pulled her close or leaned in to tell her something. Now, it surrounded him in the shower stall. Whatever brand of shampoo or body wash she used, it was tying him into knots.

Those knots tightened after he finished up his lengthy shower and stepped out. On the counter next to the sink he spotted the travel-sized bottle of shampoo standing next to a small makeup case.

At home, with other women, he always made a point to discourage such items from showing up in his bathroom. They implied too much permanence for his comfort. Technically, this wasn't his bathroom. Perhaps that explained why he found himself more curious than wary. He took the cap off the bottle and sniffed. This was it. The scent was fresh and straightforward…just like the woman.

When the knock sounded he nearly dropped the bottle.

"Yes?"

"It's Elizabeth. I'm sorry to bother you, but I was wondering if you could hand me the makeup case I left in there?" she asked through the closed door. "I want to freshen up the polish on my toenails."

Of course she did. He swallowed and glanced toward the bag as if it contained the average man's equivalent of kryptonite.

Elizabeth nibbled the inside of her cheek while she waited for Thomas to respond. Instead of replying, however, he opened the bathroom door. And not just to pass her the case. Interestingly, no steam escaped from the bathroom despite his shower, which had gone on for quite some time—hence her decision to knock. Her nails would need time to dry before she slipped her feet into the new shoes. But the lack of steam wasn't what had her full attention. The man did.

Instead of a robe, he wore a towel wrapped around his hips, hooked low on his waist, below his belly button. The towel may have been pink, but his masculinity was never in question. To think she'd found so tantalizing that mere glimpse of his abs she'd gotten while he'd slept on the couch.

Oh, my!

She should maintain eye contact, Elizabeth thought. For that matter, she should grab the bag from his hand and return to the guest room posthaste. But she stood opposite him and gaped openly, though at least she had the presence of mind to close her mouth. The man was perfection, with sculpted arms and the kind of chest and abdomen that deserved to be showcased in a fitness program's "after" photographs.

"See something you like?" There was a hint of challenge in his tone along with amusement.

Elizabeth saw no point in lying, but that didn't mean she intended to stroke his ego. "Let's just say that I see why you have no problem attracting women."

"I've always assumed it was my good manners."

"That, too. Women find a man's…good manners very hard to resist."

His lips twitched. "Does that include you?"

"Are you angling for a compliment?"

She tilted her head to one side. Her hair, which was still damp, fell across her forehead. She held her breath when he reached over and pushed it aside. Would she ever get used to his touch? Did she want to?

"An answer will do."

She was playing with fire, but instead of trying to douse it, she opted to feed it. "I don't think it's any great secret that I find you attractive, Thomas."

"Or that it's mutual," he added on a smile.

"Yes. I picked up on that as well. We have some definite chemistry," she allowed.

"Chemistry." His chuckle was dry and seemed self-directed. He rested one forearm against the doorjamb and leaned on it. "I like you, Elizabeth."

It was hardly an earth-shattering announcement, but it caused her insides to quake. Just what was he saying? The words were clear, but not their meaning, given his history. Given *their* history, brief as it was. Or maybe their conversation was nothing more than friendly banter made to seem more intimate by the fact they were both half-naked.

"I've been told I'm likeable. I took a Dale Carnegie course just out of college to improve interpersonal relationships and strengthen my communication skills."

"I also like your sense of humor," he added. "It's dry."

"You mentioned that before."

"Some things are worth repeating."

He levered away from the jamb and set the makeup case aside. She'd seen that look in his eyes before. She knew what it meant. He was going to kiss her. Without his grandmother present it wasn't going to be PG, either. And she was going to let him.

Except that he bypassed her lips and lowered his mouth to the side of her neck, working his way lower. Teeth scraped lightly across the spot where her pulse was hammering so crazily that she wondered if he could hear it. Then he was moving lower, stopping only when he reached the point where the robe's lapels crossed between her breasts.

"I'm dying to know what you have on beneath this," he murmured against her skin. His breath licked at her flesh like flames.

"I have a feeling we would both regret it if you managed to find out," she whispered, amazed that she hadn't melted into a puddle of hormones much the way his ice cream had melted earlier in the day. She'd been amused then. She was dead serious now.

Thomas issued a mild expletive that apparently served as agreement. He straightened enough that his face was inches from hers. No apologies followed his oath this time. Elizabeth considered that an odd sort of victory.

"Maybe you could just tell me then."

"Will that be enough for you?"

"What do you think?"

She knew the answer. She also knew that eventually, if things were allowed to progress between them, he would get his fill, even as she would crave more—physically and emotionally. She forced herself to remember that.

"We'd better get dressed. Your grandmother will be ready soon. She could walk out of her bedroom at any moment." Elizabeth glanced down the hall at Nana Jo's closed door after saying so.

"You're right," Thomas agreed reluctantly. Even so, he took his time readjusting her lapels, before dropping a kiss on her cheek.

Dinner was lovely. The food was superb, the service impeccable and the company…? Elizabeth had absolutely no complaints to register there. Thomas was his usual charming and solicitous self, though she caught a considering glance or two. His grandmother's presence ensured the conversation remained topical rather than intimate.

It was far from boring, though. Indeed, Elizabeth liked seeing this side of Thomas. He was so unguarded and open. And, just her luck, all the more appealing.

"You're making moon eyes at my grandson again," Nana Jo remarked on a pleased smile.

"I...I..."

"It's all right, dear. He's been making them right back when you're not watching."

The woman was sharp as a tack. And wily, Elizabeth realized after a couple of her friends stopped by their table to say hello.

"Jean, would you and Barbara mind giving me a ride home? That way these young people can stay and have dessert. It's been a long day with a lot of walking." Where she'd been bright-eyed and laughing a moment earlier, Nana Jo now yawned. "I tire out so easily these days."

Elizabeth couldn't be sure, but she thought she saw one of Nana Jo's friends elbow the other one in the ribs.

"I'll get the check," Thomas said, already raising his hand to signal the waiter.

His grandmother reached for it and gave it a squeeze. "That's sweet, my boy, but I won't hear of it. You both stay, have dessert. The red velvet cake the couple over there is sharing looks delicious." The couple in question wasn't just sharing a dessert; they were sharing a fork and very nearly a chair. From the looks of things, later on they would be sharing a whole heck of a lot more.

Nana Jo winked. "Makes me wish I were younger and not just because of my restricted diet."

"We'll get a couple slices to go," Thomas said. "You can have a couple bites of mine. Your doctor doesn't need to know."

"That's generous, but no. The two of you stay," Nana Jo insisted again, this time rising to her feet. "And don't feel like you need to rush home. I'll probably just take my heart pill and go straight to bed. Take a walk on the beach after you finish up here. Take advantage of the moonlight."

"I think we've been had," Elizabeth said once they were alone.

"Maybe." But he glanced anxiously toward the door through which his grandmother had just exited. "Still, it's hard not to worry about her. She is eighty-one."

And in better shape than some women who were half her age. But Elizabeth only nodded. He had a blind spot a mile wide where his grandmother's health was concerned. It was endearing.

The waiter came, and they ordered dessert and coffee. Elizabeth chose a tartlet topped with an assortment of fresh, locally grown berries.

"That almost qualifies as health food," Thomas teased. "Not to mention one of the recommended daily servings of fresh fruit."

"It's all I saved room for."

"That's too bad." To the waiter, he said, "I'll have the red velvet cake. The thickest slice you've got."

Once they were alone again, his teasing expression sobered. "I like that dress, by the way. And the shoes."

So he'd said. Twice now. And he'd made an interesting remark about her painted toes. Between that and his earlier stated curiosity regarding her undergarments, it was a wonder Elizabeth had gotten through dinner without choking on her grilled sea bass.

"Thank you. Mel's been after me to buy some new clothes." She plucked at the tips of the lapels. "I think she would approve. Well, at least of the color. The style is probably a little boring."

"No offense to your friend, but I'm glad your tastes aren't the same as hers. And that dress isn't boring. It, and you, have my full attention."

Even as she reveled in the words, she wished he wouldn't say things like that. They made that line between fantasy and reality keep going fuzzy. The waiter returned with their coffee and assured them their desserts would be along shortly.

"It was very kind of your grandmother to buy everything. If she had her way, I would have a new purse, too." She shook her head in wonder at the force that was Josephine O'Keefe. "I still think I should repay her."

He poured some cream into his cup and stirred as he shook his head. "She won't let you."

"I was thinking I'd just leave a check for the total in the guest bedroom for her to find after we leave in the morning."

The corners of his mouth turned down in consideration. "Nah. She'll rip it up and be insulted. They're a gift, Elizabeth. It made her happy to give them to you. Accept them graciously."

She sighed. Arguing with either of them would be pointless. And rude. "I'll send her a bouquet of flowers as a thank-you, then."

"She'll like that. Make them stargazer lilies. They're her favorite." He took a sip of his coffee.

Elizabeth added creamer to her own cup. "I don't

like deceiving her, Thomas. I said that from the outset, but I like it even less now that I know her."

"Then you understand how I feel, but—"

"But you're going to continue lying to her."

He frowned. It was guilt and concern she saw in his expression, much more than irritation. "You know my reasons."

"I do." And she knew he believed them. Just as he believed his reasons for steering clear of commitment. He was wrong on both counts, but that was something he had to discover for himself. Still… "I really think you should tell her the truth."

"What is the truth, Elizabeth?" He sounded genuinely confused.

She blinked in surprise and ticked off the obvious. "We're not engaged. We're not even dating. We barely know one another."

His expression turned oddly stubborn. Instead of denying her statements, he said, "I think I know you pretty well, better than I've allowed myself to get to know most women."

She sat back in her chair, wary of both the delight curling through her belly and the interest brewing in his eyes. "We met on Monday," she reminded him… reminded them both.

He was undeterred. "Let me give it a shot."

She lifted her hands palm-side up. "Well, then, by all means."

Before he could start, their desserts arrived. The tart, with its topping of fresh blueberries, blackberries and raspberries, looked delicious. But it was the lush confection the waiter set in front of Thomas that had her mouth watering. It was pure indulgence on a gold-rimmed china plate and every bit as tempting as the man who was now studying her.

"Where were we?" It sounded very much like a challenge.

"You were going to dazzle me with your knowledge of my person."

He picked up his fork and pointed the tines in her direction. "There's that dry sense of humor again, tinged with just enough sarcasm that you're probably already feeling guilty about it and wanting to apologize."

She popped a fat raspberry in her mouth and rolled her eyes.

"I'm not feeling guilty." *Much.*

His smile was smug. "You are and I like that about you. You're careful with other people's feelings. You're also regretting your dessert choice."

"I am not." To prove it, she cut into the tartlet with the side of her fork and then scooped both it and a juicy blueberry into her mouth. *"Mmm."*

His brows rose. Interest smoldered in his eyes. Regrets? Elizabeth still didn't have a single one.

"Maybe *regret* isn't the right word," he said. "You went with the berries not only because they're delicious, but because they're good for you. No trans-fats or whatever the media have determined the big health threat to be at the moment. You'll probably leave half of that tartlet on your plate." Okay, that had been her plan. "But you wish you'd ordered the red velvet cake."

"Then why didn't I?" she asked, a little unnerved by his accurate assessment. Not to mention unnerved by the close attention he paid even when he didn't seem to be.

"The reason you didn't is because you're the sort of woman who plays it safe."

He had her on the cake, but she disagreed with the rest. "How can you say that? I'm here with you, pretending to be your fiancée, aren't I? I wouldn't exactly call that playing it safe."

"My grandmother's gone, Elizabeth. It's just the two of us sitting here now. Well, and a room full of strangers. There's no need to pretend anything." His eyes narrowed seductively. "Or maybe that's the risk you mean since you spent the last couple days leading up to this trip avoiding me."

"We talked."

"Email, voice mail and one brief conversation during which you turned me down for a date." When she opened her mouth to reply, he held up a hand to stop her. "And last night you retreated to the guest room as soon as my grandmother called it a night."

Direct hits all. So she shot back and said, "You don't strike me as the sort of man who takes a lot of chances, either."

She was thinking of his relationships, though she stopped short of saying so out loud. The muscle that ticked in his jaw told her he got the reference anyway.

"Maybe. But we're not talking about me. You can grill me another time."

"Don't think I won't hold you to that."

"I know you will. I would never make the mistake of underestimating you, Elizabeth. You're the one who does that. I wish you wouldn't. God knows, you shouldn't. I meant it earlier when I told my grandmother how much I admire your determination and success."

Oh, yes, he paid way too close attention. Feeling vulnerable, she asked, "Are you done with your evaluation of me?"

He wasn't put off by her prickly tone. "Just starting.

You're far too fascinating to sum up that quickly. With you, I find I want to take my time."

He took another bite of his cake. Despite her best efforts, Elizabeth licked her lips. His smile was smug, but so darn sexy that she found it impossible to be irritated, especially when he cut off another bite and fed it to her. For a man who supposedly didn't do intimate, he was doing a damned fine imitation.

"I thought time was the enemy when it came to women. We wouldn't want things to get messy."

He frowned. But all he said was, "Do you want another bite?"

"A small one."

While she savored it, he continued, "You were and remain the sort of person who colors inside the lines. Taking risks doesn't come naturally to you, but you're willing to stick out your neck if the reasons suit you. You like to help people. You want to save them."

"You don't need a crystal ball to figure that out given the line of work I'm in, not to mention our current set of circumstances."

"Maybe." He went on. "You like to blend in."

She laughed as a cover for her discomfort over the accuracy of his comment and pointed out, "I'm wearing red right now. It's hard to blend in wearing red."

"Yes, but if you really wanted to stand out in that color, you would have chosen a dress that fit snugly or ended midthigh or was cut low enough to offer a peek of cleavage."

"I don't want to attract that kind of attention. Besides, I don't have the kind of figure that lends itself to the sort of dress you're talking about."

"I don't know about that." Thomas's memory reeled

back a couple of hours. "You did a pretty good job with that bathrobe earlier."

Her face turned as scarlet as the cake. "The women you date probably all look like they just stepped away from a fashion photo shoot."

"But we're not talking about me or them," he reminded her again.

"Well, I'm not in their league."

He didn't want her to be, and it had nothing to do with convincing his grandmother they were a couple.

"See, that's where you've got it backward, Elizabeth. They're not in *your* league." He wasn't trying to boost her self-esteem. It was true. "In addition to underestimating yourself, you're hard on yourself."

She didn't wait for him to offer her cake this time. She reached over with her own fork and stole some. What was it about that simple act that turned him on?

"So, I'm a perfectionist. It's not exactly a character flaw, although some people might see it that way."

Thomas shook his head. "It's not the same thing. I thought it might be at first. You have such drive, such focus. People like that tend to be compulsive in certain respects. But there's more to it in your case than seeking perfection."

She shifted uncomfortably in her seat. "I don't know what you mean."

"When we first met I asked you what made you decide to start Literacy Liaisons. Do you remember your answer?"

She laughed, though he detected nerves. "Of course I do. As I said, that was only a matter of days ago."

He didn't laugh. "You told me you saw a need."

"That's right."

"Care to tell me what exactly that need was?" He had a good idea now.

"That should be obvious, Thomas." He merely raised his brows and waited. "All around us, in a country that spends billions of dollars to provide free and mandated education to the public, there are people who cannot read. It impacts their lives, their relationships and their earning potential. It holds them back."

"Ross can't read."

"Wh-what?"

She'd spoken so little about her family to Thomas that it was clear she was unprepared for Thomas to draw lines between the random dots she'd provided and come up with a clear picture.

"Your brother. He can't read, can he?"

She set down her fork, dabbed her mouth with the linen napkin that had been spread over her lap. It was a moment before she spoke. "He can read. At a third-grade level, and that's probably being generous."

"That's why he left school and then left home."

"No, Thomas." She shook her head, her expression filled with sadness and something more damning when she told him, "He left home because of me."

"Elizabeth—"

"No. It's true. I was in college, studying to be a teacher of all things, when I found out that Ross was functionally illiterate and had dropped out of school. I was livid. I went home the first weekend I could and started in on him. 'You need to do this. You need to do that.' I drove him away with all of my pushing and nagging."

"You did it out of love."

"That doesn't matter. It backfired, badly."

This conversation was backfiring badly, Thomas realized. He'd intended to show her…hell, he wasn't sure what he'd intended to show her. Or why it mattered so much. All he knew was that *she* mattered.

"He phones our parents from time to time or has someone else drop them a note, but he's never contacted me."

Thomas chose his words carefully. "He's probably just embarrassed."

"That's what Mel says."

"What do your parents say?"

"My parents." She shifted back in her seat on a sigh. "They see nothing wrong with the situation. They never saw anything wrong with the situation, even when he was young enough that they could have done something about it."

"Are you sure they didn't try?"

"Not hard enough." Her laughter was brittle. "I love them, but their child-rearing methods, to say nothing of their lifestyle, leave a lot to be desired. Their motto was and remains live and let live. The fact that Ross doesn't have a permanent address and can't hold down a regular job doesn't bother them in the least. They actually thought it was exciting when he called from Utah a few years ago to say that he'd joined up with one of those carnivals that travel from town to town."

"Is that where he is now? Utah?"

"Honestly, I don't know." She shook her head sadly. "My parents barely pass along any information and I've stopped asking. I keep hoping…" Her laughter turned harsh. "I keep hoping he'll write to me."

"It's not your fault that he can't read. Or that he left home and has chosen the lifestyle he has."

"I went about it all wrong," she insisted. "I pushed him away."

"You can't push someone away by caring too much, Elizabeth."

Her gaze locked with his. "Yes, you can, Thomas. You're proof of that. It's the reason you've used to end all of your relationships. And, if I were to let myself fall for you, it would be the reason you'd use to end ours."

CHAPTER TWELVE

IT WAS nearly ten when they left the restaurant. Thomas decided the wisest course of action would be to head straight back to his grandmother's condo. Despite Nana Jo's claim that she planned to take her heart pill and head straight to bed, she would probably still be awake, waiting up for him much the same way she had when he was a teenager out on a date. Although this time the date in question would be coming home with him and sleeping under the same roof. But that wasn't the only reason he felt so restless at the moment, or why going back to the condo and the possibility of more conversation with his grandmother held little appeal.

He was thinking about what Elizabeth had said. She was right, of course. He had used the deepening feelings of the women he'd dated as the gauge for how soon to end things. He'd thought he was doing them both a favor that way. He'd certainly ensured that his heart remained whole and his head clear.

So, how was it possible than in a very short span of time, Elizabeth had managed to get under his skin?

If I were to let myself fall for you...

His mind kept working its way back to that phrase. It had him terrified even as it tempted him. He wasn't falling in love, he assured himself, but he couldn't ignore that his footing was far from sure.

"It's a pretty night," Elizabeth commented as they stepped outside the restaurant.

Overhead, the moon was nearly full, the sky awash in stars and the night air scented with flowers. He decided to follow Nana Jo's advice.

"What do you say we go for a walk?" When she hesitated he added, "You can work off those two pathetically small bites of my cake that you had."

"Don't forget my dessert."

"A handful of berries and that sliver of tartlet, you mean?" He chuckled, hoping to lighten the mood that had grown as heavy as the red velvet cake. "I told you you'd wind up leaving most of it on your plate."

"No one likes a know-it-all, Thomas. Trust me on that."

When she frowned, he reached for her hand. "You're thinking of your brother now."

It came as a surprise to realize how much he wanted to be her sounding board, her confidante, and to take away that line of dismay creasing her brow.

"I think of him every day."

"Have you thought of asking your parents for his contact information and calling him to clear the air?"

"Yes. And I have. But he doesn't stay put long enough."

"What about hiring a private investigator to locate him?"

"I've considered that, too." She sighed. "I'm not sure what it would accomplish, though. He's made it plain through his continued silence that he doesn't want anything to do with me."

Thomas wasn't sure he agreed, but he decided to

let the subject drop for now. "Come on. Let's take that walk. You can point out the rest of my deficiencies while we're on the beach. There's a nice stretch of it that's open to the public not too far from my grandmother's condo."

They reached his car, and he opened the door for her. She waited for him to do so this time. He used the opportunity to lean closer and inhale.

"What are you doing?" she asked.

"Torturing myself." And then he kissed her.

He drove to a public lot with access to a stretch of Lake Michigan shoreline. During the day it was dotted with families. This time of evening, it was largely deserted, although a handful of high school kids had made a bonfire and were huddled around it laughing and talking.

Since walking on sand was best accomplished in bare feet, they both took off their shoes. He left his jacket and tie in the car as well, rolling up the sleeves of his shirt just as he had the legs of his pants.

Under his feet, the sand felt cool. The water, he knew, would be cold. Even during the hottest days of summer, the lake remained chilly. Knowing that helped cool some of his ardor when he reached for her hand again. In a friendly tone, he said, "So, shoot. Floor's all yours. As promised, this is your opportunity to rake me over the coals."

"I can't think of anything."

He squeezed her fingers. "My ego thanks you, but I think you're just being polite."

She pulled her hand away, ostensibly to rescue her hair from the breeze. She gathered the wayward strands behind her nape before letting it fall free. She didn't reach for his hand again afterward. Distance. The weekend wasn't even over and she was already slipping away from him.

"You know all about being polite. And that's not a complaint, by the way. I like your manners. I mean, what woman wouldn't?"

He frowned momentarily at her mention of other women, again. He didn't want them brought into their conversation. "Since you can't think of anything bad to say about me, maybe you could just list the many things you find so appealing."

He meant it to be a joke. She remained serious.

"I do find you appealing, Thomas. And there are a number of reasons for that. I think you can figure out most of them. Surely, I wouldn't be the first woman to comment on your overall attractiveness."

His frustration grew. He stopped walking, turned and grasped her arms. "That's a stingy compliment. And I'll tell you something else I don't appreciate." Even in the dim light he saw her eyelids flicker in surprise at his impatient tone. "It's no great secret that I've dated other women, but I prefer not to have them brought up right now. I'm not out with them, Elizabeth. I'm with you."

It was the wrong thing to say. He knew that even as the breeze snatched away the last of his words. "Don't say it," he warned.

"Okay, but I think we're fooling ourselves. We're not together, Thomas." She shook her head sadly. "Not even close."

The teens up the beach set off a couple of fountain fireworks. Multicolored sparks shot a dozen feet into the air before raining down. A much bigger, professionally put-together fireworks display was scheduled for the following evening off Beaver Island in Lake

Michigan. He and Elizabeth would be back downstate by then. Back to their separate, colorless lives.

Love has a way of finding us, Tommy. Even if we never look. Maybe especially when we don't.

Nana Jo's words whispered in his head, and he jolted as if a stray spark had landed on his skin.

"Thomas?"

"I think we'd better go back."

"Now who's the one with regrets," Elizabeth said softly.

He was, Thomas thought. But he wasn't at all sure they were the regrets she meant.

Nana Jo wasn't up when they got back. A lamp illuminated the empty living room, where she'd once again set out a blanket, sheet and pillow on the couch for Thomas.

"Well, good night," Elizabeth said.

"Let me walk you to your door."

The door in question belonged to the bedroom. She turned at the threshold. "What time will we be leaving in the morning?"

"I'm in no rush." When he attempted to tuck the hair behind her ear, she stepped back. "Apparently you are."

"Things are getting…too complicated."

Something he had been careful to steer clear of in the past. He nodded in agreement. "When we get back to Ann Arbor, maybe we could—"

"No." She shook her head. "That wouldn't be a good idea. It's called self-preservation, Thomas. Ultimately, you and I are after vastly different things from a relationship."

"Is that what you want from me? A real and committed relationship?" It was a thrilling, if terrifying thought.

Her smile was sad. "I want love, Thomas, unconditional and lasting, and I want all of the pretty promises that go with it. And, ultimately, I want to stand in a church and take vows. My parents have never done that. They've always said they don't need a ceremony and piece of paper. But I do. That's something I need with the man who loves me."

He swallowed. "Elizabeth, I don't know if I can—"

She put a hand over his lips to silence him. "I know. You spelled that out in capital letters from the start. I'm the one who hasn't been clear on what I want, in part because I didn't think it mattered or that *you* would come to matter the way that you have. I love you, Thomas."

Her eyes rounded as if she hadn't intended to make that admission. If it surprised her, it shocked him to his core. More than that, it scared him. He could picture clearly his father the day of his mother's funeral. Hoyt had thrown himself on the casket after the church service.

I want to go with her. I can't live without her, his father had shrieked as Thomas looked on.

Now he was looking at Elizabeth and feeling almost as lost and desperate as his father had all those years ago.

"Does it help if I tell you that you're the first woman I've ever met who makes me question the decision I made?"

She rose on tiptoe and kissed his cheek.

"In a way, that makes it worse," she said and then closed the door.

CHAPTER THIRTEEN

"ANOTHER cup of coffee?"

Mel stood in the door of her office. It had been more than two weeks since Elizabeth had returned from Charlevoix. Thomas had dropped her at her door, thanked her and bid her goodbye. She hadn't heard from him since, unless one counted the check that had arrived. It was drafted from his personal bank account and was a couple thousand dollars more than what they had discussed.

Guilt money, she decided. And, as tempted as she'd been to rip it up, she'd deposited it. At least Literacy Liaisons would benefit from her utter stupidity.

She'd told Thomas she wouldn't lie. Well, she had. She'd lied to herself. And she'd done such a bang-up job of it that, despite the clear picture he'd drawn for her to the contrary, she'd almost started to believe she could have the fairy tale. As she'd told Thomas their last night in Charlevoix, it was worse knowing she was the first woman who had him second-guessing his no-commitment stance. She'd admitted she loved him. If that wasn't enough to change his mind...

"No more coffee for me. Any more and my heart is going to bounce out of my chest," she told her friend.

"Well, you might want to hang on to it. Thomas is here to see you."

Her friend stepped away, giving Elizabeth only a couple of minutes to get her head around the idea that he'd come to see her. She smoothed down her hair, mussed it up and then, irritated with herself, smoothed it down once more just as a tap sounded at her door.

"Come in."

"Hi."

He smiled uncertainly from the doorway. The heart she'd convinced herself wasn't even close to being broken cracked a little just at the sight of him.

"Hi."

"I hope I'm not bothering you."

Bothering her? No. Killing her more like. But she managed a smile, and motioned with her hand. "Not at all. Come in, please."

He entered the office, but he didn't take a seat. The fact that he looked nervous helped calm Elizabeth's jittering pulse.

"I was going to call. I've been meaning to since we returned from Charlevoix, but—"

"I know. It's okay." For the best even, or so she'd spent long hours during the past two weeks of sleepless nights trying to convince herself. "I got your check, by the way."

"And I got your thank-you note."

"Right. The amount, it was kind of you."

"As you said in the card. It was the least I could do."

They eyed one another uncomfortably for a moment. "Is there, um, a reason for your unexpected visit today?" she asked. *Other than torture.*

"There is." He grimaced. "I've come to ask another favor."

Her heart sank. For just a moment she'd let herself hope… "What do you need?"

"Some more of your time. Nana Jo has invited us back up for the Venetian Festival on Lake Charlevoix this coming weekend."

"Thomas—"

"Just hear me out, please." At her nod, he said, "We'll stay at the bed-and-breakfast, no ifs, ands or buts, this time. And we'll leave the following morning. Barely twenty-four hours of your time, Elizabeth, that's all I'm asking."

"You're asking for a lot more than that," she said quietly.

He nodded and had the grace to flush. "I know. Believe me, I wouldn't put you in this position if it wasn't a matter of life and death."

She frowned at that. "Nana Jo?"

"I've been in touch with a doctor. It's a heart issue," he said slowly.

"Are you sure?" Elizabeth certainly wasn't. The woman was as healthy as they came, and Thomas was hardly objective where she was concerned.

But his expression was serious, somber, when he replied, "Positive. It's definitely a heart issue. And, from what I've been told, it's not going to change. In fact, it's likely to get worse."

"I'm so sorry. Of course, I'll come."

It was late Saturday afternoon when they arrived in Charlevoix. As much as Elizabeth wanted to do this for Nana Jo's sake, it was costing her. Every smile, every glance Thomas sent her way in the car landed like daggers. Twenty-four hours, she reminded herself. Twenty-four hours and she would be back home where she could start for the second time the process of getting over him.

Or maybe she would just kill him, she decided, when a rosy-cheeked Nana Jo opened the condo door after the third knock.

"Sorry, I didn't hear you. I was 'Sweatin' to the Oldies' with Richard Simmons."

Elizabeth rounded on Thomas. "Her heart? A matter of life and death? How dare you!" Before storming away, she told Nana Jo, "I'm sorry. So sorry. But I can't stay. I won't."

As Thomas turned to follow her, his grandmother put a hand on his arm to stop him.

"Give her a minute, Tommy."

"This was a bad idea."

"I don't think so. She loves you."

"She's ready to kill me."

"Takes love to stir up an emotion that strong," she assured him.

Nana Jo smiled. In a phone call after their last visit, she'd confronted him about the true nature of his relationship with Elizabeth, taking great delight in the fact that he was every bit as smitten as he'd pretended to be.

"Love takes courage," she'd told him. She said the same thing again now.

"How long am I supposed to give her?" he asked, glancing at his watch as Nana Jo sipped from her water bottle, not a care in the world. "It's been five minutes."

She smiled knowingly. "I guess that's long enough. Go." He was at the door when he heard her delighted laughter. "Don't forget to get down on one knee."

He caught up with Elizabeth on the beach. The waves pounded the shore. A storm was brewing. How apropos, he thought as emotions crashed around inside of him.

"If you even come near me..." she warned.

He held up his hands. "Let me explain."

"You told me it was her heart!" she accused.

"Actually, I never said whose heart I was referring to."

She stopped walking, frowned at him. "A doctor. I distinctly recall the mention of a doctor."

"I said I'd been in touch with one, yes. Mine. My heart, Elizabeth." He liked the way her mouth formed an *O*. It took his mind off his nerves, gave him the courage to press ahead. "The doctor couldn't find a thing wrong with me despite this persistent ache I've been having right here." He took her hand, flattened its palm against his chest.

"Thomas?"

"I've diagnosed it myself. A chronic condition, I'm afraid." He grew serious now. "Elizabeth, I can't live without you. But I will. I won't climb into a bottle like my father and drink the rest of my life away if you're not in it. But I will feel an acute sense of loss, because I know just how much better my life could be with you in it."

"I don't know what to say."

"I was hoping for 'I love you.' The last time you said it, I wasn't ready to hear it, but I am now. I just hope you haven't changed your mind."

It seemed an eternity that he waited for her smile to blossom, her arms to slip around his neck. "I love you, Thomas Waverly."

He crushed her to his chest on a laugh that was part sob. "Thank God! I was worried I'd lost you."

"I was worried you might never find your way back to me."

"I won't make that mistake again."

He did as his grandmother suggested, going down on one knee in front of Elizabeth in the sand.

"Oh, my," he heard her murmur from behind the hand that covered her mouth.

This ring wasn't the one his father had given his mother. Too much history was attached to that one, Thomas had decided. Too many sad memories. He wanted a fresh start for the new life he wanted to make with the woman he loved, although not necessarily a new ring.

"This was Nana Jo's engagement ring," he said of the half-carat, brilliant-cut solitaire. "She and my grandfather had nearly four decades of happiness together before he died. She sent it to me via overnight post last week when we hatched this plan." His grin faltered then. "Elizabeth, will you marry me?"

"I will. Yes." She laughed as she wiped away a tear. "In fact, I thought you'd never ask."

EPILOGUE

Six months later

"Howie, stop!" Elizabeth shouted as the dog started down the street after the mail truck. "Come back here now!"

He reluctantly obeyed. They were going to have to see about installing one of those invisible fences at Thomas's home. Their home, she corrected on a grin.

She and Thomas had just returned from their honeymoon—two of the most blissful weeks of her life on the big island of Hawaii.

"I see the mail came," Thomas remarked, moving in behind her. He nuzzled her neck, sending her pulse racing. She wondered if she'd ever get used to his touch.

"Lots of junk and bills," she said, starting to flip through the huge stack that had accumulated while they were gone. "Oh, here's a card from Nana Jo." She handed it to him to open, while she continued through the pile of letters.

Thomas's laughter had her glancing over curiously. "What is it?"

"She's wanting to know when we're going to give her great-grandchildren. She's not as young as she used to be, you know. She's been feeling a little peaked since our wedding."

Elizabeth laughed too until the writing on one of the envelopes caught her attention. It was childlike and all in uppercase letters. "What on earth…"

"Open it," Thomas said quietly. "Go on."

She did and started to read the simple words only to have her eyes blur with tears. "Ross…" she sobbed.

"I found him for you, Elizabeth. A couple months ago, in fact."

"Why didn't you say something before now?" she asked, her head bursting with questions, her heart bursting with emotion.

"He wasn't able to come to our wedding, and he made me promise not to say anything until he could contact you himself. With a letter." Thomas smiled. "He's been taking night classes at a men's shelter in Seattle."

"He's learning how to read and write."

Thomas nodded and took the letter from her hands. He read the rest of it for her as tears streamed down her cheeks. Ross wasn't only learning how to read and write. He was coming home, back to Michigan. Back to her life.

"I want you to be as proud of me as I am of you. I love you, Lizzie." It was right there, spelled out in his awkward and perfect penmanship.

"Oh, Thomas," she said, pulling her new husband close. The rest of the envelopes fell from her hands and scattered over the floor. "Thank you. Thank you. You've made me so happy."

The embrace lasted, grew more intimate.

He pulled back with a wicked grin. "So, what do you

say we go try to make Nana Jo happy and fulfill her great-grandbabies request?"

Elizabeth offered her own wicked smile, grasped his hand and started to lead the way to their bedroom.

"This could take a while."

* * * * *

FAKING IT
TO MAKING IT

BY
ALLY BLAKE

In her previous life Australian author **Ally Blake** was at times a cheerleader, a maths tutor, a dental assistant and a shop assistant. In this life Ally is a bestselling multi-award-winning novelist who has been published in over twenty languages, with more than two million books sold worldwide.

She married her gorgeous husband in Las Vegas—no Elvis in sight, although Tony Curtis did put in a special appearance—and now Ally and her family, including three rambunctious toddlers, share a property in the leafy western suburbs of Brisbane, with kookaburras, cockatoos, rainbow lorikeets and the occasional creepy-crawly. When not writing she makes coffees that never get drunk, eats too many M&Ms, attempts yoga, devours *The West Wing* reruns, reads every spare minute she can, and barracks ardently for the Collingwood Magpies footy team.

You can find out more at her website www.allyblake.com

For team Arabella Rose.

Josh, Laura, Cat, David, Sam,
Kristy, Liz, Emma & Gemma.

It was an honour and a trip, with extra sauce!

CHAPTER ONE

SASKIA BLOOM FLICKED her dark fringe out of her eyes and peered through her vintage glasses at her laptop screen before madly scribbling notes on the yellow legal pad under the mouse.

"I'll eat my shoes if you're even a day under forty," she mumbled at the photo of a guy grinning inanely back at her from the Dating By Numbers website.

Undeterred, StudMuffin33 kept on smiling, as if the dauntingly athletic profile was so appealing any woman would let the age-fib slip.

Favourite Movie: The Fast and the Furious
Collects: surfboards
Who'd Play You in the Movie of Your Life? Jason Statham
Looking for: an open-minded lady with a twinkle in her eye

Good lord.
Mouse hover and click.
The photo of the next guy gave her such a fright she flinched. BirdLover28 had tufty hair, wore a grimace rather than a smile and had a chicken on his shoulder. A live one, she hoped.

Favourite TV Show: Dr Who (the original!)
Sundays are for: garage sales

Celebrity Crush: Tyra Banks
Looking for: fun in all the wrong places

Alas, Saskia would not be partaking of said fun. For, even though it had been several months since she'd been booted back into the dating pool, she wasn't online looking for The One. Or a "Saturday night special" as one possibility had so gallantly offered.

Her account with Dating By Numbers was research, pure and simple. She and her business partner, Lissy—together known as SassyStats—had been hired by the site to collate a fun statistical analysis of online dating. In order to do the best job possible, she'd jumped from an aeroplane for a piece on adrenalin junkies. Dived with sharks for a study on phobias. In comparison, creating a dating profile was cushy.

Saskia lifted her booted foot to the chair, wrapped an arm around her woolly-tights-clad knee, and, chewing on the end of a pen, shook her head at the dozen more possibilities in her inbox.

Research or not, it *was* actually pretty flattering.

With her wavy brown hair, her mother's olive skin, eyes that were kind of brown and a lean frame that puberty had pretty much ignored, under the right lighting, with humidity low, she could *just* about pull off cute. The idea that so many guys had considered her for a follow up email was a marvel.

If she'd known *this* was the response she'd get, she'd have signed up long ago! She'd met *Stu* in a *pub,* and look how *that* had turned out.

There he'd sat hunched in his old coat, looking so dark and mysterious, with pen smudges on his fingertips. He'd looked as if he'd needed a warm meal and a hug. Turned out he'd needed her mobile phone, her TV, her computers, her appliances and more. In recompense he'd left a nasty note, a huge debt and his dog.

Saskia glanced over at Ernest, the big wiry Airedale currently lying on his back, legs in the air, snoring on the dinky old armchair in the corner of her office.

With a sigh, she slid her feet back to the floor and shifted the legal pad an inch. She and Ernest might have discovered a bona fide fondness for one another, but she'd never get used to the angry red envelopes that fell through her mail-slot on a weekly basis. Never wanted to. The only way to make them go away was to work. And work some more. And then, when night fell and her bed was beckoning, get back to work.

Mouse hover and click.

Saskia lifted her hand off the mouse, ready to take notes on the next candidate, but at the sight of him her hand wobbled pointlessly in midair.

She might, in fact, have gasped at the sight, because Ernest suddenly snorted, his legs twitching like an up-ended spider, before settling back into a dream-filled sleep.

Gorgeous didn't even begin to describe the man. Drop-dead, movie star, take-your-breath-away gorgeous came a *tiny* bit closer. The shot was candid, with the man looking at something over the photographer's shoulder. Dark blond hair precision cut. Sleeves of a pale blue business shirt neatly rolled up to his upper arms, a vein or two roping from wrist to elbow. A solitary raised eyebrow, a barely there lift to one corner of a truly sensuous mouth. But who'd even notice, considering the guy had the bluest eyes Saskia ever seen.

How does a man who looks like that not have someone in his life? she wondered. Though, considering the fibs the other men had told, she couldn't count on it!

He did look resolute, as if he wouldn't be used to hearing the word no, so maybe he was plain mean. Or into cross-stitching. Or he had halitosis. Or really gnarly toenails. Or maybe he was looking for something even more outrageous than "fun in all the wrong places."

Intrigue levels rising, Saskia wriggled the blood back into

her fingers and scrolled to the mini-profile that had been sent out with the guy's initial contact.

Favourite Book: Catch-22
Drink of choice: double espresso
Thing you say more than any other: Next
Looking for: a wedding date, no strings

Pretty much bang-on to his picture, which was an anomaly unto itself. And Saskia did love an anomaly. That love had sent her from pure statistics into research in the first place. That moment reminded her why, as a seed of an idea sprang to life inside her.

Lifting her backside from her chair, she flicked through a pile of random papers till she found the press release Marlee at Dating By Numbers had sent over as part of the initial brief.

The number of people who had signed on—and only to that one site—was staggering. All of them had struggled using traditional avenues in their search for companionship, for sex, for love. Including her. And if a man who loved coffee as much as she did, had awesome taste in literature, and looked enough like a young Paul Newman to induce a drool epidemic had reached his thirties without finding someone, what *would* it take?

She'd been looking for an angle for her infographic, and she might just have found one.

When a massive Big Bang Theory mug appeared next to Saskia's elbow, she nearly jumped out of her skin. "God, you scared me half to death!"

"Not surprised. You have that weird scientist look in your eyes," said Lissy. The blue and purple tips of her long blonde locks bounced as she landed with a *whump* in the bouncy chair on her side of the paint-splattered old table they used as an office desk. "If it was legal I'd marry your espresso machine."

"Get in line." Saskia put her glasses on the desk, blinked to clear her eyes and, breathing in the rich scent of the cocoa enriched brew, let the huge mug warm her hands before closing her eyes and taking a sip. After Stu had taken off with everything she'd leased computers but bought a replacement espresso machine. Horse before the cart and all that.

"So, what are we working on?" asked Lissy. "The railway map thing? The business listing thing?"

"The online dating thing."

"Ooh, much more fun."

"I'll drink to that." They clinked mugs. "I think I've just had a bit of a breakthrough. I'm considering adding something extra to my analysis—along the lines of an equation for finding love."

Lissy stopped sipping at her coffee and blinked. "Like, chocolates plus flowers multiplied by heaps of hot sex equals never having to say you're sorry?"

Saskia laughed as she scrawled curlicues in the top corner of her legal pad, her mind whizzing now it had hit on something. "Not quite. Mathematics is natural. Love is natural. It only makes sense that it's *mathematically* quantifiable."

Lissy glanced pointedly at the pile of bills on Saskia's side of the desk which, for the first time *ever* included a late mortgage payment.

"I wouldn't be making work for myself, as I'm doing the research anyway," Saskia said. "And I think it would make a great anchor for the bottom of the infographic."

Then again, maybe Lissy was right. If Saskia wanted to wrestle back control of her mortgage payments, let alone get back to the renovations she'd been in the middle of doing when Stu absconded, she needed to focus.

Unfortunately, while Lissy was a crazy brilliant graphic artist, to her, *focus* was a foreign word. "It's never been done? This love formula thing?"

"Maybe," Saskia said, enthusiasm spiking again. "Or maybe nobody's ever tried. Perhaps somebody just needed inspiration."

"Like when Einstein was hit with that apple."

"Newton."

"Whatever. So, what hit *you?*"

"Nothing hit me." Saskia made the mistake of glancing at her laptop.

Lissy's eyes narrowed. Then, quick as a rattlesnake, she spun her chair round the desk and looked over Saskia's shoulder before she had the chance to snap the thing closed.

"Ha!" Lissy pointed. "Talk about inspiration. Who is *that?*"

Saskia's eyes skewed back to the monitor, to the bluest eyes and the hint of what would have amounted to an indecently sensuous smile if the photographer had only been kind enough to wait half a second more. "His handle is NJM."

"Handle? He's one of our online dating guys?" Lissy blew out a long, slow whistle. "Why did I let you be the guinea pig on this one?"

"Because you were dating Dropkick Dave and when he saw you smile at the greengrocer he snapped all your carrots in half."

Lissy winced at the memory. "I'll admit the guy was high strung—"

Saskia coughed out a laugh at the understatement of the year.

"—but Lordy the man knew how to kiss." With that Lissy disappeared into a daze. Saskia made a mental note to check Lissy's phone and make sure Dropkick Dave had been deleted.

With a shake of her head Lissy came to, tiptoed her chair back to her side of the table, and angling her mug at the back of Saskia's laptop, said, "Stats please."

Saskia shuffled the mouse and clicked on the link for NJM's full online profile. The sight of neat and tidy columns, of horizontal bars filled with information, of questions with answers, and she found her zen. "Six-two. Blue eyes. Dark blond hair. Financier. No interests listed."

Well, now, *that* just seemed a little sad.

"I put up my hand to give him some!" said Lissy.

Saskia laughed, then realised she was still rolling a finger over the mouse like a caress.

She lifted her hand and cricked her fingers. She was mid-knuckle-crack on her second hand when Lissy came out with, "Screw research. You should date him. For real."

Saskia's mouth twisted sideways. She noticed that her hand was on the mouse again, and it had somehow shifted till the little arrow hovered over the bright yellow button with the happy-fonted "Why not?" scripted inside of it.

Why not? "He's not my type."

"Honey, he's everybody's type. And don't even try to tell me you wouldn't be his. You've got that sexy geek girl thing that's so hot right now. And if he's on that site, he's looking for love."

"First, this is a job, not a cattle call. Second, he's not looking for love—he's looking for a wedding date. Third, for all we know this is one of twenty dating sites he's listed on and he's completely indiscriminate."

"Wow. Strident, much?"

Saskia breathed out long and hard. "Lissy—"

"I know, I know. You'll get there when you're ready. But, sweetheart, how long has it been since What's-his-name decamped?"

Saskia glanced at Ernest and in a stage whisper said, "Seven months."

Lissy whispered back. "The dog can't understand English."

"Oreos," Saskia said, this time at a normal decibel level.

Ernest woke with such a start he fell off the armchair. Three seconds later he was at Saskia's side, paws on her lap, claws stretching out the zigzags on her woollen tights in the hope of finding cookie crumbs.

"Later, baby," she said, ruffling his ears, and sending him back to the chair with a pat on the bum.

"Way I see it, this is your chance to try something new." Lissy reached out and turned Saskia's monitor so she could get a better look at the man thereupon. "Not some indigent fixer-upper, but a guy who's sexy and brilliant. A man who looks like he knows how to take care of himself for once. And take care of you, if you know what I mean?"

Lissy finished with a Groucho-style eyebrow-wiggle, then slurped at her coffee, shuffled in her chair and got to work.

Saskia tried to do the same, cracking the spine of a fresh yellow legal pad, writing "Dating By Numbers" at the top and "Love Formula" beneath. She crossed it out, tried to think of a more appropriate title and, no thanks to Lissy, couldn't.

Also thanks to Lissy, her mind kept curling back to the same conversation she and Lissy had had a million times over. Lissy postulating that Saskia's yen for needy guys came down to a childhood spent trying, without much success, to lighten the life of her clueless, maths professor, single dad. Saskia contending that she simply liked who she liked. And if that happened to be men who made her feel indispensable, then what was wrong with that?

Apart from the fact that it never lasted.

Her gaze swept back to the screen and she let it trail over every inch of *yum*.

NJM looked like the least needy man on the planet. But could he kiss a girl so well she'd forgive him for snapping her carrots? *Yeah,* she thought, tingles curling into existence inside her belly, *I have a feeling he could.*

But that wasn't why she clicked on the happy yellow "Why not?" button on NJM's email. She had a job to do—a well-paying job. NJM was an anomaly in the heretofore predictability of the remainder of subjects in her study and therefore worth investigating further.

And while she had more work than she would ever have taken on at one time under normal circumstances, a girl had to eat.

Weddings did it every time.

It had taken years, diligence and dogged immovability, but

Nate Mackenzie had finally trained his sisters to leave him
well enough alone when it came to his confirmed bachelorhood. Until a wedding invite arrived in the mail. Then all bets
were off.

He'd just hung up from his oldest sister, Jasmine, when the
twins, Faith and Hope, came at him, conference-call-style.

"She's *lovely!*" one of them exclaimed before even emit-
ting a hello.

He leant back in his office chair, executed a half turn till the
sunshine slashing past the Melbourne skyline and through the
intimidating wall of windows nearly blinded him. "I'm fine,
thanks. You?"

Ignoring his sarcasm, the twins tag-teamed. "Jasmine's
friend makes the best macaroons."

"I've seen photos. She's just your type."

He opened his mouth to ask just what his type might be, but
he snapped his mouth shut at the last second.

They were good at finding weak spots. He was better.

After all, he'd taught them all they knew: a consequence of
becoming the man of the house at fifteen.

He pressed his feet to the floor and a thumb to the temple
that had begun to throb. "I'm thrilled you are all so content in
your own lives that you have the time to stick your collective
noses into mine, but you need to focus your impressive ener-
gies elsewhere. Third World hunger, perhaps?"

"But—"

"No more set-ups. Consider that an order."

At that, a pause. Then lashings of laughter which had his
other temple throbbing in syncopated rhythm against the first.

When they shifted into a familiar tune about how his natural
born charm and adorable baby blues wouldn't get him by for
ever, Nate slowly turned his chair back to face his vast office
as his brain flicked through possible ways to convince them to
leave the subject of finding him a good woman the hell alone.
He could honestly beg work, but that was nothing new. A week-

end was something other people had. He hadn't set foot on a beach in so long he couldn't remember how sand felt between his toes. And telling them he was only keen on bad women hadn't stopped them before; it had merely expanded the pond from which they fished on his behalf.

"I'm seeing someone!" The walls of Nate's vast office seemed to heave away from him as the import of the words he'd just uttered echoed into the ensuing silence. Damn twins—they were like a pair of hammers banging at an exposed nerve. It had been bound to jerk eventually.

But when the silence deepened, Nate wondered if he'd hit on something inspired. If he oughtn't to have invented a significant other years ago—someone who travelled often, was ethically against telephones, who had lost her whole family in some tragic accident so he could therefore never subject his love to the pain of meeting his.

Caught up in his own daydreams of freedom, he realised his chance to hang up on a high a moment too late.

One twin said, "Someone who can string a sentence together without saying 'um'?"

"What the hell do I care?" he heard himself bellow. "So long as she looks good, smells nice and goes home happy."

"Nate," they said on twin sighs, with familiar waves of guilt pouring down the phone line. They *knew* they should be nicer, considering all he'd sacrificed to make sure they were well-adjusted after their father died. Knowing didn't make it so. They had stubborn Mackenzie genes after all.

"The worst part is I don't think you're kidding," said one.

"That the perfect Nate date wants no commitment, no happy-ever-after, no way," said the other.

"Find *her* for me and then we can talk," said Nate as his office door swung open. Gabe poked his head through the gap. Done with being outnumbered, Nate waved his recently returned business partner in with a brisk flap of his hand.

One raised eyebrow later, Gabe shut the door behind him

and ambled across the room to lower his huge form into a chair that would have been plenty big enough for any other man. Gabe, on the other hand, looked as if he'd need a crowbar to get out.

"I have to go," said Nate. "My ten o'clock is here."

"Say 'hi' to Gabe from me."

Then, "Tell him if it doesn't work out with Paige, he can always—"

Nate hung up before any more of *that* image made its way into his subconscious.

"The girls on the warpath?" said Gabe, as Nate once again rubbed his thumbs across both temples.

"This time, it's your fault."

"How's that, exactly?"

"If you weren't with Paige, you'd never have met Mae and Clint, who'd never have invited me to their wedding. And Macbeth's witches wouldn't have made it their life's mission to find me a woman."

Gabe's dark stare flattened. "Are you wishing away *my* woman?"

"Not," said Nate, settling back in his chair. "For years you walked around like a bear with a sore tooth. Now you're practically cuddly."

Gabe's lip curled as he as good as snarled. But then the big guy seemed to soften, sweeten, and the smile that slipped through confirmed cuddly was fine, if it meant he had *her*.

Hell.

Thankfully Nate was spared, as Gabe's mobile rang and he answered with a gruff, "Hamilton."

To think, Nate mused, it felt like only yesterday that together he and the big guy had sketched out their radical dream of a maverick venture capital business on the back of a beer coaster in a pub near uni. And now that crazy dream was a shining beacon of trust, fiscal responsibility and innovation within the morass of world-wide financial tremblings.

Nate had reached the heights he'd envisioned that long ago night, and had soared higher still. He had property all over the world, a stake in some of the most successful businesses in the country, and more money than he could count. And yet the heart of that dream, the pinnacle he'd aspired to, the moment when the pendulum of success had hit its peak and he could ease back, content with his success and enjoy the spoils, had never eventuated.

Every decision, every purchase, every paperclip was still under his tight control—as though if in letting go he'd lose it all. And it wasn't lost to him that he was nearing the age when his own hard-working father had gone to work one day and never come home.

Gabe hung up and said, "You free for lunch? The gaming guy I was telling you about is meeting me at Zuma at one, and I'm sure having us both there'll put the requisite sparkle in his eyes to get his scrawl on the dotted line."

Nate ran his hands over his face, pushing the mounting signs of frustration down deep. "I can swing by at quarter past."

"Better. Keep 'em keen." Gabe pressed himself from the chair and only when he reached the door did he look back.

"So, have you got a date for Mae and Clint's wedding, or what?" Gabe asked.

Nate lugged his stapler all the way across the room. It bounced off the wall a foot from Gabe's shoulder.

"I take it that's a no?"

Then Gabe was out through the door, leaving Nate to deal with the onset of a new range of throbs in his temples.

It *was* a no. And yet he'd told Faith and Hope he was seeing someone. When the actual truth was somewhere in between.

He'd get a damn date, if only to get them off his back for the next few weeks till the big day. But it wouldn't be anyone they knew. Or even anyone *he* knew for that matter.

Asking a woman on a date was one thing. Asking a woman to a wedding was akin to smothering himself in catnip and taking a swan dive into a pride of lionesses. There wasn't a kind way to tell someone with confetti stuck to her eyelashes that it was never going to happen.

But it *was* never going to happen.

For the six years between the day of his father's heart attack and the day his trust fund had been opened to him he'd devoted himself to being the man in his young sisters' lives. They'd repaid the favour by using his toothbrush, and wearing his shirts to bed. He'd asked them to stop and they'd acted out by dating his friends. And no matter how he'd managed to swallow it down, to let them do what they had to do, they'd cried themselves to sleep. He'd heard them, night after night, the sound tearing away at his insides. Until he'd become impervious to tears, to mood swings, to raging hormones and wily feminine ways. It was the only way he'd lived to fight another day.

Two hours after Mae had told him to "save the date," he'd tagged a research team to find him a dating website. All he'd told them was that it had to boast discretion and success; they didn't need to know why.

Since then he'd met six perfectly nice, attractive, elegant, smart women, every single one of whom had taken one look at him and sized him up for a tux, a four-bed house and a Range Rover with a reversing camera.

But time had run out.

He checked his email to find another of his "Maybes" had come back with a "Why not?"

More determined than ever, he opened the email. Her tag was Bloomin.

Favourite Pizza Topping: ham & red peppers
Favourite Music: retro grunge
If I Could Be Anywhere in the World I'd Be: right where
I am
Looking for: someone to talk to

Retro grunge? What the hell was retro grunge? Sounded dire. And yet he opened her picture for a second look. And then he remembered.

After an hour of trawling the site that first night he'd hit a point where the string of women in bikinis grinning suggestively at the camera had become a blur. He'd rather have tugged out his own eyelashes than read another thing but the very next picture that had appeared on the screen had been so unexpected it had stopped him short.

A woman in her late twenties sitting in a café, with a shaggy scarf-thing around her neck, dark hair in a messy twist that just reached one shoulder, and an old felt fedora perched on top of her head.

Nate leaned his elbow on the desk and rested his chin between thumb and forefinger. With the other hand he zoomed in till her eyes filled the screen. She was attractive, in an offbeat kind of way, with her fine chin, fine nose and soft pink lips curved into an easy smile. But those eyes of hers were something else. Wide-set, the colour hovering on the edge of brown, the long dark lashes creating sultry shadows below.

But within them was the most captivating thing about her, that one thing that had eluded him for so long… Contentment.

He wasn't sure he even knew what that felt like any more. And here, at his fingertips, was a woman who claimed to be happy being right where she was.

Without another thought he hit "Reply," picked a time, asked her to pick the place. Even if he'd built a client base on becoming on a first-name basis with some of the best chefs in town, in this case it was far better to go somewhere atypical or it would get back to his sisters.

It always did.

And a man had to have his priorities straight.

CHAPTER TWO

FOR ALL ITS family name, Mamma Rita's Italian restaurant in Fitzroy was dark, sensual and bohemian, a hotspot for artists and hipsters. If conversation was your bag the beer garden at the back rarely saw beer and reeked of the sweet smoke of the philosophical thinker. Saskia, though, loved it for the great food, and for a girl on a budget one decadent meal filled you up enough not to have to eat for another twenty-four hours.

Dolled up in her favourite batik pants, sandals made in Nepal and an upcycled scarf she'd made herself from an old T-shirt, Saskia sat fiddling with the piece of string she'd tied around her wrist to remind her of...*something* as, with scientific appreciation, she watched the man who'd just walked through the front door.

The photo of NJM hadn't lied, though it could be accused of under-representation. He looked immaculate; his dark suit crisp, the knot of his deep red tie tight, his shoulders broad and proud. And as a waitress approached the naturally provocative curve of his mouth hooked slowly into a nearly-smile. Even from across the restaurant Saskia saw the poor girl's knees buckle.

He really was beautiful. But, even better to Saskia's mind, beautifully anomalous.

It didn't make sense, and to a mathematician there was no more satisfying moment than when the seemingly senseless finally added up. Lissy dated bad boys because she wanted to

drive her rich parents crazy. Ernest liked Oreos because she'd
shared hers with him the day Stu had left. But why would a
man who looked like that need to go online to find a date to
a wedding?

Saskia ran a hand over her hair which was—by feel at
least—not doing anything overly crazy. He must have caught
the movement as the next moment his eyes found hers.

Wow, she thought, her lungs tightening and her tummy tripping over itself in rhapsodic pleasure, *those eyes should be
classed a lethal weapon.*

He lifted his hand in a wave. She did the same.

Thus unfrozen, Saskia shuffled her fork as if it was important she do so at that very moment, and told herself to get
a grip. This was research, not a real date. And if a chat with
NJM of the blue eyes, dark suit and sinfully sensuous mouth
could help her nail the angle that would take her infographic
from informative to viral, then she'd just have to suffer through
a date with the guy.

As her research subject began to stride her way Saskia made
to stand. In pressing her hand to the table, her palm landed on
her fork, sending it flying across the room.

Saskia watched, mouth agape, as it spun towards the table
of a young couple, where it landed with a series of less-than-
musical crashes, causing the girl to scream at the top of her
lungs.

A pair of waiters in black and white zipped out to clear the
mess, calm the girl, and offer free desserts.

"Need this?"

Saskia dragged her eyes from the disaster zone in the direction of a rumbling deep voice. Her eyes hit jacket button, rich
red tie, jaw carved by the gods, a mouth tilted at the corners,
a nose like something freed from Italian marble and smiling
blue eyes that made the straight lines and curlicues flittering
through her head scatter like bowling pins.

And then her focus shifted and she noticed he was holding a clean fork.

"Right," she said, shaking her head and laughing. "Thank you. Not one of my more elegant moments."

NJM's mouth curved into a deeper smile. It was a mouth made for smiling, she decided, amongst other things.

"Shall we?" he said, motioning to the table.

He waited for her to plonk into her chair before he eased his large frame into the seat opposite, popping his jacket button and running a hand down his perfect tie. His nails were as neat and tidy as the rest of him. His fingers were long and graceful, yet exquisitely masculine.

She lifted back out of her chair and held out a hand, "I'm Saskia. Saskia Bloom."

"Nate Mackenzie," he said, his nearly smile stretching out into the real thing, taking him from beautiful all the way to heartbreaking.

Maybe he had a third nipple. Or ate with his feet. But so far, Saskia saw no obvious reason a man like him couldn't find love on any street corner in the free world.

"A friend and I had a bit of fun guessing what the NJM stood for," Saskia said.

"Care to fill me in on your guesses for the *J?*"

Juicy, she thought. *Jpeg. Junk.* "Not so much."

The smile was back, and so were the curly tingles in her belly. *Charisma,* she told herself. Something chemical—hormonal, perhaps, or to do with endorphins. Not her field.

"Jackson," he proffered. "It was my father's name."

Her researcher's ear pricked. "Was?"

A beat, then, "He passed away several years back."

"Oh, I'm so sorry to hear that. Mine too. I mean, his name wasn't Jackson, but my father passed away a few years ago." When, Nate gave her nothing, just that face, and the promise of that smile, she blundered on. "I don't have a middle name, though. My mum died having me and it was all my father could do to name me at all. Even then it was after the doctor who'd given him the bad news. Or so went the story he told me every day on my birthday—"

Apparently she was going to blunder on till the end of time, as her research subject sure wasn't about to stop her. To stop herself, she reached for the massive jug of iced water, but Nate got there first. Perhaps it was gentlemanly behaviour. More likely, considering the fork incident, the guy was a quick learner. She sat on her hands as he poured her drink.

"So," she said, after managing a drink without spilling any on herself, "is this how your blind date's normally go? A slap-stick show followed by the comparison of dead parents?"

"Not so much," he said, his smile only going as far as his eyes, which somehow didn't diminish the effect one jot. "Yours?"

"You're my first."

"Ah, a virgin."

"*Noooo.* Not for a *looong* time." Then, as it sank in, "An online dating first-timer? Yep."

She wasn't a natural blusher. Not by a long shot. But something about this guy had her blood in a spin.

"Ready to order, *cara?*" asked the owner, affectionately known as *Mr* Rita—a tall, skinny man in his sixties who sported a nifty little moustache.

Saskia shook herself upright. "Um, sorry! Haven't even looked at the menu. Can you give us another five?"

She shoved a big plastic menu at Nate to distract him from Mr Rita's not so subtle winking and thumbs up, then she set to studying the menu as if she *didn't* know the thing off by heart.

As they put their orders in with Mr Rita a few minutes later Saskia's phone rang. She didn't need to glance at it to know it was Lissy, calling in case she needed a fake emergency. She quickly switched it to "Do not answer."

"Your back-up plan?" Nate asked, motioning to a passing waiter for the wine list. "That was early."

"My what?" she said, sliding her phone into the big bag at her feet.

His eyes slid back to her. Knowing. And blue. So very, very blue.

With a laugh, she admitted, "Spot-on, smart boy. Like you didn't have me pick the restaurant so nobody you know would see us together."

For the first time his eyes lost that permanent glint and he looked honestly surprised. And for the first time she felt as if she wasn't on the back foot but leading from the front, where she much preferred to be.

"Am I wrong?" She leaned a little his way, her palms flat on the table.

"No," he said, blinking. "And now I hear out loud how that sounds I feel like I ought to apologise."

She shrugged, pointed out a bottle of red from the list in his hand. "If you'd taken one look at me and walked back out the door *then* you would have owed me an apology. It was only sensible of us both to take measures. I mean, you should see the lies the other guys on the site tell about themselves."

"Lies?" he repeated, as if it had never occurred to him.

Saskia counted off her fingers. "Your photo might have been a fake. You might have been lying about your age, your weight, your occupation, your name, your reason for joining the site. You might have been a psycho killer."

With each less-than-flattering "might have been" Nate's surprise, if anything, seemed to wane. The glint was back, and he too leaned forward. She caught a hint of purely masculine spice curling above the saucy scents of herbs and garlic.

"So, if you met a man in a bar, on a train, or jogging in the park, you'd have more faith that he wasn't a psycho killer?"

"I don't jog."

His mouth kicked, as if his smile surprised even him.

Her cheek twitched in response. He noticed, and the glint in his eyes changed. Deepened. Found some kind of heat. At which point his gaze dropped to her mouth, the dip at the bottom of her neck, then moved back to her eyes.

While Saskia struggled to remember how to breathe.

But while Nate Jackson Mackenzie, with his good looks, air of money and charm that could lure a siren to dry land, was probably used to having women fall all over themselves whenever he walked into a room, Saskia wasn't most women.

Which was why, when he stretched out a leg beneath their small table, his calf connecting with hers and shooting sparks up her leg, she said, "I didn't sign up to Dating By Numbers in an effort to find my one true love."

The slight rise of an eyebrow gave her the impression he didn't believe her.

Wow. Okay. So that irked. Maybe that was his great flaw: he could be irksome.

She whipped her bag onto her lap, found a business card and thrust it in his direction. "I'm a freelance statistical researcher working on an infographic about online dating for the website."

She could have pumped a fist in the air at the surprise that coloured his eyes at that one! And then from one heartbeat to the next his brow furrowed and she saw the brain behind those dauntingly beautiful eyes whir into life. It hadn't occurred to her that he might leave, but the longer he sat there, staring at her card, the more she wondered. And hoped that he'd stay.

He finally, *finally,* pocketed her card and said, "And to think you all but accused *me* of being a possible psycho killer."

"I'm a mathematician," she said. "Not exactly the same."

"I thought the point was that people lie."

"I— *What?*" Irked didn't even touch on how *that* made her feel. Punctuating her words with a waggly finger, Saskia said, "I said I was looking for somebody to talk to, which is completely true."

One eyebrow cocked. "Safer to say it was bending the truth?"

"Not even slightly. It's not my fault if you misunderstood my meaning."

She crossed her arms, knowing she sounded defensive. But it was hard to be all sweetness and light when he was watching her the way he was. All charm and half smiles were gone as he looked her over, as if he was sizing her up for something. Hopefully not a hole in the ground.

Then he did some surprising of his own when next he said, "My motives for dating online aren't altogether pure either."

Ignoring the "altogether pure" jab, Saskia attempted to raise an eyebrow right back at him. But she'd never mastered the skill, so probably ended up looking astounded. She schooled her features back to normal. "You said you were after a date for a wedding?"

"I am. But recent events have meant my needs have altered a little."

"Do I need to call my back-up plan?"

He laughed—a deep, rumbling sound that made her knees clench together.

"The greater problem, for me, is that I have three sisters who seem to think it's their mission in life to find me a wife. Thus, I let slip that I already have a date for the wedding, and that this date and I are…seeing one another."

"Let me get this straight. There are no women in your life who would happily go with you to a wedding, so you made one up?"

"Not one who would understand that it wasn't the beginning of something more."

Okay. Now she'd met the guy, she could see that. Saskia felt herself nodding.

He went on, "What I need, Saskia, as well as a wedding date, is someone who would be willing to pretend to be my girlfriend."

Still nodding, she realised he'd stopped talking and was looking at her intently. As if waiting for an answer.

"I'm sorry, did you say something?"

"Are you dating anyone at the moment, Saskia?"

"Am I—?" Saskia thought of Lissy, Dropkick Dave and snapped carrots. "I wouldn't have signed up to a dating site if I was."

"But you've signed up even though you're not looking for 'The One'?"

Her mouth twisted. He had her there.

"So, how do you feel about bending the truth just a little while longer?"

Saskia blinked, the meaning of his words coming through slow and sluggish. "You want to do all that…with *me?*"

His nostrils flared slightly, as if he was weighing his options one last time. Well, to hell with that. She was nobody's—

"Yes," he said with a determined nod.

"Right."

Saskia so wished she had pen and paper at hand as what-ifs, problems and possibilities, questions and escape routes burst inside her head, spearing away into a million tangents.

"But…can't you just tell your sisters no? Tell them…whatever your problem really is?"

Secret wife? Secret difficulty in the bedroom? Secret identity? She itched to ask.

But when a muscle flickered in Nate's cheek and a moment later he lifted a thumb to his right temple, she thought *best not.* Best not tell him his idea was crazy either. Pretend girlfriend. *Sheesh!* Only he didn't look crazy. He looked as if he was at the end of his rope.

And just like that the curly tingles in her belly pinged into perfect straight lines.

Could it be possible that Nate Mackenzie needed her after all?

It had been months since she'd felt that flicker of purpose. Just because one man had thrown her benefaction back in her face so cruelly, it didn't mean she wasn't damn good at it.

"You're serious?" she asked.

Nate's thumb stopped rubbing his temple and he looked her dead in the eye. Saskia tried her very best to not wriggle as all that gorgeous intensity trickled through her like over-carbonated bubbly.

"As serious as a man can be," he said.

Mr Rita and his boys arrived at that moment, with plates of colourful bruschetta and fat, shiny strips of barbecued *calamari* and green salad. But, while Saskia usually had to stop herself from leaning over and kissing the plate, her eyes never once left Nate's.

"Buon appetito!" said Mr Rita.

As one Nate and Saskia said, *"Grazie."*

And then they both smiled.

Saskia took a breath. "I'm…" *Flabbergasted, bemused, actually considering this?* "I don't know how to put this, but I'm not sure if I can pull it off. You're—not the kind of man I usually date."

"You might be surprised to know you're not the kind of woman I usually date either," said Nate, laughing as if the world had finally found its natural order.

She kind of wanted to kick him in the shin. In fact…

"Oof!" he said, sitting up and rubbing at the spot.

"Sorry." She shuffled on her seat, as if that had been her intention the whole time. "So how would this work, exactly?"

"It's the first Saturday in spring. You free?"

She did the math in her head. "I believe so."

"That's how it's done." And then he smiled, as if the deal was done. Poor love. He had no idea what he was in for.

Saskia bit into her *calamari,* enjoyed every succulent drop, before asking, "So, what do I get out of it?"

"Hmm?"

"The deal. You're getting a girlfriend…" She paused when the guy actually winced at the word.

"What do you want, Saskia?" he asked, charm forming between the words like mercury.

"I want what I wanted from the beginning. To get the low-down on online dating." But if she could save time, money, by having a guinea pig do it for her...

"Here's the low down," said Nate. "It's as much of a crap shoot as closing your eyes and picking someone out of the phone book. I should know. You're my seventh."

Her mouth dropped open. "You've asked *six* other women to pretend to date you?"

His mouth kicked into a smile while his eyes came over all dark and intense, lit with that flicker of heat. "I've been on six dates," he corrected. "I asked only you."

"Oh." Well, that was kind of nice. "But I still need first-hand experience for my study—"

He shook his head, his eyes not leaving her. "No dating between now and then. I won't either. Goes without saying."

"Good to know. But I was actually going to suggest that maybe *you* could be the subject of my piece."

A muscle flickered in his cheek and she wondered how long it would be before he was rubbing at that temple of his again. "Saskia, I'm not talking to you about my dating habits. My private life is just that. Private."

He looked as if he meant it. But Saskia had always found that men liked talking about themselves. So she wasn't really worried on that score. She'd find a way to get to the heart of the man—especially if she had a few weeks to do it. At the thought of a few weeks in the company of this man the curls of sensation were back in her belly.

"So when's our next date?" she asked.

A frown creased his brow. "The wedding."

"But what if someone asks how we met? If they ask you about my home, my family, my friends, my work? What's an infographic?"

"I'm sorry—a what?"

"An infographic. It's what I am working on for the dating site."

He looked pained.

"It's a diagram that shows information—stats, links, comparisons—in a bright, attractive, easy-to-digest contained image. We need a little background to do this properly, Nate. I can put it together, if you'd like. Research is my thing."

A list of dry questions, she thought, warming to the idea, *with some curve balls thrown in.* Classic stat-collection technique. He could tell her a lot that way without even meaning to.

"Or how long will it take for your family to think you've just made me up?" When his cheek twitched again she knew she had him. "We'll need to set up a couple of meetings between now and then. Casual get-togethers. Coffee, perhaps. We both like coffee. The Art Gallery has an Impressionists exhibition. Or we could go ice-skating. I don't mind."

Keeping him thinking about places he clearly did not want to go with her gave her the chance for the other half of her brain to create the research project in earnest. Questions piled up inside her head with such speed it made her breathless.

And as she was getting excited by the research, the layers upon layers of information this man could provide for her love formula, she remembered the pile of red envelopes wavering on her desk.

Her excitement deflated like a pricked balloon. "I don't think I can do this."

"Why not?"

The *why* was like a pain in her belly—one that was lessening by the day, but would remain till the day the last red envelope landed in her mailbox. "Time, I guess. More than anything."

"An hour together here and there should suffice," he said.

"Well, now, that's about the most romantic thing a nearly pretend boyfriend has ever said to me."

His mouth did the surprise smile thing—the one that gave a hint of straight white teeth and lit his intense eyes with genuine laughter. "What's the problem? I'm a problem-solver. It's what I do. Money, time, space, audience, you need it I provide it."

"You'd be cutting into my worktime. I need to work."

"Why?"

He was so sincere, so keen, she made a quick decision to tell him the truth. Part of it anyway. Not bend the truth, just not tell all.

"I have…debts." Yet her chin lifted as she said it.

His long, slow breath in made her stomach hurt. Then, with a nod, he said, "I'll take care of them."

She shot out a laugh so loud the table shook. "Just like that? A blank cheque?" When he didn't laugh back she realised. "You're serious?"

"Deadly."

"But I haven't even said what I owe!"

He gave a slight lift of the shoulder, as if she could name her price. "Consider this negotiation, Miss Bloom."

Miss Bloom now, was it?

"You have a debt. I have the means to wipe it from existence. I have need of a date to my friends' wedding, and you seem amenable to the terms and conditions that come with being said date."

"You pay off my debt—I pretend to be devoted to you?"

He eased into a smile this time, slow and sensual. A frizzle of energy lit her belly and she felt a sudden need to swallow.

"Seems more than fair," said Nate.

"Seems like a version of the oldest profession," she muttered.

Clearly not softly enough. "I'm not asking you to sleep with me, Saskia," he said.

"Stop," she said, her cheeks feeling like little spots of heat. "Now you're just gushing."

His laughter was soft, a low chuckle. And then he leant back in his chair, watched and waited.

A pretend boyfriend. A date to a wedding. No more red envelopes. No more reminders of Stu or his letter. The time and the means to get back to renovating the first place she'd ever rightfully called home.

"For the sake of argument," she said, "would you change your mind if I told you *this* is what it would take?"

She threw out the hefty figure that covered Stu's debt only, which she knew to the nearest cent, and he didn't even blanch. Maybe if he'd flickered an eyelid, lost a little colour in that healthy face, or if his long fingers had gripped a napkin in despair that would have been the end of it. But for his complete lack of reaction she might as well have been asking for a tenner for the cab home.

And from one heartbeat to the next she considered his offer.

Seven months she'd been living under the weight of it. Seven long months of driving a banged-up car, of trawling online sales to replace every piece of electrical equipment she *needed* to make a living. Of taking menacing late-night phone calls from debt collectors, legal threats, her mortgage squeezing tighter and tighter. Of being romantically stagnate... None of the debt was her fault, but she was too bone-deep humiliated to do anything but absorb it.

Nate watched, bluer than blue eyes taking in her every breath. The guy was smart, gorgeous, clearly better than well-off. He wasn't going into this thing desperate or despairing. He was doing a deal with all the cool of a business decision. Why couldn't she do the same?

"Do we have ourselves a deal?"

"I get the feeling I'm going to regret this..." she muttered, then held out a hand. He took it and she felt a frisson of heat and something else—electricity, perhaps—shooting up her arm.

Then Nate said, "Who knows? Maybe I'll be the time of your life?"

And with that came a big wallop of charm so bright she had to blink against such brightness.

It occurred to her belatedly that while she'd thought she'd

had him on the ropes, distracting him with talk of infographics and ice-skating, he'd actually been in charge the entire time.

She waited till the buffet of charm subsided, before saying, "Who on earth filled your head with *that* rubbish?"

"Three sisters. All of whom you're going to meet Sunday week at my mother's house."

On that note their dinner arrived: steaming pasta piled high with glistening red sauce, pungent with Italian herbs. The homemade bread oozing with butter. And for the first time ever at Mamma Rita's Saskia lost her appetite.

After dinner—as always, Saskia insisted on going Dutch which, considering the amount he was about to lay down for her services, might have been a tad redundant—Nate walked her through the restaurant and outside where the breeze was brisk, the final notes of winter trying one last stir.

"Where are you parked?" asked Nate, pressing a hand to Saskia's lower back.

She actually felt the warmth of him through her top.

"I'll walk you to your car."

"I walked. I don't live far." She'd planned on walking back too, only now she could afford transport. "I'll grab a cab."

One nod, then Nate looked across the busy street and with a determined wave hailed a cab. He opened the back door for her and she leaned in to give her Brunswick address to the cabbie.

She stood to say *goodbye,* or *thanks,* or *see you soon,* or whatever a girl was meant to say to her new faux-boyfriend.

"It was a pleasure meeting you, Saskia Bloom," Nate said, taking the decision out of her hands.

She placed her hand in his to find it enveloped in his strong, steady grip. "We'll see, Nate Mackenzie," she said.

Nate's laughter was low—a rumble that slid down her arm and faded into the darkness. Leaving them looking into one another's eyes. Hands still held. Two strangers who had just made a deal to pretend to be more.

Saskia moved in for a goodnight kiss on the cheek…right as Nate let go and pulled away.

Oh, God. He'd meant to give her a handshake while she'd—*argh!*

Saskia saw the moment Nate knew it, and as blood rushed from every extremity to land hard and fast on her cheeks a smile tugged at the corner of Nate's mouth.

She opened her mouth to say… Well, she didn't get a chance to say anything, as Nate's hand slid to her waist and he pulled her close.

His blue eyes were shadowed, the street light creating a halo around his dark blond hair. He looked cool, steely, all greys and blues. And yet his touch was hot, as if a furnace burned just below the surface.

His nostrils flared as he moved in slowly, giving her time to call a halt.

But in the face of all that heat and strength, the scent of man, and after seven long months with a wiry, snoring, biscuitoholic dog her only male companionship, she wasn't going anywhere.

A small smile kicked at the corner of his sensual mouth and then, easy as you please, he brushed his lips lightly across hers.

When she didn't push him away, or knee him, he pulled her closer still, shooting sparks of awareness all over her body. Then, with another soft, tantalising press of his lips, he teased her, drawing out the kiss until her lips parted on a sigh.

He didn't waste a second, his tongue tracing her teeth before sweeping inside her mouth. She gripped his jacket as, arching against his hands, into his heat and hardness, pleasure tugged at her belly before pooling lower.

The cold night air pressed in on her back as his heat burned her front. Heat won, pouring through her as the kiss slid into something deeper. Nate fisted his hands in the back of her top and Saskia rose to her toes, sinking completely into the kiss, into him.

As she began to feel drugged, hot and flaky, nearing the edge of control, Nate pulled back.

When she finally found her breath, Saskia asked, "What was *that* for?"

"Credibility."

She glanced up the street to find a few late night stragglers looking in shop windows and ignoring them completely. "I reckon the cabbie's convinced."

Nate laughed, the sound reverberating through her still pulsing body. "So am I, to be honest. A hell of a lot more than I was five minutes ago."

Saskia blinked up into Nate's hooded eyes. When she licked her lips his grip tightened, and Saskia could feel her pulse *whumping* all over her body as her heat levels ramped up in preparation for more...

Then Nate neatly pulled away, making sure she was steady before he let her go completely. She wasn't. Steady. She was wondering if she'd bitten off more than she could chew.

Hands now in pockets, all that latent heat trapped behind a wall of cool, Nate said, "Six weeks and a bit. And a wedding." As if she might need some kind of warning.

You kissed me! She ached to throw it back at him, but she'd been all too willing to let him.

"And debts paid off," she said instead, getting the feeling it would become some kind of mantra in the weeks to come. "And if you decide to be helpful and tell me about your dating life, I'll be all ears."

"Sweetheart, I'd pay double what you asked *not* to have to talk." He held the back door of the cab as she slid inside. "I'll call you soon."

Saskia nodded, and as the cab drove away she couldn't help but look back, to find him standing on the footpath, watching her too. Tall, broad, hair gleaming under the lamplight.

She lifted a finger to her mouth, which still tingled from the attention of his wonderful mouth.

There goes a man I could forgive for snapping my carrots, she thought. *And probably a lot worse.*

CHAPTER THREE

NATE RAN TWO hands over his face, trying to get some blood flowing to his brain. He was working more than ever; the number of emails bouncing into his inbox every minute proved it.

Ignoring them as best he could, he concentrated on the contract on his desk. Bamford Smythe, the "gaming guy" whose start-up company BamBam Games Gabe had discovered, had signed an exclusivity agreement with BonAventure, and now they were in the process of nutting out the finer details of the capital investment.

Smythe was pessimistic, pedantic and paranoid that everyone was trying to steal his ideas. Thankfully he was also brilliant. Nate just had to keep him on a short leash—which was turning out to be akin to lassoing a Tasmanian devil.

A knock at the door and a glance at the watch strapped to his wrist told Nate that it was three already. *Dammit.*

Rubbing a hand up the back of his neck, he called, "Come in."

The door was opened tentatively, followed by a head poking around the door. "Hiya."

"Saskia."

After their date he'd emailed her with a half-dozen questions—basic stats about age, family, schooling. Then she'd called, suggesting they get together for a "get to know one another" in a "pretend we've had a half-dozen dates" kind of way. He'd told her to make an appointment, hoping she might waver. Alas, she wasn't easily swayed.

Nate waved her in with one hand and finished annotating with the other. "Won't be a sec," he said, glancing up as she sauntered in. But his hands stopped midscrawl when he saw what she was wearing.

Her hair was tucked beneath the same fedora from her on-line profile picture, her legs were swimming in wide calf-skimming pants that looked like they'd been cut from a Hessian sack, sandals were tied up over her ankles, and she wore a brown cardigan she near got lost in, and a scarf long enough that a lesser woman would have stooped under its weight.

A thread of tension shot through him, landing with a twitch at the corner of his right eye as he considered what his family would be expecting. Certainly not this gamine creature who looked as if she might start sprouting poetry or drawing in chalk on his office floor.

What had he been thinking?

She shot him a quick smile as she took a curious tour about the room, her wide eyes shadowed beneath her hat, her lips soft and pink. The memory of how they'd felt beneath his own hit him and hit him hard—her gentle heat, her soft sighs, her sweet response that had licked at something deep inside him. Okay, so he'd been thinking of kissing her from nearly the moment he'd sat down.

She unhooked a satchel from her shoulder and dumped it unceremoniously on the sleek cream leather couch on one side of the room, bending over to rummage through it, giving him a nice view of a pretty fine backside. She might be slight, but he'd felt enough curves as she'd pressed into him to give any red-blooded man pause.

"Gotcha!" she said, standing upright, her profile lit with a happy little smile.

Contentment, he thought again, feeling something akin to

envy at her easy pleasure. At how he'd barely swiped his mouth across hers before she'd started trembling.

He ran a hand up the back of his head several times to get his brain into gear. It was fine. Under other circumstances their unexpected chemistry might be a hindrance, but in this case it would help make them convincing.

And the deal was a good one. Saskia seemed cluey—the kind of person who just got on with things. She didn't seem demanding, or clingy, or prone to tears and pouts. The antithesis of his sisters, in fact.

His tension eased. A little.

She caught his eye, then waved a couple of folders at him before throwing them onto the coffee table, where his assistant had earlier left an assortment of nibbles for their meeting, and moving his way.

"Your desk is so neat!" she said as she moved to perch on the edge of the black chair on the other side of his desk. The chair that had made Gabe look so big only a few days before made Saskia look like some kind of waif. "How do you know where anything is?"

"It's where it's meant to be."

Her mouth twisted sideways. Then she shrugged. "What are you working on?" she asked, pitching forward. The whirls of lace beneath her cardigan scooped low, giving him a glimpse of the sweet rise of the flesh within.

"Contracts," he said, endeavouring to keep his eyes on hers even as his body reacted viscerally, remembering how she'd felt in his arms—warm, soft, all woman. "New gaming company."

"Which one?"

He hesitated, old habits dying hard.

"I'll know them," she promised, misunderstanding his silence. Then, pointing at her chest, said, "Maths degree, remember? Nerd girl."

She looked so expectant, which only made him clam up more. It was a spontaneous reaction, brought on by years spent with women and their need to ask questions, to talk, to pry, to get to the heart of every damn matter. The more they wanted, the less he had to give.

He saw the moment she realised it. Her eyes widened and her lips pursed into a small O. "You're not going to tell me, are you? Is it confidential? No? Okay. But what will I say if anyone asks me about your work? That you keep a tidy desk?"

He laughed before he'd even felt it coming.

If nothing else, he liked her. Honesty and decency shone through the quirkiness. And even beyond the signs of attraction that had led him to email her in the first place aside, their kiss had been natural, raw, effortless. And wanted. By both sides. This *could* work.

"BamBam Games," he said.

Her eyes widened, her mouth twisting as she gave a long, low drawn-out, *"Reeeeally?"*

All that lovely cocky certainly was swept away. "Problem?"

"Not necessarily. Bamford Smythe is a genius. He's going to change the world." Under her breath she added, "Or destroy it from the inside of a cave somewhere."

Nate cricked his neck. "You know the guy?"

"Of him. Lissy, my business partner, did some work for him once. The logos and icons on his website are her work."

Nate clicked over to BamBam's website for a quick reminder. It was slick, cool, with an aura of hipster that Bam-Bam…*Bamford* had never given off in person. Now he knew why.

Then he realised Saskia was still talking.

"…and M&M'S. The guy is spookily addicted to M&M'S. So good luck!"

"Right. Thanks."

"Finish your thought and then we can get started," said Saskia, pressing herself to her feet, ridding herself of her long cardigan and tossing it towards the couch.

When she rounded his desk and headed to the wall of windows in only a lumpy lace tank, the beige pants and bondage sandals, Nate found himself watching her walk. Relaxed, easy, a neat little sway to her hips.

Not a mote of self-awareness about the woman—as if it didn't occur to her he might be paying such close attention. That from his angle the afternoon sun sluiced through the window making the buildings glow gold and rendering her lightweight pants all but see-through.

Her silhouette showed off lean legs, gently curving hips and a round, high backside. He curled his hands into his palms till the nails bit deep. Despite the test kiss, she wasn't his to touch. It hadn't been part of the deal.

Her hands went to that waist and she stretched out her shoulders, as if opening to the sun. His blood rushed every which way but loose.

"Shall we do this?" Nate said, his voice gruff.

Saskia turned and he waved a hand to the couch.

Saskia picked out a strawberry before unwinding and kicking off her shoes, taking off her hat, ruffling her hands through her kinky dark hair. Then she sat in one corner, leaving the length to him, one foot under her backside, the other curling its toes into the thick white rug.

She made it look so…comfortable. He wasn't sure he'd ever had anyone barefoot in his office before. He was pretty sure he liked it.

"So?" she said.

"You called this meeting, Miss Bloom," said Nate as he took the other corner. "You have the floor."

"Miss Bloom, is it? Well, then, we are all business."

Her gaze dropped to his mouth, her lips closing around the red fruit. Then, with a soft sigh, she picked up the two neat leatherbound folders with leather ties from the coffee table and handed one to him.

"Flash," said Nate, amazed that his tongue worked when it felt as if it was tied in knots.

"Stationery addiction." She waved a hurry up hand, practically bouncing in her seat as she waited for him to pull out whatever was inside. "I know it's a little more than we agreed to but I'm a sucker for a new project. There's nothing like it— blank paper, freshly sharpened pencils. Anything's possible."

"Before real life gets in the way?"

She shrugged, as if she was still convinced one day things really could work out as she hoped they might. An optimist was Saskia. With Pollyanna tendencies. Nate made a note to remember that.

He opened his folder to find his emailed questions, only she'd expanded them to include a slew of small details, rich details—the kind of details and funny stories people tended to discover about one another on the first few dates. And his were all filled in.

"You researched me," he said, eyes widening as he read on. School subjects, overseas trips, friends past and present, sports played, prizes won, legs broken and a full list of companies he'd invested in, complete with links to interviews he'd given to financial magazines and websites.

"Don't get too excited. I do this for a living, remember. I just found what was out there."

"I'm not sure *excited* is quite the right word." He looked up to find her nibbling at her lower lip.

"I've overstepped the mark, haven't I? *Argh!* Lissy calls it my Puppy Syndrome."

She held up her paws and panted and Nate's blood rushed south with such speed he had to grip the couch.

"But I just like being helpful. Here, give it back. We can start over. Pretend it never existed."

Was she kidding? She'd just saved him *hours*. In Nate's world that made her akin to the perfect woman.

He pulled his dossier out of reach and looked down at hers, gripped in her hot little hand. He found himself...not excited, exactly, but intrigued as to what was contained therein. "Swap."

She blinked, her lashes jerking against her cheeks, then did as she was told.

Nate opened the first page, speed-reading past schooling— state run. Tertiary education—scholarships. Work—applied mathematics with government agencies, before she'd moved on to build her own business—research with a bent towards the statistical.

He slowed when he hit her favourite books, movies, TV shows, as a tumble of odd and wonderful nuances meshed together to form a picture of not just a set of sultry eyes and kissable lips but a woman. *The Princess Bride* nestled alongside *Aliens* and *The Breakfast Club,* Ray Bradbury butted up against Sophie Kinsella and John le Carré. And a litany of real-life adventures flew before his eyes.

Compared with him, she'd lived three lifetimes.

"You've really eaten live witchetty grubs? And—" he glanced down "—you were an extra on *The Hobbit?*"

A smile hooked the corner of her lips, soft pink and warm. "All of the above. They taste better warm. Like nuts. Witchetty grubs, I mean. Not Hobbits," she corrected.

Laughing, Nate said, "Who knew statistics could be so much fun?"

That just lit her up—eyes bright, smile wide, cheeks pink, she glowed like a touch-lamp on level one. He wondered what it would take to light her up all the way.

Clearing his throat, he closed the folder.

Just in time for her to add, "My dad was a maths professor, so we lived in university housing, holidayed on campus. He never left his rooms if he could help it, while I'd sneak out and find people to talk to about things other than chaos theory. To ask about dinosaurs and rainbows and France. Being a university, there were always people happy to oblige. I found there's always potential to learn something new. You only have to ask. So I never say no to possibility."

"Never?"

That earned him a sassy grin. One he felt right deep down inside.

"What was your father like?" she asked. "Was he a lot like you?"

"A good deal." *Worked a lot, took responsibility seriously, blue eyes that laughed easily.*

"How did he and your mother meet?" Her chin rested on her knee, her eyes the picture of innocence. But she'd forgotten, he had three sisters. Her nugget about her own father suddenly made perfect sense. She wanted to get inside his head. He almost felt sorry for her that she was going to waste her time trying.

Nate said, "If it's not in the dossier let's consider it extraneous to the project."

Thwarted, she twisted her mouth.

"So," he said. "Tell me something about me."

"You're testing me?" she said, sitting straighter.

"If you can't pull it off what good are you to me?"

"Fine," she said, crossing her legs on the couch, eyes burning into him, bright with challenge. "Bring it on."

"Favourite colour?"

"Blue." She looked around his white, silver and pale blue office and said, "But you'd have to be colour blind to miss that. Pick up your game, Mackenzie. You're dealing with a pro." She crossed her arms beneath her small breasts, pressing them up, creating swells above the neckline of her top.

"Pets?" he said, his eyes lifting to stick to hers.

She snorted out a laugh. "I'd bet my life savings that you're not home enough to keep a cactus alive, much less a goldfish."

Considering he'd wire-transferred *those* life savings into her bank account only a couple of days before, he knew that wasn't much. But she was right. "You?"

"A dog."

"Really?"

"You don't like dogs?"

"I like them just fine. So long as someone else is in charge of feeding, washing, walking, cleaning up after them. What kind of dog? Please tell me it's not the kind that fits in a handbag."

"Ha! He's an Airedale named Ernest. He belonged to an ex who thought he was going to be the next Hemingway. Turned out he was more opportunist than writer—he left Ernest behind as payment for the TV and stereo he took in his place."

"Ever get them back?"

She shrugged as if it didn't matter. But he was a master of body language, knowing when to attack a deal and when to take a breath, and by the hunch of Saskia's small shoulders it mattered.

"Charming," said Nate, his tone belying his sudden desire to find out the guy's name and hang him from a balcony till he coughed up the goods.

"I came out with the better end of the deal."

"Good dog?"

"Sheds like nobody's business, has a wonky ear, will take a man down for an Oreo. But he's never gonna steal my TV."

Finding it hard to reconcile the woman before him being involved with the kind of man who could do that kind of thing, he moved on. "Family?"

She rolled her eyes. "You're a middle child—older sister, younger twin sisters."

"A psychologist's dream."

"I'm an only child, remember, so get in line."

He laughed and settled back in his corner of the couch. She settled back in hers. *Game on,* her smile said as she spoke. "Your mother is still about. Your father died when you were fifteen. A day before your fifteenth birthday, in fact."

Nate's throat closed over at that last part—a small fact he usually left out, as if it was one intimacy too far. But he'd brought up the subject of family. He'd asked for it.

She opened her mouth as if to say more, but he quelled her

with a look. Then she brought her knees to her chest and snuggled in against the cushions as if she belonged there.

"Women?" Nate asked, even while he wondered instead about this woman, about the kind of men she normally dated. No doubt men with goatees and sandals swarmed around her in droves. Unless she preferred her men clean-cut in suits.

"Your tastes run to brunettes," she said, curling a lock of her own brown hair around a finger, "mostly. Though there have been blondes and the occasional redhead."

"I'm an equal opportunity date."

A flicker of a smile, then, "No serious girlfriend that I could find." That got him a pair of raised eyebrows, meaning *fill in the blanks, please.*

Instead he went with, "Until now."

When her brow furrowed, her sweet mouth turning down, he nodded towards her and saw the moment she got his meaning. Pink rose up the soft column of her neck.

"Though we haven't really touched on that as yet. Are we that serious?" he asked, watching as the pink moved north to land in her cheeks. His palms warmed, as if he could feel the heavy beat of her blood from there. "Or just messing about?"

"A little serious," she said, but only after licking her lips. "Or what would be the point?"

Once his eyes had landed on her mouth there they stayed. And this time, as the memory of how she'd tasted, how she'd opened up to him and kissed him with such easy release came back to him, it did so with a great hot thud. "There's something to be said for messing about."

"Nate," she said. Her lips opened as she said his name.

"Yes, Saskia?"

"Maybe we should talk about the kiss."

With that, his eyes slid back to hers. When it came to his "feelings," *talk* was a four letter word. But if she wanted to describe, in any kind of detail, the kiss, then who was he to stop her? "Talk away."

She carefully put her feet back on the floor, as if needing to ground herself. "What I'd like to talk about is limits."

"Limits."

"Requirements and…restrictions."

God, she looked so earnest he couldn't help but grin. "My hand may brush your hip but must move no higher than your waist? Kissing allowed, but no under-clothes action?"

Her resultant stare was understandably flat.

"We're both grown-ups, Saskia. You know what I want. I know what you want. I think so long as we both get what we want the boundaries can be fluid."

She breathed in long and deep, and he felt himself breathing right along with her.

"So, kissing…" she said, her voice husky as all get out.

"Needn't be off the table. Unless *you* want it to be."

Did she? He'd live if she put a kibosh on it, but he found himself going very still as he awaited her answer.

A few long moments later she sat up straighter, shook her hair from her face and with a small shrug said, "Never say never."

That's my girl.

"So whatever happens…"

"…happens."

"Till the wedding."

"Right." Nate jerked a little at the fact that she'd been the one to say it. Then he shifted closer. "No point knowing about one another's childhood pets if basic chemistry isn't believable."

She sat stock-still, as if they'd been forced together by a fateful turn of Spin the Bottle. She frowned at his smile, which only made him smile all the more.

"What's so funny?" she asked, her voice husky, giving her away.

"You."

"If the thought of kissing me is *that* funny, maybe we ought to cut our losses right now."

"Sweetheart, the thought of kissing you is out there now, like a flashing red light right in the middle of my forehead. I can't stop thinking about it. As far as I know there's only one way to fix that."

"Right…" she said.

He moved closer again, till his thigh touched hers. Her bare feet curled into the couch. Her scent shifted in the air around him—soft, natural, making his nostrils flare and his blood pump so hard through his body he could hear it behind his ears.

He slid a hand into her hair, the softness spilling over his fingers. He turned her head till she was looking at him head-on, to find her lashes at half-mast, her eyes darkened with anticipation. Not a flicker of light was to be found in their bottomless brown depths.

He leaned towards her and smiled as she did the same, till her breath washed across his mouth, hot and ready.

Her chest lifted and fell quickly, as if her breath was getting away from her.

And then he pressed his lips to hers.

Such sweetness, sweeter than he'd even anticipated, as he fed her slow, aching, gentle kisses. And then there was her taste. He'd somehow forgotten that part; the lush, wholesome taste of her that was familiar and unique all at once. Her small hands lifted to grip his shirt. Soft sighs escaped her hot lips.

As her tongue slid across the seam of his mouth his brain turned to wild red mist. He returned in kind, their tongues dancing, chasing, creating the most delicious friction, and wave upon wave of heat rained through him.

Her arms wound around him and her body lifted to his, as if she couldn't get close enough. He felt trembling, though it couldn't possibly have been *him*.

When he wound his hand deeper through her hair, tugging it back, she opened to him as if she'd been unlocked, and all that sweetness was swept aside beneath the flood of heat that erupted between them. Her sweet, hot mouth was like a drug, pulling him under. When one bare foot ran down his leg it was all he could do not to come then and there.

Needing air, he moved his mouth to her jaw, to her sweet neck. God, she tasted like cupcakes with butter icing—sweet and decadent all at once. He slid a hand up the curve of her hip, then beneath her top to her waist. Her mouth opened on an intake of breath as he found skin. Such warmth, such satisfying softness.

When he circled his thumb beneath her ribs she writhed beneath his touch. Hell, the woman was all response. She made his blood pump too fast through his body, until kissing didn't seem like nearly enough—

He heard the phone ring in the outer office and remembered where he was: the company he owned was humming uncompromisingly on the other side of an unlocked door.

He pulled away with less haste than he'd intended. His hands took their time to leave her body. His mouth trailed back to hers for one last taste.

Then, using every ounce of self-control he was able to muster, he leaned back on the chair, as far away from this strangely compelling creature as possible.

Her eyes fluttered open and she stared at the ceiling, her legs twisted, her clothes askew. "Well," she said. "I'm sure glad we got that sorted."

He laughed. Then laughed some more. And thanked his lucky stars he'd found Saskia Bloom.

She pulled herself up to sit, ran a hand through her hair and only managed to make it look more rumpled. Provocative little thing, she was. He wondered if she had a clue.

"We done for today?" he asked.

"And then some," she said, shooting him a smile still lazy with lust.

While Saskia heaved herself from the couch Nate glanced at his watch, saw it wasn't even four. He had hours of work left to do, but knew without a doubt he'd be lucky if his concentration strayed above fifty percent capacity.

"I'll walk you to the lift," said Nate, picking up the dossiers.

"Keep them," she said, grabbing her hat, her cardigan, her huge bag. She was soon lost inside them again. "Some light reading for you. And if you feel like I've missed out any important details in your file feel free to jot down notes."

Nate pressed his thumb into his temple.

"You do that a lot," Saskia said. "Rub your temples. Or run a hand up the back of your hair. I wonder if you keep your hair so short so you don't tear it out."

She sat to retie her shoes, crossing the straps over her small ankles. When Nate found himself staring, imagining himself dropping to his knees and undoing them all over again, he distracted himself with his dossier, opening it to a page labelled "Identifying Marks."

Hello!

"You have a tattoo?" His eyes drifted over her lean form, landing on spots that might sport a tattoo of some breadth. "I should probably know what it is. And where."

Her eyes narrowed slightly. Then she set her feet on the floor, walked around the table. She turned away from him and lifted the loose top to reveal a small tattoo at the top of her shoulderblade.

A swathe of her hair was in the way, giving him no choice but to move it to one side. Her skin contracted under his touch. His gut tightened at her reaction. And the urge to kiss her, right there, came with a powerful push.

"A rose?" he said.

"My mother's name. Rosetta, actually. She was holidaying from Spain when she met Dad."

Her mother—who had died giving birth to her.

Losing his father had been horrific. Life-altering. Every dynamic in his life had shifted overnight. Even while Nate's mother drove him crazy he couldn't imagine not having her in his life. And yet Saskia Bloom, was, for all intents and purposes, an orphan of the world.

She lifted her shoulder away from his touch and let her hair fall back to her shoulder. "Not what you expected?"

"I was all prepared for a Chinese symbol for…something."

She rolled her eyes at him. "Unless I know a language intimately I'm not letting some biker with a needle write it on my skin."

A biker? Who *was* this woman?

Whoever she was, she was smiling at his shock. And in a flash he saw fearlessness behind that smile. A girl without a mother. A woman without a father. Alone in the world. And yet she was bright with effervescence, drive, gumption, humour and fearlessness. Looking into her lovely brown eyes for a moment, he could feel wind in his hair, the sun on his face as he left the world behind.

"Do you have any tattoos?"

He blinked, came back to the real world. "I do not."

"Want one?" She leaned forward, grabbed her bag and a grape, popping it into her mouth, where she rolled it around with her tongue before her teeth sank into it with an audible pop.

"I'm sorry?"

"A tattoo," she said, licking grape juice from the corner of her lip. "I know a guy who'd just love to get a hold of all that nice clean skin of yours."

"You think I have nice skin?" he asked, his voice dropping a notch.

Her head tilted, as if she was considering answering. Fearlessness won. "I think you could do with some ruffling."

"Ruffling?"

"You're so clean-cut. Even your background is pristine. No parking tickets."

"I fob those off on my driver."

She laughed—a husky sound he felt as a tightening in his gut.

"No restraining orders."

All she got for that was a raised eyebrow.

"I've taken out three. Two of them against the same guy."

Again Nate found himself sideswiped by the sudden urge to tear a complete stranger limb from limb. Time to call this meeting over. He pointed a hand towards the door. She hitched her bag and headed that way.

"You've clearly been dating the wrong kind of men."

"Tell me about it."

He got a knowing grin over her shoulder for his efforts.

"I certainly have a type."

"What type is that?" he asked.

She thought about it a moment, her mouth twisting. "Men with needs I can't help but fulfil."

He gripped the doorjamb to stop himself from fulfilling his own rabid need to dive his hands into her hair and ravish that mouth till she could no longer feel her legs.

When she hitched up her big bag again Nate slid a finger under the strap and tucked it over his own shoulder instead. Then he stepped through the door, dragged in a lungful of air filled with the scent of cleaning product and money and inside his head started listing stock exchange codes…alphabetically.

"Anyway, that's by the by," she said, smiling at his assistant as they passed by her desk. "I'm with you now."

Nate's assistant raised her eyebrows at Nate, who mouthed, *Get back to work*.

They walked companionably towards the lift. Nate nodded to any staff they passed, each one casting glances at Saskia, no doubt desperate to know who she was. He wondered if any thought they might be a couple.

"How about you?" Saskia added as they hit the vast foyer.

Nate put a hand to her back to ease her around the scattered chairs. "Do I intend to fulfil your needs?"

"Identifying marks," she said with a smile.

For once it didn't seem too much to ask. "I have an appendix surgery scar and a birthmark on my inner thigh."

"Shape?" she asked.

Her eyes slanted to his lap. Nate had never had cause to wonder about death by abstinence, but in that moment he was beginning to imagine the possibility.

"Texas," he lied, and thanked God when her eyes shot back to his. "Kidding. It's roundish."

"I guess I'll have to take your word for it."

The lift door opened and she held out her hand. He was half a second from taking it, using it to drag her in for one last kiss, before he realised she wanted her bag back.

He waited till the lift was clear bar anyone but her before saying, "So, next is my family lunch on Sunday."

Her shoulders flicked to her ears. "Nervous?"

"Not a bit," he said as the lift doors began to close.

"Liar." She grinned.

His laughter continued even when he was looking at nothing but the lift door.

"So that's your date?"

Nate turned to find Gabe leaning against the reception counter, his eyes on the lift. Nate made a beeline for his office, not keen on having this conversation in the foyer.

"Not what I expected," said Gabe, falling into step.

"What's wrong with her?"

"Not a thing. She just seemed...normal."

And even though Nate knew he was being baited he rose to it before he could stop himself. "What she is is cool. And funny. And mouthy." He pictured her standing in his window, hands on her hips, opened to the city view, the light shining through her clothes. "But mostly she's got this level of contentment I never even knew was possible."

"I think Nate has a crush on his pretend girlfriend."

Nate shook his head. "What Nate *has* is a contract to read for the third time."

Gabe winked at Nate's assistant, who giggled like a school-girl, then stopped in the office doorway, grinning. Nate pointed a sharp finger at his business partner. "*You're* going to Vegas."

"I am?" Gabe asked, standing straighter, his dark eyes shining with thoughts of treasure.

"With Bamford Smythe."

"The hell I am."

"He likes M&M'S. You're taking him to Vegas and getting him a private tour of M&M'S World. And when he's nice and high on chocolate fumes we're getting the nitty-gritty of this damn deal locked in."

Nate could feel Gabe reacting to being told what to do. They were equal partners, after all. Had been since day dot. But after Gabe had disappeared all those years before, leaving Nate to pick up the slack, Nate had never used the "You Owe Me" card. Not once.

Even while he couldn't believe it himself, Nate felt it shimmer on the air between them now. Over Bamford Smythe.

For reasons of his own Gabe took it on the chin, striding off towards his own office to make it so.

Nate thumbed his temple and stalked behind his desk. When he realised what he was doing he pulled his thumb away. If even Saskia, whom he'd met twice, had noticed his stress, he needed to take a break. And soon.

Or he was seriously going to crack.

CHAPTER FOUR

SASKIA STOOD LEANING against Nate's car—a glam silver sporty number that would have gone down well in a Bond movie—on the street outside a massive Stonnington Drive home. Its three clear storeys of gabled roofs and picture windows gave its imposing façade familial warmth, even while the shade of a hundred-year-old oak in the front yard added to the late winter chill.

No wonder Nate had looked so relieved when he'd picked her up at her door a half-hour before. The poor love had probably expected her to turn up in hemp and a hat. Instead she'd gone for a little lipgloss, a little more mascara, fitted jeans, layered tops, a tailored jacket and ballet flats. He didn't need to know the frilly scarf that hung to her knees was a million years old, second-hand and homemade.

"What a beautiful home," said Saskia, having a Molly-Ringwald-in-a-John-Hughes-movie moment.

"Mmm."

His tight response was so chilly she literally shivered. She gave herself a good mental shake. Then a physical one—stomping her feet and shaking the blood back into her hands.

"What are you doing?" Nate asked, his voice tight, his whole body stiff as a board.

"Trying to relax."

"Try harder."

He was serious. Which only made her laugh. Hard. Giving the butterflies in her belly a good workout.

"Enough already! How do you *expect* me to act? Faking it in front of a guy's family is hardly a common occurrence in my life. How about yours?"

His sensuous mouth grew flat, his stare much the same.

"Didn't think so. Because *you're* not doing such a bang-up job of looking like a guy who likes a girl enough to bring her home."

His jaw clenched so hard he was in danger of breaking a tooth.

"Here." She reached for the top button of his shirt, and stopped when he flinched.

Jeez, the guy was so wound up that if she flicked lint off his jacket he'd probably self-combust. She spared a glance at the door of the beautiful-looking home perched at the end of the perfect white gravel drive and wondered for a second what she'd let herself in for.

But it was too late for all that now.

She'd promised to help, so she'd help. She'd be such a great amount of help he'd never forget it. Maybe he'd be so touched he'd open up a little, give her fodder for her study.

"May I?" she asked, hand hovering an inch from his chest.

"May you what?"

"Ruffle you up a little."

"For what purpose?"

"For the purpose of making you look like a man on a date, not like an undertaker."

He breathed deep, his chest lifting till the weave of his luxurious woollen jacket brushed the hairs of her arms, creating skitters of…*something* all the way to her elbows.

His gaze finally left the house to connect with hers. The tangle of blue was enough to take her breath clean away.

"Ruffle away."

She purposely lowered her gaze from his eyes, not quite

sure what to do with the warmth that seemed to have seeped in there from one second to the next.

Instead she focused on the top button of his shirt and slid the button through the hole. When she saw he wore a crisp white T-shirt underneath—heck, even that had been ironed—she undid another button, and another. Her fingers slid beneath the collar as she softened out the starch. The backs of her knuckles brushed against the warm cotton of his T, and the beat of his heart didn't feel so steady.

Because of what he was about to try to pull on his family, she told herself. For the less than steady beat of hers her excuse was less clear.

"You have a good reason for doing this, right?" she asked, flicking her gaze to his to find him watching her fingers. Intently. She pulled them away, tucked them into the back pockets of her jeans. "For lying to them. For their own good? For yours? For world peace?"

He sniffed out a laugh and looked up at her from beneath his unfairly long lashes. "What if I told you the reason was less altruistic?"

What if? she thought. But she didn't have any qualms. She trusted his heart was in the right place. Or right enough. Her allegiance was with him.

She slid her hand into the crook of his arm, her hip bumping his companionably. "Come on, lover. Let's go make them believe."

She pushed away from the car and escorted him up the path, the scent of roses clear and lush on the crisp air. He unhooked his arm and slid it around her waist. She did the same to him, his body heat pressing in on her.

They walked side by side up the steps. Eyes on the big white double doors with a great lion's head knocker snarling back at them.

Saskia looked at Nate, waited till he looked back at her and made sure he was listening. "This thing between us is new, so if I don't know something I'll say so. All you have to do is throw me a hot glance every now and then. Undress me with your eyes a little. They'll eat it up."

He stared at her for longer than was comfortable.

"What?"

"Hell, Saskia," he said, his voice a growl as he ran a hand up the back of his hair—a move she was already familiar with.

She slipped her hand into his and gave it a squeeze.

Then when he looked down at her in question she lifted onto her toes and kissed his cheek. The rasp of his stubble tickled her lips. The scent of him slipped down the back of her throat.

Which was when she might have hummed.

The flicker of heat that sparked to life in Nate's eyes made her sure of it.

He lifted a hand to her cheek, his thumb running slowly across her cheekbone before his fingers disappeared into her hair. Brow furrowing, his eyes roved over her face, leaving *her* eyes to rove over his. And what a face. Noble nose, thunderbolt eyes, lips just made for kissing. She'd tried not to remember just how good they were at that particular job, but it was an impossibility.

So much so that, when his tongue darted out to wet his lips and he bent towards her Saskia was so filled with anticipation she began to tremble.

Which was when the front door swung open, letting out a shaft of golden lamplight and noisy chatter.

Nate blinked as if coming to from a spell, then as one they looked up as a gorgeous blonde rolled her eyes at them.

"Get a room!" said she.

"Faith," Nate growled, taking Saskia's hand and holding it tight behind his back as if he was her human shield.

"Nate," said Faith. "And you must be this new girl we've heard about. Glad to meet you."

"Saskia Bloom," said Saskia, but Nate had her in such a tight grip she was forced to hold out her left hand.

Faith took it, laughed, shook her head, then waved a hand to usher them in.

She bounded off, her long blonde hair swinging, but Nate kept Saskia back a moment.

"Thank you," he said, his breath brushing her ear as he leaned in close.

"I haven't done anything yet."

"Yes," he said, waiting till her eyes found his. "You have."

Then he stepped back so that his eyes could slide down her form, touching on her neck, her wrist, her thighs, before slowly meandering back to her eyes.

"Now, let's do this," he said, then winked—quick, brief, but potent—before he led her into his family home.

And while Saskia tried to get over the fact that gorgeous Nate Mackenzie had just well and truly undressed her with his eyes, for a brief moment she imagined running. Far, far away.

But Saskia was a stayer. Through thick and thin. You could take her stuff, call her names, ignore her through an entire childhood and still she'd never leave you. It was her defining quality. And, no matter that Nate Mackenzie was proving to be a trickier proposition than she had at first realised, she wouldn't let him down.

In fact he'd be so impressed with her awesome girlfriendness he'd open up and give her all the research material she'd need to do her piece. To write her love formula. To understand why some people found love every day of the week and others didn't no matter how hard they tried and how much they wanted it.

She just had to keep one step ahead of him or she'd turn into a puddle of lust on his mother's floor.

Saskia's coping mechanism was sophisticated, but surrounded by the females of the Mackenzie clan, her nerves were just about shot after less than an hour.

They were all gorgeous, like Nate. His mother effortlessly

charming, like Nate. So it should have occurred sooner that Nate's family would be as sharp as he too. As dogged. As tricky.

Interweaving questions about her, and Nate, and her and Nate, with talk of current affairs, reality TV, school friends she'd never heard of, keeping her spinning in circles till her inner ear was on its last legs.

"You're not his usual type," the one with the silver earrings—Faith—threw into the middle of an argument about the men in *True Blood.*

Nate's older sister, Jasmine, pinched Faith till she cried out, and then looked sweetly at Saskia. "What she meant was you're a real woman."

Hope rolled her eyes and stuck a rum ball in her mouth.

Saskia said, "As opposed to an imaginary one?"

Faith stopped rubbing at the pink mark on her arm, her eyes cutting to Saskia before she barked out a round of raucous laughter. "You know something we don't?"

Sure do, Saskia thought. But she just shrugged, looked Faith right in her big blue eyes, and said, "Nothing I'd share even upon threat of torture."

Faith grinned. "I like you. Stick around, if you can manage it."

They *liked* her, Saskia thought, making her wonder how they treated those they were less than keen on.

Later, cradling a much-needed coffee, she found a quiet corner, slowly sweeping her eyes over the great room at the rear of the house. The women were chatting, gossiping, sharing their favourite books. Saskia felt herself watching them as if they were the subject of a nature documentary: Women of the Mackenziegeti…

The guys were watching footy—black and white versus blue. Jasmine's twin boys had turned the dining table into a fort. Nate, on the other hand, was nowhere to be seen.

The whole afternoon he'd kept himself apart, just beyond the edges of conversations, hiding behind a coffee, or a beer, or a nephew. While she'd watched them all in open-mouthed awe.

Growing up, she'd wondered what it might be like to have a big family, and watching the shifting dynamic of this group of people, the vibrant debate beneath the warm glow of the beautiful home, she felt a twinge of envy. A kick of regret. And her first pang of guilt.

She was on Nate's team. No matter what. But she wasn't sure Nate's team was doing the right thing. Whatever it was that kept him at arm's length from his family, that made him think he had to lie to them rather than have it out with them, he certainly didn't seem willing, or able, to fix it himself. The only outcome she could see was that one day he'd be so removed *he'd* be the one feeling he was on the outside looking in.

She found him in the kitchen, which was surprisingly devoid of action. He was swishing his thumb over his phone, brow furrowed. His other thumb was pressed into his temple, and not for the first time that day.

Her fingers itched to rub it for him. To make everything all better.

Instead she leant in the doorway and said, "Howdy, stranger."

Nate looked up from his phone, expecting his mother, or one of his sisters. He could never seem to go five minutes without one of them tracking him down, making sure he was happy, that he hadn't disappeared.

When he saw it was Saskia, her soft mouth smiling indulgently, the clench in his stomach unwound and he put his phone away. "Howdy yourself."

"I wasn't sure if you trusted me to hold my own or if you'd just gone into hiding."

"We can go any time you please."

"I'm fine. Honestly. They worship you."

"Hmm."

She leant a hip against the sink. "Poor Nate. To be so adored."

He turned to face her. "Want to swap?"

She glanced back to the swing door, where noise poured through the fretwork above. All too late he remembered she had no-one.

"Saskia—" he said.

But Faith bustled into the kitchen before he had the chance to take it back.

"Nate? Oh, there you are," said Faith. "Half-time. Game-time."

"No."

"What's game-time?" Saskia asked.

Nate held out a hand to shield Saskia, but it was too late. Faith took her by the hand and dragged her through the door. "You're going to love this."

Faith shot him one last look before the door swung closed—and a grin that left him worried for Saskia's safety.

Knowing he'd left her alone too long already, he followed, leaning quietly in the doorway of the lounge, arms crossed, nursing a beer as his family went about their loud business around him.

Usually he took these moments to think about work, to disappear inside his head and pull himself away from all that energy. And history. And emotion so thick it clogged his throat.

This time they seemed to have forgotten to try to include him, now that they had a new victim to bat about, so he let his eyes rove over the scene, taking it in.

Hope was midargument with her girlfriend Tanya—a wholefoods wholesaler—about which kinds of flour were gluten-free and which weren't. Poor Tanya, so earnest, while Hope's eyes were gleaming, her Mackenzie genes loving every second of the battle.

Faith pinched her fiancée on the backside on her way to the kitchen with an empty salad bowl.

Jasmine was washing down the face of a toddler with a baby wipe, calling him back when he tried to leave before he was picture-perfect. Nate found himself wincing in sympathy.

The Mackenzie women were tough, uncompromising. He felt a small, swift kick of pride at the fact, considering where they'd all been twenty years before—the way it might have all turned out so differently if he hadn't done everything to make sure they felt safe, secure, loved, protected. If he hadn't given every ounce of his heart and soul, and then a little more, to give them the safety net from which to leap out into the world.

He breathed into the void it had left inside him, the vacuum where empathy and love had resided once upon a time.

"Look what you did."

Nate turned to find his mother behind him, her eyes taking in the same picture as his. He stood straighter. "I think you'll find they're all yours."

"We're all *ours*," she corrected, leaning her head on his shoulder as she gave him a squeeze. Then she lifted her head to look him in the eye as she said, "I like your girl."

It was on the tip of his tongue to say, *She's not mine,* but he caught himself in time, offering a small smile before he brought his beer to his mouth for a swig.

"You know what I like most?"

"What's that?" he asked, pretty sure it wouldn't be the same thing *he* liked best.

"She makes you laugh."

"I laugh plenty."

She laughed at his frown. "You *smile* plenty. A mere glint in those eyes of yours and you can get away with anything. But it's always taken a lot to make you laugh. And today you seem more…relaxed." She tugged at the open collar of his shirt. "It suits you." Then, after a long, slow breath in and out, she said, "Have I told you lately how proud I am of you?"

"Half an hour ago."

"Okay, then." She gave him a kiss on the cheek before heading into the fray with a tray of cookies.

Leaving Nate with the same sense of ruefulness he always felt when they looked him in the eye and said, *Well done, you.* As if it was as important to them as it was to him that he'd made something of himself. And just like that he felt a pressure headache building behind his left eye.

It was why he gravitated to women whose appeal was surface-deep. Who wanted him for surface reasons. His money, his touch, his charm. Replenishable resources all.

He glanced across at Saskia. Her motivations for being with him were simpler still, and yet far more complicated than he'd envisaged. Because compared with his usual dates, Saskia was...*real*.

Reality was scrappy. It was dirty, hard, complicated. It asked everything of a man and then some. His father dying young, leaving him with four women in varying stages of grief to look after, had given him a closer dose of "real" than he ever wanted to encounter again.

And yet here this woman was, real from the top of her wavy hair to the tips of her now bare feet and her short fingernails— a couple bitten to the quick. He looked at her slight figure. The way her right foot rubbed up and down the back of her left calf as if it might bring forth inspiration as she stared at the scrap of paper in her hand. She was first off the mark in Faith's game of high-speed half-time charades.

Saskia looked up at him then. Two little lines showed above her brow, her bottom lip was disappearing and reappearing from between her teeth. There was entreaty in her gaze.

He tilted his head in question. She flicked the paper in her hand. Two weeks they'd known one another, yet there was a shorthand there. An understanding that he couldn't remember having with another woman.

Maybe it was because there was no pressure. No demands.

Maybe it was because they both knew it was a few weeks, a wedding. And out.

But even while he felt his twin sisters' eyes swing to him at the same time, even while he knew they were smart enough to know there was something different about this one, Nate put down his drink and went to her.

And he had to admit, as Saskia threw herself into the game with gusto and a complete lack of success, that those twenty odd minutes were some of the most fun he could remember having in that house in a really long time.

After lunch Nate found Saskia looking out of the French windows in the library, watching Jasmine's husband and kids playing chase in the backyard. She was leaning over the back of a couch, her backside pointing nicely his way.

He shoved his hands into his jeans pockets.

"Come here often?" he asked.

She came to with a start, as if from a million miles away, before a smile stretched across her face—which had his eyes zeroing in on her mouth, making him wonder when they could get the hell out of there.

"That the best line you've got?"

"I don't usually need any."

"I don't doubt it."

He might have let it go if not for the fact that her cheeks had turned a completely gorgeous shade of pink. "Really?" he drawled.

She rolled her eyes. "Like you don't *know* you're gorgeous."

She said it so matter-of-factly, and yet her admission slid through him like a wave of heat. And when her eyes connected with his awareness surrounded them like a net—heavy, tight, confining.

"So…" Saskia said, moving around the couch, clapping her hands together and using them as a shield.

Interesting. She was aware of him. She liked the look of

him. Clearly. And now she was trying to pretend it didn't mean anything.

Maybe it didn't, he thought.

Then again, maybe it could.

It was four weeks till the wedding, and he didn't see why they couldn't enjoy themselves in the meantime.

He took a step her way and her eyes flickered.

He took another step until she'd backed herself against a bookshelf.

He put a hand on the shelf above her shoulder and very much enjoyed her shiver at his near touch. The rise of her chest, the way her lips fell apart. At a noise in the hall Saskia's gaze cut sideways, leaving him room to whisper against her ear, "We want them to walk in on this."

"We do?" she asked. Then, as an afterthought, "Walk in on what?"

"This."

He pushed her hair aside and kissed the soft skin of her neck. Her scent poured into him like pure pheromones. He pressed himself against her. Thank God she pressed back. Her hands lifted to his shoulders, where they gripped for dear life.

"Nobody's watching," she said, her voice a rasp as he trailed kisses along her jaw.

He dropped a kiss on the corner of her sweet mouth. "Then consider it practice."

Her hand slid to curl around the back of his neck, her hips rocking against his and making him see stars.

Even while his body screamed at him never, ever to stop, he knew things were fast getting out of hand. Having his sisters and mother believe he was attracted to Saskia was one thing. Being caught with the evidence in his pants was quite another.

"Come with me," he said, grabbing her by the hand and dragging her after him without waiting for a response.

Up the stairs he went, two by two, with her keeping up behind. They hit the hall and he just kept on walking till they reached his old bedroom.

With his hand on the doorknob, he balked, realising how long it had been since he'd been inside. Years. Decades. Maybe his mother had turned it into a guest room. Or an after-hours seniors disco. Hell, he hoped so. And he hoped not. It had been his refuge during the hardest years of his life.

He pushed the door open and as the ghosts of his past rose up and surrounded him with such complexity, such vividness, he felt himself sway.

Saskia shot past him. "Oh, my God," she said, laughter in her voice. "Is this your room?"

His eyes on hers, Nate felt his tension ease back a notch. He crossed his arms across his chest and looked right on back. "Not anymore."

"No? You *don't* live at home still, then? I know you own like a million houses, but we never did touch on which one you live in…"

"Funny girl."

Saskia gave him a curtsey before taking a slow turn about his room, forcing Nate to follow. The room was big; the bed-spread, dark wood furnishings and the nautical wallpaper were the same as they'd been the day he'd left.

When Saskia ran a finger and thumb softly down the sail of an elegant three-foot yacht on the chest at the end of the bed, Nate said, "Dad and I made that one when I was about eleven."

She shot him a glance. Then she kept walking, as if it *wasn't* as important an admission as it clearly was. "Good with your hands. Nice to know. Anything else? For the dossier, of course."

A good listener was Saskia, he warned himself, and an eager one, with an ulterior motive. And yet still he said, "He made the small ones downstairs too—the ones in the bottles. It was his favourite hobby. Mine too. Until it wasn't."

Her eyes swept back to him—open, warm, filled with un-derstanding. "Nate…" she said, her voice husky.

His thumb pressed against his temple.

"You need to stop doing that," she said, pulling his hand away.

"It helps."

"Find another way. How do you relax?"

"I don't. I work." He glanced up at her, then admitted, "Occasionally...yoga."

"Hardcore relaxing. Does it work?"

"If I let it. Which isn't as often as I ought."

"Why not?"

"I have...responsibilities."

"As do we all."

"I have over a hundred employees who depend on me. Every decision I make affects them. And their families." Nate lifted a hand to the back of his neck, but stopped it there. How had that happened? He'd walked away from being responsible for four souls only to become responsible for hundreds. No wonder he never took a day off.

"Nate, you might be their boss, but they are, each and every one, responsible for themselves. On the other hand, I wonder if you spend near as much time worrying about yourself."

Saskia's eyes roved over him then. Over his eyes, which he knew looked as tired as he felt. Over his shoulders, making him feel the tightness of the muscles bunched therein.

She reached out, slid her small hand back into his and led him to the bed. There she pressed him down with gentle hands at his shoulders.

He sat, bouncing on the mattress, looking up at her.

She smiled a little before lifting her hands to run them through his hair. Front to back. Her fingers sliding across his scalp with perfect pressure. The touch was such a surprise he blinked at her. Speechless.

"I've been wanting to do this since I first saw your picture," she murmured.

Then, when her hands moved back through his hair, against

the grain, tugging slightly against the short strands, he closed his eyes with the complete and unexpected pleasure of it.

When her thumbs moved to his temples, making small insistent circles right where he needed it most, he groaned at the sweetness. He put his hands behind him on the bed and gave himself over to the sensation. The pure relief.

There they stayed for seconds, minutes, until the constant pressure that lived inside his head ebbed away.

As her hands moved to his neck, kneading at the tight muscles bunched there, her knees bumped his. He opened them to let her closer.

When her outer thighs brushed his inner thighs all relaxation fled in a heartbeat, leaving him unquestionably aware of himself. And her.

His eyes swept open to find her watching herself work, concentrating, with those little lines above her nose. Clueless to the fact that she was trapped between his legs. That her breasts were at his eye level. That she was so close that when he breathed deep through his nose he could smell her—not just her shampoo and her soap but her skin. Her heat. Her essence.

When he lifted his hands to her waist she flinched with surprise.

She braced her hands against his shoulders. Her eyes flickered to his. Her next breath in was deep, her breath out lush. As if she'd known that touching him would lead to this.

Her thumb grazed the outside of his neck, sending shivers through him. Leaving him baffled that this lean, soft, down-to-earth woman could create such anticipation, such rich layers of desire coursing through him with no more than a brush of her thumb.

And surrender in her eyes.

One hand at the back of his neck, she leant down and pressed her lips to his.

He knew to expect sweetness, to expect warmth, to expect

her clean, honest taste. What he got was a jolt of heat so thick that the blood rush to his head near wiped out all thought.

He wrapped his arms around her to drink it in. All of it. All of her.

She opened her mouth to him, sank her body against his, and all that softness and warmth pulsed through him till he wrapped his arms so tight about her there wasn't a millimetre of daylight between them.

Yet for all that he wasn't close enough. He wanted to be inside her. Inside that heat and ease and peace and sweetness. He wanted her with a level of need he hadn't felt in a long time.

As if she felt it too she pressed nearer again, till he tipped back, taking her with him. Her hair tickled his cheeks. Her mouth was like a siren song, drowning him till his brain was a haze of red, and sex, and Saskia.

Nate rolled until he was on top. Looking down at her. The dark waves of her hair splayed out on the plaid bedspread, her cheeks flushed, her lips dark pink and plump, her eyes drunk with desire.

"Having flashbacks?" she asked, her voice husky, her fingers playing with the back of his hair. "I'm betting I'm not the first girl you've made out with in this room."

She was right. And she had him so hot he felt seventeen all over again. Clumsy, desperate, on the verge of losing himself in her.

He shifted till his hardness was nestled against her and her eyes fluttered closed.

He ran his thumb down her cheekbone, traced her bottom lip, the dip in her chin. "Would you have played hooky with me back then?"

"Not on your life. I was a good girl. Classic only child. Pleaser. Head in a textbook. Didn't have my first real kiss till uni. Marty Grantham. Chemistry major."

Again Nate found himself gripped with a desire to track this Marty down and clock him one, even though by the lift of her mouth her memories of *him* were all good. Sweet kid she must have been then. All alone. The desire to protect her, from that and more, swelled from some place deep down inside him and landed like a punch to the solar plexus.

Saskia didn't leave him any time to dissect it as she slid a hand to his neck and dragged his mouth to hers.

Desire, and thunder, and instinct pounded him from all directions. Nate tried to keep his head, but pleasure ripped through him as her tongue slid neat and clean along the edge of his bottom lip, before she found his tongue and traced it with hers. Lust pressed against the outer edges of his skin, raw and rabid, nothing neat about it.

Her hands were clawing his back, his backside. Her leg around his waist, then her hand moved between them, cradling his length. A groan spilled from his mouth as he pressed into her hand, relishing the feel of her around him, beneath him.

A fog of rich red lust swarmed over him, wiping out everything in its path. Control, order—gone. Screw it. Screw it all. All he wanted was this. Her. *Now.*

"Nate? Are you in there?"

He heard his mother's voice all too late.

"Oh," she said, before the bedroom door slammed shut.

Nate could only hope she was on the other side of it.

The fog cleared faster than it had come over him, leaving the world around him crystal-clear. The glow of the old red lamp on his bedside table, the dust on the edges of the shelf with books and old toys leaning against them, the grain of the bedspread digging into his wrists.

He glanced down at Saskia to find she'd slapped a hand over her eyes, her body tensed like a rubber band stretched to its outer limit.

His mother's muffled voice came through the door, "Just letting you know Jasmine and the boys are heading off if you want to say goodbye."

"We'll be down in a minute!"

"Rightio," said his mother, with more than a little laughter tingeing her voice before her footsteps padded away.

"Saskia," Nate said, once he was sure they were alone.

"Mmm-hmm?" she said, trying to roll up in a ball beneath him.

"She's gone."

"Mmm-hmm."

A smile creased his face. "Just because you couldn't see her didn't mean she couldn't see you." He peeled her hand from her eyes to find them wide and wild. Heat still lingered. More than lingered. It pounded behind her eyes. Drenched with desire.

He felt the same pounding rekindle deep in his belly. The drumbeat of lust was pulsing through him as she shifted beneath him, the length of him cradled between her legs.

He heard Jasmine and the boys downstairs, calling out their goodbyes, and he bit out a curse as he pushed himself away from Saskia. He heard the bed creak and turned to find her straightening up, running a hand over her bed-tousled hair. She might as well give up. She looked well-tumbled.

If only, Nate thought, then caught himself, thanking heaven they'd only gone as far as a kiss. If what they'd been doing before his mother had stumbled upon them could be called something so simple as a kiss.

"Hell," he said, running a hand over his face.

"Think they'll believe we're an item?" said Saskia, her bright eyes cutting to his.

And he realised she didn't think it as funny as he did. In fact she looked more than a little shell-shocked.

Swearing again, Nate moved to sit beside her, taking care not to touch. Touching this woman was not a smart idea unless he intended following through.

"That's not what that was," he said, running a hand up the back of his head. "That wasn't for their benefit."

She sucked in a quick breath. "I know."

"Do you?" he asked, reaching out to tuck a kink of dark

hair behind her ear. So he couldn't help himself. That much was fast becoming clear.

Saskia looked from one eye to the other and Nate felt himself being weighed and measured. And for a man who'd long since been in a position where nobody who judged him could find him lacking it was a strange sensation indeed.

"I really wanted to kiss you," she said simply.

"I wanted you to kiss me."

"I got that feeling."

"Did you, now?" he asked, a smile easing across his face. The relaxing of his shoulders showed him how tense he'd been. How concerned that he'd been that he'd stuffed things up royally. How much he wanted things to continue…until the wedding. "Though as I recall, heavy petting on my childhood bed wasn't part of the original deal."

"Let's call that a renegotiation."

At that Nate laughed so loud his sides hurt. "You're a savvy operator, Saskia Bloom. In fact, why don't you work for me?"

"I like being the boss."

"Mmm, woman after my own heart."

When he'd first come upon that picture of a girl in a hat with big, sultry eyes, he'd struggled to believe them the same species. Yet the more he got to know her the more alike it seemed they were. Stubborn, determined, captains of their own destiny. Equals in very many ways.

Then with a saucy little lift of her shoulder Saskia was up, heading for the door. "The sooner we face them, the sooner the mortification will be over and done with."

"You're one hell of a woman, Saskia Bloom," said Nate as he took her hand.

"Don't you forget it."

CHAPTER FIVE

"You what?" Lissy yelled to be heard over the sound of The Cave's house band who'd just started up a grunge version of "Perhaps, Perhaps, Perhaps."

"I kissed him," Saskia said, the words no easier to spit out second time around. *Stupid, stupid, stupid,* she sang inside her head along with the chorus.

"I thought you already had. By the cab. And at his office."

"I kissed him again."

"Where?"

"At his family home. In his childhood bedroom, with sailing ships and baseball mitts watching over us."

"You hussy."

"It's worse. My hand was on his…you know…when his mum walked in on us."

Lissy clutched her stomach and fell to the couch they had staked out at The Cave a couple of hours earlier.

"We barely spoke on the way home after," Saskia said. "Then he walked me to the door, kissed me on the cheek and went on home."

Between clutches at breath Lissy managed to get out, "You tell me I crave dysfunctional relationships—but, honey, you take the cake."

"It's not dysfunctional. We're merely…renegotiating the terms of our mutually beneficial agreement."

"Until one day I come to work and find a tie hanging on the door handle."

"No," Saskia said. Then, "I don't think so anyway. We haven't discussed it."

"You haven't *discussed* sex? Sweetie, I saw his photo. You don't *discuss* sleeping with that. You just hold on tight and enjoy the ride."

Saskia swallowed. Not that it helped. The lump in her throat at the thought of holding on to Nate Mackenzie, enjoying Nate Mackenzie, *riding* Nate Mackenzie was immovable. Much like the guy himself. From the second he'd come knocking on her email he'd loomed larger than life.

"It was right that we stopped," Saskia said, straightening.

"Why on earth?" Lissy asked, eyes large with astonishment.

"It's complicated."

"It's really not. You take your clothes off, kiss a bit, he puts his—"

"It's temporary!" Saskia nearly shouted to stop Lissy from putting any more images in her head. Nate was *naked* in there now, as it was, his hot-as-a-furnace skin all glistening with sweat.

"The majority of love affairs are temporary, hon. But that doesn't diminish the possibility the next one might become something more."

"Nate's not a possibility, Lis. He's like the door of a bank safe—all big and hard and shiny and tempting, but impossible to get through."

"Knock harder. There's treasure behind that there door."

"Maybe," Saskia said, frowning.

"Oh, sweetie," Lissy said, dragging herself upright to hold Saskia by both cheeks. "You should see the mope you have on right now. You *like* the guy. For real. He might be pretending, but you're not."

Saskia shook her head—hopelessly, as it turned out, because Lissy had caught the arm of a busboy and was flirting him into getting fresh drinks for them. Leaving Saskia to think it out on her own.

She *liked* kissing him. The man had skill.

She *liked* pretending to like him. It was great fun. A caper.

She *liked* Nate too. How could she not? Every layer she managed to laboriously shave away only revealed more to like beneath. And more to make her certain that despite the perfect appearance, Nate was a true fixer-upper.

But… But what if she found the combination to unlock that door and discovered that his odds at finding and keeping love were as dim as the rest of the poor saps out there? What hope did she have then?

"Good God," Lissy uttered. "No wonder you felt him up all over."

Saskia blinked and turned to Lissy who was staring at some point over Saskia's shoulder.

"Here's a love formula for you: those shoulders plus that jaw line plus oh, my word, what a mouth equals…"

Right as the band hit a crescendo of onerous drums, screeching sax and groaning bass guitar, Saskia turned and found herself looking right at Nate Mackenzie. He was making his way through the crowded bar, smiling at anyone who caught his eye, and unless it was a coincidence of the highest degree he was looking for *her*.

"What's he doing here?" Lissy asked.

"I have no idea. I mean, I might have mentioned I'd be here tonight, but not in an invitation sort of way."

"Well, he's here—and he's not alone."

Saskia dragged her eyes away long enough to see Nate had an entourage: a collection of shiny gorgeous things behind him, looking around The Cave, taking in the mismatched chairs, the shabby old couches covered in faded velvet, the bad acoustics, the scratched and dented vintage signage.

Her heart thundered against her ribs as her hand went to her hair, which had long since gone to curl. Her skinny jeans, ballet flats and layered tanks were good only for dancing, which meant the likelihood was that her mascara had long since turned to panda eyes.

Finally Nate's eyes found hers. Dark, blue, intense. She lifted a hand and his mouth cocked into a half smile which was different from the one he bestowed upon strangers. Gentler, warmer—just for her.

I know this man, she thought in a moment of wonder. *I've kissed this man. I'd really like to kiss him again.*

Lissy was right, she thought with a groan. She wasn't one hundred percent pretending any more.

She stood as he approached; his suit was slick, he had not a hair out of place, and a beam of light slanted across his stunning face, picking out his sensuous mouth and sapphire eyes.

"Beautiful," she thought. But before she could catch the word she realised she'd said it out loud.

Nate's brow furrowed a moment, before it cleared and he laughed. As if hearing such a thing from her wasn't so unexpected after all.

A loud clearing of the throat brought Saskia's attention back to Lissy who was standing behind her batting her lashes. At Nate and at the big guy behind Nate.

"Nate," said Saskia, "this is Lissy—my friend and business partner. Lissy Carmichael—Nate Mackenzie."

"Love Formula research bunny, in the flesh," Lissy said, giving Nate's hand a good shake.

Saskia could have killed Lissy. She honest to goodness could have thrown her over the back of the chair for that one. But she had to put on a smile as Nate's gaze skewed back to her.

"Better than a lab rat," she said.

Thankfully that brought laughter which hummed across her chest. "True."

Lissy sat down and grinned over her cocktail.

"More trouble than she's worth?" Nate murmured against her cheek as he moved around behind her.

"You have no idea."

When his entourage appeared through the haze like a band of perfection Nate placed a hand in the small of her back. There was no suppressing her shiver at his light touch. Nate must have felt it. Might even have liked it, if the way he spread his fingers around to her waist was anything to go by.

"Saskia Bloom, this is Gabe Hamilton—*my* friend and business partner."

Saskia looked up—and up—and shook hands with about the biggest man she'd ever seen.

"Pleasure," said Gabe in a voice as deep as he was tall. He drew an attractive blonde to his side. "This is Paige. My fiancée."

"Next up we have Mae and Clint," Nate said. "It's they we have to thank for bringing us together."

Mae grinned, while Clint seemed to be eyeing the bar.

Saskia waved them all onto ottomans and over-soft couches—whatever they could drag around the low coffee table.

Clint's backside had barely hit a chair before Mae put in her drinks order. "After the dinner we've just had I need a big blue jug of something sweet and deadly."

Saskia watched all this with Nate's hot fingers pressed against her side, pretty much diffusing everything else to about half strength.

Then he said, "And you know Bamford, of course."

Well, *that* got Saskia's attention. She hadn't even noticed the scruffy-looking gaming king off to the side of the group, sorting the M&M'S in his palm into colour blocks and then throwing them into his mouth one at a time. From the corner of her mouth, to Nate she said, "I've never met him before."

Nate's eyes widened. "But didn't you say—"

"I said Lissy had worked on his website for a time. And found him a pain in the ass."

Nate ran a hand up the back of his head and swore, looking comically pained.

She asked, "What's going on here?"

"Celebratory dinner. The contract's all done, signed. Thanks, in part, to you."

"Me?"

"You inspired us to schlep him over to M&M'S World in Vegas and it put him over the edge."

"Wow. I mean…that's fabulous! Do I get a finder's fee?"

His blue eyes snagged on hers and his hand dropped from the back of his head. His mouth kicked up into a half smile. Anxiety forgotten. *It's a gift,* she thought, glowing from the inside out.

"What you get," Nate said, eyes smiling deep into hers, making her glow brighter still, "is the chance to help a friend get through this night before he strangles someone."

A friend, Saskia thought, liking the term a whole lot. Because the truth was she really liked Nate Mackenzie. And friendship sounded a heck of a lot less disastrous than the feelings buzzing around inside her, starting where his hand rested possessively against her hip.

"Dinner was atrocious," he continued. "The guy complained so much, about everything, I kept waiting for the chef to appear from the kitchen brandishing a carving knife. Then I remembered you'd be here. You were my last hope to make this evening anything other than horrendous."

Wow. If Saskia hadn't already thought herself on the other side of pretending, the guy had just pushed her over the edge with a neat little shove.

She widened her eyes in warning that he owed her for this, and moved to meet Bamford Smythe.

"I'm Saskia Bloom of SassyStats. My colleague did some work on your website last year. It's an honour to finally meet you."

Bamford blinked as if coming to from another plane. And

then Saskia saw the direction of his gaze. His eyes were all on Lissy, who was bouncing in the chair as the band lurched into a grunge version of "Dancing Queen."

"Did you meet Lissy? She did the graphics for your site," Saskia said, nice and loud.

Lissy looked up from her cocktail, her straw caught between her teeth. She saw who Saskia was talking to and her jaw dropped. Saskia knew her friend well enough to see the war going on behind her pale green eyes. Bamford was famously difficult, but in their circles he was a god. And behind the scruff he was actually pretty cute.

Lissy twirled the straw with her tongue, just once around the rim of her glass, before she pressed to her feet and thrust herself deep inside the computer genius's personal space. Saskia sent out a word of prayer on Bamford Smythe's behalf.

Saskia turned back to Nate with a smile. "How's that?"

Nate leaned in so as to be heard. "You are my very own little miracle-worker. Again."

"It's a knack."

"One of these days I'm going to have to repay you for all this. Properly."

Right, Saskia thought, flinching on the inside. And there she'd been *liking* the guy, because somehow she'd let herself forget that at the heart of everything was the deal. Not friendship, not desire. Just a tenuous arrangement that stretched between now and a wedding.

"It's fine," she said, waving it away. "Happy to help. Puppy Dog–syndrome, remember?"

Nate angled his head, motioning to a quieter part of the bar. Saskia grabbed her beanie, scarf and her ex-army jacket with all its helpful pockets for money, ID and the like, hooking it over her arm, extricating herself from the group and following.

"Drink?" he asked, once they'd found themselves a spot at the end of the bar.

"Ta," she said, perching on a bar stool.

"I'm paying," he shot back as she reached into a pocket.

"Honestly, you don't have to. Thanks to you, for the first time in months I have money to burn, remember?" There, now he'd been reminded too.

"Doesn't mean a guy can't buy you a drink," he said. "I insist."

She'd never had a guy *insist* before. Pretend to, sure. But the difference was clear. And it felt unexpectedly nice. *Oh, what the heck?* she thought, and let him.

"In recompense I'll even let you take notes just this once," he said with a smile as the bartender slid them each a bottle of imported beer. "'Nate's Moves on a Date.'"

"So we're on a date all of a sudden, are we?" she asked, spinning to press her back against the bar and then taking a swig.

"You tell me."

She opened her mouth to tell him...something. But nothing came out. At the directness of his gaze, the glimmer of something warm and relaxed deep in his eyes, his nearness, his latent heat, her tummy was twisting and diving too much for a quick comeback to occur to her.

"Some place you've got here," he said, letting her off the hook with a grin that offered a now-you-see-it-now-you-don't dimple. "It's got a good energy."

Saskia leant her elbows back on the soft old wood and sighed. "I love it. Since uni it's been my home away from home. They make the fattest, crunchiest fries on the planet and their coffee is the absolute best."

"Only one thing—"

"What's with the music?" she finished.

They both listened a moment to the dissonance of deep rumbling ABBA lyrics cranking out of the fuzzy old speakers.

"I think it's meant to be ironic."

"It's terrible."

Saskia's teeth gripped the lip of her beer bottle as she grinned. "Yeah, I know. It's a dive. The lead guitarist in the band is the owner's nephew to whom he pays nothing. But I think there'd be a revolt if it ever changed."

Nate's eyes dipped to her mouth, then to her throat as she took a swig and swallowed. She tucked a foot onto the long metal footstand running around along the bottom of the bar and held on with all her might.

Nate's eyes remained narrowed in her direction, his fingers tapping on the bar, as if he was deciding whether or not to say what was really on his mind. Then a muscle twitched in his jaw. "I've been meaning to call to thank you for coming to lunch with my family."

"They were convinced?"

"Convinced I don't deserve you."

"I am rather adorable when I want to be."

His mouth kicked at one corner again, but there was no humour in his eyes. Dark clouds had swirled in, taking too strong a hold. His hand lifted and he brushed a knuckle down her cheek. "I think you're rather adorable even when you haven't a clue."

"Nate," she said, in warning, or maybe in entreaty.

Either way, Nate lifted himself from the stool and moved around in front of her slowly, till she was trapped between the man and the bar, the heat of his skin sending her nerves into meltdown.

She tried to tell herself they'd done more than enough renegotiating. That friendship was all she wanted. That she feared the treasure behind the vault doors was too rich even for her.

But then his fingers slid beneath her hair and he bent down till his lips were a whisper away from hers. "I need to kiss you, Saskia. Right now."

And before she knew it he *was* kissing her—as if his life depended on it. Her hands slid up the back of his jacket and her leg twined around his strong calves, till she disappeared into heat, desire and sumptuous sensation.

He pulled her to her feet. Her flat shoes landed on the sticky floor with a thump. And when his mouth moved to her ear, sweeping a shot of breath over the lobe, her knees all but gave out from under her. His arm was at her back, dragging her against his body, and his readiness, his need, had her biting her lip to stop from whimpering.

Then his voice, deep and insistent was at her ear. "I lied. I didn't come here because of Bamford. I have not been able to stop thinking about you since last weekend. About your warmth, your sweetness, your glorious mouth. There's this light inside of you, Saskia Bloom, and all I have to do is touch you and it burns me up right along with it." He lifted away, just enough to take her face in both hands, look deep into her eyes and say, "I want you. And I'm not enough of a gentleman to pretend I don't know you want me too. Let's get the hell out of here."

Saskia's eyes flicked between Nate's, lured by his incessant heat. He wanted her. While her whole body throbbed from wanting him.

Yet a little voice in the back of her head whispered just loud enough to be heard above the rush of blood. He might want her now, but this was not a man who would ever wonder how he lived without her, which was ultimately what she wanted.

She licked her lips, and when he looked like he was coming back for seconds she put a hand to his chest. Fighting the urge to hook her finger through his shirt and lose herself in his kiss. In his everything.

"Nate?" she croaked.

"Yes, Saskia?' he said, his voice not much clearer than hers.

"I'm not sure this is smart."

"Screw *smart*."

Her blood filled with liquid fire, meaning she had to gather every last shred of sanity she could find and said, "I'm not sure I have it in me. I finished high school a year early, I have first-class honours in Applied Mathematics; smart is my fallback position. And I think we *should* fall back."

He fell back not an inch. In fact he might even have pressed a little closer. Close enough that the scent of him filled her nostrils and made her head spin.

She'd told Nate once she *never said never,* but the less fanciful truth was she simply found it hard to say no. And with Nate leaning into her, all hot and male and husky with desire, she'd never wanted to say no less in her entire life.

But from nowhere some kind of latent self-protection mechanism rose out of the mist. "It's not real."

He blinked at her. "You sure as hell feel real to me," he ground out.

"Would your friends agree?" she asked. He looked at her as if she was making no sense. While she felt more sensible in that moment than she had since she'd spied him slinking through the crowd. "I mean, do they know the truth about us?"

He might have flinched, but she couldn't be sure.

"What does it matter?"

"*Do* they?"

He shook his head, as if clearing away cobwebs, before he looked at a point over her shoulder. "Gabe knows."

"And what does he think?"

His eyes shot back to hers. Still hot, still rippling with desire. Only now there was a thread of desperation beneath. "He thinks I'm a fool. He's love struck and out of his head. He's not the man he used to be." He pulled back. Ran a hand through his hair and swore, convincingly.

"So if he knows then Paige knows?" Saskia said, not backing down.

"Probably."

"Mae and Clint too?"

"I don't understand the big deal," Nate said, exasperation tingeing his words. "I'm not going to gather them together and let them know we went home together, if that's your concern."

"It's not." In fact it was the opposite of her concern. His friends assuming he was sleeping with the woman in his life was *normal*. "It's fine that your friends know. Better, actually. Lissy knows. And, like Gabe, she thinks we're crazy. And this…" She touched his chest, felt it heave against her palm, pulled away. "This is probably why. If we take this any further we'll be blurring the lines so much we'd be the only ones who no longer knew the truth."

It was more than she'd meant to reveal about her nascent feelings for the guy, but she was scrambling.

Then Nate had to go and turn his intense blue eyes her way and hit her with, "What if we *weren't* faking it?"

"Nate, don't."

"A date. For real. You and me. We've done dinner. You've met my family. I'm not seeing anyone else, just like we agreed. So what do most women consider a perfect second date? Paintball? Paris?"

"I'm not most women."

"Tell me about it."

He looked so solemn. Hot, a little angry, and a whole lot turned on. But it was the solemnity that made her like him—and want him—even more. With a ferocity that stole her breath clean away.

"We'd date. We'd end up in bed. But to what end?" Saskia asked, her voice gentling.

The heat in his gaze gave her imagination some idea of his answer. But it wasn't the one she was looking for.

"This was all fine in theory, Nate. Getting to hang out with a hot guy for a few weeks and maybe even pretend to be like most women for a bit."

He opened his mouth to say something about that, but she held up a hand in front of his face.

"But the truth is I'd like to meet a guy, date him, meet his family for real, swap keys, move in together, get married, have kids—"

Nate came over all pale and swallowed as if his mouth was filled with sand.

"And there we have it, folks."

"What?"

"You look like you're about to pass out!"

"Do you blame me?" he asked, pacing. "You're three steps from walking me down the aisle—which is exactly the kind of hell I was hoping to avoid in finding a date online."

"Thanks so very much."

The look he shot her was dark. Her heart thumped against her ribs. She was liking the darkness. She needed professional help. "Nate. Honestly. Do you want that? A wife? Calm down!" she said when he started to pale all over again. "Not me, *per se,* but someone? Some day?"

"Are you really saying that if I said that I was all about the 'Australian Dream' you'd come home with me?"

Ignoring his attempt to sidetrack her, Saskia said, "Have you even ever come close?"

The darkness in his eyes deepened. Worse, it cooled. And right there she had her answer.

He might be hot to the touch, but at his core Nate was untouchable. And Saskia had already spent more than half her life desperately doing everything at her disposal to make someone love her, never to be quite sure if he did.

And Lissy's postulations had been right; Saskia did keep repeating the same relationship pattern, over and over. But in that moment, she realised that for all the wrong he'd done her, Stu had changed that.

She'd pretended not to notice that he didn't really love her, that he was using her, because it felt better to have someone in her life than not at all.

Never again. And if that meant steeling her heart against Nate Mackenzie—a man whose very kisses spun her emotions so far out of control she felt like flying—then so be it.

"I like you, Nate." *More than is in any way sensible.* "And once this is over I'd like to look back on our crazy caper with a laugh. I have enough regrets about my past relationships, and I'd rather not feel that way about you."

Even while she could see it physically pained him to do so, he listened. He really did. She had to give him props for that. But what she *wouldn't* give him was her body. Her heart.

"I like you too," he said finally, with a physical effort obvious at admitting even that much. "But I have my reasons for not wanting to go down…*that* route. Good ones."

"I'm listening," Saskia said, softening.

His mouth twitched at that, but the smile didn't reach his eyes. "You women and your need to talk."

Saskia's mouth twisted into a smile. Maybe this was a good thing. Maybe they'd needed this moment to finally find their boundaries. They could go on from here as friends. Funny, though, it didn't feel quite enough this time around.

Nate turned to face the bar, his fingers gripping the edge, his gaze far away. "So what do you suggest we do from here?"

"Maybe we stop renegotiating and stick to the plan?"

"Yeah," he said, propping his head between both hands.

She held out a hand, making sure to keep an arm's distance from the guy. "Deal?"

His eyes slanted to hers. Beautiful, blue and a little bit tortured. Poor love had probably never been turned down for sex before. She steeled herself and even managed to conjure up a smile.

"Deal," he grumbled, taking her hand in his. His heat skittered through her. She knew he felt it too. Struggled to contain it. Whatever it was. But this time he didn't do anything about it. Till he said, "At least you have to let me see you home."

"The two of us? In the back of a cab together? How do you think that'll turn out?"

"Yeah," he said again, his voice a growl.

He downed his beer with three large gulps. Then he shook his head at her.

And after one long last sweep of his hot blue eyes down her

body and back up again, leaving her feeling as if he'd stripped her bare right there in the middle of the bar, he turned and walked away.

Leaving Saskia shaking all over.

Feeling as if she'd won some kind of battle.

And lost it all at the same time.

It was a couple of hours before Nate took a cab back to the office. Another again before he slid behind the wheel of his car and headed home.

As he slowed before a red light he switched on the radio, clicking past Tom Petty singing about bad boys and breaking hearts till he found Duran Duran singing about hunting and hunger, and his mind spun through the hours spent trying to be charming, and gracious, and the perfect host to his new client.

It shouldn't have felt like so much hard work. He'd been to more client dinners, celebrations, parties, all out raves than he could remember. He'd lived them, rocked them, until they'd gone down in legend.

But that night, when Nate had pointed out that Gabe had spent more time talking to Paige than to their star client, the two of them had near come to blows. And it had taken for Gabe to tell Nate to calm the hell down, as Bamford—with Lissy on his lap, hand-feeding him pretzels—was having the time of his life.

The light turned green, and when the car in front didn't pull away instantly Nate's fist landed on the horn. He overtook the first chance he had, the gears shifting hard and fast, the sports car rumbling deep and throaty beneath him.

He was so damn tense, if he didn't do something about it, soon, he'd get into fisticuffs with his best friend. Or tell a client what he really thought of them. Or do something really stupid, like join an online dating site for real.

Taking a corner a little sharper than safe, he eased his foot from the accelerator.

He'd start small. Take a day off. Go fishing. He and his dad had loved fishing. The peacefulness. The contentment. There was that word again, only this time it had context. Was the last time he'd felt content? Could it really have been when he was twelve years old? That had to be fixed.

Problem was, he knew exactly how he wanted to get loose. With Saskia Bloom beneath him. Up against a wall. In the back of a car. So long as she was hot, and naked, and making those sweet gasping sounds she made whenever he kissed her neck.

Saskia, who'd put on the brakes.

The city lights swept across his windscreen in time to the beat.

It made no sense to him why they shouldn't explore that in the short time they had. In fact the natural end to their relationship made taking every advantage of their chemistry seem the most uncomplicated decision possible.

He turned into his street, where large homes nestled behind imposing fences. He pressed the remote to his wrought iron gate, before gliding up the curved drive and pulling to a stop outside his front doors.

He rolled his hands over the leather steering wheel as the car ticked and cooled beneath him.

He was not known for backing down at the first hurdle, and just because he was considering dropping a line in the ocean at some point in the future, didn't mean he'd gone soft.

It was a little under three weeks till the wedding. That gave him twenty days to charm the pants off her. Literally. To show Saskia that a man and a woman could like one another just fine, and could also tear each other apart in bed, and it didn't have to mean anything other than a good time.

He was the best damn negotiator in town, and if he couldn't negotiate that he didn't deserve the title.

Feeling better about things than he had an hour ago, Nate

pulled the key from the ignition, leapt from the car and jogged up the front steps. Whistling "Fame." Or maybe it was "Footloose." Whatever it was it brought a smile to his lips, which had to be a good thing.

CHAPTER SIX

ANOTHER WEEK OR SO went by before Saskia and Nate saw one another again.

He was busy; she was hiding out. Or maybe she was busy and he was hiding out. Either way, Saskia kept herself busy.

With Stu's debts all paid—and, oh, what a liberating feeling it was finally to put that whole sordid business firmly in her rearview mirror!—she had real money in her bank account for the first time in months. Money with which to get back to turning her crumbling little house into a home.

And, like a woman who'd been kept away from chocolate for months, and then been given the key to the Cadbury factory, she might have binged. Just a little.

Furniture. Paint. Fixtures. Tiles. Her house smelled like a hardware store. And she couldn't have been happier!

Spring was a little over two weeks away, and it was pouring outside. Typical of Melbourne's contrary weather. At least it gave Saskia the excuse to start a fire in the brand-new fireplace she'd helped fit the day before. Music played softly through her new wireless speakers. And she switched on a couple of her new lamps: leadlight and ridiculously romantic. She'd fallen in love with them at first sight.

Looking around at the eclectic, bright, functional, vintage pieces mixed in with state-of-the-art electronics, emotion swelled in her throat.

The truth was she couldn't have done it without Nate. For

that—for him—she'd for ever be thankful. As for the fact that she wondered where he was and what he was doing several times a day and dreamed her raunchiest wishes into existence at night…that was something she'd have to hope would fade in good time.

She downed the last of her coffee, covered her usual attire of multi-coloured tights, oversized sweaters and ugg boots with a smock, and was halfway up a ladder in her bedroom when her phone beeped.

It was a message. From Lissy.

Chinese or Indian?

Lissy had been fixing a client's website on site all day and was coming for dinner.

Whatever goes best with scent of paint thinner.

Indian then. See ya about seven.

With Lissy out, Saskia had painted the bedroom earlier that day. The wall above her bed was now dry, so she measured for the picture she'd had leaning against a wall for months. Tape, spirit level, pencil in hand, she measured vertically, horizontally, then stood back and looked at the dot with a view to the wall as a whole. Her tummy gave a happy flutter. Symmetry was a beautiful thing.

Yin and yang. Balance. Not just in art, but in life. In love. She was the active participant in her relationships, drawn to people who were content to be more passive. It made mathematical sense. At least she'd always thought so.

Till Stu.

The taking of all her things had been a pretty proactive thing for him to do. The hurtfulness entirely deliberate. As evidenced by the note he'd left on her kitchen bench. In ten short lines, including three spelling mistakes, he'd taken apart

everything she'd done for him and thrown it back in her face
like a bucket of acid.

"Emasculating," he'd called her. "Bossy…stubborn…a pain
in the ass."

She'd only been trying to help. Believing that was what he'd
wanted. What he'd needed. Believing he'd love her for it. If he'd
just told her, asked her to back off… She'd probably have been
so shocked her brain would have short-circuited.

Had all the men in her life thought that way about her? That
she was stifling? Unbending? That she was so used to taking
care of herself she didn't know how else to be?

She was still staring at the dot on her wall, the pencil in her
mouth, when there came a soft knock at her door.

Cursing softly around the pencil, she rid herself of the
smock, washed her hands then, with one final pointless run of
her hand over her hair, which was curling madly in the heat of
the now roaring fire, she opened the front door with a flourish.

And there stood Nate, a day's worth of stubble covering his
hard jaw. A few sparkling drops of rainwater stuck to his short
hair. A few more dried on the grey T-shirt stretched across his
impressive chest. A casual jacket gripped his broad shoulders
and faded jeans clung so lovingly to his thighs she couldn't
even allow herself to notice properly for fear she'd start to hy-
perventilate.

For the first time since she'd known him, he looked…*ruffled*. And, boy, did it suit him. It made him seem more ac-
cessible, somehow. Her perverse heart gave a happy little
thumpety-thump.

Then Ernest bounded out of nowhere and stuck his nose in
Nate's crotch.

"Easy," Nate said, laughing, surprise crinkling his eyes.

"Ernest!" said Saskia, lunging for his collar.

But Nate was down on his knees at that stage, rubbing behind Ernest's the collar in the spot he liked best.

"He must smell these," Nate said, tossing her a small blue

box which—miraculously, considering her lack of dexterity—she caught.

She stared for several seconds at the box of Oreos. Then at Nate. Then at wiry Ernest, who was by now staring into the middle distance, tongue lolling out of the side of his mouth, back leg slapping against the floor in ecstasy.

"You've done that before," Saskia said.

"I'm a man of hidden depths."

Don't need to tell me, she thought, while trying not to appear as flummoxed as she felt. "Come on, kiddo, you've taken advantage of the man quite enough." Saskia clicked and Ernest gave Nate's hand one last lick before trotting back into the lounge room.

"Bossy," said Nate.

After her trip down amnesia lane she felt her eye twitch at Nate's choice of that particular word. "I find it gets the job done."

Nate pulled himself to standing, his eyes creasing into a smile as he said, "Hi."

"Hi," Saskia said back, hating that she had to clear her throat afterwards. "To what do I owe the pleasure?"

He broke eye contact as he reached down for the dossier he'd dumped on the floor so he could pat Earnest. "I finally got around to adding some bits and pieces. Thought you might like a look."

He held it out. She took it. And *flummoxed* didn't even begin to name how she felt at that. It was a small miracle.

"Now?"

"Unless you're busy?" He glanced over her shoulder and she realised she was blocking the entrance as if he was trying to sell her something.

"No. Nothing that can't wait. Come on in."

He squeezed past, his scent—hot, spicy—washing over her till she had to grip the door handle for support. And she couldn't help thinking of the last time she'd seen him, the look he'd given her, as if it had taken every bit of civility in his arsenal not to throw her over his shoulder and take her back to his cave.

"Coffee?" she asked, her voice husky.

His eyes crinkled again. "Why not?"

She turned towards the kitchen, leaving him to follow, and couldn't deny the little thrill scooting down her spine at the sound of the door shutting softly behind him. "What gave you the sudden urge to dive into shark-infested waters?" she asked, waving the dossier over her shoulder.

"I had some free time."

"So says the man who made me consider keeping smelling salts on my person in case he passed out at the mere mention of anything deep and meaningful."

She switched on her machine, set up a pair of espresso glasses and reached for a pitcher of milk. She came out of the fridge and leapt out of her skin when she found Nate just behind her, his eyes roving over her hair.

When he reached out to her, her wide eyes followed his hand. And just like that she was back in the bar, her heart racing, warmth tugging low in her belly, not able to quite catch her breath. Wondering how she was possibly going to find it in her to deny him a second time...

"You have paint in your hair," he said, pulling forward a strand that was white from root to tip.

Right.

"I'm renovating," she muttered, moving quickly to her new butcher's sink to madly wash out the paint. And to silently yell at herself to *get a grip!*

Nate had agreed to move into a holding pattern. The fact that he was here with the dossier proved it. He was trying to uphold his end of the deal. Perhaps even going the extra mile to "repay" her in other ways, as he'd out-and-out told her he'd wanted to do.

Glancing up from beneath her wet hair, she saw him taking

in the gorgeous new wooden cabinets she'd installed herself, the deep turquoise walls and tiny red tiles, and the old vinyl floor she'd yet to replace, before his bluer than blue eyes landed on her. And her now dripping hair. She tucked it behind her ear.

"New?" he asked.

"As of about three days ago."

"And I can smell paint."

"That was this morning."

"You've had a house full of contractors?" he asked, both eyebrows lifting towards his hairline.

"I did most of it myself."

"*By* yourself?" he asked.

"Mostly. I haven't tackled the electrics, so don't panic. You're safe."

His mouth kicked at one corner. Safe? As if he'd felt unsafe before? Afraid she might jump him at any instant? Maybe he was right to worry. He nearly filled her small kitchen, and catching his scent with every breath was making her head spin.

She gripped the sink and leaned back. "It came to a bit of a standstill after my ex took off with all my stuff, so I've gone a bit crazy this week because it's the first chance I've had to do so in so long."

"I thought you said it was just your TV?" he said, his eyes pinning her to the spot.

"And my surround sound."

"And…?"

She twisted her mouth, wondering if she oughtn't just blow him off, change the subject, flash her boobs, anything not to have to talk about *that*. But he was looking at her in that way he did—interested and protective. As if should Stu be in the room he'd no longer be attached to his man parts. And then there was the fact of the dossier, sitting on her small red Formica kitchen table.

She checked the coffee grounds, then rested her hands on the settings. And in a rush of breath, she admitted, "And my computers, my books, CDs, DVDs, coffee maker, toaster, every piece of furniture. He wiped out my bank balance and took all my shoes. My neighbour saw him back up the truck, and thought we were moving. He left Ernest, a couple of tins of the only brand of dog food that he *doesn't* like, a phone bill in my name that would cripple a small country and backed the truck into my car before disappearing into the sunset."

She turned on the coffee machine so it filled the air with the noise of coffee beans crushing and the delirious scent of the same. When the coffees were made she turned back to find Nate had shoved a hip against the kitchen bench. His thumbs went into the waistband of his jeans, so his hands framed the contents therein.

He said, "Hence the debt?"

"Hence the debt."

Nate looked around again, seeming to see her place with a fresh eye. "Have you tracked him down?"

"Stu? Good God, no." The note he'd left had been more than she could take. "I'm fine now. I have a job that's getting more and more successful, I have a roof over my head, I have a cute sugar daddy—what more do I need?"

Nate's eyes were slanted to her, a frown above his nose—until her meaning dawned and the frown turned into a smile. And then a deep laugh filled her small kitchen, before bouncing around inside the cavity of her chest awhile.

Needing something to do with her hands other than place them on the big man in her kitchen, she shoved a double espresso at him, grabbed her own coffee and the dossier and ducked past him back into the large main room, which was now blistering with heat from the fire. At least she assumed it was the fire. But there was no way she was about to dim it—that would be as good as saying *Is it hot in here or is it just me?*

"The place was barely inhabitable when I bought it," she said, giving him the grand tour. "Decades-old wallpaper dangling off the walls. Holes in the ceiling. A bathroom floor near rotted through. The ultimate fixer-upper."

"And you are a sucker for a new project?" he said, pulling from nowhere a comment she'd made in passing weeks back.

Once again Saskia had to remind herself—just because he looked a little ruffled, and rumpled, and faded, and warm, and cuddly, and was saying nice things about her home, it didn't mean he was any closer to wanting what she wanted from life than he was a few days ago.

"Impressive," he added, finishing his turning circle close enough that she could smell the rain on his clothes. Feel the heat of his skin pressing in on her even more than the fire at her back. He smiled down at her, as if oblivious to the effect he was having. "A woman who can change a lightbulb all on her own."

When, under the effect of all that nearness, the ground felt as if it was tipping under her feet, Saskia blurted, "I can't cook to save my life."

Nate laughed, the sound filling the room. "Good to know."

She led him to the third bedroom, where she'd set up the office. It was cooler in there, and her skin thanked her for the respite from the stuffiness of the rest of the small house.

The desk—a reclaimed wood dining table covered in paint splotches and pen marks and nicks and notches sat in the centre of the room, her chair and computer on one side, which was covered in teetering piles of notes on yellow legal pad paper, with colour-coded notes stuck all over them. To anyone else it probably looked like a disaster waiting to happen, but Saskia knew where every single scrap of paper was. Lissy's computer and chair were on the other side of the huge table, which, incongruously, considering the person who used it, was clean as a whistle.

The rest of the room was all cream paint and raw furnishings. Built-in shelves were filled with rattan baskets found at flea markets; soft-furnished guest chairs held cushions and throws. Sprays of stripped willow in an array of huge vases filled up the far corner. A dog-eared copy of *Catch-22* nestled amongst her other favourite books.

"Great room," Nate said, his eyes skimming too quickly to settle on any one thing. "Love the lighting."

"The original fixtures were hideous—straight out a horror movie. I do believe you're *actually* interested in my renovations. I'd be a little worried if I didn't know better."

Nate's eyes slid back to hers, laughing, vibrant, lit with something she hadn't seen there since she'd known him. "The BonAventure offices were refurbed a couple of years back," he said. "The same decorator did my apartment, and I was so busy at the time I let him go nuts—which is why I live in what looks like the home of a sixty-year-old big game hunter. I worked more closely with him at the office."

"Nate the interior decorator? I'm shocked."

"Gave Gabe a laugh."

"Maybe because he's more manly than you?"

"No argument there," Nate said, which only made him seem manlier still.

Ruffled, rumpled, even a little rugged, she thought, staring at the scuff on his boots, then at the loose thread on the collar of his T-shirt.

A skitter of something new and sweet and just a little frightening trickled down her spine. Shaking it off, she waved a hand at a guest chair which was nudged up against the short end of the table. "Work first, food after?"

"Sounds fair—work?"

"The dossier. You've come to the party on my end of the deal, right?"

He looked at the folder in her hand, then at the guest chair as if it might bite, before lowering his length into it.

Saskia sat in her soft pink bouncy office chair, one foot sliding to rest next to her backside. She twisted back and forth and stuck a pen in her mouth. The mixed feelings that came with having Nate so close edged away as she slid into work mode.

Popping her vintage glasses onto the end of her nose, she grabbed the dossier and opened it to the first page. But she'd already filled that out.

"What are you wearing?" Nate asked.

Saskia went cross-eyed as she looked at the incongruously big glasses perched on her fine nose. "They're for reading."

"They look like you nicked them from your grandfather."

"Never met either. And they're vintage." She went to turn the next page when Nate interrupted again, "What's that?"

Sighing, she took off her glasses and glanced at her monitor and a big hot pink rectangle with *Electric Dreams: Finding Love in the Digital Age* scrawled across the top in curly girly font that Lissy had started fiddling with. "The infographic. The carcass at least."

"Does it have to be pink?" Nate asked, looking as pained as if she'd handed him a set of knitting needles and asked him to make her a pair of bootees.

"Pink's romantic. And hot-pink's...well, *hot*."

Nate muttered something that sounded along the lines of, *This can't possibly be worth it.*

"I've got some great stuff to work with so far: one in five singles have tried online dating. Less than one percent believes a movie is a good idea for a first date. More than half of women think dinner is a good first date, and that the guy should pay—"

"You refused to let me pay."

"I'm not most women."

"So you keep reminding me."

"Here." She dug through the pile on her left, found the legal pad dedicated to that job, and threw it to him.

He moved the chair closer. Close enough that when she next swung back her knee brushed his. Thick wool rasped against old denim and the friction shot through her as if she'd been hit with a cattle prod.

His eyes widened as he flipped page after page of the questions she'd come up with in her research. Some of them she'd already put into a survey she'd added to the Dating By Numbers website, and given to a handful of online magazines—men's and women's. Others were just of interest to her.

She glanced down at the pages, reading words such as *sex, love, lies, oral, psycho killer, back-up plan*. She slowly slid a pen towards Nate. "It's the intimate details that lift a piece from dry statistical analysis to something that resonates with people. So if you have anything you'd like to add—thoughts, experiences, anything—feel free. Start simple. Like, are you a leg man?"

Nate's face began to turn green.

"Eyes, then? Hair? Little toes? If you picked me, clearly it's not about chest inches. Or is it something more intangible? Something chemical?"

His eyes shot back to hers at that, so blue, so quick, so effortlessly seductive, and she could have kicked herself for getting cocky.

He put the notepad back onto her desk, holding her gaze the whole time. "You really want to know what I like?"

She did. She really did. "Hit me."

"I like drinks—casual, no promises. I like parties—more people to talk to if talking to *her* is like pulling teeth. I like night time—it has a built-in end point."

"Wow. That all sounds so…hopeless."

"You asked," he said, grabbing a box of paperclips and shaking it by his ear as he leant back, his knees pressing deeper under her desk, crowding her, leaving her nowhere to move.

"Yeah," she said, tucking herself into a tighter ball on her chair, "I did." Then a thought. "Okay, then, what are you hoping for when you meet a woman? And I don't mean the 'built-in-end-point.' I mean *ultimately*."

His eyes narrowed and his jaw clenched. So many walls, she thought, wondering how he managed to connect beyond superficially with any member of the human race. The guy needed more than ruffling. He needed disentangling.

"Is this going to end up in your piece?"

She thought about it, and then shook her head. "*I* want to know."

"Why?"

She threw out her hands, her feet collapsing to the ground so that her knees bumped against his. "Because it's the human condition, Nate. Biological imperative. Haven't you ever had the urge to clobber some woman over the head and brand her as yours?"

Seeing the darkness in his eyes, she was pretty sure he was allowing himself a moment to imagine how his life might be better off if he clobbered *her* over the head.

He leant forward and put the paperclips back on the desk, then rested his elbows on his knees, his gaze settling at some point in the middle distance. He said, "This isn't for the piece. This is just for you."

She nodded. Swallowed. Gripped her mouse for support.

"After my father died I spent six long years of my life looking after the whims and needs of four very emotional, very demanding, very much loved women—and it near wiped me out. I've done my time on that score. I have no desire to 'settle down.' To marry. To 'make a life with someone.' Whatever you want to call it. I like women. Adore many. Love a handful. But I like my independence more. Ultimately I will protect it with my dying breath. How's that?"

"Thank you," she said, even as his words felt like little needles all over her skin.

"Your turn. Why do you care so much about what I want?" he asked, his long fingers tapping a soft beat on the table, his blue eyes roving over her face.

"That's not how this works."

"Says who?"

"Me."

"You think you're the boss in this scenario?"

"I'm the boss in *every* scenario."

His grin showed teeth, straight and many, and that rare and delightful dimple. "Well, sweetheart, in my world so am I. So what are we going to do about it?"

She had to swallow before she could get a word out. "I think you're a good guy, Nate. But when it comes to relationships you're screwed in the head. I think I can help."

"I'm beyond help. Do you want to know what I *need?*"

Saskia hoped he had no clue about the button he'd just pushed. That she was sitting there humming with the desperate need to know what he needed. What any man needed. She'd been searching for that answer her whole damn life, without success, and Nate was about to hand her the key.

She nodded, even while the look in his eyes told her she was agreeing to way more than she could ever have bargained for.

"I took the day off today."

She found herself oddly disappointed. "Are you okay?"

"I'm fine," he said with a low rumble of laughter. "I didn't go to work. That's the first weekday I've had off work in seven years. I looked it up. That's what I spent an hour of my first day off in seven years doing—looking up how long it had been since the last time I'd played hooky."

"So why did you play hooky?"

"You. Badgering me about relaxing more."

She got two raised eyebrows with that, which she could only meet with blank shock.

"And partly because I've known for a long time if I don't ease back I'm going to burn out. So I thought about going fishing, even drove down to the pier at Sorrento with grand ideas of dropping a line for squid. Turns out I'm a total wimp—it was just too damn cold so I turned around and came home. And of all the things I could have done with my day I came here. To see you. Do this."

He reached out and ran a hand down her hair. A curl gripped his finger before he gave it a gentle tug.

"And this."

His hand moved to her neck. His eyes followed as his thumb ran down her throat.

"And this."

His hand roved over her shoulder, sliding her oversized sweater right along with it till her shoulder was bare. He swept his thumb over her collarbone and she shivered, pleasure pulsing through her.

With that he grabbed the arms of her chair and tugged till it was between his thighs. Anticipation raged inside her. It had been building since that night at the bar, and she'd used up the last of her resistance.

"Kiss me," he insisted.

She didn't need to be asked twice. She was in his lap, her hands in his hair, her mouth on his, before he took his next breath.

No testing this time. No figuring one another out. They just opened to one another—mouths, lips, teeth, tongues, breath intertwining as sexual tension wrapped about them like a tight coil.

Then, with a final slow swipe of his tongue along hers, Nate pulled back, his forehead leaning on hers. Their stilted breaths matched, mingled.

"Are we done here?" he asked, his voice like an echo deep inside a cavern.

"In what capacity?" she asked.

"I don't want to talk about other women."

"I don't want to hear it."

"Good."

Then, with a speed that defied the guy's impressive size, Nate slid an arm beneath her and lifted her into his arms. With a wholly unladylike *whoop* Saskia flailed her legs madly and she gripped his neck so hard she was sure she'd leave a mark.

His eyes slid to hers, dark, devilish, dangerous. "I'd be very happy to sweep everything off that desk of yours right about now."

"No!" The computers were leased, and she'd never get her notes back into order! "My room!" she said, pointing the way.

Nate hitched her as if she weighed next to nothing. "No, wait, it's being painted." She tugged at the near-dry curl curving against her cheek.

"Sasssskia…" he growled.

"What?"

The glint in his eye said everything.

"Screw it," she said, and wriggled out of his strong arms.

She pressed him right to the wall in the hall, tugged at his sweater, her mouth going dry at the flash of sinew and muscle, the smattering of golden hair on his chest, the darker trail curling about his navel before disappearing down the front of his jeans, and the eye-popping bulge a few inches lower.

She practically tore his T over his head, her hands at his chest, running eagerly down the bumps and planes. Her mouth followed, revelling in his taste, his insane heat, the thunder of his heart.

When she reached Nate's belt line he had other ideas.

He spun her about, pressing her against the wall, making a newly hung picture down the hall bounce precariously. Nate braced his hand against the wall by her head, wrapped the other around her back. The press of his hard body left her in no doubt as to how much he wanted this. Wanted *her*.

Desire rose inside her, scraping at her insides.

She slid a hand behind his neck, lifted onto her toes and kissed him for all she was worth.

"Why do you always taste so amazing?" he groaned against her neck.

"Goats' milk soap," she breathed. "It's my one descent into unadulterated decadence. Have to drive to the Dandenongs to buy it. Costs a mint."

This was met with silence.

"It's lush. You should try it."

"Don't worry. I am." With that his tongue lapped the rise of her collarbone, sending shivers so hard and fast through her body her knees gave way.

Luckily Nate was there to slide his knee between hers, pinning her to the wall.

"I got you," he said, and proceeded to show her just how by lifting both arms above her head and dragging her sweater off in one swift move, leaving her in a pink bikini top and a wave of goosebumps which Nate proceeded to kiss until each and every one melted away.

"Your grand renovation include a pool?" he said, his thumbs running along the underside of her bikini top.

"Laundry day," she said, her voice croaky as a whole new wave of goosebumps followed his touch. This time he let them be, till she squirmed at the pleasure and the pain.

His hands learnt her curves, what little there was of them, but the hitch in his breath, the reverence of his touch made her feel like a pin-up. The pulse of desire between her legs now so insistent it was a wonder he couldn't hear it.

And then his head dipped to kiss the swell of her breasts. When his teeth grazed her nipple through her bikini top, and then he sucked it into his mouth, leaving the fabric moist in the fiery air, her hands moved to his head, desperate to stop the ache, desperate for more.

Then he was down on his knees, kissing each of her ribs, dipping his tongue into her navel, rolling her tights down her legs, scraping his teeth over a hipbone, hitting every sweet spot and a few more she hadn't even known she had.

As he came back up his hands slid over the backs of her legs, behind her trembling knees, caressing her weakening thighs, grabbing her ass and pressing her against him—which was when she came to from the drenching red haze of desire enough to realise he was naked too. And ready. So ready.

She ran a hand over his perfect backside, glorying in the heat of him, the hardness, the pure and utter masculinity. She wondered how she'd ever thought him cool, untouchable. This was as real as it got.

He lifted her knee to wrap it about his hip. The heft of him was nudging at her core. She bucked at the sensation, her body pressing back, moving with him of its own accord, desperate to bring all this swirling need to completion.

She jumped into his arms, trusting him not to let her fall.

His eyes found hers—so hot, so dark, so intense—as if awaiting her final *yes*. She kissed him—open-mouthed acquiescence.

With his hands on her backside and a groan at her mouth, he pressed into her achingly gently, with more restraint than she could have managed. When she sighed, and pressed back, he finally drove into her, deep, full, a millimetre from too much. Then deeper again, till she had to pull away from his kiss to catch even the tiniest breath.

She closed her eyes, blind to all but the thick, rich, heady sensation pummelling her every which-way. It was too much. It was impossible. It was everything. And all too soon every skerrick of feeling contracted to a single point where her whole world stilled, throbbed, pressed in on her like the most beautiful pressure she never wanted to end.

But end it did—in a splintering of sensation that rent a shout of pleasure from her so loud her own ears rang.

Nate took her scream in his mouth, muffling the sound with a kiss so lush, so tender, she felt lost. As if she'd fallen anyway. Was falling still—even as he held her tight and pinned her to the wall with his final thrusts before his release came.

Trembling, spent, her muscles quivering in afterglow—or aftershock—she held on tight, her hands gripping his slick shoulders, her legs clamped to his hard hips.

He let her down slowly, easing out of her with infinite care—not as if they'd just had blinding hot sex against the wall, but as if she was something soft and precious. Even as her feet found purchase she was shaking so hard there was no way she'd be able to stand upright.

"I got you," he said again, hands on her hips, forehead resting against hers, keeping her steady.

She could feel the deep staccato beating of his heart, and was overwhelmed to find it as erratic as her own.

Real, she thought. He felt so real. And for a silly little moment she wished it *was* all real. Him, this, her feelings. Everything.

Which snapped her smartly back to real life. To the fact that she wanted it all and he wanted nothing. To the fact that he was so fanatically independent he'd never budge enough to let someone take care of him. And that that was all she knew how to do.

"That was some renegotiation," she said, trying to snap the moment before it snapped her.

A beat bled by in which she wondered if she'd gone too far, made light of something too significant. Then his laughter rumbled through them both, deep and satisfying. "Wasn't it just?"

Nate trailed his hand from hip to arm and back again, and Saskia found it hard to hang on to reality at all.

"Why the hell did we not do this earlier?" he asked.

"From memory, we were being smart."

"Yeah? You're probably right." He bent down, gathered his gear. "Bathroom?"

She angled her head down the hall. "Second on the left."

He laid a kiss on her neck, followed by a quick swipe of his tongue, then walked that way, giving Saskia a superb view of beauty incarnate. A sexual dynamo. A frustrating, hardheaded, stubborn example of a man. A danger to the heart of any woman who crossed his charismatic path.

She was in so much trouble.

At the door he looked back. A grin spread across his face—a happy grin—leaving in its aftermath a clench in her belly that pierced the pleasure-induced numbness that held sway all through the rest of her. Then he shook his head once and disappeared.

Slapping a hand across her eyes, Saskia thanked her lucky stars the fire was still roaring as the night air cooled her damp skin. She was also thankful that she'd shaved her legs.

Crushing on Nate from afar was one thing. Sharing a few kisses was flirting with danger. But what had just happened—that inferno of desire, that wanton drive to take and be taken… It was still too soon. Her body was still humming from the effects, all of her too damn raw, to decipher what that was.

The old cuckoo clock in her lounge room cuckooed—seven o'clock.

Lissy!

She reached for her phone to turn Lissy around before she arrived with Indian, then realised she was butt-naked and her phone was nowhere to be found. In a flash of inspiration, she grabbed her bikini top from the floor, quickly opened the front door and hung it from the handle outside and slammed the door shut.

It was no tie on the door, but it would have to do!

When Saskia turned back, Ernest—tail wagging, eyes bright—met her nose to nose.

"Hey buddy," she said. "Did you catch any of that?"

Ernest gave her nose a gentle lick of support.

"I know, the guy brought Oreos. This too shall pass, but we can have some fun till then, right?"

Ernest thumped his tail on the floor before sliding across the floorboards to his possie in the lounge. One thump was for yes, right?

She heard the shower being turned on. Her head kicked in that direction. That shower was touchy. Only right she should show her visitor how it worked.

CHAPTER SEVEN

FIRST THING MONDAY morning Saskia sat in the foyer at Dating By Numbers, humming to herself. Her eyes roved happily over the golden-framed artwork, the fresh flowers on every surface, the discreetly frosted glass walls, the thick white carpet that must be a bitch to keep clean.

With many online businesses run from a home offices these days, instead the dating site took up the top floor of a beautiful old building in elegant Kew. It seemed there was a lot of money to be made in facilitating the search for true love. And in random hook-ups, one night stands, invites to friends of friends' weddings...

"Saskia? Marlee Kent," said a tall, elegant woman with a slick dark bob. She could have been aged anywhere from early forties to late fifties.

Saskia pulled herself from the overly soft couch and shook the woman's hand, before following her through padded velvet doors into a discreetly elegant office beyond, where on a tidy desk sparkled two big glass bowls—one filled with Baci chocolate kisses, the other with condoms.

"So you joined the site?" Marlee asked as they sat, her long red nails wrapped around the handle of an old-fashioned china coffeepot as she poured without asking how Saskia liked it.

Saskia reached into her bag for her yellow legal pad. "I did. A few weeks back."

"And what did you think?"

"It's very thorough. As a researcher, I like thorough."

Marlee's smile didn't reach her eyes. "And you've found someone?"

"Excuse me?" Saskia said, wondering if it was written all over her face that she'd been on the receiving end of some very hot and thorough loving only a couple of hours before, when Nate had turned up at her door before work for a breakfast special.

"You mentioned a case study in your email?"

"Oh. Yes. Well, studying him, getting the man's perspective, has been most helpful."

"I see." Marlee clearly saw plenty, as that time the smile did reach her eyes. "Then my job here is done."

"No," Saskia said, her cheeks threatening to ripen like a tomato. "It's not like that. We're not…romantically involved." Financially, sexually, mutually helpingly, at times frustratingly, but *not* romantically.

After he'd left that first night she'd found the dossier. Her heart had fluttered as she'd opened it, her stomach tumbling as she'd giddily imagined what he'd revealed to her only to find a few random titbits such as his favourite footy players, how he liked his coffee, the phone number of the best dry cleaner in East Melbourne. She'd thought he'd turned a corner. Instead he'd given a lollipop to quieten a noisy toddler.

And while Nate might be charming, hot as the sun and could make her melt with a whisper of breath, the touch of his lips, the slide of a hand, even *after* he'd given her the most exquisite sex of her life, she didn't feel any closer to breaking down that door.

"So, honey," said Marlee, gently breaking into her reverie, "what do you need from me?"

"Well, okay," Saskia said, pulling herself together. "I have the preliminaries down. Stats nearly done. The who, how old, how many—the dry substance. But it always helps to have a hook. A cheeky bite to get people talking over the water cooler. I had a crazy idea for a formula—"

She shook her head. It wasn't going to happen. Not right now anyway. Maybe one day. Maybe she'd have to rely on her own experience to nail that one.

"Now I'm thinking about the lies people tell in the search for The One."

"Such as?"

"Age, weight, interests, experiences. From what I saw, people lie about everything. But how will they ever be able to find someone who loves them just the way they are if they're not being honest about who they are?"

"You're a romantic."

"Aren't you?"

Marlee's laughter twinkled with just the right quality. Saskia shot her eyes to the glass bowls, afraid they might shatter.

"We discourage it, of course, in our welcome pack—lying about oneself, not romance—but you can't stop people from morphing the truth. It's human nature. I blow-dry my hair, put on make-up, wear high heels. I've laughed at jokes told by men who simply weren't that funny. We create an outer identity to hide our innate vulnerability. But even deeper, it springs from the most primal desire we harbour—to land the alpha male."

Saskia looked down at her notes, her pen hovering, but she wasn't sure where to start. Marlee's claim made scientific sense, and yet *she'd* never tried to land an alpha male. The men she dated were barely even betas.

Funny, she'd picked on Nate for fighting against the human condition, the biological imperative, and it seemed she was doing the same. Huh! At least now she'd gone alpha, she could see the appeal.

Putting Nate out of her mind as best she could, she said, "So you think it's natural to lie? Even when looking for love?"

Marlee steepled her fingers beneath her chin as she looked

Saskia dead in the eye, her heavily made up eyes hypnotic. "Are *you* looking for love, Saskia?"

Saskia swallowed. "Oh, sure. Of course. Well, not right now. There have been…men. And it hasn't worked. For myriad reasons." *Like grand theft.* "But I'm sure I'd welcome it if it came calling. Wouldn't we all?"

Marlee shrugged—a spiky lift of her sharp shoulders. "Everyone's different. Some people want it so badly you can see the desperation pouring off them in waves. Others want it less than root canal. You, on the other hand, confuse me, Ms Bloom. You have a neat little figure, just-rolled-out-of-bed hair, with a little more make-up your eyes could be stunning, and yet with all that potential you dress like you've walked off the set of *Oliver*. I'm a scholar of human body language, and you don't give off the usual signs at all."

While Saskia reeled under this blatant and not altogether flattering character assessment, Marlee brought her coffee to her red lips, her dark bob swinging precisely against her cheek as she took a sip. "What does love look like to you, Saskia Bloom?"

Saskia's mouth popped open before slamming closed. Because the truth was she had no idea.

"Perhaps the thing isn't lying about who you are, but misrepresenting your true desires—whatever they are."

Saskia's brain sifted through all this new information as if it was creating a fresh Rolodex.

"So, does your young man know how you feel about him?"

"My young *who?*" Saskia said, shoving her legal pad back in her bag and practically shoving her head in with it to hide the rush of blood to her cheeks.

"Darling, this is my field, and I make a fine living at it. Lie to me, lie to him—I don't care. Just don't be silly enough to lie to yourself."

Saskia closed her eyes shut tight, stopped fiddling and with a sharp outshot of breath that flicked a curl skyward she looked at Marlee and asked, "How?"

"Take a breath. Still your mind. Forget yourself. Follow your heart."

"Now *you* sound like the romantic."

"Do I?"

Saskia left not long after, her head spinning with everything Marlee Kent had given her. There were nuggets of gold for the infographic, quotes galore she and Lissy could weave into the piece. But as for the rest?

She knew she wanted to love and be loved. Growing up near invisible to the only family she'd ever had, she'd known that since before she even knew what the want deep in her belly meant.

As for what love *looked* like? On that score she'd done what she'd always done and used her head. She'd played the numbers, and shortened the odds by choosing men according to how her skill set would complement theirs. She was energetic, organised, liked being in charge and was quietly terrified that she was unlovable. And therefore had gravitated to a string of losers who'd…proven her theory over and over again.

Forget yourself, Marlee had said. *Follow your heart.*

Once at her car, Saskia stuck her key in the driver's-side door—the remote locking hadn't worked since Stu had hit the thing with the moving truck—then bumped the crumpled panel with her hip to pop the door open.

Take a breath. Still your mind.

She'd tried that after Stu had left, she honestly had. Even going so far as to attend a couple of Lissy's power-yoga classes, which had sounded like a contradiction in terms and turned out to be exactly that.

But she'd been burned so badly she'd not have found love if it had jumped up in front of her with a flashing sign telling her what it was.

At least she was back on her feet financially and would soon be able to cut back on her overwhelming workload. She'd have time to breathe, time to date again. And maybe this time she'd give herself half a chance; with a little less fear, a little more forethought, a little more faith.

After the wedding.

After Nate.

She stuck the key in the ignition and then let her hand drop.

Marlee had told her not to lie to herself, and the God's honest truth was that with the swarm of foreboding the woman had whipped up inside of her, *all* she wanted to do was go to Nate.

It was the strangest feeling. In fact it close to feeling a heck of a lot like *need*. Her hand shook a little as she dialled his mobile number. Shaking her hair from her ear, she waited for him to pick up.

"Saskia," he said.

And even while she told herself it was mental, financial, sexual, mutually helpful, at times frustrating, his voice sent happy goosebumps all over her skin. "Can I come over tonight?"

When silence ensued she clamped her eyes shut tight and said, "Ever since you described your place I've imagined a deer head on the wall above your bed. I can't sleep for not knowing if I'm right."

"Well," he said finally, "I'd hate to be the reason you can't sleep. How's eight?"

"Eight's great."

"Bring your PJs. For helping with the sleeping."

"One problem with that."

"Hmm?"

"I never wear any. No word of a lie."

"Texas," Saskia said, her voice far away, drowsily running her finger around the edges of the birthmark on Nate's naked thigh. "I honestly see Texas."

"It's roundish," he murmured, lifting his heavy head a half an inch off the padded edge of his big deep tub before letting it drop. His fingers never stopped trailing lazily up and down her feet, which were propped on his shoulder.

Saskia slipped an inch lower, revelling in the hot water, the decadent bubbles, the dreamy sound of Nat King Cole playing through Nate's fancy system, too deep in afterglow to do much more than blink fuzzily at the fake—as it turned out—rhinoceros head suspended on the stark grey wall over Nate's shoulder.

"Unless you're a contortionist," she said, "or handy with a mirror, you'd never know."

"I've been told. By women of good authority."

"How's that? Did your sisters pin you down and measure it out?"

"Never happened," he rumbled in warning. "I might be outnumbered, but I'm smart. And crafty. And strong."

Before she even felt him move he tugged, nearly dunking her under the wash of spicy-scented bubbles. She came up spluttering as he pulled her feet apart and drew her towards him till there was nothing to do but straddle his thighs and grab his big shoulders.

"Evidently," she said, settling. The hairs of his legs rasped against all too sensitive skin.

She wiped the bubbles from her hair, and twisted the length over her shoulder.

Nate's eyes followed the movement, changing to a darker shade of heaven as he watched the trail of water wavering down her collarbone, over the rise of her breasts where bubbles slid south. His knees lifted, pressing her forward, nudging her centre against the thickness of his.

"What was it like?" she asked. "Growing up with sisters."

As soon as the words came out of her mouth she stilled, waiting for him to shut down. For the worshipping touch of his eyes to cloud over.

"Loud," he said, surprising her.

Saskia breathed out.

"I'm not sure if it's a female thing, or a Mackenzie female thing, but no matter how I laid down the law they could never keep their hands off my stuff."

Saskia didn't have any sisters to compare them to, but she thought of Lissy, of the pieces of Lissy's clothing hanging in her closet, the books and DVDs of hers lost in the depths of Lissy's apartment. "Female thing, I think. Bonding, perhaps? Nesting, maybe?"

"What was it like growing up with no sisters?"

"Quiet."

He cocked a half smile.

"Especially when my father would have preferred to spend a beautiful spring day in the university library rather than playing in a park."

"And what was she like? Your mother?"

"Dad didn't talk about her much. Only when he saw her in me. When I was acting 'too colourful,' as he put it."

"He never married again?"

"He never married at all. From the bits and pieces I managed to gather I came to think of my mum as a free spirit—his one brief shining moment and his cautionary tale." She'd seen them try though—students, fellow scholars, even a Dean or two, but her clever, handsome, distant father had remained impassive. Married to his work, they'd all sigh, only Saskia had seen the rare flashes of pain that would pass over his eyes when he looked at her, as if he was seeing her mother…the one who ruined him for all others. And knowing it, she'd tried harder to make it all better.

"I at least had my dad till I was into my teens. Long enough to identify what it meant to be a man," he said, surprising her again.

Saskia swallowed at his words. At the thought of a boy of fifteen having to take on that mantle. When his eyes found hers, she said, "It was what it was. Maybe easier because I never knew any different."

"Maybe. Now, promise me…"

Anything. "Mmm?"

"Not a single thing we've done together had better end up in that damnable pink thing of yours."

"Hmm…" His eyes connected with hers, a smile curling at the corner of his sensuous mouth.

Then his hands left her hips to dig into the flesh at her waist. Saskia's eyes fluttered shut, her mouth tipping open as he rocked her forward, creating the most gorgeous pressure inside her.

But her head was filled with so many more questions. About his childhood, his family, his relationships, his choices. How they'd all intertwined to make him who he was. To keep him from getting close to someone special. Because whether it was the water, the lethargy, the bubbles, the fact that they hadn't stopped touching one another for even half a second, *something* had relaxed him, given him ease.

When his hand lifted to run down her torso, from collarbone to belly, the questions fled. When he took her hips, his thumbs sweeping her inner thighs, she struggled to remember her own name.

He lifted to kiss her neck, nip at her shoulder, to draw her wet nipple into his mouth. His hand moved between them, sliding along her seam with gorgeous restraint. Another finger followed, with less restraint, and while a minute before she would have considered herself spent, from one heartbeat to the next she felt drenched with desire. Her eyes were unseeing, her breath a mere instinct. She wrapped her arms around his head, pressed against him, took his fingers inside as he held her tight, and rode the arc of exquisite need.

There was that word again.

"Nate?" she whispered.

"Shhh…" he said, before taking her mouth with his, his hot, slick lips feeding her the most devastating kisses of her life.

And any disquiet dissolved into a haze as he pulled back and locked his gaze to hers, the stunning blue so dark with desire emotion rose thick and fast within her, expanding till it filled her all the way to her throat. There it stopped, as pleasure and pressure built inside her, and from there it was released, and the roar of his name echoed off the walls as she fell apart.

Truly spent, Saskia collapsed into Nate's arms. He held her there, a hand tracing her spine, the other twisting her hair as wave after beautiful wave of aftershock trembled through her.

Feeling the pound of Nate's heart against her own, Saskia took a breath, stilled her mind, forgot herself and heard her own heart.

This, it said.

And she knew exactly what it meant.

Nate Mackenzie might not talk about himself as much as she wished, but when she was with him he was more present than any man she'd ever known.

He was the first man who'd ever been with her not because he needed to be but because he *wanted* to be. And that made more of a difference than she'd ever imagined.

But not Nate, she told her heart. *Not him.*

It said nothing back. It seemed her heart had exhausted its wisdom for the moment.

"We ever going to actually make it to a bed, do you think?" she said, her voice thick.

"One of these days."

She felt Nate's smile against her shoulder. And then his teeth scraped over her rose tattoo before he replaced them with a gentle kiss. She didn't need to count to know exactly how many days they had left together. It was permanently imprinted on her brain, like the ticking of a time bomb.

"In fact…" said Nate, and he dragged himself upright, bubbles and water slewing over his glorious golden skin, till he stood before her, a supreme example of manhood in every which way.

Then he pulled her to her feet, threw her over his shoulder,

and padded out of the ridiculously large *en suite* bathroom,
into his bedroom which, with its elegant striped wallpaper,
leather-backed bed and dark wood trim, looked as if it had
come straight out of the set of *Mad Men*.

"Wow!" she said, her hands on his hips. "Testosterone central."

"The faux rhino wasn't evidence enough? Told you—the
designer went mad."

He gave her bottom a kiss before throwing her on the bed.
She bounced and settled, still covered in bubbles, and watched
as he found a condom, slid it into place, his eyes roving over
her wet, naked form as if he couldn't decide where to start...

Later, Saskia lay sated beneath luxurious sheets. Nate's arm
was slung heavily across her hip, hooked so his hand settled
between her breasts, and the tips of his long fingers were close
enough to kiss.

In that soft place between awake and asleep, with the hot,
hard length of him nestled in behind her, the last thing that entered her mind before consciousness finally eluded her, was:
This.

Saskia woke to the sound of a phone ringing. One eyelid at
half-mast, she reached out for it—only to knock over a big
rectangular lamp with an elephant built into the base, and an
Art Deco clock from a low mahogany bedside table.

Nate's bedside table.

Her eyes popped open like a Pop-Tart in a toaster. She'd slept
over? She'd slept *over*. Oh, God! She'd only meant to drift off
for a few minutes, regain some strength, then kiss him to distraction before heading off into the night as if what they were
playing at was nothing but fun and games.

Not...not what her heart had hinted at the night before. The
same heart that now gave her an unfamiliar little squeeze hello.
She shut the thing down and glanced over the side of the bed at

the clock on the floor to see it was some time after ten, meaning Nate would be long gone.

He could have woken her, though, sent her on her way before he left. She couldn't help but feel a little chuffed that he'd trusted her enough to leave her be. Unless he had really good security.

Her phone rang again, and she kicked at the charcoal-grey bedding hooked around her legs, then rushed naked to the chunky leather *chaise* in the corner of the huge room. Rummaging in her massive bag, she found her phone. Withheld number. Probably a client.

Sitting, naked, with a *whump* on the edge of the couch she answered, "SassyStats. Saskia Bloom speaking."

"Hi, Saskia!" twin voices shouted down the phone.

No. It couldn't be.

"It's Hope," said one.

Then, "And Faith. We nicked your number from Nate's phone the day you came over. Anyhoo, we have a free morning and thought how nice it would be to get to know you better—considering."

Considering what? That she was sitting on their brother's *chaise* naked? She grabbed a deep red afghan and covered herself to her neck.

"We thought coffee at Chadstone?" said one.

The other added, "Then shopping. Hope's a stylist, so she'll find you the perfect thing."

"For…?"

"The wedding! Two birds with one stone."

Saskia wondered momentarily what these two birds would do with a stone if they knew her relationship with their beloved brother was all a lie.

"Please say you'll come," Hope said hopefully.

Saskia nibbled at her bottom lip.

Saying no would seem plain rude, which wouldn't help Nate's cause. And she'd not actually considered what she'd wear to the wedding. Clothes weren't really her thing, and considering her finances it had been months since she'd been able to afford even to update her undies.

And then it hit her—she knew how much Nate hated talking about himself, so using him as her infographic/love formula test bunny had been harder than getting blood from a stone. But he'd never expressly asked that she not talk to his family.

Three birds with one stone...

"I do need a dress," she said, and Faith near deafened her with excitement as she barked orders down the phone as to when and where they'd meet.

Only after she'd hung up the phone and was taking advantage of Nate's enormous dual-headed shower—keeping her back to the fake rhinoceros head which seemed to watch her no matter where she was in the room—did she wonder if she should have checked with Nate first.

But, no matter how it looked, he wasn't her boyfriend. So as long as she kept within the bounds of their agreement he didn't get a say. Besides, he would have said, *No way in hell.*

She wasn't as convinced that she'd made the right decision an hour later as Faith and Hope curled their grips into the crooks of her elbows and dragged her all over Chadstone.

"You even smell like him, you know," said Faith, as they hit the top of the escalator and headed towards designer row.

Saskia sniffed her shoulder, and realised she did. "Must be his shower gel," she said, a moment before realising what she'd just given away. "Too much information."

"No. You have no idea how happy it makes me." Hope gave her a happy bump with her hip. "We were all beginning to think he was actually *serious* in his efforts not to settle down. And then you came along and we all let out a long, thankful breath."

"Oh. Right." Saskia bit her lip to stop herself saying anything more. Even while she knew Nate would be thrilled to the tips of his designer socks that his sisters were so far off the scent, she'd never counted on the fact that they'd see her as anything other than the last in a long line of future exes. That they'd care.

A little twinge of guilt took up residence in her belly.

Saskia was down to her bra and undies in a change room when Faith's voice sing-songed from the other side of the curtain. "Think of the babies you two would make. Sweet, serious little things that'd charm a lolly out of a candy machine."

Saskia poked her head around the edge of the huge velvet curtain as the guilt began to churn. "Faith, I—" *God, how to put this?* "Nate and I are having a really good time together, but *babies* are…not on the agenda. Yet. For a good long while. If at all. Okay?"

"We *know*," said Faith, holding the netting of a fascinator over her eyes as she pulled kissy faces at a nearby mirror.

The way she said it made the guilt churning in Saskia's stomach turn to lumps.

"You know *what,* exactly?" Saskia called, grabbing at the heavy velvet curtain which kept slipping out of her grip.

"About the pre-engagement," said Hope, who now came at her from nowhere with a filmy, frilly red dress that looked like something out of a gangster movie.

Saskia held out a finger to take the hanger. "I'm sorry—the pre-what?"

Hope angled her head behind Saskia and she glanced back to see that her cotton-covered backside was in full view of the store in the mirror at her back. She let the curtain swing closed and looked at herself, cheeks pink, hair a tumble, the red dress clutched to her front like a great figurative scarlet letter.

CHAPTER EIGHT

"You told your family we are *pre*-engaged?"

Nate looked up from the conference table, where he and Gabe were knocking back double espressos and doughnuts as they strategised the next step in landing a new account, to find Saskia barrelling down on him, her face a mask of fury.

Too many things hit him at once.

First, Saskia was looking about as damn cute as any woman had the right to look, even in an odd get-up of tight army pants, cropped leather jacket, mottled scarf and huge floppy beanie.

Next, Saskia's brow was furrowed, her sultry eyes wild, cheeks pink, lips a deep red—as close to how she looked when she fell apart in his arms as he'd ever seen her in daylight.

Lastly, Saskia had apparently been talking to his family.

"Pre-engaged?" Gabe repeated, when Nate said nothing at all. Then Gabe laughed, the deep sound echoing off the walls of glass enclosing the imposing room.

Saskia's fiery gaze shot to Gabe and she stuck a hand on her hip and nodded. "I know, right? What the hell is *pre*-engaged anyway? A man made that up, for sure. As a way to get out of ever actually being engaged."

"You got that right," Gabe said. "If you want a woman you get married. No in between."

"Thank you!"

"What kind of bling do you get for being pre-engaged?" Gabe asked, turning in his chair to direct that one to Nate, his dark eyes laughing their proverbial asses off. "Semi-precious at best."

Nate angled his head at Gabe then towards the door. *Out. Now.*

"Oh, no, no, no," Saskia said, waggling her finger at them both. "Of all the men in this room right now I like him best. So he can stay. Why not? He might know more about our 'burgeoning relationship' than I do."

Wheels in his head whirring back to life, Nate stood, planted his hands on the table with a thump, and said, "Enough, Saskia. Calm down. Sit."

"Excuse me?" she said, her eyes like twin flints.

He should have known better than to tell her to calm down, what with having three sisters, but this woman messed with his synapses. And *hell* if seeing her all riled didn't turn him on...

He eased back in his chair with a studied air of submission. "Have a doughnut."

Saskia blinked. Then her eyes cut to the tray of doughnuts on the table beside the mini-espresso machine. She licked her lips. Once. Enough for Nate to feel it in his groin. Then she shook her head so hard the curls below the edge of her beanie slapped her in the face.

Nate felt Gabe wince beside him.

"Sit," he said again, then after a breath softened it with, "Please? And we'll talk. Alone."

"Fine, fine."

Gabe dragged his bulk from the chair and ambled out— but not before planting a kiss atop Saskia's head. And for that Nate wanted to crack *him* over the head with the nearest chair.

Saskia took a deep breath through flaring nostrils before she sat. Once she did, she seemed to deflate, head in hands, toes just touching the floor, as if she was trying to make herself as small as possible.

Swearing beneath his breath, Nate unclenched his hands from his chair's armrests and rounded the table, took the seat beside hers. "Start at the beginning. How is it that you were talking to my family at all?"

She drew her hands down her face—eyes smudged, cheeks now devoid of colour, lips turned down at the corners. He actually wished the banshee was back.

"The twins rang this morning and invited me out shopping to find a dress to wear to the wedding."

His sisters. His deal. His fault. He took her hands in his. Compared with his hot fingers they were soft and cool and small. "So you got a dress?"

"I did," she said, delight flaring in her eyes, colour swarming back to her cheeks, her mouth turning up gently at the corners. *She's something,* he thought. *Like there's a light inside of her determined to shine no matter what.* And he bet she hadn't a clue.

She looked up at him then, and breathed in deep, even a little shakily. "Why do they think we're engaged, Nate?"

"Pre-engaged," he said, unhooking a stray curl from her eyelash. "I have a small idea. Jasmine rang this morning— asking about you, about how things were going."

He'd been standing in his bedroom doorway at the time, wondering whether or not to wake Saskia. She'd been curled up in his bed asleep, hands tucked under her chin, knees drawn to her chest, toes coiled around one another, her riot of hair splayed across his dark pillow, her soft lips parted, her face clear.

He shifted imperceptibly on his chair and said, "I might have told her something along the lines of 'they're going in the right direction.'"

Saskia breathed again—a little more shakily, a little deeper.

He continued, "Then one of them—Faith, probably—called and asked when the 'Save the Date' cards were on their way. I said I had no clue what she was talking about. She explained, I said she was a good couple of steps ahead of herself and—"

"She took a natural two steps back and landed on pre-engaged."

"So it seems. The others are persistent, but at least they are vaguely sensible. I'm not sure where I went wrong with her."

Saskia turned his hands over and gave them a little squeeze. She must have hit a nerve, because warmth shot through him with all the subtlety of a bolt of electricity.

"Nate, I like your family, and I'm not sure how I feel about lying to them any more. Fudging a few dates is one thing, but *engaged?*" She leaned into the huge bag on her shoulder and pulled out a folded piece of paper. A cheque. Rumpled at the edges as if she'd worried at it some. "If you could wait a couple of months before banking it…"

As realisation hit panic swelled inside him. He clapped his hand around hers. "No!"

"Nate," she said, her eyes beseeching.

"Do you want more money?" Her head rose so slowly he knew he'd said the wrong thing. "I take that back."

"I can't believe you just said that!"

He ran a hand up the back of his hair. "Me either. I'm sorry. It's just…this was meant to be simple."

"And it's not, is it?" she asked, looking him right in the eye.

Brave girl. Braver than he. He gave himself a mental shake and simply refused to go there.

"Our initial contract was fulfilled the moment you stepped over my mother's threshold."

"But—"

"I mean it. All I really wanted them to believe was that I was seeing someone. You made that happen. Every moment from that point on was above and beyond."

"So the wedding…?"

A moment hovered in front of him—a moment during which he could have thanked her for her efforts and sent her on her way.

A savvy businessman, to say the least, he knew when to

take such moments. Cut ties and move on. The world was a big place with a million new deals to be made. And yet in that moment, even while they were surrounded by glass walls, with people walking past, glancing in, no doubt wondering who the small brunette with her foot tucked up on a chair, looking unblinkingly into their boss's face might be, the world felt about two metres square.

He looked into Saskia's big nearly brown eyes and heard himself say, "Tell me about the dress."

"Red," she said, swallowing. "Floaty. Gonna knock your socks off."

"I'll be sure to wear two pairs."

Her breath was released on a big sigh. He did much the same, only he was far better at hiding it.

"Okay," she said, frowning a moment, before adding, "But your family—"

"It's not a lie, Saskia. Not any more. The pre-engagement is Faith being Faith. But as for the rest…? You might not have noticed, but we're sleeping together. And we're exclusive. That's about as close to a relationship as I've ever been."

He actually held his damn breath as he waited for her response. Those big eyes were searching for the loophole. Poor kid. She'd been screwed over so many times by men who'd just wanted something from her she couldn't see when someone was being honest. And he was. He wanted her as his wedding date, and he wanted her in his bed until that day. Exclusively.

When her answer came it was, "Wow! A more romantic proposal I never did hear."

At which he laughed. Laughed till his sides hurt.

Then came a smile so sweet and unexpected it near broke his heart. Thankfully the thing was unassailable, tough as old leather, or he might have begun to worry.

"Why do I get the feeling I should have fought harder to cut you off?"

"Low blood sugar," he said, sliding the platter of dough-nuts her way.

Rolling her eyes, she lifted her backside off the chair and took one, biting into it with relish. "You're trouble, Nate Mac-kenzie. I should have known it the minute I saw you walk into Mamma Rita's. Heck, maybe I did see it and just didn't care."

"You're no walk in the park either, Saskia Bloom."

At that, she grinned. "Maybe we should shock them all and just get married. You can keep the losers from my door and I'll keep infuriating matchmakers from yours."

She was joking—he knew she was joking—and yet for a brief shining moment the simplicity of it made a perverse kind of sense: her contentment, her warm body, the way she made him laugh.

Until memories of skimpy underwear hanging over the shower rail began to flick through his mind. And *Pride and Prejudice* marathons, and drips of red nail polish on the bath-room sink, and never being able to find a piece of chocolate in the house as once it crossed the threshold it became fair game. And the tears. So very much rich, thick, swinging emotion to navigate every single day.

If you want a woman you get married. To Gabe it was that simple. While Nate's skin began to itch as if he'd come out in hives.

He stood, took her hands, and drew her to her feet. "Get out of here, Ms Bloom, before I take you up on that."

She hitched her bag over her shoulder and gave him a wonky smile. "No wonder you're so good at what you do; for a second there I nearly believed you."

Together they walked to the glass door. She tried to tuck her hair behind her ears but it sprang back, a mass of wild curls. The lift of her arm raised her sweater, exposing a sliver of skin, the dip of her waist. And as her hand reached for the handle he touched her there. His hand at her hip his thumb found skin,

and her light body melted into him as if it had been waiting
to do just that.

He let her go, and without a backwards glance she opened
the door and walked away.

"I just had a terrible thought."

Saskia grinned as Nate's voice rumbled down the phone line.
Phone tucked under her chin, she grabbed a corner of vinyl
from the kitchen floor and tugged. "Do tell?"

"It's just over a week away and I still haven't got a wedding
present. Mae didn't do the normal thing and send invites weeks
before the wedding with a registry card attached—"

"You know a lot about weddings, my friend."

"I'm beloved. I get a lot of invites."

Saskia gave up, shucked her gloves and plonked herself on a
red vinyl chair in the corner of the kitchen. "Any reason you've
included me in your terrible thought?"

"You're a woman."

"Why, thank you for noticing."

"Sweetheart, I think we can safely say I would not have
kissed you by the cab that first night if I hadn't noticed that
pretty quick-smart."

"And I thought that was just for credibility."

A pause, then, "You probably believe in fairies too."

Saskia laughed, then sighed, then curled up on the chair and
gave herself over to the bliss.

After the pre-engagement blow-out they'd hit a kind of
flirty, easy peace. That night she'd gone to Nate's to watch a
movie and eat takeaway. After a half-hour they'd both decided
they ought to be doing something else, and had spent the better part of the night doing just that.

He'd turned up at hers with Chinese and red wine the next
night and they'd managed to eat about half before other more
pressing matters had taken over.

When he'd refused to take her money back she couldn't

remember feeling more relief in her whole life. And it hadn't been about the debt. Not even a jot. It had meant she had another week and a bit with Nate in her bed. In her life. In her heart. She'd always thought herself a smart woman. Clearly she'd been mistaken.

"So, what does my womanhood have to do with your shopping dilemma?"

"Would you care to do the honours?"

"Not on your life." It occurred to her a split second later that in the past she would have said yes. Without hesitation. Saying no felt…good. Evolved. A blessed relief that she'd said it and her world hadn't ended.

"But—"

"You have three sisters, Nate. And a mother. Any one of whom would jump at the chance to help."

That shut him up. It was kind of nice to know she could still render the man speechless.

"Mae's your friend now as much as she is mine."

Saskia's mouth twisted at that. She'd been to Mae's hen night the night before and had the time of her life. A pub crawl through the Irish pubs of Melbourne had turned into something else entirely when Mae had taken it upon herself to stop every man they met and ask him about their internet dating experiences. It had given Saskia—who always had a yellow legal pad on hand—enough in-depth research from the male point of view to create three infographics.

It had been a blast, but it had also meant she'd not seen Nate at all.

"Okay. Then care to come shopping with me?"

Saskia looked down at her overalls, her sticky hair, her paint-splattered hands. "Sounds like a treat. But no. Can't. I'm tearing up my kitchen floor."

Another pause. "On your own?"

"Unlike you, I don't see the need to hire people when I'm perfectly capable of doing it myself."

"Would you even know how to ask for help?"

"Sure," she said with a shrug. "If I didn't think I could do it better myself."

"I've never met anyone like you, Saskia Bloom."

"Nice try. Get the gift yourself." She hung up, the sound of his laughter still humming through her.

A week, she thought, staring at the sun shining through the small collection of red glass bottles lined up on her kitchen window. A week more of Nate and then…*nothing*. That was pretty much what she felt like when she let herself hear the clock ticking in the back of her head. As if the place he had in her life would leave a hole too big to fill.

Because what would happen post-wedding? Not just with Nate but his friends? She liked Mae. Genuinely adored Gabe's fiancée, Paige. Would she see them again? *Should* she?

She knew Nate wouldn't try to stop her. But could she, knowing they ran in the same circles as Nate? Something gave her the feeling that going cold turkey would be for the best. A little something that tightened around her heart every time she thought about it.

As if he felt her impending gloom Ernest came padding in and she threw him the crust of her ham sandwich which she'd saved. He sniffed the air, smelled that it wasn't an Oreo and padded away, his claws slipping on the part of the floor which was now down to raw wood.

The blessed kitchen floor, she thought, dragging herself from the chair. Another reason she loved doing the work herself. Keeping busy had always meant not having time to think about all the things missing from her life.

No mum, a barely there dad, soon no Nate…

She donned her gloves, grabbed a hunk of vinyl and ripped for all she was worth.

Nate knocked on Saskia's front door.

He couldn't stand still, rolling his shoulders and shifting

from foot to foot. It was ridiculous; he couldn't remember being this unsure about dropping in unannounced on a woman since he was seventeen-years-old and all fired up to ask Lily von Krum's police commander father if he could take Lily to the Scotch College formal.

Women liked him. Always had. He couldn't remember a time when women hadn't stopped in the street to gush over his baby blues.

But Saskia was different in myriad tiny little ways he found himself struggling to pin down even while they hummed around him like a field of fireflies. She wasn't easy, but neither did she go out of her way to be hard. She was just…who she was. And the equanimity at the heart of her still gave him a kick.

A kick in the pants to yank himself out of his own rut and be more a part of the real world—which was why he was standing at her door.

He'd moved to knock again when a scrambling from inside stopped him. The door bumped, then swung open to reveal a mass of kinky curls atop Saskia's dark head, her knuckles white as she gripped her dog by the collar, his wiry body shaking with glee.

"Hey, buddy," Nate said, stepping in to help.

"Nate?" she said, looking up in surprise at the sound of his voice. Then, "Your suit!"

Which was when Nate realised he probably ought to have made a detour to change.

"Dime a dozen," he lied, not about to tell her it was his lucky suit. Not *date*-lucky—he rarely had a problem there. More like deal-of-the-century-lucky. Too late now. He gave the dog a rub. Crinkly doggie hair came off in droves.

"Ernest! Be gone!" she said, and like that the dog was off.

Nate stood, as did she. In overalls three sizes too large. Her feet were bare, bar the chipped paint on her nails, and her hair had been dragged off her face by a headband with a feather poking out of the top.

Her eyes slid down his torso with a thoroughness that sent a surge through his bloodstream. But when she blew a curl from her forehead with a quick stream of air from the side of her mouth it hit him hard, right in the solar plexus. She looked…like she always looked. Soft, vibrant, her wardrobe choice more than a little off centre. And yet there was no denying his certainty that she was one of the most gorgeous women he'd ever known.

He reached out and flicked the feather. She crossed her eyes at it before sliding it from her hair, her cheeks pinkening.

"Ernest found it outside," she said, playing with the fronds. "He gave it to me as a gift." She glanced over her shoulder. "I really can't shop, Nate. Not right now. I'm in the middle of something."

"I'm not here to ask you to shop," he said, moving past her since she hadn't asked him in. "I'm here to help."

Her hand still on the door handle, she blinked at him as if she didn't even know what the word meant.

"Help," he repeated, pulling off his jacket and tossing it onto a pale green cabinet in the entrance hall, noting it was new. As was the heavy round mirror above it. He rolled up his sleeves. "As in pull vinyl. Or lay tiles. Or re-roof the joint. Whatever you need." When she continued staring at him as if he was talking Swahili, he said, "Have you never had a man offer his services before?"

At that she shook her head. And he believed her. In that moment he wished she had a little black book—just so he could track down every man who'd ever hurt her, used her, abused her, taken all she had to offer without taking the time to let her know she was appreciated, that she was something special. What he wanted to do to them was possibly excessive, but then if a man didn't aim high, then what was the point of aiming at all.

"I don't need help," she said.

"I don't much care what you think you need, Miss Bloom, so you're going to have to put up with me."

"Aren't you meant to be at work?"

"I'm the boss. I can be wherever the hell I want to be."

"Yes, sir," she mumbled.

"That's more like it."

"Ha! Don't get used to it, buddy."

"Hmm, the day I do will probably be the day we're done."

She flinched as if he'd slapped her. Then schooled her face as if nothing was wrong. He wanted to slap himself.

He couldn't help himself. Since the blow-out in his conference room, when he'd had the perfect chance to end things amicably and hadn't, he'd been all over the shop. Wanting her with a ferocity he couldn't contain, while at the same time constantly reminding her, and himself, of their imminent demise.

He peeled her hand from the door handle and slammed the door. Then he led her past the newly painted hallway—where did the woman find the time?—into the kitchen, to find a disaster area.

Bits of vinyl torn up all over, bits still stuck, a few gouges out of the floor as if she'd taken to it with a mallet and a chisel.

He looked over his shoulder to find her frowning at the floor. "We seem to have met an impasse."

The magnitude of the job hit him. Along with the fact that she ran her own business, and that he'd been stealing every spare moment she had, while hampering her work by refusing to help her out by being her lab rabbit.

He'd thought *he* worked hard, but the woman didn't rest. And as he watched her frown at the floor, as if her entire self-worth was wrapped up in whether or not she could strip vinyl, it occurred to him why. The loser boyfriends, her distant father and getting things done were all she thought she was good for.

It put his own reasons for working his ass off to shame.

"It's a big job, Saskia. Maybe you should call a tiler—"

"I can take care of myself."

"I know you can," said Nate. "I get the feeling you've done just that your whole life."

Looking into those big bedroom eyes, over that soft pink mouth, twisting sideways as she tried to deny the undeniable, Nate said, "Today it's my turn."

It wasn't a question. It was a promise. And after only the slightest of hesitations Saskia nodded, her eyes melted and she let him.

With a tear in the front pocket and a stain that might or might not be dog food on his knee, the pants of his lucky suit were officially ruined. But the vinyl was gone—every last dot of the damn stuff—and, covered in the sweat of a job well done, Nate felt amazing.

He'd ditched his shirt an hour before. Saskia's overalls hung from her waist, leaving her in a tank top. Her hair was plastered to her neck and cheeks with sweat and her cheeks were smudged with dust.

When she realised they were done she brushed her hands together and let out a great sigh. She looked up at him and grinned.

"Happy?" he asked.

"Delirious! Thank you," she said, shaking her head as if she was amazed at herself for having let him help at all.

He ran a thumb over a smudge on her cheek. "Partners in grime."

She laughed again, the sound husky. Her big, dark, sooty-lashed eyes blinked up at him. Filled with more than thanks. Filled with so many things he'd barely pinned one down before it floated dreamily to the next. And even while he was smart enough to understand them, and hard enough not to want them, using a finger to tilt her chin he kissed her.

Her hands fluttered to his bare chest, the soft touch searing him. And like that they kissed—gentle, sweet, exploring kisses—for so long he lost track of time.

Her hands slid over his shoulders, deep into his hair, and she lifted onto her toes, taking the kiss deeper. He lifted her, desire pouring through him like a relentless waterfall, and pressed her back till she hit the bench. He tore her overalls down her legs, lifted her tank top, fell to his knees. He kissed her belly. Her salty taste hit the back of his throat and he groaned. Her fingers drove tracks through his hair as his teeth found her hipbone. His tongue her belly button. His mouth her centre.

With such sweet sensuality she melted in his arms, coming with a shudder he felt mirroring his own.

Then he lifted her into his arms, her slick skin sliding against his as he took her into her bedroom. He peeled off her damp clothes. Pressed her hair from her face. Wiped away the grime with her tank, leaving her clean and glowing. So fresh and beautiful he felt it pierce his heart.

"What will you do when you don't have me around to do that to you?" he asked, steeling himself against the sensation, against her. Brutal as it was, he wanted to know she'd miss him. Needed to know she'd feel it when he was gone.

Her eyes narrowed. Glinted. And then her hands began a slow trek down her naked sides, dipping into the dips, curving over the curves, driving him into near insanity.

"I can take care of myself," she said, her voice low and clear. "Been doing so my whole life."

Nate's smile came from deep within. "Today it's my turn."

This time there was no hesitation. Saskia lay back on the bed, her arms behind her head, her eyes cloudy with desire as she let him take her to oblivion and back.

Her eyes, those gorgeous brown depths, lit with passion and need and bone-deep tenderness, looked right into him as he buried himself inside her slick heat, and he came harder than he remembered coming his entire life.

* * *

Nate lay in Saskia's big soft bed, staring at the rainbows shifting across the pale pink ceiling—moonlight glinting off the chandelier of colourful plastic discs. Her smooth, lean leg was entwined around his, her breath was shifting the hairs on his chest, the soft heat at her centre pressed against his side.

She sighed and he tilted his head to look at her.

"What's up?" he asked, his voice barely a croak.

"I will miss this," she croaked back, her fingers playing with the hair on his chest.

"Don't blame you."

"Though I'm not sure why I ever thought you charming," she said with a laugh.

She snuggled closer. And he let her. He'd miss it too. For a while. Then he wouldn't. That was how it went. Though when he tried to imagine going about his days without her in them, his nights without her warm body melted against him, he didn't like what he saw.

For a split second he allowed himself to imagine an *after*. A few more dates, a few more DVD sessions, a few more drinks with friends, a few more nights like this. Then he stopped himself.

He might be selfish, but he hoped he wasn't a selfish bastard.

He knew this was getting harder for her. He knew her feelings for him weren't purely sexual. She just wasn't that good a liar. But, while he'd be happy with a little more contentment in his life, she wanted happily-ever-after. And that wasn't something he was willing to deliver.

Start as you intend to finish, he told himself. *Be honest, friendly, and most important be resolute.* It was past time to begin the great unwind.

"The charm thing," he said. "It's all an act."

She moved onto her elbows and looked into his face, her eyes fierce as she said, "Don't you believe it."

He took her hand and held it at his chest as he tried to find the words he needed. The words he knew she'd need, which somehow mattered more.

"After my father died," he began, his eyes on the ceiling again, "after the effort of the following few years, I was running on empty. If I was ever going to run a business without being attuned to every employee's emotional up-and-down I had to…stop caring. It worked. I did what I had to do to— charmed, led astray, hedged, profiteered—to carve a life for myself. The life I wanted. And I have that. And it's enough."

"You need to give yourself more credit."

"I think I'm awesome. How's that for credit?"

Her eyes narrowed and her mouth twisted to one side. Cutest woman he'd ever known, he thought. He stroked his thumb across the corner of her mouth and her eyes closed dreamily.

He let his hand drop, kicking himself for undoing any headway his little speech might have made. But he'd get there. He had no choice.

"Promise me something?" he said. "When this is all said and done…"

"Anything."

"You'll give *yourself* more credit."

"I can do that. Promise *me* something."

Anything. It hovered on the tip of his tongue, but he couldn't offer that. "Hit me."

"Stay ruffled."

Then she lifted a hand and ran it through his hair gently, fondly, with an intimacy he wasn't sure he'd felt since he was a kid.

"Unruffled, you're pretty cute. Ruffled, you're just plain irresistible."

She was ruffled, soft, pink-cheeked. Her hair mussed, her eyes hot and wanting. She was the definition of irresistible. This precocious creature, this spark in his day, the laughter in his thoughts, the wild cat in his bed, with her pushy little digs she was the incitement to spread his wings.

He lifted his hand to her cheek, waited till she looked him in the eye, and said, "Resist."

She breathed deep, her shoulders lifting, and said, "I'm trying."

And then, belying her words, she slid over him, her softness melting into him, turning him hard as a rock.

She lifted to her knees, holding her hair from her neck as she sank over him. Arching her back, she lifted, nudged again and again. The touch sent her head rocking back on her neck, her mouth open, her skin pink all over.

He gripped her hips, took control, stroking her even while he throbbed with pressure that beat to the point of pain.

"There," she said on a gasp. "Right there."

"Bossy."

Her eyes focused on his and her cheeks came over all rosy as her eyes dropped to his mouth. "You like it," she realised, letting him an inch inside before pulling away.

"Yeah," he said through gritted teeth, "I really do."

And with that she slid over him, all silken and gorgeous demand, and pleasure tore through him like liquid heat, twisting him inside out. She rocked, making his whole world spin, till it imploded where their two hot bodies met.

As exhaustion and completion dragged him to sleep Nate knew. Helping her pull up her kitchen floor clearly wasn't enough. He had to do more. Make her understand how grateful he was. Know that she meant something to him even as he told her goodbye.

CHAPTER NINE

NATE WASN'T SURE how long he sat on the edge of Saskia's soft bed early the next morning, watching her sleep, remembering how he'd held her in the night, her head beneath his chin, his hand on her hip. But at some point she'd curled into a little ball on the edge of the bed. He wondered if she always slept that way or if she'd been making room for him.

Figuring it was too early for philosophising, he padded down the hall and into the main bathroom to splash water on his face.

And there, amongst the stash of pens and paint samples on her bathroom bench, he saw a yellow legal pad. Even at a glance he recognised the Dating By Numbers study, the questions he'd managed to avoid answering. Though apparently at some point somebody had—many had notes against them in a different-coloured pen, some with something that looked a heck of a lot like the words *Pub Crawl* scrawled in the margin.

Intrigue and a healthy dose of jealousy—because some other man had given her what he wouldn't—made him read on to find questions about intimacy, love, attraction, fear and faith. The kinds of things he'd rather eat dog than talk about at length.

And yet seeing her happy, curly scrawl racing all over the page it seemed to him a small thing she'd wanted—a few simple truths in exchange for all he'd asked of her.

He gazed down the hall to where she slept.

She'd put herself out there with his family, his friends, risking exposure, putting up with his irascibility. The woman had

had her faith in people trodden on time and again, and yet her generosity was so hardwired she'd do the same thing all over again if he asked.

While *he'd* thrown a few bloodless titbits into the damn dossier as if they were some kind of gift. Because without thought, without care, he'd hardwired himself to *resist* anything remotely intimate.

He gripped the legal pad tighter in his hand as he was hit with a wave of disappointment. In himself. He *was* a selfish bastard. A wholly self-made one at that. Independence was one thing—grudging self-interest quite the other. That wasn't the kind of man he'd hoped to be one day—not even within spitting distance.

He found a pen, then, taking a deep breath, went through the list, jotting down notes, sometimes paragraphs, giving her the answers she was missing, moving on to the next before he had a chance to think about the one before in an effort to outrun the horror.

When he'd finished he let go a shuddering breath.

Then he padded into her room and kissed her on the shoulder, leaving the pages on the pillow beside her.

She *still* didn't budge. Sleeping the sleep of the content. Of someone whose life was just as it should be.

He ran a hand over her shoulder, feeling the innate warmth that flowed just below the surface, like the crushed petal of a rose. In touching her, a soft milky scent rose up to him. The tattoo on her shoulder brushed rough against the pad of his thumb. He traced it distractedly. And then not so distractedly.

She deserved better. More. He wanted her to know it. Needed to know she was as amazing as he knew she was. And there was only one way he could think of to tell her. To show her. To make her see.

Spurred, he pressed himself to standing, pieced together his clothes, threw them on only as decency demanded, and headed out through her door, closing it softly behind him.

* * *

The following Tuesday evening Saskia brought a hot chocolate into the lounge and sat, curling her toes beneath the skirt of her maxi dress.

Ernest padded in from wherever he'd been foraging and turned three times before settling on his doggy bed. The fire crackled softly, now she'd got the hang of it, and her new second-hand lounge chairs were gorgeous: red-and-white checked, with pale green and baby blue and soft yellow floral cushions—a riot of spring colour. *Busy,* her dad would have called it, and frowned, thinking of her mother, claiming it gave him a headache. Saskia would have exchanged it for something less lovely. Less *her.*

She'd added touches of riot everywhere the past few weeks, fancying up the relatively blank canvas until it looked to her like the very image of happiness.

Thanks—very much—to Nate. He'd not only given her the opportunity to get out from under the weight of her debt, he'd pulled her from the even more debilitating hit she'd taken to her self-esteem after Stu. And those who'd come before.

She picked up the slightly rumpled pages of yellow legal paper covered in her swirly writing and Nate's sexy scrawl— rumpled because she'd rolled over on them when reaching out for him to find not him but this gift.

She couldn't for the life of her fathom what had changed his mind about answering her interview questions, but he had. He'd written about his interactions with women—the respect, the intrigue, the unashamed temptation. But she could feel his desire to be better. Do better. To become the man he hoped to be. And giving her this he'd given her himself.

No wonder he was always rubbing his temples in frustration, she thought, with all he had in his head. No wonder he worked himself to distraction. No wonder he'd come looking for her.

And Saskia couldn't have loved him more for it.

It had been coming, brimming, easing, falling, pressing in

on her from every angle. Her love for this man who had no clue that he gave so much and took so little for himself. This man who knew his strengths but couldn't see his worth.

How could she know him and not love him? And she'd be so good for him. Take care of him. Relax him. Show him contentment. Make him happy. Love him all his days and nights. If only he'd let her.

Never having been there before, she had no idea what came next. So she sat in the middle of it, feeling it, living it, revelling in it, till her backside turned numb from sitting in the same spot too long.

Ernest leapt from his doggy bed and took off. A moment later a knock sounded.

By the time she reached the door Saskia's heart was thumping through her chest at the thought that it might be Nate. What would she say about what he'd given her? Would he even know what it meant to her? Could it be why he'd done it?

"Earn your keep, Fido, and learn how to open the door!" Lissy called from the other side. Then added, "Men suck!" as she spilled through the door, arms laden with grocery bags—hence the non-use of her key. She gave Ernest a perfunctory cuddle with one foot as she trudged in.

Not all of them, Saskia thought, the bliss riding high again.

"More than usual?" Saskia asked, padding into the kitchen to make another hot chocolate.

"Bamford dumped me."

Wow. Lissy, of the glorious mane of blonde hair with its now hot pink tips, the big blue eyes and curves for the ages, was a bombshell. Crazy, for sure, but men didn't seem to care. As if they couldn't use their brains while their tongues lolled out of their mouths.

"Did he say why?"

Lissy waved a dismissive hand over her shoulder. "Something about compatibility. A lack of seriousness. Blah-blah-blah."

As Lissy upended her bag of groceries on the kitchen table Ernest thought he'd died and gone to heaven—caramel popcorn, butterscotch ice cream, boxes of Oreos.

"You disagree?" Saskia said, plopping a mound or two of chocolate powder into a mug.

Lissy deflated into a chair. "I'm not sure, to tell the truth. Bam was fun. A crazy kind of challenge. But when I see you and Nate together—the chemistry, the way you complement and challenge and fit—there's this aura, like the glow of possibility, that gleams around you. I want that."

Stunned into silence because it really wasn't all in her head, Saskia flinched when the door was knocked upon again. She glanced in its direction, wanting to press Lissy for more about the glowing and the aura.

The knock sounded at the door again.

"If that's Bam, I'm not here," said Lissy as she plonked herself at the kitchen table.

"Why would he think you were?"

Her eyes narrowed a moment. "I told him this was where I'd be if he realised he'd just made the biggest mistake of his life and decided to send flowers or diamonds."

Saskia shook her head at the logic, or lack thereof, then in a kind of daze went to answer the door.

She didn't even notice Ernest was nowhere to be seen until she swung the door open and found herself face-to-face with—

"Stu?"

"Hey, Sas. How's it hangin'?"

Chagrin had brought dimples to his cheeks. Add that to the elegant height, the puppy-dog eyes, the Byronesque mien, the guy was better-looking than a man had a right to be. But looking at him now—at the way his eyes darted anywhere but at her, at the defensive slump of his shoulders, the shuffling of his feet—Saskia wondered how she'd ever dated him at all.

"Aren't you gonna invite me in?"

Her heart beat in her ears and her vision narrowed to about

a square metre in front of her eyes as, watching Stu she felt like Alice watching her old life from the other side of the looking glass.

"Why on earth would I do that?"

He blinked.

"What are you doing here, Stu?"

When he didn't look as if he had plans to go anywhere else, she let him in. Then followed in a kind of haze as he walked into her apartment, making appreciative noises about the work she'd done. He poked his head into her lounge room, glanced at her new TV—not as big as the last, but new all the same—then at Ernest, who was curled up in his cosy bed, pouting. It seemed she wasn't the only one hanging onto reality by a fingernail.

"Hey, boy," Stu said, taking a step Ernest's way.

But Saskia put herself bodily between the man and *her* dog. "Hands off."

He backed up in shock. "Steady on."

"Steady...?" She barked out a laugh, encroaching while he continued to back away. "Stu, you stole from me. And more than just my things. You're so lucky I felt like so much of a fool after you left that I didn't press charges."

His soft brown eyes slanted back to hers before flickering quickly away.

"You know it too. So why on earth have you come back?"

He looked at her, hard, and she saw the cool beneath those warm eyes. The calculation. God, the guy must have seen her coming from a mile away.

"And if you even dare say you missed me—"

"I wasn't going to."

She flinched, but she didn't let him see it. "Spit it out, Stu, and then you can get the hell out of my house."

He took a breath, his lean chest lifting and falling, his expression more hangdog than puppy dog. "I'd like to repay my debt."

That time there was no hiding her shock. As long as she'd

known him he hadn't made a cent from anything other than unemployment benefits. "Wow. Did you sell something? Apart from my gear, I mean? Did you sell your book?"

The flicker of surprise in his eyes told her he'd probably not written another word of the mysterious text.

"Then how? Five dollars a fortnight out of your dole payment? It would take you years."

He lifted his chin as if she'd wounded his pride. "If that's what it takes."

The idea of having this man in her life for all that time, of getting fortnightly reminders of the fool she'd been, made her want to rip her new TV off the wall and give it to him if it meant never to having to see him again. And by the look of him he'd have taken it too.

"You should know I am so pissed off right now—even more than when you left if that's at all possible. So before I tie you to the chair and call the cops, tell me: why are you here? Honestly."

"It was made clear to me that this was my only option."

"*Clear?* By *who?*"

A flash of malice crossed his face before he reached into the back pocket of his torn jeans and pulled out a business card. A card with "BonAventure Capital" written in a perfect black font on a perfect white card.

"I don't understand."

"That guy Mackenzie came and saw me yesterday. We had a conversation about responsibility and recompense."

If the card hadn't convinced her Nate was involved in Stu's reappearance, that did.

"He told me to come here, to pay you back, to…*apologise,* or else."

"Nate *threatened* you?"

"Not in so many words. He made it clear he was a better judge of my priorities than I was."

The irony was not lost on her. She'd spent the better part of a year believing—erroneously—that she'd convinced Stu she was the better judge of what was good for him, while Nate had actually convinced him with one conversation.

She didn't realise she was rubbing at her temple until she'd pressed her thumb to the spot hard enough to leave a mark. Why? Why would Nate have done this to her?

Did he want *his* money back? It made no sense.

Her phone rang. She instinctively rose then she heard Lissy take it. She'd forgotten Lissy was even there. It brought her back to reality with a thud.

"I'd like you to leave, Stu. And this time please don't ever come back."

"But—"

"I'll deal with this," Saskia said, flicking at the corner of the business card.

"So that's it? You're not calling the cops?"

"You really think I would have strapped you to a chair?"

He glanced at the plump love seat behind her, and of everything he'd told her that day it was the only thing that made her smile. Despite all his nasty words, he actually thought her strong enough to take care of *herself*. From that moment on she was certain she'd never forget it either.

"Go," she said, pointing at the door, "before I change my mind."

He nodded. Smarter than she'd ever given him credit for. Then, as he made to move, he said, "You're different. It suits you."

"While you're exactly the same."

He took it as the insult it was meant to be, then walked out through her door. And this time she couldn't have been happier to see him go.

On wobbly legs Saskia moved to the lounge and sat. Ernest uncurled himself from the bed and came over to rest his chin on her knees. She rubbed his soft wiry ears. "I know, boy. I know. But this is better. Beyond better."

A minute later Saskia felt Lissy sink down on the chair beside her.

"You okay?"

Saskia lifted her head to look into her friend's big worried eyes. "I'm fine. We're both fine—aren't we, Ernie? We're survivors. We'll be just fine."

"Men suck," said Lissy.

"Some," Saskia said, as she rubbed noses with Ernest before he padded off to the kitchen in search of crumbs. "Some stick up for you when you least expect it. Who was on the phone?"

"Nate."

Nate.

"I said you'd call him back."

Saskia let out a long, slow breath. One man situation sorted; a whole other one to endure. She'd thought her relationship with Stu was complicated, but now it seemed two-dimensional and black-and-white compared with the situation with Nate.

When Saskia made to stand Lissy pressed her back to the couch. "Leave it for a bit. Catch your breath. Have a glass of wine. Hell, have a bottle. Nate can wait."

"You know what?" Saskia said, standing. "I'm done waiting."

She felt as if she'd been waiting her whole life for men to make up their damn minds. A little pressure here, a nudge or two there, giving them the time, the place, the opportunity, the incentive, the dossier with its encouraging white spaces, the yellow legal pad covered in blatant questions so that they'd open up to her, let her in, love her. And none of it had worked.

She tossed a jacket over her maxi-dress, pulled on the closest pair of shoes at hand, stuck a scarf round her neck and a hat on her head and grabbed her bag.

It was time she did this face-to-face, woman to man, to stop tiptoeing and just have it out.

Saskia worked her way through the maze of Nate's home, up three stairs, turn right, down seven, split levels and closed doors, thinking how hard the guy made it to get into his home, much less his life.

Finally she was out in the wide open living area, all blonde wood trim and gunmetal-grey paint. The ceiling was all vicious angles and the place smelled of chopped wood and leather and a spice she couldn't name. No warm-blooded human being would ever choose to live there. And yet Nate did.

She saw him in the kitchen, tasting something he was cooking on the stove. It stopped her short. He cooked? How had she not known he cooked? And it smelled…amazing. It smelled like the best of Mamma Rita's.

But she was not to be deterred by the fact the man could cook…

When Saskia threw her bag—containing the legal pad and dossiers for incontrovertible proof should she need it—on the slab of rock that constituted his kitchen bench, Nate looked up.

"Men suck!"

He stood taller, wiping a towel across his mouth. "Why, thank you."

"Bamford dumped Lissy, you know."

"I didn't, in fact."

"Yet you don't seem shocked. Why? Lissy rocks. He was lucky to know her, much less…the rest!"

"She does. He was. But you have to admit they were an unlikely couple."

Unlikely? No more unlikely than a hippy statistics maven and the King of Collins Street. At that she began to pace.

"Would you like a drink?" he asked, tilting his chin at a bottle of red wine. "Can I take your hat? Scarf? Jacket?"

She glanced down at her outfit and blinked. From the floppy felt hat to the floaty beige dress, the dressy caramel jacket, ancient multi-coloured scarf and the knee-high ugg boots she only ever wore at home, she looked like the result of a market stall explosion. Whipping off the layers and tossing them at a bar stool, she wondered what she'd been thinking. *Oh, that's right...*

"On the subject of men sucking…"

She pulled the card from her bag and tossed it to him. Damn jock snapped it out of the air easy as you please.

"Why?" she asked, and that one word was filled with more emotion than she'd thought any one word could be. Because his response would give her the answer she'd wanted more than any other in her entire life.

"Closure."

And like a whip across the face she got it. *Closure.* Of course. Right in the moment she realised she was in love with the guy he was plotting his extrication. The end. *Finito.*

It was Stu all over again. Only this time he wasn't making off with her TV while she was out working. He was taking her heart, in broad daylight, right in front of her face.

Knees buckling, she sat on a wooden barstool. Hard.

Nate moved around the bench and slowly slid to the stool beside hers, his knees close enough that she could feel his latent heat.

"Why?" she said, needing more, needing every last skerrick of data to understand fully.

"You're better than him. Better than any man who needs a restraining order to keep him away from you. Better than every damn bozo you pass on the street. I thought you needed to look Stu in the eye to see that. To know you're better off without a TV, without a fridge, without a coffee maker if it means not being with a man like him."

Her eyes flickered to his to find his blue eyes serious. No

charm, no pretence, just Nate. And even while everything inside her felt as if it was unravelling her love for him was like
a constant warm hum.

"Then you didn't find him to get your money back."

His raised eyebrows reminded her he'd met the guy.

"Or in the hopes I'd want to get back together with him?"

This time Nate looked as if *he'd* been slapped. Better at her
at the dissembling thing, he pulled himself together far quicker,
his jaw hardly clenching as he said, "Why? Are you?"

"Good God, no!"

He breathed out long and slow, and his voice was a little
raw when he said, "You don't let me get away with anything,
and yet you let him get away with what he did. So I wondered
if maybe it was because he…he meant more."

"No," she said. The warm hum was getting louder, fuelled
by a new and faint hope that maybe, just maybe, Nate actually
cared. "He didn't. He doesn't."

"Okay, then."

Only fair he had all the data too, Saskia looked at the hands
twisting in her lap. "Stu wrote me a note, you know."

"Today?"

"Back then. That was why I didn't chase him down and kick
his ass. I didn't want to have to face that…hatred ever again."

"What did it say?" Nate asked, his voice now less raw, as if
had Stu walked through the door he'd not have got another foot
without having his manhood kicked up into his neck.

It helped. It really did. Especially as she made herself remember the words she'd tried so hard to forget. "He called me
emasculating. Controlling. He said that I only ever pretended
to care."

"Hell, Saskia—"

"He was right. In his way. I never loved him, and yet I let
him move into my home. I do that. I try too hard to be what

I think people need me to be. Because what I am has never been enough."

"Saskia," Nate said again, his eyes fierce as they roved over every inch of her face, "Stu's an ass. A petty, sad, small-minded toad. He tried his damnedest to take something away from you—something he knew he'd never have—your fierce spirit. But he failed. Fool only made you shine stronger still."

She wanted to believe him. She wanted it more than she'd wanted anything in her whole life. To believe not just the words but the sentiment, the tenacity, the *possibility*... But if the men in her life had taught her anything it was that potential was a pipedream.

Take a man as he is, or don't take him at all.

"You think I shine?"

"I know you shine."

"You couldn't have just said so?"

No, his expression said, *he couldn't.* Almost as if he knew she'd read too much into it.

But, hand to his heart, Nate said, "I'm sorry to the tips of my very everything that I forced you to have to see him again."

Her mouth twisted and she couldn't drag her eyes from the hand across his heart. "Do you plan on tracking down all the men who've wounded me?"

"If that's what it takes."

She laughed despite herself. "I keep telling you I don't need you to take care of me."

"And yet once in a while it would be nice if you just shut up and let me." His brows knitted together. Then, "Odd."

Not odd, she thought. Sweet. Darling. But the fact that he couldn't see it, didn't understand what it might mean, scared her silly.

"It's not your job to make up for their shortfalls," she said.

"Not yours either."

"Yeah. I guess you're right."

"I am right. Always."

She coughed out a laugh, her eyes landing on her bag with the legal pad therein—all the things he'd revealed whether he'd wanted to or not.

"Not always."

"Oh, really?"

"Every mistake I've made has been in a full-bodied effort to find my place, my people. While you have it all, right at your fingertips, and you're determined to throw it away."

She felt Nate still even before her eyes swung back to his.

You have me too, she said with her eyes. *If you want me.* But the stillness didn't abate. If anything it cooled about ten degrees, and she knew she had her answer. Even if he saw, even if he had any kind of sense of how she felt, he clearly didn't want to.

"I appreciate it," he said. "I do. From afar."

She'd never seen him look more like granite personified. He looked as if he'd been born of the grey walls and blond wood, and faux taxidermy. Maybe that was what the designer had seen. The *true* heart of the man—cold as any stone.

"I wonder if you know how far away you are. You're way over there. And you don't let anybody come close. Not your gorgeous family, who adore you to their very ends. And certainly not me. Paying me off, bringing me Stu, reminding me every two seconds that the end is nigh. Love isn't poison, Nate. It won't kill you. It's natural, it's complicated, its crazy-making, but it's a fact of life."

"Like death and taxes."

Saskia threw her hands in the air and swore like a sailor. "Why the hell am I bothering? You're a lost cause. I knew it, and still it didn't stop me."

"Stop you, what?"

"Oh, no. All you're getting from me any more is exactly

what I want to give—which right now is less than diddly-squat."

She wouldn't have thought a man could be as still as Nate was in those next moments. While she had so much energy pouring through her she wanted to stamp her feet and throw her arms in the air, he didn't even blink.

Then he said, "You constantly—and I mean constantly—amaze me."

Her eyes cut to his.

"Such a little thing, with so much fight in you."

"It's not fight. It's passion. Verve. *Joie de vivre.*"

One eyebrow slid north. If she'd had a bow and arrow and any kind of athletic skill she'd have shot him between the damn things.

"Nate," she said, her hands out in supplication. *Give me a sign. Give me a break!*

He caught her hands to him and didn't let go. "Cards on the table."

Her heart stopped. From one beat to the next—nothing. Then she curled her fingers into his and her blood began to race. "Fine. You first."

He laughed, the sound soft, raw, the loveliest sound in the entire world. "You started it, sweetheart. Tell me what you came here to say. It'll be okay. I promise."

Saskia breathed out hard. The man had more charm in his little finger than the rest of the population of Melbourne combined. Maybe she could tell him that.

He looked into her eyes. She'd never felt him more present, never seen the real him so clearly in the beautiful fathomless blue.

"I'm just a man, Saskia. Flesh and blood and instinct. I don't know what you want unless you tell me."

She could tell him. She could. It was simple after all.

Name: Saskia Bloom
Age: twenty-eight
Looking for: a way to tell the man sitting before her that
she's in love for the first time in her life

She took a breath. Tried to still the centrifuge in her mind. To forget herself. And it was like one of those dreams where she felt a scream rising inside her but no matter how wide she opened her mouth no sound came out.

Nate's eyes flickered between hers, then they softened. He turned her hand over in his and lifted it to his mouth, kissing one palm and then the other before letting her go. "Just as I thought. You're no more ready for this than I am."

No! she screamed inside her head. *I'm ready! I've been ready. For ever and always!*

It was just after Stu's awful visit, and Lissy being dumped, and the surfeit want, the need, the desire—it was all a big mess inside her head. A big mess with a solid centre. When it came down to it the thought of laying her heart on the line and being rejected was more than she could bear.

A tear plopped down her cheek before she'd even felt it well in her eye. She wiped it away with the back of her hand, but another followed.

"Don't cry," Nate said.

It was the closest to begging she'd ever heard from the man. "I can't do tears."

Which only made her cry more.

With an oath, he pulled her into his arms. She struggled against him, knowing if she softened she was gone. And she was all she had.

"Hush," he said, his breath against her hair.

A second later, maybe ten, the effort of keeping herself strong crumbled.

He kissed her on the forehead and then, as if it simply wasn't enough, lifted her face with a finger beneath her chin and pressed his lips to hers. The silken heat of his touch flowed through her, even while her whole body was rent with tension.

His kiss was lush, lovely, lost in time. Her mind was a whirl of sensation and sadness.

With a groan she slid off the stool, threaded her hands through his hair and sank against him, imprinting herself on him, and him on her, as if it might be the last chance she'd have to commit him to memory, pouring every ounce of love she felt into that kiss in the hope he'd feel it, know it and understand it without having to be hit over the head with it.

When he pulled away the tears kept on coming.

Love me, she thought, *love me, love me, like I love you.*

Smiling—*smiling!*—he pressed her hair from her cheeks. "You'll be just fine, Saskia Bloom. I know it. I knew the first moment I saw your picture. You're content. You have your house, your dog, your work, your friends. Your life is in a groove that's made for you. I envy you that."

"I want…more," she said, as close to admitting anything as she'd come.

He shook his head once, then, looking her right in the eye, said, "When you told me what you wanted in a relationship, back at The Cave that night when you refused to come home with me…?"

Saskia nodded, astounded that it felt like such a long time ago.

"You talked about meeting a guy, moving in together, getting married?"

She nodded again, knowing as she pictured all those things that even then she'd imagined those things with him.

"You never once mentioned being in love."

Saskia stopped nodding. The glorious self-pity fled and she shook her head a little as she tried to unearth that memory in its entirety. "Of course I did."

"No," Nate said. "You didn't."

But she *did*. She wanted to be in love and loved with so much of herself her lungs tightened to fists at the very thought. And yet she couldn't open her mouth and say so.

But *he* was the one with the walls, not her. She wanted him, she loved him—couldn't he damn well stop talking rubbish and look at her? It was pouring out of her!

But with a kiss to the end of her nose he extricated himself from her embrace and stepped back, then another step and then he moved around to the other side of the bench to check his pasta sauce and it felt as if he'd walked a mile.

And his words finally came through. *You'll be just fine,* he'd said. Meaning she'd be just fine without him.

She stood on shaky legs and collected her things. She waited until her throat wasn't so tight she could barely swallow, then said, "Nate?"

He turned, faced her across the kitchen. And she wondered if he knew what she was going to say before she did.

"I don't see how… I'm so sorry, but I can't go to Mae's wedding with you."

"Yeah," he said, frowning at his shoes before looking back at her, all dark and impenetrable, his thoughts kept from her behind the deep, dark tunnel of his eyes. "I wondered about that too."

She just looked at him in silence. Her throat a dry wasteland where words could apparently no longer pass.

"Consider this my breaking off our agreement."

He lifted his hands and tore the air and her heart snapped right in two. She heard it. *Ping* and *crack*. And then a *swoosh* as air filled the crevasse.

"Thank you," she said.

He'd broken her heart and she'd *thanked* him. She might not have pressed charges on Stu, but she'd never thanked the guy! She was clearly way more screwed up than she'd thought.

Nate said, "It's been my absolute pleasure."

And with that she turned and walked away.

As she drove off in her newly fixed old car she was glad it seemed to know the way home because her mind was anywhere but on the road.

Reliving every second, every nuance, every touch, every glance, she felt as if Nate had known why she'd come, and he'd carefully turned her about until she no longer knew what she was thinking.

Before she'd gone over there it had felt so much like love. Now it hurt like love, it burned like love, but with her genetic make-up—a transient femme fatale and a shut-in who pined his life away—who the hell was *she* to know?

CHAPTER TEN

NATE SAT ON the couch in his office in battered old track pants and a tank, trainer-clad feet on the coffee table, head resting on the back of the couch. His yoga mat remained curled up in the cupboard, along with his free weights and a folded-up rowing machine, while the sun set over Melbourne, sending long shadows across the room and turning his blue-and-white office a dreamy pinkish-gold.

Nate nudged his shoes off by the heels and slowly lowered his feet to the carpet. It was even softer than it looked. No wonder it had cost a mint. Hitching his pants, he curled his toes into the pile and closed his eyes.

And not for the first time in the past few days, behind his closed lids he saw Saskia.

This time it was barefoot, not five metres from where he sat, the sun shining through her unassuming clothes, revealing a figure you'd never guess would be hidden underneath that op-shop exterior.

Then he saw her lying back in his bed, dark tousled hair splayed out on his pillow, eyes sleepy and sensual as she looked up at him, hooked a hand behind his neck and pulled him down to make love to her.

He saw Saskia, her eyes fierce as she told him to loosen up, to open up, accept ruffling, to be a human being.

He saw Saskia, her face mottled with tears as she told him it was over.

"Here you are."

Nate looked up to see Gabe, laptop bag over his shoulder as he prepped to head home for the day.

"Where else would I be?" It was meant to be a joke, but in the beat of silence both were all too aware it was the blatant truth of Nate's life.

"Beer?" Nate asked.

"Don't have to ask me twice." Gabe dropped his bag and liberated two bottles from the bar below Nate's bookshelves. He snapped the tops off the bottles, sank down on the other end of the couch and said, "So, out with it."

Nate finished a mighty swig, then said, "With what?"

"The reason you're sitting here pouting like a little girl."

No point denying it. "Saskia and I broke up." Knowing it was one thing. Saying it out loud made it feel real. Right behind his ribs. He took another swig.

"She with whom you were never actually going out?"

"Seems we were in the end."

"Yeah, I know."

"How's that?"

"Gut told me. And Paige confirmed it. According to her, you're seriously cute when you're in *lurve*."

"I'm not in…*anything*. As evidenced by the fact that I am no longer seeing her."

"Lady's choice?"

Nate thought back to their conversation a few nights before. Okay, so he'd thought it over a lot. Over and over. The twists and turns, the moments when he'd felt as if it was about to fall the other way before it flipped again, leaving his chest tight. He'd thought clinching an impossible investment deal was a rush, but being with Saskia was that times a thousand.

Had been, he reminded himself. Then took another swig.

"Yeah." Gabe answered himself, giving Nate a thump on the shoulder. "Man, I'm sorry. I liked her. Paige liked her. Mae

162   FAKING IT TO MAKING IT

was on the verge of asking her to be another bridesmaid. Now, *that* woman is off her tree. If she wasn't Paige's best friend…"

"Poor Clint," they said in unison.

Laughter followed and Nate knocked his bottle against Gabe's. Friendship healed. And it felt good. A relief, even. A need met.

Even while he told himself he needed nothing but the business he'd built, the independence he'd earned, life was better with Gabe in it.

In fact life had been better these past weeks than he remembered it being in a long time. Simpler. Lighter. Easier. He'd seen more of his family than he had in months. His circle of friends—not merely acquaintances but actual friends—had grown without him even realising it, and it felt good.

And he'd had Saskia to thank for it all.

"Wedding's Saturday, remember? So who's the lucky girl you'll be taking now?"

Nate sat forward, rubbed his hands over his face. "No one I guess. I'll go alone."

"Don't say it too loud. The Mackenzie women *will* hear."

"Tough luck. I'm done."

"No more breaking hearts and taking names? Love her, don't you?"

Beyond feigning ignorance as to whom Gabe was referring, Nate moved his gaze to a spot in the middle distance. "I like her. I like being with her. I think about her when I'm not with her. She's bossy, and I like that. But…" The fight seeped out of him as the truth seeped in. "Not that I have anything to compare it to."

"Comparison's not the point, mate. You don't love her or you do."

The sun must have dropped below the horizon because the sensor lights in his office flickered on, casting a cool glow over the room. "Not that it makes any difference. As much as we drive each other crazy…we'd drive each other crazy."

"And that's a bad thing?"

It was messy, challenging, a fight he couldn't always win. It was full-on, distracting, time-consuming. It was emotional, painful, exhilarating. It was anything but bad. It was the most fun he'd had his entire adult life.

"Welcome to the club, mate; your pass and monogrammed towel are in the mail," said Gabe.

"Too bad I spent my last hour with her carefully convincing her there was nothing between us then."

"Ain't over till the fat lady sings."

"So why do I get the feeling I've turned up at the opera house a day late and a dollar short?"

Gabe gave Nate a pat on the back and curled him into a bear hug that thumped the breath from his lungs. Then, clearing his throat, pressed to his feet with a speed that belied his size. "You're coming Saturday." It wasn't a question.

"I think the best gift I could give Mae and Clint would be my *not* coming."

With a final slap on the cheek, like an old Italian mamma, Gabe left Nate to his misery. To the knowledge that he loved a woman who didn't love him. Or, by the dawning realisation in her eyes, didn't love him enough.

He sank his head into his hands and rubbed at his temples. Damn her big brown eyes. She'd turned him soft and then sent him off into the world a great big marshmallow.

Only it didn't make him feel soft. He felt strong with it. As if he'd been running on quicksand his whole life and now the ground beneath his feet had solidified, letting him slow down, see the world as it happened not as a blur as he chased the future.

Saskia. Sweet, interfering, dogmatic, stubborn, gorgeous Saskia. Who'd lived her life on quicksand too. He wondered if she knew it. If she felt it. If that was what she'd seen in him. A like soul. Her match. His complement.

Yet still she'd walked away.

And he'd let her go.

It was the night before the wedding and, as Nate tended to do, he leant in the doorway while the women in his life took over his mum's lounge room—Jasmine with her eyes flicking to her twin boys, playing with his old train set, making sure they weren't hatching plots for world domination, Hope reading an eBook with her legs hanging over the leg of the couch, Faith flicking channels on the TV so fast it made Nate's head spin.

When his temple began to throb he did something about it, grabbing the remote out of Faith's hand and switching off the damn TV.

Faith's "Hey!" got everyone's attention.

Good. He had something to say.

They wouldn't like it. In fact they might all turn on him. But he couldn't not say it. He'd *not* said quite enough things the past few days, and it was eating him from the inside out.

"I have a confession." With that four sets of sharp feminine Mackenzie eyes swung his way.

Jasmine spoke first and, grinning, said, "Do tell, oh, brother mine."

"It's about Saskia."

"I *knew* it!" Faith said, her squeal near breaking the sound barrier.

Hope, meanwhile, gave him a small smile, a tilt of her head, encouraging him to go on.

"Saskia and I were never actually dating." No, not exactly true. And this was a time for truth. The idea of anything else made him feel more exhausted than a man with his youth, stamina and ripping good health had a right to feel. "Not in the way we made you believe we were."

"I don't understand," his mother said as she came to sit on

the arm of the chair nearest him, her forehead creased with concern, her heart in her eyes.

The threat of emotion swarmed over him, but rather than pressing it back, pretending it didn't exist, he merely held it at bay, letting it lift and subside like a lunar tide.

"I found her online with the express purpose of taking her to Mae's wedding as my date, merely to keep you lot from finding one for me."

Silence stretched to the outer reaches of the big room, broken only by the click and whir of the old wooden train set, whose batteries were winding down.

"I don't understand," said his mother.

"It was fake," Faith said, as if trying to make sense of it herself. "The relationship. The affection. The attraction. All of it."

Not all of it, no. But he knew them well enough to know any flicker of hope would be fanned into a flame. So he chose his words carefully.

"We made a deal that was mutually beneficial to us both."

"Good God, you *paid* her?" Faith asked, incredulous.

"Don't say it like that," he bit out, turning on Faith so fiercely her eyes bugged out of her head. He reined himself in a notch. "Don't even think it. The details of our agreement are none of anybody's business but our own. But, since we involved you in the ruse, it's fair that you know the only reason she went along with it as long as she did was because she had this crazy compulsion that I needed her help."

"If anyone needs help it's you, brother." That was Hope.

Nate puffed a laugh from his nose, grateful she was in the room. Grateful they all were, to tell the truth, and that he could finally say what he had to say. And by the way they were listening they would know he meant it.

"I wasn't thinking anything bad about her, Nate," Faith said, drawing his eye. "I've met her, remember? She's way too cool for you. But I *am* flabbergasted that my darling, dashing big brother actually thinks any woman would need an inducement to be with him."

God, was that a tear? He couldn't take tears.

"Faith, you've missed the point. I went miles out of my bloody way to find a woman to *not* be with me."

That met with silence.

"I don't want marriage. I don't want a partner." His hand was running up the back of his hair before he could stop himself. "I want to date who I want and when I want; without you all—or anyone, in fact—expecting it might one day lead to me settling down. It's just *never* going to happen."

"Why?" his mother asked, rising now to take his hand, to look into his eyes. "The truth. All of it."

Jasmine had one of her boys, was hugging him tight, as if telling herself her own son would never feel that way. Faith watched, tears at the corners of her eyes. Hope breathed evenly, smiled softly and simply waited, as if she'd been waiting for the truth—all of it—all her life.

"I was there," Nate said. "After Dad died. Missing him, mourning him. I still think about him every day." He fisted a hand in the front of his sweater. "But I don't *ever* want to feel that much need and hurt and empathy and rage and love and fear again."

Hope slid gracefully to her feet and came over and gave him a hug. Then punched him hard enough on the arm to hurt. "We know. We watched in dazed amazement how our little big brother handled himself. You were the glue and we may have overused you. For that I apologise. Profusely."

She looked to the others, who all nodded with her.

"But, for the record, while you're stuck with us—interfering, emotional and fabulous as we are—finding that one person out there in the big wide world who you *choose* to be with…well, that's something else entirely. Love is scary and magical and bittersweet and special and hard and wonderful and the best thing that can ever happen to you in life."

He looked around at his sisters—all strong women. All nodding. All of whom had come out the other side, able to throw their hearts into the ring. All hopeful he might still.

And even while he ought to have been setting up a whiteboard, with graphs and charts and a loud hailer to explain how and why it was different for him...all he could think of was Saskia.

Saskia, whom he'd chosen to be in his life, even if only for a finite time. Saskia, who pushed him and challenged him and laughed with him, made room for him. Saskia, who made him feel light and funny and free. Saskia who made him *feel*.

Bittersweet didn't even begin to describe the pleasure and the pain. The pleasure of knowing her. The pain of losing her. *Hell.*

"I have to go," he said, his voice raw.

"Yeah, yeah, yeah," said Faith as she gathered up the remote.

Hope shot him a wink before sliding down onto the floor to play train smash with the boys. And Jasmine, relieved of duty, leant back against her wall and closed her eyes.

"We heard you, darling. No more matchmaking," his mother promised as she walked him to the door. "Though you can never make us promise not to hope you'll one day find her. Or that maybe you already have."

"Mum—"

"You've said your piece. My turn. You always were such a stubborn boy. Once you put your mind to something—whether it was building the best linen fort ever seen, or looking after all of us after Nathan died—that was it. Your father was stubborn too, you know. But his stubbornness was inclusive. And even though he died too young, he died happy. Nurtured. Inspired. Deeply touched by love. I'd hate to see you regret any choices you might have made in powering that stubborn streak with fear, not love."

She gave him a kiss, then near shoved him out through the

door—likely so his womenfolk could dismantle every word he'd said. Either way, he *had* said his piece.

Crazy that the hardest part had been admitting that he and Saskia had been faking it. Maybe because amidst the hard truths that was a big fat lie.

He waited for dread to set in at the very thought, but instead felt…nothing. As if the tide of emotion that had swelled earlier had abated, leaving him bereft. Empty. Missing her. Her warmth, laughter and charm. The way she kissed, the way she melted against him, her feelings for him gleaming from her honest brown eyes.

He shoved his hands in the pockets of his jeans and took a deep breath of fresh air—and reminded himself of the likelihood he'd never see her again.

Now she was gone. Gone from his life. His days. His nights. His everything.

And like *that* the dread was there. Engulfing him like a wave of fury that he could have been so stupid.

His mother was right. And Hope. And even Faith.

He *did* use his obstinacy as a shield. He *did* need help. And Saskia *was* way too cool for him.

And yet he was in love with Saskia Bloom. He loved the woman with a conviction and certainty he could no longer deny. And he'd seen it in her eyes, felt it in her touch, tasted it in her tears—she'd been right there with him in every possible way.

Afraid to love, afraid not to.

"Hell," he said, this time out loud, and he kicked the porch so hard he limped out to the car.

Saturday morning Saskia headed to Dating By Numbers, her infographic in tow.

She could have emailed—it would have taken five seconds flat—but she wanted to see Marlee. The woman might be part shark, but she was smart, she had knowledge, and she'd seen through Saskia in a red-hot second. If anyone could smack her out of this funk it would be the wizard behind the pink curtain.

"Saskia," Marlee said, with honest pleasure in her eyes before she hid it behind a cool smile.

"I wanted to give you this." Saskia had framed it. It was a work of art—quite simply the cutest thing Lissy had ever whipped up.

Marlee's eyes roved over the hopeful colour, the joyful curlicues, the straight stats and romantic hooks, a smile lighting her eyes as she saw "follow your heart" scrawled across the bottom.

"Thank you. It's darling."

"So glad. Take a day to look it over, in case you want any changes, then I'll send it to the digital marketing team and get it moving."

Marlee looked over at Saskia, her eyes narrowing as she took the whole of her in. It seemed jaunty knee-high boots, skinny jeans, winsome floral top and fabulous faux fur jacket had been pipped by blurry eyes and a permanent crease above the nose.

"Coffee?"

"Sure." Why not? She had nowhere else to be.

Saskia followed Marlee into her office. Bit her lip. Held her breath. Then spat out the question that had been hovering on her lips since the moment she'd decided to come calling. "Can I ask you one last thing?"

"What's that?"

"How many find The One?"

"You want numbers?" Marlee asked, a red talon flicking towards the screen of her computer.

"I want...*hope.*"

Marlee turned, coffee forgotten. "Then the numbers don't matter. The odds against only exist because of the odds for. In the end all that matters is you. And your guy. The rest is gravy."

"Gravy."

Taking Saskia by the hands, Marlee led her to a big squishy white couch in the corner. "I wasn't going to say, but last time you were here I would have bet my fortune you'd been struck by cupid's arrow. Now you look like you've been hit by a truck, which then backed up and ran over you again. What happened?"

What happened? Even she wasn't sure. She'd thought over that last conversation so many times, yet couldn't get a grasp on what had gone wrong. What she'd missed. She just felt right deep down in her gut that there had been a moment when she could have had it all, and instead she'd let it slip through her fingers.

She'd been so sure she loved Nate—until he'd convinced her otherwise. And yet days later it still felt like love, it still hurt like love, burned like love and yet she still couldn't be sure.

Saskia took a deep breath, then said, "I met a man—"

"On my site?"

Saskia nodded. "I met a man, dated him, fell in love—and screwed it all up."

"Happens every day."

"Heartening."

"Mmm. You know what else happens every day? People realise the errors of their ways and make up for it."

"How?"

"Any which way they damn well can."

"You're good at this. Are you married? I'm sorry. It's none of my business."

"No, I think that's a fair question, considering what I peddle. I *was* married. Many years ago. To a bear of a man with a big prickly beard and a laugh that stopped time. He passed away too young. And I've never found it again. Maybe because I had my one chance, or maybe because I've never put myself out there."

Saskia looked at the woman. Beneath her class and elegance and her sharp tongue she nursed a broken heart.

"My father lived with a broken heart," Saskia said, "his whole life. I always thought it rather romantic. And thus spent my whole childhood trying to make up for it, getting nothing in return. I thought that was love, but now I wonder if I haven't been completely reactionary—treating every relationship as an 'I'll show you, you mean bastard.' As if even *one* of them loved me it would prove, to a dead man, that I was right and he was wrong."

"Understandable," Marlee said.

"Yeah—'understandable' has pretty much driven me my whole life. But it hasn't helped me sleep much the past few days."

"In my experience nothing beats a warm pair of male arms for that." Marlee patted her on the hand and went to get the coffee.

Marlee was right—each person reacted as they chose to react and each had to live with the consequences.

As she thought about her choices to date and their consequences, and Nate—out there, loved and not knowing it. For her there was no choice.

"I want love," she said out loud. Then louder, arms out to the world, as if she'd been born again, "I'm Saskia Bloom and I want to love *and* be loved."

Marlee hovered in the doorway, her smile soft before it spread into a grin. "Now, this poor fellow we quite purposely have neglected to mention, is he a man of unparalleled excellence? Is he a man of manners and charm and fantastic genes? Is he a possibility partner for life?"

She'd never looked for a partner.

Sharing herself, leaning on him, taking his advice, listening to him—none of that had much come into it. Until Nate. That strong, blind, charming, heartbreaking, stubborn, oak of a man had never let her get away with steering on her own. He'd imposed himself as much on the relationship as she had. In equal measure.

As if the curtains had been parted and the light let in, suddenly a whole new possibility opened up to her—the possibility of a life not for him but *with* him.

It felt like a brave new world. Was she brave enough to see it through? If any man had made her feel safe enough to try it was Nate. Vulnerable enough to love it was Nate. Happy enough to let him take care of her as much as she took care of him it was Nate.

She didn't need Marlee to give her hope. She had more than enough to push her from the chair, give Marlee a hug and a kiss, and walk…no, *run* from the room.

It was just after ten on the first Saturday in spring. She had a date.

CHAPTER ELEVEN

THAT WAS A hundred-dollar blow-dry wasted, Saskia thought as she wobbled down the stone steps that led to Blairgowrie Beach, one hand on her hair, trying to keep the once slick waves from turning wild in the whipping wind.

As for the dress—foxy, floaty, seriously *va-va-voom* and chosen to blow Nate's socks off—it suddenly felt too fantastical, too sexy, too lacking in fabric for a beach wedding on a blustery spring day. Not surprising since she'd bought the thing when high on burgeoning love.

Goosebumps danced up and down her arms. But there was no going back now. She was there on a mission. She was a strong woman, a business-owner, a home-owner, a DIY decorator who had laid her own bathroom tiles. She had a tattoo and had swum with sharks. She could tell a man she loved him even if there was no certainty she'd hear the same back.

Holding herself together—just—she scanned the crowd scattered along the narrow beachfront.

She spotted Paige and Gabe, chatting to an older couple—Mae's parents, judging by the twin sets of vibrant red hair. Lissy and Bamford were there together, but as friends, not lovers, and the two of them were cheerfully laughing at something Lissy had said. Even Clint and Mae were about—Clint chatted with friends in suits, many wearing no shoes, and Mae was on the other side of the crowd, spinning in a slinky backless number, the cool sea air clearly not touching her at all.

And then the crowd parted and there he was. The man she loved.

Seeing Nate after being sure she'd never see him again amazed and terrified her. As for the bone-deep knowledge that she adored the guy and had every intention of making him believe her... That made her knees positively quake.

Especially when he looked the antithesis of ruffled—clean-shaven, with sunlight glinting off his neat dark blond hair, in a suit that made the most of the glory beneath it and with his eyes covered with sexy sunglasses. He looked...perfect.

He brought a glass of champagne to his lips as he turned to survey the crowd, and she knew the moment he spotted her. His hand stilled, his mouth kicked at one corner, and his chest fell as he breathed out long and slow.

The tinkling of laughter, the clinking of champagne glasses, the soft *swoosh* of waves lapping at the shore—faded till all Saskia could hear was the thundering of her heart.

He excused himself, put his champagne on a passing tray, shoved one hand in a trouser pocket and walked towards her. She ditched her heels as they kept sticking in the soft sand and walked towards him, meeting him halfway.

When he came close he took off his sunglasses and she could see the smudges under his eyes, the worry lines etched at their edges. And, since he looked just how she felt, her heart gave a thumpety-thump because it might have something to do with her.

"Hi, Nate," she said, her voice hearteningly strong.

"Saskia."

He leaned in to kiss her cheek and stayed there a beat past familiar. A beat into want. She let her eyes close, filled herself with his warmth and his heady scent. Before she did anything stupid like throw herself into his arms, she pulled away.

"Credibility?" she asked.

His eyes didn't leave hers as a small smile curved the corner of his mouth. "Not this time."

Her heart thudding like a runaway hammer, Saskia glanced over his shoulder at the wedding party in the distance. "I had to come. I couldn't disappoint Mae. She did help me finish my online dating research, after all."

He tilted his chin in understanding and the smile curving at the corner of his mouth kicked a little higher. "Well, I'm glad you came. In fact I have something for you. Brought it just in case."

She looked down to see a small silver bag with frothy silver paper poking out of the top. "You do realise the bride and groom are the only ones meant to be getting gifts today?"

"We got them a toaster."

"Did we, now?" she asked, cool as she pleased, even while her stomach soared at his use of "we." She tried to mentally slap it down but it continued to buzz along happily.

Paige waved to Saskia across the beach, started to move, then saw she was with Nate and took a ninety-degree angle away from her.

Saskia's hand shook as she took Nate's gift. His finger brushed hers and a spark shot between them—the same spark that had been there at the first meeting. The one she'd clung to as she'd fallen deeper and deeper under his disarming charm.

She peeled away the soft silver wrapping to find a solitary bar of goats' milk soap. Her one downfall into decadence. She'd mentioned it maybe once and he'd remembered. And sought it out. And it was near impossible to find. That little shop in the Dandenongs was about the only place you could get it. Meaning he'd gone looking. With her in mind. In an effort to make peace? Or more...?

Blinking, she looked up at him, clueless as to what to say.

"It came in a pack of two," he said. "I kept one for myself. My skin's never felt better."

He smiled his innately charming smile, only this time there wasn't any performance in it. Just him, his eyes roving over her face as if he couldn't quite believe she was there.

When his eyes landed back on hers—blue, hot, hungry—her whole body began to pulse. "Thank you," she said, her voice thick.

"You're most welcome. Now, since I haven't quite got around to finding a standby date, would you care to accompany me?"

He held out his arm; she slid her hand in the crook.

They walked in no particular hurry towards the rest and Saskia said, "I knew you hadn't asked anyone else."

"How's that?"

"Your sister rang just before I came."

"Oh. What did Faith say?" His hand came down on hers, their fingers entwining, and his thumb ran over her wrist, sending waves of heat and hope all through her.

Saskia breathed out, even laughed a tad. "She told me about your family meeting. I'm so proud of you, Nate. Now, hold onto them with everything you have. Know how lucky you are to have them at all."

"I will. I do."

And since he'd given her an opening she saw no reason not to take it. "She also said you were pining."

Nate laughed. "Terror."

"She's softer than you think, you know. She's..." *Hang on a second.* "How did you know it was Faith?"

"I'm sorry?"

"It could have been Hope who'd called. Or Jasmine."

"Hmm?"

Saskia tugged at his arm, pulling them both up short. She held a hand to her eyes to shield them from the sun. Noticing, Nate moved to shield her all on his own.

And then it hit her. "You *asked* Faith to call. To casually let slip you were coming alone."

He looked over her shoulder a moment, before his eyes slanted back to hers. "I figured what's the good of having bumptious sisters who won't butt out of my affairs unless I use them for my own nefarious purposes?"

The sun created a halo around his golden head, leaving his eyes dark smudges in his perfectly carved face. But there was no mistaking the glint, the gleam, the need, want, desire, all shifting below the surface.

"Considering how we left things, I wasn't sure you'd have listened to me."

"I'd have listened, and I'd have come." Saskia grabbed a hold of his lapels and gave the big guy a shake. "And not because of any contract. Just because you asked."

While she still held his jacket so tight, not wanting to let him go ever, Nate lifted a hand. It was millimetres from her cheek, a whisper from her skin, when Mae came barrelling up.

"My God, you two look gorgeous. Don't they look gorgeous?" she said to no one in particular. "I just want to stick you on top of my cake and eat you with a spoon. Later, though. It's all about to begin. If you want to join the crowd over there somewhere I'm about to marry the man of my dreams!"

With that she skipped away, her red hair a riot against the blue sky.

Saskia looked back at Nate to find him watching her, his gaze intent, as if his eyes had never left her. "This isn't a dream," he said. "You're really here."

Happiness tugged at her belly and her heart felt too big for her chest. "I'm really here."

"And you do look gorgeous. Beyond gorgeous. In fact—" He lifted his trouser leg to reveal two pairs of socks. "In preparation for having one pair knocked off."

Saskia laughed, the sound floating away on the sea air. "You were confident I'd come!"

"Hopeful," he said, his hand finally landing on her cheek with such care and affection she leant into his touch, into him.

"To hell with it," he growled, enfolding her hand in his and leading her up the beach and up a grassy sandbank behind a bright blue beach hut with a red roof. He turned her to face him and said, "I drove for an hour to go to a shop to buy stuff to make me smell like the milk of a goat. Washed myself in the stuff for days. Because I missed your scent. I missed you. When what I really should have done is this."

And then he kissed her. Hauling her in tight and drinking her in like a drowning man. Only she was the one drowning. In lush waves of pleasure that swirled behind her eyelids like a kaleidoscope of colour and pulsed through her veins all the way to her toes.

When the kiss softened, slowed, till its sweetness nearly broke her apart, Saskia dropped her head to lean her forehead against the solid wall of his chest, the not so steady beat of his heart mirroring the not so steady beat of her own.

"I'm sorry about the other day," she said. "I was in a messy head space—lots of thoughts clashing. And it's not your fault I fell in love with you. You were very clear about what you wanted. I was the one who stepped outside the rules of the game."

"You what?" His hands went to her cheeks, lifting her face to look into his.

"Stepped outside—"

"The other bit."

She swallowed, thought one last time about feigning amnesia then squared her shoulders and looked him right in the eye. She saw so much possibility and potential in him, in her life with him, and it was too amazing to resist.

"I'm in love with you."

Saskia's mouth fell open. It had been Nate who'd spoken. Nate who now had his hands on her upper arms as if he'd sensed her knees had given way.

"You okay?" he asked.

"Not so much."

Looking around, he found a park bench tucked into a private copse of rough-leaved trees on the edge of the beach, and paid the skateboarders perched thereupon a bunch of notes to rack off.

"You love me?" Saskia said as she sank to the bench, the words thick and unfamiliar on her tongue.

"Yeah," said Nate as he perched on the edge of the seat beside her, "I do."

A glance her way, then he ran a hand up the back of his head. But not in a frustrated way—more in a chagrined way. As if he knew he should have said so a hell of a lot sooner. Then his hand fell to hers, wrapping it tight.

"Saskia, I was living in a tunnel, with no light at the end. Then you came along, and suddenly I noticed when I could smell fresh air, when I felt sunshine. I began to notice the stars and the ground at my feet. You, Saskia Bloom, are my earth."

So much emotion swelled inside her there were no words. Just feelings. So many wonderful, tumbling impossibly beautiful feelings. And the knowledge that she held Nate's heart in the palm of her hand. She knew then that she'd take better care of it than she had of anything else her whole life.

"Before I met you," Saskia said, turning to bump knees, to slide a hand onto his smooth cheek, to look deep into his spellbinding eyes, "I was like a mouse spinning on a wheel—fully expecting to reach my desired destination so long as I kept going in the same direction. And then along came you. You showed me another way." She ran a hand through his hair, smiling when the wind took over, ruffling it just a tad. "I'm not sure what I was ever so afraid of."

"Me either."

"This, perhaps?" she asked, sliding her arms around his waist.

"Not so scary."

"How about this?" she said, sliding her hand over his shoulder as she straddled him. Light played through the trees above, shadows dappling eyes not able to hold back the gleam.

His hands went straight to her backside, held on. "Nope. Not that. How about this for scary: I choose you, Saskia Bloom. If you'll have me."

Scary? Try the very meaning of perfection!

"I'll have you, Nate Mackenzie. And have you and have you and have you."

She dipped her head to kiss him. Shock and awe subsided as he kissed her back tenderly, surely, ravishingly. Her very own big, beautiful, sweet, kind, bold master of the universe.

The hum of music rolled over the sandbank and skimmed the edges of Saskia's love-drenched mind. A grunge version of "Wishing and Hoping."

It was Nate who pulled away and said, "Is that…?"

Her ears pricked up. "The band from The Cave!"

"Mae is a crazy woman."

"I like her."

"Yeah," Nate drawled. "I can't quite believe it, but I do too. Meaning we'd better go do this thing."

Nate lifted her off his lap, placed her gently on the sandy grass and helped her back into her shoes. Then, standing, he put the silver bag in one of Saskia's hands and wrapped his arm about her waist, snuggled her in against his side.

When they hit the beach Saskia marvelled at the crisp, perfect blue of the sky, at the sweet fluffy white of the clouds, at the way the sand sparkled like glitter, and asked the one question she'd wanted an answer to that she hadn't put in her dossier.

"Why did you choose me?" Saskia asked. "From the site, I mean."

"The urge to know what retro grunge meant." He waved a hand at the band rocking barefoot by the waves. "That and the fact you had the sexiest eyes I'd ever seen, the sweetest mouth, the most incongruous hat…"

He leaned down to brush a kiss against her mouth and soon Saskia thought breathing was overrated.

They pulled up at the back of the group, and Nate waited until Mae had skipped down the makeshift aisle before asking, "So why did you choose *me*?"

Saskia almost laughed out loud before she realised he was

serious. Sweet man. "Oh. Well, I near didn't. Don't get me wrong—you were adorable. Got me all tingly with one photo. But you looked so uptight." She looked at him now, pink-cheeked from the wind, hair ruffled, tie askew from her ministrations. *Yeah*, she thought, *he so needed me.* "The only thing that made me think we might have anything in common was that *Catch-22* is your favourite book."

Nate looked at her blankly.

"You said so. In your profile."

"I did?"

"It's not?"

"I work a lot. I don't have much time to read."

"Ha! And to think that tipped the odds in your favour. Imagine if you'd gone for *Valley of the Dolls*. Or *Spot Goes to the Park. Twilight*. Ooh, now *that* would have brought you a whole other type of woman calling."

Nate's warm, strong, insistent arm around her waist tightened, his fingers sinking into the flesh at her waist in warning. As warnings went, it only made her want to ramp things up.

Until he looked deep into her eyes and said, "I don't want another type of woman."

Saskia's breath left her lungs in a whoosh. "Do you always know the exact right thing to say?"

"Famously." He grinned, and his charm beamed across the beach till it outshone the sun. "You'd better get used to it."

He planted a kiss on her mouth, sealing the deal.

As heat blossomed inside her Saskia had a funny feeling she'd never get used to Nate. His kindness and his ambition. His loyalty and resolve. His easy smile and deep convictions. His hot touch and the love that blazed in his eyes.

When Gabe noticed they were behind him he made space and smiled at them in a way Saskia was only just beginning to understand. She looked at Nate to find he was watching her.

Love you, he mouthed.

She snuck in a kiss in response, and it occurred to her she'd found her love formula after all. It was as beautifully simple as all the best formulas: Find someone you love who loves you right back.

Then, as Mae married Clint on that windy sunny beach, Saskia lifted her face to the dappled sun and breathed deep of the sea air, her heart filled with such light, such happiness, she wasn't sure she'd ever get used to either.

Though she was going to have a damn fine time trying.

EPILOGUE

NATE CAUGHT THE toast as it popped out of Saskia's ancient second-hand toaster. He knew what to give her for Christmas. Or maybe he'd just bring his own top-of-the-range one over. He spent most nights at hers, after all. Her espresso machine was a thing of the gods.

But it was more than that. Something about the hot little fireplace and the riot of colour, and the over-soft bed it was simply too difficult to get out of in the morning—especially when it was filled with warm, sleepy Saskia. It was a combination far more him than a fake rhino head on the bathroom wall and stuffy leather.

He lathered the hot bread in chocolate spread, popped a corner and threw it over his shoulder, unsurprised when it didn't hit the floor. The thump of Ernest's tail was as good as asking for more.

"Enough," he said, attempting Saskia's stern but loving tone. Ernest just looked at him as if he was kidding. He threw the dog another corner and took off before the canine had the chance to point those big glistening eyes his way.

Saskia looked up from her computer and smiled. Nate's heart squeezed in his chest. It happened every time he laid eyes on her, and yet he found he couldn't get used to it. Hoped he never would.

He pressed a kiss to her waiting mouth. Her willing heat was no surprise. "I'm off."

"Gabe and Paige are coming for dinner."

"Am I invited?"

She rolled her eyes. "You kidding? You practically live here. I should start charging rent. Or maybe you can just bring your toaster over as a down payment. Mine's on its last legs."

It was a done deal. He perched on the edge of her desk. "Should I consider this the start of negotiations?"

"Sure," she said, her mouth kicking up at one corner. "If that floats your boat."

He pulled her out of her chair and into his arms. "*You* float my boat, Saskia Bloom."

When she'd caught her breath, she said, "Lucky, because you float mine." Her sultry eyes darkened as she leant in for another kiss. Soft, sweet, and soon rocketing into something scorching.

Nate pulled away with a groan. "I have to go. Promised Gabe I'd tag-team. New investment prospect has him in a lather."

Not trusting himself, or her, he pressed her back into her chair. Her feet were tucked instantly up under her, and she snuck a pencil between her teeth. *So damn cute,* he thought. *And sexy and smart and sweet and stubborn.* All must-have traits on his new list for the woman in his life.

She grinned around the pencil and began to swivel her chair back and forth, her knees rubbing against his. Lucky he had a car coming for him in five minutes. He wasn't sure he'd be able to drive in his current state.

As he turned to leave she grabbed him by the sleeve of his shirt, her hand curling around his wrist, sending shards of heat up his arm. To think this hot little gamine creature was his. All his.

He already knew he was never letting her go again.

He'd tell her so later, when she was naked in his arms. Trapped. She tended to be more amenable, less stubborn, after he'd loved her into a pile of molten limbs.

"New gig's just come in," she said, pointing the pencil at her flash new computer monitor.

Completely unable to help himself, he leaned over her, sucking in lungs full of her soft morning scent as he looked at the screen. "What am I looking at?"

"Pegasus Motors have taken us on to do a series of infographics. For starters it seems I'm going to *have* to test-drive their entire range of sports models. You can come along if you like."

"I *knew* there was a reason I loved you."

"Just one."

"Okay, two. Maybe three."

One last kiss, he told himself as her hand snuck around his neck and pulled his mouth to hers.

Three quarters of an hour later he zipped his pants and made a run for the door, cold toast between his teeth, Saskia's old copy of *Catch-22* under his arm for the car ride, and ignoring the constant buzzing of his phone.

He told himself Gabe would have to wait.

Hell, the whole world could wait for all he cared.

A man had to have his priorities straight, after all.

* * * * *

THE WEDDING
MUST GO ON

BY
ROBYN GRADY

One Christmas long ago, **Robyn Grady** received a book from her big sister and immediately fell in love with Cinderella. Sprinklings of magic, deepest wishes come true—she was hooked! Picture books with glass slippers later gave way to romance novels and, more recently, the real-life dream of writing for Mills & Boon.

After a fifteen-year career in television, Robyn met her own modern-day hero. They live on Australia's Sunshine Coast with their three little princesses, two poodles and a cat called Tinkie. She loves new shoes, worn jeans, lunches at Moffat Beach and hanging out with her friends on eHarlequin. Learn about her latest releases at www.robyngrady.com, and don't forget to say hi. She'd love to hear from you!

CHAPTER ONE

THE worst possible person at the worst possible time.

Peeking through a gap in her back-room door, Roxanne Trammel admitted that looks weren't the problem. The guest waiting at her Sydney wedding salon's point-of-sale counter was over six feet tall, delectably masculine in demeanour and build...those lidded ice-blue eyes and coal-black hair would set any woman's heartbeat tripping a thousand to one, including her own.

Roxy wanted to shrivel up and die because she *knew* that man. Knew him and more. That she'd slipped into this wedding gown moments ago was only the icing. The not so funny punchline to a bad joke she'd sooner forget.

Out by the counter, a line creased between the dark slashes of Nate Sparks's brows before he caught the time on his Omega then rubbed the back of his neck...the same strong neck Roxy had clung to with such fervour that fateful spring evening when they'd shared their first and only kiss. If she closed her eyes, she could still smell his woodsy scent...feel the graze of his sandpaper jaw along her cheek. The magic his touch stirred deep inside had transported her to another time. Another place. She could admit that she hadn't wanted that kiss to end.

But it had, and in the most cringe-worthy way imaginable.

'Anyone there?'

Angling those linebacker shoulders in their immaculate suit jacket, her visitor called out, then checked behind the counter, around a potted palm, while Roxy bit her lip and wished him gone. She had nothing to say to Nate Sparks and only a limited amount of time to solve the problem surrounding this gown she wore. Make that *problems*—plural. At least three people's futures depended on some answers.

Outside, Nate found some Perfect Dress notepaper on the counter and extracted a thin gold pen from his jacket's inside pocket. Gazing off into the middle distance, he tapped that pen against his strong cleft chin, then, with a swift sure hand, began to write. Roxy poked her nose closer and exquisite Duchess satin rustled against the white-gloss frame.

What could he possibly want to say? *Forgive me for treating you so abysmally. Please come out to dinner.* Not likely. His exit speed would've left a navy torpedo green with envy. Not that he hadn't enjoyed their kiss as much as she had. No one could fake that kind of intensity, even a man who, by all accounts, wasn't short on potential partners. There could be only one explanation for his behaviour that night.

Given they'd met at their respective friends' engagement party and she'd spoken of her profession within the wedding industry in such passionate terms, he must have worried that she'd naturally want to take their amazing first kiss a whole lot further. Like straight down the aisle.

In reality, Roxy believed marriage was an institution not to be taken lightly. Experience said that sustaining a relationship took a whole lot more than the immediate sizzle of emotions and naïve wish for a fairy-tale life. Still, while she might not care to set Nate Sparks straight on her opinion, neither could she hide behind this door for ever. Her sense of dignity, for one, wouldn't allow it.

Shucking back bare shoulders, Roxy filled her lungs, fanned open the door and entered the main room, a long satin stream swishing proudly behind. Nate's attention snapped up and those ice-blue eyes near fell out of his head. Above the knot of his cinnamon-coloured silk tie, his Adam's apple bobbed. A heartbeat later he remembered to smile.

'You're here. I was leaving a note.' His gaze dropped and eyes widened before he pushed out a throaty, nervous laugh. 'Uh, nice outfit. Do you always serve people wearing a wedding gown?'

She couldn't help but bait him.

'Only when I'm feeling lonely.'

When Nate's eyes widened more, Roxy grunted. He didn't know whether to relax and pretend to be a good sport or swap those Pitt Street lace-ups for runners, repeat history and get out while the getting was good. He needn't worry. She'd sooner burn down her shop and play in the ashes than allow him anywhere near her lips again.

Head high, Roxy slipped off her twinkling tiara and set the veil down.

'What can I do for you, Nate?'

'Greg told me this morning. I guess Marla would've told you too.'

She unclipped both diamanté earrings, then weighed them in her palm. After a year-long courtship, 'Their wedding is off.'

The person for whom Roxy had lovingly made this dress was no longer tying the knot. She felt gutted, for Marla's sake mostly but, in truth, also for her own. This gown was the most beautiful she'd ever created…a dress guaranteed to garner interest within industry circles and at a time when she needed it most.

Nate's deep voice lowered more as his gaze intensified. 'Greg's a good friend. My *best* friend.'

'Ditto Marla and me.'

'Dammit, those two belong together.'

'After Marla was slapped in the face by those pictures,' Roxy said, 'she's convinced that they aren't. Frankly, I have to agree with her.'

Roxy's heart flipped over. She knew a little of how Marla had felt. The week after that engagement party incident, Nate's photo had appeared in a gossip magazine. Obviously in his element, he'd been snapped charming a big-breasted woman with swollen lips and hair the colour of rich dark chocolate. Roxy had been so angry—so hurt— she'd torn out the page and ripped it in two.

His jaw tightening, Nate admitted, 'Those photos were incriminating.'

'Her fiancé, intoxicated and handling a near naked woman...' She huffed. 'I don't know what Greg's so-called friend was thinking, publishing those shots on his social media page. And don't you dare say that the "indiscretion" happened at Greg's buck's night. That's no excuse.' Narrowing her eyes, Roxy crossed her arms over her crystal-beaded bodice. 'Where were you anyway? Aren't best men supposed to stop those kinds of things from happening?'

Not that they should ever get anywhere near started.

'I had a meeting early the next morning. I couldn't cancel.'

'I wish things were different—' for more reasons than one '—but Greg did the wrong thing and, frankly, I don't appreciate you showing up here unannounced trying to convince me otherwise.'

She hated seeing Marla so puffy-eyed and bereft. She wished there were some way to help, but listening to a man she already didn't trust, a man who was adept at minimizing bad behaviour—that wasn't the answer. Yes, Greg had always seemed so devoted; however, Roxy knew better than most, sometimes the ones you should be able to rely on were the very ones to watch out for. Given her own past growing up, Roxy supported Marla's decision one hundred per cent. Still, that question remained.

What would become of this gown? She'd held such high hopes for it. For her big designer future.

For months the bridal industry had been abuzz with talk of an incredible opportunity—a contest. The winning gown would take its bow on the Parisian catwalks and feature in *Wedded Bliss*, the world's glossiest wedding publication. Plus, its creator would be awarded a sizable lump sum *and* a year's apprenticeship with New York's leading bridal salon designer.

Roxy had lain awake at night dreaming of claiming the big prize. Since junior high, she'd only ever wanted to design wedding dresses, all kinds of creations to suit all kinds of brides. She couldn't imagine a more exciting or rewarding profession. Five years ago, after completing a number of courses and experience at other shops, she'd set up her own business. But Roxy ached to learn more. *Be* more. All that she could be.

This contest was her chance.

She'd put two hundred per cent into her entry. Last week she'd made the top fifty. She'd bubbled with excitement. For hours had walked on air. But before she could let Marla in on her good news, her friend had broken down and announced that the wedding was off. Since all entries were required to take their big walk down the aisle by the thirty-first of this month, this amazing gown was no longer eligible for final judging. No wedding equalled no apprenticeship. No big prize money either. Suddenly Roxy's recent run of decreased sales and increased bills seemed all the scarier.

Now, while she set the earrings on their red velvet cushion beneath the counter, deep in thought, Nate paced up the length of the counter and Roxy's attention drifted to his hand sliding down the glass surface. It was just a hand, she told herself. Big. Tanned. Four fingers and a thumb, five very neat nails. And yet, despite how he'd embarrassed her that night, she couldn't deny that even now memories of the way he'd held her released a slow wash of tingling warmth deliciously low in her belly. For those few moments when he'd kissed her so thoroughly, her every inch had glowed and come alive, a phenomenon that had left her feeling hot, light and slightly giddy.

A little like she felt now.

Damn the man!

Her cheeks burning, Roxy siphoned down a breath, gathered herself and caught the last of Nate's comment.

'…must be something we can do to get them back together.'

Closing the counter drawer, she refocused on her friend's situation as well as her own. Lifting her chin, Roxy made herself clear.

'Whatever you have in mind, count me *out*.'

As Nate held Roxanne Trammel's determined gaze he knotted his arms securely over his chest.

Of medium height. Nothing bombshell about the body. Voice on the soft rather than smoky side. Her gestures weren't exceptional. Neither were her walk or her laugh. And yet *something* about this woman was incontestably, frustratingly alluring.

Nate accepted that reality same way he accepted that

steel softened at a predetermined temperature. A similar temperature to the one his blood had reached when he'd given himself over to Roxy's lure six months ago. He'd hated leaving her looking so confused and pained that night, but he'd also vowed that their first kiss would be their last: should they happen to come within each other's orbit again—at a mutual friends' wedding, for example— he would not permit a repeat performance, no matter if the continuation of the human race depended on it.

That outfit she wore now ought to be reminder and turn-off enough. He was a self-determining man, a bachelor who intended to stay that way. And yet looking into those thickly lashed, sparkling green eyes now, he had to concentrate to keep from reaching out and making mammoth mistake number two. Only this time—if he caved and brought her crushingly close again—he wasn't certain he would stop.

Crossing to the end of the counter, she said, 'I don't know why you're stepping up now to defend him. Greg's responsible for his own actions, even if he obviously needs a watcher.' She shrugged. 'Hope your meeting was worth it.'

'Depends if you count a huge opportunity for launching a business venture that both Greg and I had worked on for months worth it.'

'You're becoming partners? From what Marla's told me, Greg's committed to the family business.'

Nate held that breath. He didn't want to lay bare any secrets. But he did need her help to get those two reunited, which meant coughing up some answers and rebuilding a little good faith here. So, when Roxy in all her finery moved to lift a small cardboard box from the floor, he stepped up to help at the same time he replied.

'Greg's wanted to break out on his own for a while.'

He took the box from her arms and set it on the counter, after which Roxy opened the lid and extracted a frilly mauve garter. Nate's gaze zeroed in on the lace and words came to mind. Seductive. *Sexy.* Guess a bridal salon sold all kinds of accessories.

Mulling, Roxy ran the silk loop around her index fingers once, twice. 'His family owns a big steel company, right?'

'PrimeSteel. A manufacturer and distributor of steel and finished steel products. I work in management for a rival company.'

As he spoke she opened a nearby drawer and, peering through the counter's glass ceiling, arranged the garter on its own rumpled satin bed.

'Greg and I met through industry contacts,' he went on, his voice a little deeper than before. 'We shared similar views about the future of steel, more specifically, colour-bonded products. Given the economy and environmental issues, we think the opportunities in *less expensive* and *environmentally effective* are endless.'

He expected to hear back regarding the most relevant patent application soon, then they could truly move forward.

'So you joined forces?' Roxy asked.

When she moved to extract another goodie from that box—a gossamer-thin, ultra-short negligee—Nate blinked and, in a heartbeat, imagined her wearing it. He saw the swell of her cleavage, a taut midriff too. He knew her skin would be smooth and warm, just as the sweep of her lips had been that night.

With a start, Nate blinked again…brought himself back. While Roxy arranged the negligee beside that garter, he cleared his throat and, diverting his focus, brushed down then inspected the tail of his tie.

'Greg and I decided that we needed a big investor to do this and do it right. Last week, a prospective investor landed in Sydney. On the phone, Bob Nichols liked our business model, was interested in hearing more but, having hundreds of balls to juggle while he was here, he was short on time. Before heading back to Texas, he made himself available at five a.m. last Sunday—the morning after Greg's buck's party.'

'How does Greg's father feel about his son leaving the family business?'

'Mr Martin's not happy. He's supportive of Greg but in exchange for that support he expects total loyalty, to the family, to the company.'

Returning to the box, she extracted a white satin triangle no larger than a skewed playing card. With its thin elasticized straps dangling from her fingers, she moved to lay that piece beneath the counter too—alongside that garter and X-rated slip.

As her hand smoothed over the display Nate's pulse quickened and beat in his ears because now he imagined Roxy standing in a dimly lit room wearing it all—garter, nightie, that provocative scrap of a thong. In his mind, while he lowered to kneel before her and shaped his palms over her hips, she sighed out his name, filed her fingers through his hair and, stepping closer, brought his head near.

From far away, he heard her ask, 'So, was your Mr Nichols still interested after your meeting?'

The real world faded back.

'Absolutely. Not that it matters. Greg and I spoke this morning. Since Marla called the wedding off, he's lost all motivation. For the time being Greg's staying on at PrimeSteel.'

'Why not go ahead on your own? With Mr Nichols, I mean.'

Her tone added, *And leave me alone.*

'This was *our* project and I know Greg will be sorry if he pulls out now.'

She cocked a brow. 'And?'

He exhaled and gave it up. 'And two heads with steel manufacturing knowledge are better than one.'

He was comfortable with his abilities but in business—in life—a person needed as much reinforcement as possible. It was a slippery slope into failure and obscurity. His own father's descent into near poverty had taught Nate that lesson well.

Roxy dipped a hand back into that box. Before she could pull out God knew what, Nate swiped that box of goodies off the counter and set it safely on the floor.

'I think,' he said, 'if we get Greg and Marla alone, she'll hear his side of the story and accept that those pictures painted him in an unfair light.'

'Oh, gee, you think?'

Studying her mock pitying look, knowing there was something more behind it, he said, 'They'll work this out.'

'Then they'll keep their date at the church,' she surmised, 'and you'll get your business partner back.'

Correct. 'Question is—are you on board?'

'You must be hard of hearing. I already said count me out.'

'Give me some time and I'll convince you.'

Her too-kissable mouth tightened.

'No.'

He growled, cursing under his breath. 'Five lousy minutes. I have a plan. It could mean the difference between your friend's ultimate happiness and a lifetime of loneliness.'

'So dramatic.'

He frowned. 'Yeah, well, it's pretty damn important to them.'

'And Mr Goodie-two-shoes you has nothing at stake.'

This time he bit back the growl and pierced her with a judgmental glare.

'This isn't about Greg and his buck's party, is it? It's not about whether you want to help stop your friend from making perhaps the biggest mistake of her life. You're being obstinate and surly now because of what happened between us all those months ago. You felt jilted and you're prepared to let your friend suffer because you have a beef with me.'

Her eyes rounded with affront and anger. 'If you think that argument will help your cause, you have more ego than even I gave you credit for. Ever hear the saying, water finds its own level? You treat women like chattels. Chances are you choose friends of a similar nature. But neither of you like being called out for it.'

Words burned on the tip of his tongue, but he wouldn't give her the satisfaction of acting the way she anticipated and cutting her down. He was ready to tell her to forget he'd even suggested she help, forget he was ever here.

In fact, she could go to hell.

He strode for the exit, swung back the door and barely refrained from slamming it shut behind him. He was half-way down the busy city block, near colliding with oblivious passers-by, when the steam clouding his brain cooled a degree and his locomotive pace slowed down. As much as he was attracted to Roxanne Trammel, she was a giant thorn in his side. He'd be wise never to see her again, under any circumstances.

But, if he were truthful, he understood her upset over

his departure that night. He'd never done such a thing before and apologizing as he'd hightailed it away didn't rub off any of the tarnish. But Roxy didn't want a confession. She did, however, want to help her friend. He was convinced that Marla should at least hear Greg out, and that wouldn't happen unless he swallowed his pride, turned around and tried to persuade Roxy one more time.

Roxy was still standing at the counter in that wedding gown, staring blindly at the accessories under that glass counter, when the doorbell tinkled and, hat in hand, he edged inside the shop again. She looked over and, straightening, opened her mouth. But he held up a hand.

'Before you run me out of town again, let me say I was a jerk for bringing up that other night. It won't happen again. But I can't walk away without asking you one more time to help give those two the chance they deserve, the chance Marla would want if she were thinking clearly.'

'Maybe she *is* thinking clearly.'

Weary now, he exhaled. Her middle name was stubborn. 'Just give me five minutes to tell you what I have in mind.'

She tilted her head, thought some more.

'Five minutes?' she finally said. 'That's it?'

'Won't even take that long.'

She almost grinned. 'Anyone would think you were sure of yourself.'

'About this, I am.'

She set her hands on her satin-clad hips. After another tense moment, she visibly relaxed and inspected her dress.

'Let me change first.' Her lips twitched. 'I don't want to give you hives.'

Moving through that back door again, she lobbed a final remark over her shoulder. 'If someone happens to walk in looking for their perfect dress, tell them I'll be right out.'

But it was well after five on a Friday—closing time. 'Why don't I just flip the sign over?'

'Don't you dare.' He barely caught her last words as she disappeared out back. 'I need every sale I can get.'

People in business had to be aggressive, but the energy behind that last remark was one hell of an admission. The way she'd spoken six months ago, Roxy lived for the thrill of owning this shop—for the privilege of personally contributing to the 'magic of marriage'—but it sounded as if her enterprise wasn't doing so well. Would she want to go ahead with helping Greg and Marla when she knew his plan? That she'd need to leave her shop unattended or alternatively manned for a few days? Perhaps if the deal included watching him being hung, drawn and quartered…

Admittedly, his behaviour that night had been less than chivalrous, but God knew he'd had his reasons for leaving, just as Roxy had had hers for latching on the way she had. Clearly she was in the market for a serious partner of her own. What was so wrong with letting her know he wasn't up for grabs? Surely that was better than leading her on.

The bell above the door rang and two women edged inside; from the age difference and resemblance, Nate suspected mother and daughter. He strolled over to a rack of dresses and feigned interest. Roxy might be difficult, she might play havoc with his equilibrium, but, even if her shop were raking in millions, he wouldn't get in the way of a possible sale. People liked space. He imagined that went double for brides searching for a wedding dress.

So he thumbed through some size six to tens while going over the points of his plan for Marla and Greg yet again. Aside from needing to vacate Sydney for a few days, he wondered whether Roxy would entertain the idea of taking on such an active role or even if Greg and Marla would fall for it. Marla would then need to get past the mistrust and hurt those pictures had caused.

On the other side of the room, the women were involved in a hushed conversation. Eavesdropping wasn't Nate's style; however, the words he caught worried him enough to push scruples aside.

'We won't find anything,' the daughter bemoaned. 'It's suburbia. You saw the sign. My God, she sews them herself.'

'We're here, Violet,' the mother encouraged. 'Let's look a while. You never know what you'll find.'

Coat hangers clicked down a steel rod. Satin and silk rustled, and Violet sighed. 'No. No. No. No.' A second, more impatient sigh. 'A waste of time.'

Nate hadn't a clue; women's fashion wasn't his forte. But ignorance and prejudging were two different beasts. Clearly Violet had made up her mind before entering the store. If she took off her blinkers, bet she'd find something worth another look. Perhaps even worth buying.

Roxy had said she needed every sale. Given she was at least prepared to listen to his plan, why not return the favour and see if he couldn't help here?

With a dress in hand, he rotated around and, as impatient as that woman's sighs had been, his was filled with satisfaction.

'This is perfect. My God, she'll love it.' His smile big, Nate nodded a greeting then apologised to the ladies. 'Sorry. Thinking aloud.'

Curious, Violet looked around. 'Is your fiancée in a dressing room?'

'I asked her to meet me here. I can't wait till she sees this dress.'

One of the mother's pencilled eyebrows lifted. 'I've never heard of a groom choosing his bride's gown.'

'Emma's been everywhere, including interstate. She was thinking of having one made and a friend recommended this place. She was so disheartened. She'd even talked about calling the whole thing off.'

The daughter gasped. *'No.'*

'She's the woman of my dreams,' he said. 'I want to have babies with Emma. Lots of them.'

Now Violet and her mother's eyes were shining with approval, so Nate hammed it up. He hadn't been given his senior production's lead in *Ali Baba* for nothing.

'I never thought I could love someone like I love my Emma. I just need to help her find that perfect dress.'

'That's what this place is called,' Violet whispered in her mother's ear loud enough for Nate to hear. 'The Perfect Dress.'

'It is a pretty gown,' the mother agreed, taking more notice of Nate's impromptu choice.

'Don't ask me how I know but I do.' With an enamoured air, he shrugged. 'My Emma will look like an angel in this.'

Having moved to another rack, Mother drew out a gown.

'Sweetheart,' she called. 'Look. This beading is exquisite. Did you say the owner sews these all herself?'

Violet examined the dress, draped it close. When she began to sway back and forth, searching for a mirror, Nate intervened again. A sign hung over the entrance to a nearby corridor.

'The change rooms are that way,' he said with a slant of his head.

But now Violet had found the price tag and told her mother, 'I know you said not to worry about cost, but…' When Violet mouthed the amount, Nate overheard and near fell over. Did women honestly spend that much on a single dress?

Fortunately, Mother didn't bat an eyelid. She dashed away Violet's concerns with a wave of her diamond-clad hand and both women had trundled off when Nate's ears pricked at a persistent *pssst*. He pivoted around.

Hiding behind that door, Roxy was madly waving him over. Nate hung up the dress and crossed the room—not fast enough, it seemed. Her hand shot out and hauled him inside.

'What are you doing?'

Gathering himself as she shut the door, he lengthened his neck and straightened his tie. 'Drumming up business.'

She looked as if he'd admitted to eating chocolate-covered tarantulas for lunch.

'You can't lie like that.'

'It's not lying.' The way he saw it, 'I'm creating an opportunity.'

Horrified, she leaned back against the door. 'I hate to think of the opportunity you've concocted for Marla and Greg.' Gathering herself, she pulled up tall. 'You can't come waltzing in here and making up stories. This is my place of business. I depend on my reputation.'

'How did I harm your good name?'

'If those two ever find out and take it further, the legal term I think is *fraud*.'

'They'll never find out.'

She held the bridge of her nose. 'Maybe I should go out and just come clean.'

Outside, the desk bell pinged. Roxy jumped, called out, 'I'll be right there,' then glanced down at the gown she still wore.

Which, frankly, looked great on her. The white satin suited her skin's natural glow. The sweep of her waist in that bodice was hypnotic.

Not that he would allow himself to be concerned with

any of that. He was here to get his plan on the table and any bugs ironed out before they went ahead with Operation Back Together.

He said, 'I thought you were changing.'

'I couldn't get a hold of the zip.' She whirled around. As the train slapped his shin, he was presented with a tantalizing rear view. 'You'll have to help.'

Alarm bells—red and flashing—went off in his head. An invitation and bare flesh equalled temptation. Sure, what Roxy proposed seemed innocent enough but, in essence, she was asking him to help her undress. To open himself up and be vulnerable to the call of his baser urges, which he had trouble enough containing where Roxy Trammel was concerned.

He held up his palms. 'I'll pass.'

'You can't *pass*.'

Believe me, 'It's safer I don't.'

'I trust you not to do any damage.' When he didn't budge, she groaned and muttered, 'Okay. Time to get this out in the open.' Her fists finding her hips, she rotated again. 'I won't lie and say I didn't enjoy the kiss we shared that night because, while I'm loath to admit it, I did. And I admit my reaction was…enthusiastic. But if you think I'm so desperate that I'd use sex to manipulate a marriage proposal, think again. And if I *were* to do such an abhorrent thing—' her nose rose a regal notch '—it wouldn't be with you.' She hesitated, then went on. 'In fact, I've been kissed since and, frankly, yours pales in comparison.'

Nate's gape turned into a smirk. And she called *him* a liar. He knew just how much she'd enjoyed that kiss. Almost as much as he had.

Still, if she could play this Arctic ice-shelf cool, couldn't he? Hell, it was only a zip. She wasn't asking him to slip off a garter or nightdress or that itty-bitty pair of silk panties—which he'd best not think about right now.

When he lifted his chin, she lifted hers. He twirled his finger—*turn around*—and, hoisting up her skirt, she whirled again.

The dress's back was scooped low and, with her long fair hair twisted up, Nate was greeted by an unobstructed, blemish-free landscape. Delicate twin shoulder blades bracketed a sweep of smooth tan skin and two accidental curls spiralled either side of the dent of her spine.

Pleasant warmth pooled then solidified high on Nate's thighs. But he took a deep breath and, focusing not on the view but the task, doggedly searched. After a full-on few seconds, he huffed. No wonder she couldn't find it.

'There *is* no zip.'

'It's invisible,' she told him. 'Feel around inside the bodice facing.'

Nate scratched his head. Did she say invisible? And, 'Bodice *what*?'

'Slide your finger up and down the inside top of the seam.' She dropped a wry look over one shoulder. 'You do know what a seam is, don't you?'

'A rich deposit where minerals are found.'

She rolled her eyes as if to say, *Men*. 'Just don't tug too hard.'

When she turned back, Nate shook out his hands, rubbed his palms together. Not sweaty. Not cold. All good. He edged one fingertip inside.

Her skin was toasty-warm and smooth as the satin. And now he was aware that she was wearing the same perfume she had that fateful night. Subtle. Something with lavender? Whatever the ingredients, the scent was light and fresh and…

Nate filled his lungs.

The kind of bouquet I could breathe in all day.

He snapped open eyes that seemed to have drifted shut.

Roxy had implied that she'd dated since their evening together. Leaning closer, he slid his thumb down and felt around. He hated himself for needing to ask but couldn't a guy be curious?

'So, I take it you're seeing someone.'

'No one in particular.'

Chewing that over, he found something small and difficult to grab high at the top of the crease. Squeezing just enough to get a grip, he added, 'And yet *someone's* swept you off your feet.'

Those curls tickled the back of his hand as she purred. 'I've been swept off several times since that night.'

His bite tightened and grip firmed more. He was jiggling in earnest when, outside, the desk bell rang again.

'I'll be right out,' Roxy called pleasantly, then to him, 'What's taking so long?'

'Inexperience,' he growled. With a wedding gown, at least. This darn thing didn't glide as it should.

'Don't force it,' she told him.

'I'm not forcing anything.'

Shifting, he began to work it in a hopefully more fruitful and earnest kind of way. Clearly this exercise needed a little more of the ol' Nate Sparks finesse.

Three seconds later, she complained, 'You're too rough.'

'Relax.' His fingertips rolled, then tugged and rolled again. 'Just a few seconds more.'

'Nate, not so hard.'

'Almost got it—'

The zip suddenly gave.

Actually what gave was the fabric splitting either side.

While Roxy stiffened, Nate's heart stopped beating as he held his breath and stared.

It wasn't much of a tear. Really barely noticeable. But when Roxy turned around, her expression said it all. Her face was a mask of disbelief, anguish. *Rage*. And her eyes, which had looked merely annoyed earlier, now spat green fire.

'Tell me you didn't tear the dress,' she groaned. 'You didn't, did you? Not *this* dress.'

The anger in her eyes turned to fear then they edged with moisture and Nate felt the walls press in.

'It's not too bad.' He indicated with his fingers. 'Maybe an inch.' Maximum two.

That call from outside came again.

'Anyone there?'

'Coming,' Roxy said, but this time her voice cracked.

What could he say? If he could take it back, he would.

'Roxy…'

Her eyes filling, she inhaled and in a heartbeat all her angst and energy seemed to drain away. She pressed her lips together. Swallowed. Shrugged.

'Doesn't matter anyway,' she muttered and he frowned.

'What doesn't matter?' When she swished out of the room, he followed. 'Roxy, answer me.'

'It doesn't matter,' she replied, 'because this gown is— or was—Marla's.'

Nate gaped. He'd wrecked his mate's fiancée's gown? Not a good omen. And why was the bride's best friend wearing it anyway?

When he joined Roxy out front, she was looking around an empty room. Seemed those potential customers had given up and gone home. But then that same enquiring voice rang out again, this time from the direction of the dressing rooms. A moment later, that older woman appeared. On seeing them, she clasped her cheeks with glee.

'Oh, my. This must be your beautiful bride-to-be. And

you're right,' the woman went on before speaking directly to Roxy rather than Nate. 'That gown suits you to a T. My Violet thinks she might have found the right one too.'

'Really? That's wonderful.' Roxy's disappointment at that accidental rip transformed into a frail but hope-filled smile. Then she evaluated her own gown. 'But this dress…' Her cheeks pinked up and she rubbed her brow. 'Well, it's a little hard to explain.'

The woman angled in. 'No need. My Violet went through the same thing,' she confided. 'Anxiety. So many decisions.' Her shoulders squared. 'But when you've found a man who's so obviously in love with you, so committed, how can things not fall into place? You're a lucky woman.' She slid that smile Nate's way. 'A lucky couple.'

Nate smothered a wince. The woman had it wrong. Roxy wasn't Emma. There *was* no Emma and wouldn't be for a very long while, if he could help it.

The woman looked between the uncertain two, then slanted her head. 'Is there something wrong with the gown, dear?'

'Oh, no,' Roxy said. 'I *love* it. More than any gown ever. The satin's as soft as rose petals. Every line is exquisite. It's just that this dress is—'

'Beautiful,' Nate cut in when he knew he ought to have let her finish and set the misunderstanding straight. But the dress *was* stunning, he thought again, drinking in those satiny curves and falls, whether Marla ended up wearing it or not.

When Roxy's slow smile said she appreciated his compliment, a kernel of heat bloomed in his chest, a sensation he enjoyed as much as he spurned. Then she turned and admitted to the woman, 'But I'm not this man's fiancée.'

The woman blinked. 'I don't understand.'

'I own this salon. I'm Roxanne Trammel.'

The woman absorbed the news and, nodding absently, introduced herself as Ava Morris before her focus swung to Nate. 'Where's your bride-to-be? Nothing's wrong, I hope.'

Nate scrubbed his jaw. He'd only meant to help—to give Roxy a hand up with a potential sale. But duplicity, well intended or not, had caught up. Nothing for it but to face the music.

'Actually,' he began, 'my fiancée's—'

'Out back,' Roxy said, cutting in. 'Emma's choosing accessories.'

Mrs Morris held her stomach and breathed out over a relieved smile. 'Well, that was quick!'

'Happens like that sometimes,' Roxy said, slipping Nate a 'you owe me' look.

A call from the dressing room. *'Can someone help with this?'*

Picking up her skirts, Roxy went to hurry off but Mrs Morris put up a hand.

'I'll help Violet. You see to your other matter.'

Mrs Morris rushed away while, sheepish, Nate tugged his ear. 'Sorry about the Emma thing.'

'You shouldn't have lied. I in no way condone it.' Roxy's expression lightened a smidge. 'But I do appreciate you trying to help. I didn't need to embarrass you.'

As he'd embarrassed her that night?

But she didn't look half as ticked off as she had a moment ago. In fact, her eyes were almost smiling, somehow reaching out. And he liked the positive change. Liked it way too much.

Nate cleared his throat and hauled himself back. 'We'll need to see each other again. To discuss the Marla-Greg plan,' he clarified quickly.

'I'll give you my email address.' She cut across the counter and slipped a business card from a holder. 'Why don't you send over your ideas for Greg and Marla? I'll be with Violet for a while yet hopefully.'

'I'd rather toss around ideas face to face.'

'I don't know what time I'll be free.'

'I could hang around. Help out some more. Maybe do some zip repairs.' His weak smile faded and he tucked in his chin. 'I really am sorry about that.'

She tried to hold her scowl. 'Guess you can't help if you're too strong for your own good.'

'I should have taken more time.' Thought ahead.

Hell, maybe he shouldn't have come at all. But he believed in Greg and couldn't abandon him. He believed in their business too, and he definitely wouldn't abandon that. There seemed no other way around this bind, and to pull this make-up plan off he needed help. He needed Roxy.

Looking radiant beneath the lights, she offered over the card, but Nate found his attention drawn instead to the side of her throat where a tiny pulse popped. Strange, but at this moment he seemed to feel that heartbeat as well as he felt his own. Steady. Deep.

Hot.

When she tipped closer, still offering the card, Nate extended a hand and accepted. He hadn't meant for his fingers to linger, to stretch that bit further and brush over hers. And in that instant he saw the pulse in her throat beat faster and her gaze grow heavy while his dropped to her glossy parted lips.

Time and again, he'd wondered what would've happened if he'd stayed that night six months ago. What principle of physics decreed that he would share his father's fate, as well as his grandfather's, and back on down the line? But as he continued to drink in Roxy's curious gaze the world fell away and a series of snapshots flashed through his mind...

His parents on their wedding day, two months after they'd met. His grandfather and grandmother in tails and lacy veil six weeks on the heels of a first date. If ever he mentioned the myth, his father would simply shrug. When a Sparks man found the right woman—the one who left his senses reeling and blood crashing like giant rollers on a shore—nothing else mattered. He might as well surrender. The toll of wedding bells was imminent. Marriage and domesticity a foregone. So, it would seem, was lack of personal growth and motivation for building security for one's future.

After marrying, his father had given up his dream of finishing medical school and becoming a surgeon. Instead he'd taken a job as a hospital wardsman, which meant less income to support the five kids that came along but more time to spend with his beloved wife, the only thing in his life that seemed to matter. Not always as romantic as it might sound.

Nate couldn't forget the weeks his mother had spent convalescing after a car accident when he was twelve. The children had needed leadership, strength, hope. Instead, their father had stopped eating, stopped communicating. He'd all but pined away for love. Or the time his father had had the chance to return to his education but had decided to support his wife's dream of becoming a renowned painter when, hell, they could barely afford to feed themselves, let alone buy art materials and exhibition space.

Similar stories of Sparks men and their women had survived…hasty marriages followed by a lifetime of Byronic devotion. Was it genetics or a curse? Of course it could all be coincidence.

It was only when Nate realized his other palm had curled around the satin cinching her waist—when Roxy

trembled and his head dropped deliberately over hers—
that he knew the truth.

Coincidence had nothing to do with it.

He should have run while he could.

CHAPTER TWO

WHEN his throat made a gravelled wanting sound that resonated like beautiful bass chords through Roxy's bones, memories of the dreams that had tormented her these past months wrapped around her like a run of steamy veils. A heartbeat later, his mouth captured hers and inhibitions concerning Nate Sparks and his dubious affections spread their powerful wings and flew far away.

In the smoky recesses of her mind she understood she'd submitted without a whimper of protest. More so, she was aware of her breasts, suddenly so full and sensitive, rubbing against the front of his business shirt…against the hard broad plateau of his chest. After all her talk, after the way he'd escaped that night, she ought to be ashamed by her surrender now. She should be *horrified*.

She was anything but.

The magic of his kiss was still as strong. In fact, the pleasure he stirred up within her had only grown. The verdict was back, approved, stamped and sealed. Their lips were a perfect fit, and the desire pulsing through her veins was a better than fair indicator that their bodies would join just as well.

She focused on individual sensations but absorbed them all at once…the graze of his jaw, the drugging pull of his scent, the mesmerizing way he seemed to *consume* her.

The sensations were so pure, it was nothing short of sweet torture. Then his palms ironed up and over the curve of her back, pressing her that much closer, and Roxy dissolved even more.

No man could compete with the depth of longing Nate Sparks had brought out in her. Ridiculous as it might seem, she was helpless to deny it. She wanted him to make love to her—*take* her. After one craze-filled moment, she wanted that so completely, she couldn't remember a time when anything had mattered more.

Of course, something did.

His kiss shifted then lightened so that rather than covering, his mouth was now brushing hers. On a dreamy smile, she held his bristled jaw and murmured, soft and sexy against the bow of his lower lip, *'Gotcha.'*

Nate stiffened. His eyes flew open, enlarged pupils shrank, then he jumped back as if someone had rammed his stomach with a stick. His lips pressed together while he drove a hand over his scalp, leaving usually neatly groomed hair nicely dishevelled.

Roxy's smile widened.

Damn, it felt good to be right.

'What the hell are you doing?' he rasped.

Satisfied, she slapped her hands as if removing grit. 'Proving something.'

'Proving *what*?'

'That the world didn't end.'

Nate's face thundered and his jaw clenched doubly tight.

But then the fury and shock cleared, the tension locking his stance visibly eased and his eyes took on the gleam of a wry smile. All in all, he looked rather pleased with himself.

'You *are* right,' he said. 'The world didn't end. The sky wasn't ripped open by a thousand raging thunderbolts.

There's nothing wrong with physical reaction to stimulation. Sexual arousal happens every day.'

And *that* was why he'd run that night six months ago. Why he was acting overly cavalier now. Which was fine by her. She had enough going wrong with her life without inviting in more trouble.

'Hope you don't take offence,' she said in a flat tone, 'but I need to follow up on Ava and Violet.'

Giving a curt nod, he dug out a business card of his own. 'Ring when you're finished here.'

'That could be late.'

He flashed a thin grin. 'I'm a night owl.'

After slapping the card on the counter, he strode out and the invisible band squeezing her windpipe eased.

She'd daydreamed of how she might one day turn the tables and make Nate feel as small as she had that night when he'd left her quaking and embarrassed as she'd never been before. Seeing his reaction now had been worth the price of stirring up all those wonderful, dreadful feelings again. Primal emotions that demanded immediate attention but needed to be shut down and ignored.

Still…

Remembering, Roxy touched her tingling lips.

No one kissed like Nate Sparks.

'Hey, buddy, great game.'

Rounding up a squash match at Greg Martin's private home court, Nate clapped his friend on the back as they moved into a change room that boasted three showers, a sauna and facilities for remedial massage. Nate hadn't mentioned Marla and their bust-up yet but he planned to. He was committed to helping mend Greg's fractured life—both personal and professional—even at the risk of exposing himself to public enemy number one. The girl with the lips.

Shaking off the residual effects of his and Roxy's latest bombshell kiss, Nate grabbed a towel while Greg dropped his racket on the bench. The clatter echoed around the ceiling and walls.

'I played like a dog,' Greg said before dragging his shirt up and over a crop of sandy-coloured hair. 'But I appreciate the company. The alternative was dinner with the folks. Don't think I could stand my mother's questions tonight, or my father turning red, trying to contain his relief.'

Happy that his son was staying with the family firm, Nate surmised, stuffing his racket into his bag.

'We're going to sort this out. You didn't hire that stripper on your buck's night, you didn't call her over to sit on your lap and you certainly didn't ask for those shots to be snapped in the brief window of time she was there. Woody Cox did all that.' One of Greg's buddies since university. Nate had always thought that guy needed a leash. 'Hell, he even admitted to putting the evidence on the Net.'

'He apologised as soon as I balled him out.'

'Not soon enough.' News on social media networks spread quicker than a wink. Sometimes a great thing. In this case, just plain dumb. 'But Marla can't stay mad for ever.'

'You think? A few words on the phone—her crying, me begging—and she refuses to see me again, let alone marry me.' Greg's towel swiped down his unshaven face, around the thick column of his neck. 'I've sent a truck full of flowers, a diamond bracelet to go with the ring. I even hired a scaffold and played a slideshow of all our best moments outside of her second-storey window. She pitched our framed engagement photo at the screen. Tore a two-foot rip down the middle.'

Nate forced a Pollyanna smile. 'After getting that out of her system, she might be ready to talk.'

'When she emailed our guest list and said the wedding was off, what could I do?'

Seriously? 'Not *give up*.'

There was a reason he and Greg were friends. They thought the same. Shared similar values. Nate knew Greg would never cheat on a woman because Nate, himself, would never do such a thing. Not that he was naïve enough to think indiscretions between couples didn't happen.

At the engagement party six months ago, he and Roxy had been talking out on the restaurant's balcony when she'd mentioned her father and his exploits. She hadn't belaboured the point but had rather only said enough to make her situation growing up clear. Life was confusing for a kid when your dad was a womanizer and your mother refused to see the situation for what it was: a betrayal not only to wife but also to child.

Guess there were some advantages to that blasted family curse, Nate thought as he drew the sweat-damp shirt off over his head. Despite the downsides, he was thankful his parents' marriage was a solid one. They didn't argue over anything more important than where to spend their next vacation. If their trust should ever be tested, neither would look at the other with suspicion. Not that his dad would ever come close to cheating. And neither would Greg.

His friend was jamming his shirt into his bag, muttering, 'Hell, maybe Marla's better off without me.'

'Like Sparks Martin Steel would be better off without you?'

Greg's dark gaze edged over. 'I know you're disappointed but, believe me, it's best you go that alone. I'm no good to anyone right now. I'd only let you down.' He headed for the exit, his six-plus height barely missing the lintel. 'I'm going to take a shower inside.'

Nate punched his arms through the sleeves of a fresh shirt, then followed Greg out. Time to set down the first layer of his plan.

'Why don't you and I get away for a couple of days? You had time pencilled out anyway.'

Time off to finalize wedding stuff with Marla.

'I'd be sorry company.' Outside in the evening cool and beneath path lights, Greg turned and sent a wan smile. 'I'm beat. I'll catch you later in the week.'

As Greg made his way down the path that led to his separate quarters on his parents' extravagant Potts Point estate, Nate set his jaw. Dammit, he wasn't giving up on that wedding. He certainly wasn't giving up on his and Greg's partnership. This was only the first round and, no matter the setbacks or complications, he was in for the long haul.

When his cell vibrated and buzzed in his sports bag, Nate checked the ID and his heartbeat began to crash. Speaking of complications...

Shoring himself, Nate connected and Roxy Trammel purred down the line.

'Is that Luscious Lips?'

'That's not funny.' Neither the nickname nor her tone. He'd done the wrong thing that night, but couldn't she show him a little mercy six months on? He'd fallen hook, line and sinker when she'd given herself over to their embrace. Now her voice was tease enough.

If history was anything to go by, it wouldn't take too many more embraces like the one this afternoon to have him looking cross-eyed, thinking he was in love and arranging a whole new set of priorities. The mere thought of the way her body had moved against his could make him break into a sweat that had nothing to do with the energetic hour he'd just spent on the court. If it killed him—and it probably near would—from now on he'd keep his hands to himself.

'Are we still on for tonight?' she asked.

Regarding Marla and Greg? 'You bet. Have you eaten?'

'I have a craving for sushi.'

Sauntering to his car, Nate winced. 'Raw dead fish.'

'Who knew you were so cultured?'

'I vote Chinese.'

'Done.' She suggested a well-known restaurant.

'Say, thirty minutes? I need to change.'

'Just for you, I'll change too. All this white satin is getting heavy.'

He heard her laugh before signing off and, despite his mood, Nate couldn't help himself. He laughed too.

Roxy arrived at the China Town restaurant bang on time.

The expansive room was bordered by tall arched windows, smelled of fine Asian cuisine and was illuminated by a sky of glowing pumpkin-shaped lanterns. A slender woman dressed in a red full-length cheongsam led her to a table and when Roxy pulled in her chair, she knew Nate would appreciate their location: dead centre of the restaurant, in plain view of everyone. That second kiss had been even more unsettling than the first; neither she nor Nate needed to be tested by sharing a darkened corner tonight. Her outfit had also been chosen with those same boundaries in mind.

A 'tailored black trousers, loose-fitting black silk shirt with matching casual vest' combo was more 'business' than 'come hither'. Spiked sandal heels were a staple with this outfit but tonight it was boots. No sheer silk stockings either. Thick, black, to the breastbone tights, as well

as her ugliest bra. Who could get turned on wearing old
stretched cotton? Amazing what a person found stuffed
at the back of their lingerie drawer.

Roxy glanced across at the entrance—no Nate—so she
filled her water glass from a centre pitcher then inspected
the table setting. Skimming a fingertip over the symbols
printed on her Chinese zodiac placemat, she smiled. The
years indicated she was a tiger! Powerful, passionate.

Reading on, she frowned.

Restless, *reckless*? What sign would Nate fall under? An
agile rabbit might fit. Or an arrogant monkey. She huffed
and flicked out her napkin.

Bet he was a loner snake, waiting for some unsuspecting victim to mesmerize.

When he strode in five minutes later, looking drop-
dead amazing in chinos and casual button-down, Roxy
skulled her ice-water to keep her over-heated imagination from going up in flames. So much for the power of
pathetic underwear.

His dark hair was post-shower damp and his shoulders tonight appeared even broader. He'd forgone a shave
and the bristled shadow smudging his strong square jaw
only served to make his presence all the more entrancing.
Knowing he was near, she felt tingles race over her skin,
brushing her most sensitive spots and making them glow.

Could a man grow sexier in a matter of hours?

He caught sight of her and crossed over with a fluid
strong gait that had every woman in the room blindly setting down chopsticks and turning her head. At the table,
he beckoned a passing waiter at the same time he dragged
in his chair.

'I'll need something a little stronger,' he said as she
refilled her water glass. 'Care to share a bottle of red?'

'No alcohol for me.'

'Need to keep your wits about you?'

She blinked at the tease glittering in his lidded blue eyes. But after her 'luscious lips' comment earlier, she'd allow him one ace. Frankly, she didn't need her inhibitions weakened tonight. Not that she would admit that now.

'I have to be in the shop early,' she said. 'Busy week coming up.'

'Actually, I wanted to talk to you about that.'

Before he could explain, that waiter arrived and Nate ordered a glass of Cabernet Sauvignon.

'To have any hope of enticing Greg and Marla back together,' he said as the waiter moved off, 'you need to speak with your friend about getting away from Sydney for a few days. Somewhere isolated where she can't jump on the next plane out and escape before really hearing him through.'

'Sorry.' Shutting one eye, Roxy turned her head slightly. 'Think I'm having auditory hallucinations.'

He spoke up. 'We'll need to send Greg there too, of course.'

'Without either of them knowing?' Roxy fought the urge to laugh. This was his plan? 'Are you crazy? A, they'll hate you for ever for tricking them. B, short of leading them by the nose, they'll never go.'

'Precisely. I'll take Greg. You take Marla.'

'You want me to take Marla out to some isolated destination so she can meet with Greg and verbally tear his head off again?'

'I want to see them together so they can work through this. We'll keep them on track.'

'We. As in you and me? You expect me to leave Sydney, my shop, to go trekking off to God only knows where with *you*?' Astonished, she sat back. 'I have a business to run.'

'Put someone else on at the shop.'

Roxy wanted to get up and leave, then and there. He really was an arrogant son of a…

Dragging down a calming breath, she put her thoughts back on track.

After Violet's deposit this afternoon, the books were almost square. When the minor alterations were done and the dress delivered, the balance would put her business back in the black. That didn't mean she could afford to slack off. The economy was dead. People cut corners, even on must-haves like a perfect wedding dress. She had to keep her eye on the bottom line.

'If you need some funds,' he said, as if reading her thoughts, 'to see your way through, I can help.'

'You really are mad if you think I'd accept anything from you.'

'You're being obstinate.'

She exploded. 'You don't *get* it. I'm not going *anywhere* with you.' She crossed her arms. 'And I'm not lying to Marla.'

'Even if it means helping to secure her future happiness?'

'That's your story. I'd like to think Greg is innocent but…'

That was being naïve, gullible, as her mother had been for too long. Some guys liked it on the side, no matter how devoted they might outwardly appear, her own two-timing father, case in point.

Nate was folding a shirt cuff back up over his wrist…a bronzed, corded forearm. It looked so strong, so lawlessly masculine, she found herself remembering how completely lost she'd felt when they'd kissed this afternoon and, irrespective of knowing that she would never approve of this man, would never agree to anything he might scheme and plan, Roxy found herself asking.

'You want me to abandon my shop and fly off to where exactly?'

'I'm thinking the Outback.'

Her arms unravelled and she sat straighter. 'Really?'

'That appeals?'

'I'd like to experience the red dust and sweeping plains at least once in my life.'

'What about snakes and scorpions?'

'I thought you wanted to talk me into this.'

'Right.' He put on a serious way-too-cute face that sent her pulse rate spiking. 'The carols of kookaburras will wake you each morning, you'll enjoy a panoramic view of rust-coloured hills and fiery sunsets every night, not to mention the magical allure of those endless starry nights. How am I doing?'

She inwardly sighed. *Fabulous.* But it was far from that simple. Remembering her disgust when she'd happened upon the picture of Nate canoodling that woman just days after he'd left her stranded on her doorstep, she pinned her shoulders back and made clear again.

'I only want to do whatever's right for Marla.'

The waiter arrived and poured a wine sample. Nate tasted, voiced his approval and, thoughtful, set his glass down for the waiter to fill.

'Can I ask you something?'

'Thought you already had.'

He ignored her tone and asked, 'Why were you wearing Marla's dress today?'

'I'm a tactile person.' She shrugged. 'I thought wearing the gown, feeling the fabric against my own skin, might help give me an idea or two.'

'More information needed.'

She pressed her lips together, but talking about a bad

situation couldn't make it worse, even if she was talking to a man she didn't trust.

'That dress is entered in a contest,' she admitted. 'First prize includes a showing in Paris, among other fabulous things.'

'And yet you look unhappy.'

'One of the conditions of the contest is that the gown must take its stroll down the aisle by the end of this month. With Marla and Greg's wedding off, so is any chance of that dress taking out the number one spot. Or even a coveted place.'

'What did Marla want you to do with the dress?'

'She doesn't care. As long as she doesn't have to see it again.'

'So someone else could wear it. You could put out an ad or something so long as the nuptials are sealed before the thirty-first.'

'I thought about that, but this dress is special. I couldn't give it away to someone who might not appreciate it.'

'Even for a shot at that contest prize?'

Even if she explained, he wouldn't understand. People didn't value what they got free. What they didn't have to fight for or respect. That gown deserved to be adored.

Besides, 'What if Greg and Marla do get back together?' She collected her water glass. 'Not that I'm saying it'll happen. But in one breath I'm supposed to be working to reunite them and in the next I'm giving her gown away.'

'If those two reunite, all our problems will be solved, *including* your gown's. Greg was caught in an unflattering moment. It can happen to anyone.'

'It's never happened to me.'

He looked as if he might say, *Me either*, but then thought better of it.

'I'm convinced he's meant for Marla and vice versa.'

Nate's glittering gaze took on a distant look. 'A man falls in love only once in his life.'

'Wow. Such conviction. Anyone would think you're an expert.'

'You don't want to know how big of an expert I am.'

Elbows on the table, she set her chin prettily in the net of her thatched fingers. 'But I really, really do.'

That shadowed jaw shifted and he took another sip of wine. He set down the glass, his chest expanded on a breath and he finally said, 'Truth is, I'm the product of a happy family.'

That was it? She sat straighter. 'More information needed.'

'My father fell in love with my mother at first sight,' he went on. 'They married a matter of weeks later. I've always known they were happy together. Were meant to be. The looks they share... Marla and Greg look at each other the same way. It's not something you can fake.'

Roxy's throat swelled. She felt sad and envious as well as pleased for Nate all at the same time. What must it be like to have grown up in such a stable, predictable world and obviously, from Nate's face, not appreciate it nearly enough?

'Must be great to have parents who really get it.' She swallowed as that familiar dark feeling gripped her stomach. 'Think I mentioned my dad's been married three times.'

Nate gestured for the waiter to bring another glass for Marla. 'And your mother?'

'She has a circle of good friends.'

'But none of the male variety?'

'She doesn't believe in love any more.'

'And her daughter creates wedding gowns?'

'My mother supports what I do.' Roxy relented and

sipped her wine, which coursed a warm pleasant path down her throat. 'She often says how proud she is of me.'

'What about you?'

'Of course I'm proud of my career.'

His tone dropped. 'I meant do you believe in marriage?'

The question took Roxy aback. She thought he'd already pegged her as a huge fan—a woman who stuck her claws in at the first opportunity and didn't like to let go. And she wouldn't lie now.

'Pardon the pun but *I do*. I also believe that making it legal shouldn't be rushed.' His eyes took on a new light as those broad shoulders seemed to lock. 'Sounds like your parents lucked out,' she went on, 'but mine married after a whirlwind romance too and they bombed out badly.'

'So it'll be a long engagement for you?'

'I have a career to nurture. Places I want to visit. People I'd like to meet. I'm a long way off from wanting to get serious with someone.' Particularly the *wrong* someone.

'That's exactly how I feel.'

Her grin was wry. 'I kinda guessed.'

As his gaze roamed her face, the awareness glistening in those crystal-cut eyes sent her heartbeat tripping all over itself and her mind wandering to places it shouldn't. She already knew she loved the feel of his mouth on hers, the heat of his amazing body pressed close. She also knew developing feelings for Nate Sparks was completely, totally out of the question. Her mother might have been weak and fallen for a rogue who thought only of himself, but, dammit, she never would.

'I have an idea,' he said, collecting his glass as if ready to make a toast. 'If you agree to be part of this plan and Greg and Marla *don't* make up…'

His head went back as if he were having second thoughts but now, despite it all, she was curious.

'And if they don't make up…?'

'If they don't make up, I'll walk you down the aisle in that dress myself.'

Her vision tunnelled, the world tipped upside down and Roxy forgot to breathe. When she did fill her lungs, it was with a gulp. Then she coughed and had to cover her mouth with the napkin.

'You must have a temperature,' she said over the square of linen. 'You're delirious.'

'You have everything to gain, nothing to lose.'

'Except Marla's friendship when she bans me from her life for deceiving her.'

'I'm betting she'll name their first girl child after you. If not—' his smile softened '—she'll understand. That's what friends do.'

Slowly, Roxy set her napkin down. 'You'd really commit to walking me down the aisle in that dress?'

'It's for a good cause. Besides there's such a thing as annulment.' His laugh was a little too quick. 'We're not talking for real here, Roxy, just a means to an end. We both agreed. Neither of us is after that kind of commitment.'

She blinked and felt her cheeks go horribly warm. Well, of course that was what he'd meant. This proposition was simply another of his angles to get to where he wanted to go.

'Was that a yes?' he asked.

She held her brow. She hadn't said that. She *couldn't* agree. 'That's too wild of an idea.'

'Way I see it, for you it's a safe bet.'

Roxy looked down at her placemat and that big striped cat flashed a challenging grin. Was she like that tiger? Powerful, passionate? *Reckless?* Nate had already said it wouldn't be a *real* wedding…if Marla and Greg didn't make up and it even came to that. One part of her was

shouting, *Do it! He's right. What have you got to lose?*
Another part was shuddering, warning her, *Don't be an idiot. This can only blow up in your face.*

Roxy gnawed her lower lip, shifted in her seat. 'I don't know...'

'No decision should be made on an empty stomach. Let's order and discuss it later. After all—' looking more commanding and handsome than ever, Nate swept up his menu '—we have all night.'

Below that ceiling of lanterns an hour later, Nate slid the leather bill folder the waiter had dropped off over to his side of the table. 'I'll get this.'

The wallet hadn't left his back pocket before Roxy swept the folder over to her side.

'We're going Dutch,' she said, curling hair behind an ear as she concentrated to study the bill.

'I never let a woman pay.'

When he swept the folder back, she sent a dry look that only made her green eyes sparkle beneath the lighting's soft glow all the more. 'Nate, don't argue.'

'Going Dutch wasn't the way I was brought up.'

'As old-fashioned as it might sound, if you'd invited me to dinner for other reasons, I'd let you get the tab. But this is not a date.'

Her tone said, *As long as I have breath in my body, nor will there ever be a date.*

She reached again. He caught her hand. The contact of his skin touching hers sent a surge of blood rushing through his veins. Low down, he came alive and the part of him that was plugged into 'me caveman' throbbed and demanded an audience. The rush of testosterone was natural, uncomplicated. Its intent was also out of the question.

Throughout the evening, and what had turned into a

small banquet, they'd discussed the Outback and had also digressed into travels abroad, ending on federal politics, usually a subject he avoided. People had their own opinion and sometimes a comment could turn into an overly heated, less than pleasant discussion. But he and Roxy shared similar views there too. At one point, he was so engrossed in their discussion regarding new tax implications on fledgling businesses, he forgot the reason they'd met tonight—to sort out their friends' situation. He was sure Roxy had forgotten she was supposed to disapprove of him, which boded well for getting her on board with his plan.

But, Lord above, he should never have touched her. The feel of her hand only made him want to touch more. From the alarm in her wide eyes, Roxy felt the same heat and uncertainty too. Then she did something he couldn't. Her shoulders easing back, she siphoned down a breath and dragged her hand out from beneath his.

'Guess we got sidetracked,' she murmured.

Try as he might, he couldn't take his gaze from her lips. 'Guess we did.'

'Thing is, to get back to it, if I agreed to this Outback plan of yours, Marla would either love me for ever or never talk to me again. When I can't be sure of Greg's intentions that night, I simply can't take that risk.'

Although he capitulated on the bill—they paid half each—he wasn't prepared to accept her decision to bow out of the plan. He meant to convince her and convince her tonight. He simply needed a little more time.

A few minutes later, strolling through Chinatown amid a high-energy Friday night crowd, Nate was focusing on his next move when she stopped at the kerb. Hitching her handbag higher on her shoulder, she raised a hand to flag down an approaching cab. He moved to lower her hand but, remembering that earlier sizzle, thought better of it.

Instead he stated, 'I'll drop you home.'

That cab whizzed by, but she waved at another. 'I can find my own way home.'

'I insist.'

'So do I.'

'I surrendered on the bill,' he pointed out. 'It's your turn to bend.'

'It's not my turn to do anything.'

When a second cab ignored her hail and, stubborn, she only looked for another, he checked out the growing city crowd, then his wristwatch. 'You do realize we could be here all night.'

Roxy opened her mouth to disagree. But then the logic must have interceded because the fire in her eyes faded and eventually she sent a contrite smile in spite of herself. 'Friday night's not the easiest time to get a taxi.'

'No, it's not.'

'Don't suppose you'll take five bucks for gas.'

She was joking. He should laugh. And, truth was, he found her need to be self-sufficient extremely attractive. But the past shaped us all and he wondered if maybe the biggest reason Roxy was Miss Independence now was because she hadn't been able to rely on the person who should have had her back when she was young. Her philandering father. The reason *he* was so driven stemmed back to his father too, but for vastly different reasons.

With traffic whirring by and people rolling past, he stepped forward and smiled down into her beautiful expectant face. Thankfully, she didn't baulk and move away.

'I won't take your money,' he said, 'but you can do something in return.'

A frown pinched her brow. 'Like go to the Outback?'

'I was going to say tell me more about the time you were invited to base-jump in Switzerland.'

Despite the fact she didn't like him—or at least pretended most of the time that was the case—her expression changed now, opened up, and the sparkle he'd seen earlier in her eyes returned.

'By that couple who wanted to spend their honeymoon jumping off cliffs with similar-minded friends,' she clarified. 'Needless to say, I declined.'

'A bat suit not flattering enough?'

'I have a problem with heights.'

As she explained more and they set off for the parking lot, he instinctively went to rest a palm on her back to help guide her through the crowd. At the last moment, he reconsidered. It might be the gentlemanly thing to do, the way he'd been brought up, but as Roxy had said: some risks simply weren't worth taking.

Twenty minutes later, Nate swerved his car in front of Roxy's quaint cottage of a house. The hedges were still maintained, the picket fence still upright and strong. Everything was just as he remembered from six months earlier. Including the sense of physical awareness cracking like an electric whip between them now.

Over the last few minutes, banter had ceased. He couldn't say for sure what she was thinking, feeling. But the only thing rumbling through *his* mind was recalling how he'd felt the last time he'd driven her home. Hyped. Taut with anticipation. That night he'd known he was going to kiss her. He simply hadn't known how darn good it would be.

But he'd already decided he and Roxy would not kiss again. He wasn't ready to take a chance on turning into a hobbled married man overnight like Sparks men were wont to do. Although…

If Roxy was against the idea of settling down as much as he was, didn't that make a difference? Even if the world went mad and he asked her for her hand in a matter of weeks, given what she'd told him earlier, it would only be for the competition. The marriage could be easily dissolved. She was not looking to get tied down. She was a career person, like him.

Nevertheless, when Roxy found the car door release, where he would normally have walked her to the door, Nate stayed glued to his seat. Etiquette was one thing, stupidity versus self-knowledge and survival quite another.

From beneath lowered lashes, she said, 'Thanks for the lift.'

Gripping the steering wheel, he nodded once. 'I'll be in touch.'

'Nate, I am sorry but I—'

Anticipating her words, he cut her off. 'Please. Think about my plan for Marla and Greg overnight. If you're still not convinced, I won't bother you again.'

Did she know he was stretching the truth? Not only was this a good plan, it was the only one he had. With persistence—some subtle persuasion—Roxy would come around.

In the street-lit shadows locked within the car's cabin, her uneasy expression eased and their gazes held for a powerful moment. He gripped the wheel tighter, set his toes into their inner soles more, but that pleasant sensation burning high on his thighs didn't leave him. If she tipped half an inch closer, the fight would be over. He'd have to kiss her—at least just once more. Hell, if she didn't come right out and belt him, kissing her and staying with it might even help his cause.

But then the car door whooshed open and closed and in a blink she was gone, striding down a path that led to her door while the throbbing in all his main arteries pulsed on.

Still, as he watched her retreat, a small smile hooked up on one side of his mouth. He liked the way she walked, particularly in those black tailored trousers. That silk blouse was sexy too. And boots…he'd always been a fan. What kind of lingerie was she hiding beneath that ensemble? He'd bet French lace. *White* sexy-as-hell French lace.

A raucous laugh, loud enough to penetrate his window's glass, grabbed Nate's attention. On the other side of the street, two youths were strutting down the footpath, jeans falling off their backsides, bright coals from cigarettes dangling from their lips. A chill chased up Nate's spine and he shot another glance Roxy's way. Standing outside her front door, she was digging around in her bag for a key. And now those guys had stopped to check out his car. Or were they eyeing the babe standing alone among those convenient shadows?

His heart thudding low in his chest, Nate wrung the steering wheel and waited while Roxy fished around more. When the youths swapped hushed words, laughed again then ambled across to Roxy's side—*his* side—of the street, Nate made an executive decision. He didn't care if those guys were A-grade citizens out for a harmless stroll, which he doubted. He wouldn't leave until Roxy was safe inside.

Nate shoved open the door.

The noise earned the boys' attention. Standing in the cool night air, Nate challenged their wary gaze. After a few seconds, one flicked his butt at the gutter before both continued leisurely past and down the street. Nate almost bared his teeth. *Good riddance and don't come back.*

When the pair was a block away, he focused on Roxy again. Had she lost her keys somewhere? Did she have a spare for the house? He couldn't leave until she was inside, which at this rate might take all night.

As Nate approached the house Roxy pulled her nose out from her bag and her expression opened in surprise.

She stammered, 'Wh-what are you doing?'

'Helping to find your keys.'

'They slipped to the bottom, but I have them now.' She withdrew a set from her bag and jingled.

'Right. Good.' Glancing over his shoulder, Nate craned his neck to be sure that unsavoury element was indeed gone. 'You ought to get inside.' He crowded her back towards the door. 'It's late.'

'I've lived on my own for a while now.'

'Be that as it may.' He took the key she'd chosen from a half-dozen looped on the ring, then unlocked and fanned open the door. 'Remember to lock up behind you.'

Her eyes twinkled with amusement, as if she was less irritated by his edict and maybe more touched.

That menacing laughter rang out again, distant but not nearly far enough away. Hackles rising, Nate headed towards the street to make his presence known again. The Sparks were a family who paid attention to hunches, good and sometimes bad feelings that were in no way limited to choosing a spouse. He trusted his instincts. This one made his gut clutch and the back of his neck go hot.

'Nate?'

He dragged his attention back to where Roxy stood outside her now opened door.

'It's still early,' she said, and her gaze dipped before meeting his again. 'Would you like to come in for a drink?'

At her words, that earlier warmth rose to fill his chest and, for a moment, he couldn't think of one reason he shouldn't. He'd never met a woman he could speak with more easily. He liked her wit, her intelligence, the way that tiny dimple winked in her left cheek whenever she grinned. But if he took up her offer, the night might start with a drink but it sure as heck wouldn't finish on one. Still, she knew now precisely where he stood. And he knew where she stood too. Neither of them wanted 'serious'.

He didn't have to go the whole way and actually *sleep* with her…although some pillow talk leading into the Outback scheme couldn't hurt. But simple truth was— right this minute—he wanted that drink. Wanted that kiss.

'How does coffee sound?' she asked.

'Just coffee?'

'I have hot chocolate. Tea too, I think.'

'Is that all?'

'What else would you like?'

He took two measured steps towards her. 'That's up to you.'

She blinked twice and fast because there was nothing ambivalent about his tone or the intent he was certain shone in his eyes. A small smile quivered on her lips.

'Well, this is a turnaround.'

'Nothing's changed. I wanted to come in that night six months ago too.'

'Except you were dead certain I wanted to throw a rope around your ankles and drag you down the aisle.'

'Now I know better.'

While she peered up uncertainly into his eyes, he soaked up the last of the anticipation, then reached out and took what he couldn't deny either of them a moment more.

CHAPTER THREE

ROXY's head was swimming. In a matter of seconds, a situation she'd had under control had spun a three-sixty and now Nate was going to *kiss* her.

Of course, she'd felt the possibilities—the attraction—building between them all night. Perhaps she'd asked him in because deep down she wanted to face this irresistible force and get it over with. But was she truly game enough to see how long these sparks could fly before multiplying out of control?

She was still angry over the way he'd left her standing here on this very spot six months ago. Still secretly fuming over that photo taken of him enjoying himself with some other woman only a week later. On the other hand, she couldn't deny she'd never felt this strongly about anyone before. She'd never known this kind of intensity existed. Maybe these kinds of feelings were the reason her mother had let her wayward husband come back again and again. Why she'd never had any sense where his obvious shortfalls were concerned. Roxy had been so annoyed by her mother's blindness…her incurable weakness.

Nate's mouth was a hair's-breadth from hers when strength returned to Roxy's legs, she spun around and, still light-headed but seeing more clearly, managed to step over the threshold. Working to catch her breath, she came up with a suitable throwaway line that sounded almost unaffected.

'I think I have some chocolate to go with the coffee.'

'Something sweet sounds good.'

His deep sure tone sent her pulse rampaging all the more. But she didn't want Nate to know the tumult she was in, although by the confident smile she saw smouldering in his eyes when she flicked on the light, she supposed he already knew.

Bolstering herself up, she closed and locked the door, then headed for the kitchen, which was part of the open-plan living area.

'Guess you bring your work home,' he said as she found the coffee grinds and he strolled into a lounge room littered with a designer-slash-seamstress's ware.

'Some might call it messy,' she told him. 'I prefer the term *inspiring*. I have a sewing room here as well as at the shop. Fabric, patterns, lace and buttons… It all kind of spills out around the place.'

Edging around two partially dressed mannequins, he pretended to shudder. 'I feel like I'm being watched.'

'Wait till they start talking to you.'

He shot her a wry glance. 'Just assure me you don't talk back.'

Roxy didn't admit that, late at night on a deadline, sometimes she thought they did.

While she thumbed on the kettle and worked to rationalise her feelings—what she truly wanted from tonight, why she wanted it, whether she was in any way like her mother—Nate wandered around more.

'Where do you get your ideas?'

'I keep abreast of present fashions as well as past.' She flicked the tap and rinsed the plunger out. 'When I'm commissioned to design a dress, I try hard to get inside the bride's skin, so to speak. Understand what tone she wants to relay and capture it as closely as I can.'

Looking larger than life in her usually uncomplicated space, Nate had stopped to study a magazine spread on spring brides opened on the couch. He ran a hand through his coal-black hair as he leaned forward to focus more on the page.

'Ever get it wrong?' he asked, leaving the magazine to head for the kitchen where she was pouring boiled water.

'I had a client once who wanted to look like a bunny.'

'As in Playboy or Bugs?'

'As in big front teeth, carrot loving, fluffy ball of tail. We talked extensively and I came up with sketches and ultimately a gown I thought captured her dream about her walk, or should I say *hop*, down the aisle.'

'Then she decided to go as Bambi, right?'

'Oh, no. This woman was focused. Picture it. A winter theme. The bolero jacket lovingly sewn from imitation fur. A veil that, as best I could manage, resembled bunny ears. A fluffy ball secured the train at the back.'

'And she hated it.'

'She loved it!' Roxy set the mugs, sugar and some cream on a tray. 'In fact, it wasn't enough. She wanted whiskers attached to the veil. You know, the part that covers a bride's face before the groom kisses her.'

'Forgive me for saying, but, *Wacko*.'

She plunged the coffee. 'I said I could do the whiskers… somehow. But then she had another brilliant idea. A bouquet of fresh carrots and she wanted all the guests to wear carrot buttonholes and corsages.'

'Like I said…' He wound a finger around near his temple before moving to help with the tray.

She indicated he should set it on the coffee table and admitted, 'The groom had had enough.'

Roxy lowered down on one side of the three-seater while Nate took the couch's other end—a relatively safe distance from each other, although given how close he'd come to capturing her on the doorstep a few minutes ago, she wasn't certain that would last, or whether she really wanted it to. With a remarkably steady hand, she poured his coffee and handed it over.

'This guy said he loved her carrot cake and fluffy bunny feet slippers, but no way was *he* wearing carrots. Enough was enough. The disagreement escalated. The wedding was called off. The bride wouldn't blame her fiancé or herself so she blamed me for not delivering.'

He frowned before his gaze filled with disbelief, then compassion. 'You're serious.'

'It's not up to me to tell a bride what her expectations of her big day should be—' she had her own ideas…romantic, tastefully unique '—but I've learned that sometimes it's best to follow instinct and suggest perhaps another designer.'

While stirring in sugar, he cast another curious look around and Roxy forced her focus away from the rhythmic motion of his hand and how that smattering of dark hair filtering down one side made her feel a little weak and definitely wanting. Which was a far cry from the stand she'd taken over the preceding six months when she'd sworn they would never lock lips again.

Concentrating to fill her mug and contain her seesawing feelings, she passed another look over the fabric samples and mannequins, and frowned. They really were everywhere.

'This must look incredibly unnecessary to someone who doesn't know how to thread a needle.'

'So you presume.'

About to sip, she arched a brow. 'Don't tell me you know how to sew?'

'My mother tried to teach me to hem once. She said domestic chores weren't purely women's work.'

'What did your dad say?'

'I think he was busy ironing at the time.'

Roxy chuckled. 'Did you learn to hem?'

'I'm relieved to say she gave up on me. Threading that eensy-weensy needle near drove me mad.'

A common dilemma. She set down her mug. 'Let me introduce you to a common trick of the trade.'

After sourcing a needle from a nearby sewing box, as well as a length of thread and her trusty needle threader, she moved to sit on the padded arm of the couch nearest Nate, but then stopped. Wasn't she inviting trouble?

On the other hand—if she put a zipper on the voice inside her head—wasn't a teeny taste of trouble what she wanted?

Implements in hand, she shored herself up and set her behind down on the padded couch arm. She angled slightly so that her doubtful student could see every step.

'You slot this looped wire through the eye of the needle, like so.'

His head going back, Nate squinted. 'See. Right there. Already I need a magnifying glass.'

'You'll never thread a needle any other way after this.'

'I'll never thread a needle again, period.' Gifting her a dazzling grin that made her insides squeeze and quiver, he took the needle, the threader. He shut one eye, pulled his mouth a certain scrumptious way and poked the wire through. Chuffed, he sat back. 'Now what?'

'Run the thread through the opening of the looped wire.'

One eye closed again, he guided the thread through, then let out a deeply satisfied sigh. 'Next?'

'You pull the threader back through the eye of the needle and it's done.'

'It can't be that simple.'

She'd been concentrating on the threader, on the process. But now she felt her hand lightly touching his—or, more precisely, that sexy smattering of dark hair—and a tingling bright sensation fell through her middle, settling into an all too pleasant heat at her core. Had Nate noticed that her breathing was coming slightly faster, that she was leaning that bit closer?

As her heartbeat rushed in her ears, carefully she lifted her gaze.

Nate was looking not at the needle and thread but at her. From the smoke in his usually clear blue eyes, he'd guessed at her avalanche of feelings. When a pulse beat once low on his cheek and he tipped closer, his gaze gravitating to her lips, the brushfires coursing through her blood threatened to turn into an inferno. A knowing grin lifted a corner of his mouth while his gaze stroked her like a lover's touch.

'Nope. I still can't quite seem to get it...'

Short on air, Roxy managed to swallow. Damn the man. Neither could she. Did he want to kiss her or not?

He must have read her mind. Blindly he set the needle and thread on the coffee table, then one big palm curled around her nape while the other cupped her shoulder, winging her gently in. His head angled and gaze intensified as if he was giving her time to truly grasp what was about to unfold, then his essence seemed to fill every part of her, her eyes drifted closed and his mouth at last met hers.

That familiar drugging warmth filtered through her system as Roxy slipped into a state of both blessed relief and spiralling passion while the wet tip of his tongue traced over her lower lip, then slid past her teeth to wind deep and hot inside. With him holding and exploring her, her arms went out to draw him in at the same time any oxygen left in her world evaporated and she surrendered without reserve. As much as she'd like to deny it—deny him—wasn't this the moment she'd been waiting for?

As she savoured the embrace and his chin grazed her cheek, he manipulated her around until she'd drifted to lie near horizontal, draped over his lap. With one palm cradling her head and his chest rumbling with satisfaction, he proceeded to kiss her more thoroughly than she'd ever been kissed before. Still she needed more.

Drowning in sensation, she reached across, found the hand gripping her shoulder and slid his palm down her upper arm, then over towards her breast. When his fingertips brushed the peak beneath her blouse, her womb compressed and beat a rhythm that released a hot surge of longing at the apex of her thighs. He rolled and plucked the sensitive tip until the throbbing in her belly grew to a point where she only wanted to rip off her clothes and have him finish feeding this mind-blowing want. It was official. She'd lost her mind.

But then the crush of his kiss eased enough for him to murmur against her parted lips.

'Mmm…this *is* sweet.' His smile feathered over her mouth. 'Very sweet, indeed.'

His mouth claimed hers again while that hand ironed down her side, over the ticklish slope near her hip and across to that part of her that begged for attention. Over the fabric of her trousers, his long fingers curved down and pressed between her legs. When she melted more, his touch rode slightly higher to circle a spot that felt three heartbeats away from catching light and consuming her whole. Her every cell floated higher while her core squeezed and pulsed and reality shrank down to only this. To only Nate and only now.

When the pressure of his touch, of his kiss, lightened again, Roxy groaned as some of what the world had been before filtered in. She couldn't care if Hollywood's most celebrated female celebrity were knocking on her door desperate for a million-dollar dress. Her only thought was to have him back. Have him kiss her again and again.

His scratchy cheek came to rest alongside hers as his deep velvet voice rumbled at the sensitive shell of her ear.

'I'm glad we worked out our differences.'

His mouth gravitated to her throat and nibbled down while she sighed and murmured, 'Me too.'

'I vote we take this to your bedroom.' His tongue looped around the hollow at the base of her throat. 'Call me cautious but I'm not a friend of stray needles.'

Spreading her fingers over his shoulder, she arched towards him and, as if the world were about to end and this would be their last, he scooped under her back, lifted her higher and kissed her again. The raw sensation he mined from deep inside left her mind blank but for the stars. His next words were muffled and rough as he spoke against her lips as if he couldn't bear to leave them.

'Which way?'

She was prying his shirt tails out from beneath his belt. 'Which way what?'

She felt his grin. 'Your bedroom.'

Oh, yes… She hummed out a smile. She longed to sprawl out on cool sheets while he flicked open her blouse buttons, wound the silk from her shoulders, peeled the bra from her…*from her*…

A sudden heart-stopping fright seized her chest and Roxy's eyes flew open as ice-cold dread fell like a lead weight through her middle. She'd totally forgotten. Beneath her blouse, her chemise, she wore underwear a prim great-aunt would be ashamed of. She couldn't let him see her in granny pants. But now they'd come this far, what could she do or say to get around it? Maybe if they went to the bedroom and kept the lights off…

She blinked and came back to the here and now. Nate was peering down at her most curiously. Her face beginning to burn, Roxy eased up and sat alongside him while he studied her face, then carefully cupped her cheek.

'You went all stiff,' he said. 'Did I do something wrong?'

'No.' *God, no!* 'I was just thinking, ah…thinking that I should, um…' She searched her panicked brain, gave a quick smile and a shrug. 'That I should go freshen up.'

'Well, sure.' He cleared his throat, siphoned down a settling breath, then looked at her closer still. 'Roxy, are you sure everything's okay? Because if you're uncomfortable with us getting together like this—without any added strings, I mean—tell me. I'd rather know.'

She took in the earnest slant of his brows, the cautionary tone in his voice, and more of those glorious got-to-have-you feelings fragmented and floated away. Pulling her mouth to one side, she brushed hair back from her face and replied.

'Nate, I don't need to be told that this is sex for sex's sake.'

His expression softened as his eyes dropped to stroke her lips once more. 'You know that's not the way I see this.'

In a skilled fluid movement, he angled to bring her against him again. But a flattened palm against his hard chest stopped him dead. She needed to know.

'How *do* you see this?'

'As two like-minded people moving forward, coming together.' His hot mouth brushed and tickled her ear. 'Hopefully coming a lot.'

Cute. But not the answer she was looking for.

When a knuckle drew a confident line up her throat and urged her chin back—when she found her mouth a breath away from his again—unease rose higher, her throat closed off and, decided, she got to her feet. Straightening her blouse, she tried to gather her jumbled thoughts. One day he was running and the next he was all over her, but making doubly sure that she knew this meant nothing beyond the physical. A quick romp in the sack. No doubt the same kind of tumble he'd enjoyed with that brunette from the photo, and how many more since.

'Is this how you treat every woman you're attracted to?'

He looked insulted. 'Of course not.'

'Then why *me*?'

'Because, unless you hadn't noticed, I'm not simply attracted to you.' A line formed between his brows before he rubbed his palms up and down his long hard thighs. 'It's complicated.'

'Unlike a quick shag in my bed tonight.'

'No, actually, that *is* complicated.' His gaze and voice dropped. 'More complicated than you could imagine.'

To keep her heart from dropping any lower, she knotted her arms over her waist. 'I need some answers, Nate, and I need them fast.'

'You wouldn't believe it.'

Her eyes narrowed. 'Try me.'

He squared his shoulders, rubbed his thighs again.

'If you really want to know,' he said, 'my family is cursed, although *cursed* is an interchangeable term. My parents and grandparents would say that we're blessed.'

She edged away. 'Okay. Now you're freaking me out. Do you all turn into snarling wolves on a full moon?'

'Only Great-uncle Stuart on my mother's side.' Her mouth dropped open and he grinned. 'Now you can laugh.'

She glared but refrained from telling him to forget she'd ever asked. A curse. Well, at least he had imagination.

'Go on,' she said. 'I'm listening. Although I'm not certain why.'

'From as far back as anyone can remember,' he said, pushing to his feet, 'Sparks men have been hit hard when Cupid's arrow strikes.'

'That doesn't sound so tragic to me. In fact, it sounds rather romantic.'

'Romantic, lucky, decisive. All those things and, apparently, all good for those who have come before me. Dad, Grandfather Sparks and on up the line…they've all fallen and for the right woman, it would seem. Each couple has tied the knot within weeks of starting to date. Nine months on, like clockwork, the first child comes along, and any plans for a career, for a solid future, is put on the back burner indefinitely. My father could have been a surgeon. Instead for years he cleaned bedpans.'

'And that's the curse's fault?'

His chiselled features hardened more. 'My predecessors have given up everything for love. Career. Health. In some instances, their sanity. Call me selfish or an egotist but I don't want to be a hospital wardsman or the road maintenance guy who holds up slow-down signs when I can work in a professional field that I'm good at. That I enjoy.'

Roxy eyed him up and down. This was hogwash. Curses weren't real. Intelligent men weren't bewitched by women who sucked out their souls. This must be another scam, like when, earlier, he'd manipulated Ava Morris into believing he was a genuine guy with a fiancée he adored. Having said that, she would concede she was beyond grateful for the sale. At least she could pay some outstanding bills.

And yet as she continued to study him Roxy couldn't help but be halfway convinced by the resignation shining in his eyes. Could he have been brainwashed from child-hood into accepting this family curse junk? Common sense wasn't a factor when you were taught from birth what to believe. What was truth. Like, *Your father does love us. If he didn't, he wouldn't come back.*

'This has really got you convinced, hasn't it?'

'I grew up dirt poor,' he said, 'which I can more than handle. The really hard part was having a father who couldn't function without his other half. I'm saying if my mother had died, he would have died too. When you have five kids to consider, I don't care how many love stories you've seen, that's not romantic. It's—'

Growling, he bit off the word.

'You're the only son,' she said. *The oldest.* 'What do your sisters say?'

'They never had careers to consider. And before you pounce, my respect for a woman doesn't hinge on whether she has a career or not. I'm just saying.'

Being the only other 'man' in the family, perhaps Nate felt the responsibility—the link with his parents—more deeply or differently than the girls. She had to ask.

'Sure there's not a little Oedipus syndrome going on here?'

He pulled a pained face. 'But even if there were, fact remains, I'm not ready to settle down. Fall in love. Gamble my future or throw it away.'

Her smile was thin. *Nice.* 'I pity the poor girl you end up proposing to—properly, that is.'

'That's a long way off.'

She studied the firm set of his mouth and for a heart-beat she wanted to comfort him. Seemed his childhood wasn't as rosy as she first thought. He'd grown up feeling pushed to the background. Feeling as if he and his siblings didn't matter as much as they should. At least when her father had been home, he'd showered her with affection. Her dad was a charismatic man, the kind who didn't self-analyze or register any guilt.

But as much as Roxy sympathized with 'Nate the boy', a stronger part of her said, *Enough.* A whole new stream of commitment phobia could be named after 'grown-up Nate'. Whether he was justified in his negative stand regarding love and marriage, she wasn't in a position to say. She hadn't lived his life and didn't own anyone's opinions. She could only look after her own best interests and more than ever they seemed clear.

Roxy shored herself up. 'It's certainly been an interesting evening.'

The tension in his face, in his stance, seemed to ease. A grateful smile hooked one corner of his mouth at the same time long warm fingers curled around her hand and, just like that, a bevy of sparks spiralled up her arm, stole her breath.

'So you *do* understand,' he said.

'Frankly, I'm not sure if I do or I don't. I only know I don't feel as convinced about having you stay as I did five minutes ago.'

On a logical level, she knew that at this point in their lives neither wanted anything as serious as marriage. But she simply couldn't sleep with someone who made it sound as if she was little more than a release for sexual cravings. Yes, she'd been as turned on as Nate, but, now that she'd had time to take a breath, she knew this scenario was all wrong. She wasn't after phone calls every night; however, neither would she accept, *Thanks for the hump. I'll call if I call.* That was too darn close to the treatment her mother had accepted. She had more respect for herself than that.

His grip and jaw tightened even as his grin grew and

he joked. 'I could go with the curse turning me into a wolf if that'd help.'

She couldn't see anything would.

Feeling flat but resigned, she slipped her hand away from his. 'I need for you to go.'

CHAPTER FOUR

SITTING on the verandah of Marla's third-storey apartment late the next day, Roxy slid another Scrabble tile onto the game board and in a supportive tone asked her friend the question that had hung in the air since she'd arrived.

'How are you holding up?'

'All things considered…' Absently studying the board, which had been handed down through her family from the fifties, Marla shrugged. 'It'll take a while.'

'Have you heard from Greg?'

'Not since that slideshow.'

Greg running slides of their most romantic moments from a projector onto a screen outside her apartment had been an inventive way to reach Marla when she wouldn't take his calls. The upshot, however, was that the shots had reminded Marla of those despised pictures she'd seen on the Net. She'd been less than impressed.

'Greg broke my heart,' Marla went on. 'I don't know if I'll ever trust a man again. I wanted to spend the rest of my life with him, have children together.' Shaking back her auburn locks, she put more steel into her voice. 'I can't believe he was groping a near-naked woman behind my back, and who knows what else? A lot more happens at those buck's nights than some women might think. A *lot* more.'

Surrounded by sweet-smelling umbrellas of Jacaranda blooms, Roxy mulled over Marla's heartbreaking situation as well as Nate's suggestion they ought to get the couple together to give them time to sort it out. When she'd asked Nate to leave last night, Roxy had been determined that would be the last she'd ever hear of him or that plan, and Marla's response now only validated her decision. Her friend needed time to heal, not a web of lies that would hurl her into the face of the person who had shredded her heart.

Good or bad, images stuck. Heck, *Marla* had never been snapped fondling another person's private parts.

Although…

Roxy remembered at the hen's night, as part of the show, a nicely built topless waiter had flirted with the bride-to-be unashamedly and Roxy had laughed and cheered as hard as the rest. What would Greg say if he were to watch a tape of that? Was it a once-in-a-lifetime situation, a bit of harmless fun or something best kept concealed? One day when the right man came along, no doubt she would enjoy a hen's night too.

But if what Nate said was true, a Sparks man didn't care to celebrate a buck's night so much as make a commitment to the woman he adored. And in truth, despite being annoyed, frustrated—hurt—Roxy had to wonder. When he got over his angst and did allow himself to fall in love, would Nate make a devoted husband? Someone a wife could be proud to have at her side? Would it be a case of 'like Sparks father like Sparks son'?

Each deep in their own thoughts, the women played a few more words before Marla spoke again.

'I wasn't going to tell you until plans were set, but it's only a matter of a week or so now.'

Curious, Roxy glanced up from collecting more tiles. 'What plans?'

'I'm leaving the country. I've told you about my brother and his IT firm in California. He suggested I go stay with him a while. Learn something different. Make new friends.' Marla reached over and caught Roxy's arm. 'Not that I don't value the ones I have here.' She tried to smile. 'You understand, don't you, Rox?'

Feeling giddy, Roxy had to sit back. She knew, despite the distance, Marla was close to her brother, but this decision had left her reeling.

'How long will you be gone?'

'A year. Two.' Marla shrugged. 'I'm not sure.'

On one hand Roxy was pleased Marla had decided to take a firm grip on life's reins and move forward. Neither of them was the type to wallow in self-pity and, given that Marla earned a living as a freelance business consultant, she didn't have any concrete employment ties. On the other, Roxy would miss her friend like crazy. They did so much together, had shared so much.

And there was Greg, a man who had pledged his innocence...just as Roxy's father always had.

But was it possible that Nate was right? What if Greg *had* been a victim of circumstance and he and Marla could get over this major bump in their road? That would never happen with ten thousand miles and two years or more separating them.

Until a moment ago, she'd been better than okay with letting matters take their own course. But with Marla deciding to leave—and so soon—suddenly the way ahead didn't seem quite so clear.

Roxy set down the last tile in her word—an *H*—and summoned the courage to ask. 'What if you woke up tomorrow morning and found out it had all been a horrible mistake. That Greg hadn't done anything wrong and you could still go ahead with the wedding?'

Her eyes glistening, Marla sighed. 'If that were to happen, if I could somehow truly find that faith again and get those pictures out of my mind…well, I'd be the happiest, most relieved woman in the world.'

Then, with a wan smile, she set down three letters after Roxy's. The word spelled HOPE.

'You *have* to come to the anniversary party. Mum and Dad will be crushed if you don't.'

Nate turned away from his sister—the second eldest of the Sparks siblings—to resume a seat at his apartment's dining room table; he'd been sorting out reports before Ivy's unexpected visit. He didn't mind being interrupted. He simply felt uncomfortable about the reason.

'I never said I *wouldn't* go.' He dragged over a pile of papers. 'It's just I probably won't stay long.'

'If you have a hot date lined up, bring her.'

'I don't have a hot date.'

'Then maybe you should find one.'

He sent her a look. 'Don't start on me about finding a nice girl and settling down. I get enough of that from our father.'

'I'm not talking about *till death us do part*.' Ivy's blue-grey eyes filled with needless sympathy. 'I'd simply like to see you get out from under your grindstone and let your hair down a bit. We all would. You've been so focused on getting this business of yours off the ground, you barely take time to eat.'

'I eat. *And* I have a personal life.'

She arched an eyebrow and looked over the papers. 'So, what's this you're busy with?'

'I'm sorting out performance charts for reps as a function of purchasing patterns and meeting bi-annual budgets.'

Ivy emptied her lungs. 'The perfect way to spend a

Sunday.' She crossed her arms over the waist of her pink cotton dress and pegged out a leg. 'When was the last time you went out to dinner? And I'm talking attractive female, not wheeling and dealing with some boring businessman type.'

'Businessmen aren't boring,' he eyed his colour-coded charts and mumbled, '...necessarily.'

'So when?'

'As a matter of fact, I took a lady out night before last.'

Ivy's gaze sharpened. 'Have you seen her before?'

'Affirmative.'

'Plan to see her again?'

He thought for a moment and admitted, 'I'd like to.' Irrespective of the disappointing way the night had ended—how much Roxy obviously still didn't trust him— simple truth was he'd like to a lot.

'Ohmigod.' Ivy sank into the chair beside him. 'It's serious.'

'Don't go choosing bridesmaid's shoes just yet. I would never let it get that far.' *And neither would Roxy.*

Before tossing him out, she'd made herself clear. Roxy was attracted to him physically, intellectually, but she didn't want to rub shoulders with his demons. Perhaps she thought he used his family history as an excuse, a trick so she wouldn't expect him to call—at least not regularly.

He hadn't stopped thinking about her since and, for the first time in years, he was questioning his beliefs. Still, curse or not, he did *not* want to get hitched. But he *did* want to spend time with the woman who his mind respected and his body craved—more every minute.

'So, will the family meet this mystery girl at the anniversary dinner?' Ivy asked. 'I mean before you whisk her off somewhere quiet and romantic, away from your terribly supportive dreary family?'

Shoving the reports aside, he moved to a glass slider's view of Sydney's cityscape and Harbour Bridge. 'She's not going to that party.'

Even if he did decide to brave the endless questions from family members—their over-the-top encouragement—and ask her, Roxy wouldn't accept.

Ivy sniffed. 'Anyone might think you're ashamed of us.'

'You know that's not true. It'll be the same old crowd going over the same old stories. The food will be more extravagant, the fireworks brighter and higher, but the couple of the moment will still be trying to set me up with some woman or other. Drives me *nuts*.'

They'd grown up poor but five years ago a distant relative had left his mother a stack of money, so the anniversary parties were the same—only *bigger*.

Ivy grinned as she had when they were kids and she beat him at checkers. 'They won't try to set you up if you bring someone of your own along. I for one am dying to meet her. What does she do for a living? Blonde or brunette? Is she wildly in love with you already or playing it cool?'

'Depends which day it is.' When Ivy's ears seemed to prick, Nate waved his hands. *Scrap that.* But he did have something he wanted to share or, rather, ask. A question that had eaten at him since leaving Roxy's place so abruptly Friday night.

'Ivy, what do you know about the Sparks family curse?'

'Don't call it that. It's a—'

'Blessing. Right. What do you know?'

'It stems from an epitaph Great-grandfather Sparks found on an ancestor's gravestone back in England. Read something like…*"I live only for your heart and wither without your love."* The wife was buried one day, her husband a month later. More ancestral research led our great-grandfather to the conclusion that we have a history of falling in love quickly and staying that way.' Her sigh eased into a soft faraway smile. 'I get such a buzz from telling the kids how Nan and Grandad fell in love at first sight just like a prince and princess from a fairy tale.'

'Our grandparents too,' he said, crossing back from the view.

'Don't you melt whenever you see those two walking hand in hand? I hope Cameron and I are still cuddling when we're eighty-five.'

Nate didn't doubt Ivy and her husband would be. Those two adored each other, and their two children. Another happy family Sparks success story. But that wasn't what he wanted to know.

'So, is there anything in it? Is the curse real or not?'

She blinked and then her eyes widened to saucers. 'You *are* serious about this girl, aren't you? You're afraid you'll beg for her hand, the curse, as you call it, will be awakened and all the effort you've put into this business hope will come to nothing because you'd have found something that matters more than money.'

He held onto his groan and asked again. 'Do you think there's some kind of voodoo involved or it's just a matter of, well…emotion?'

'Maybe it's both.' Gazing down, she twirled the gold band circling a finger on her left hand. 'Falling in love is a magical experience.'

He sat down at the table again. 'There's nothing magical about wearing patches to school.'

'Your pants may have been patched from time to time but it was a good school. A *private* school. You got a great education, Nate. We all did.'

'It wouldn't have been such an almighty struggle if Dad had finished his own education.'

'I imagine children from divorced families struggle more than we did. Money was tight—'

'We couldn't afford to have the phone on. The electricity sometimes.'

'Which is an even greater testimony to our parents' dedication.'

What about their father's obsession with their mother to a point where nothing else mattered? Husband, fathers, were meant to be strong. Why couldn't his father have been a man as well as an enamoured spouse?

'I guess you and I see things differently,' Ivy said. 'Maybe because I'm happily married and...'

When her lips pressed together and her gaze veered off, he prodded.

'And what?'

She shrugged. 'I'm sorry, Nate. It's not something a person can explain.'

He assessed his sister's pitying smile and growled, not at her as much as himself. Would he still be torn this way at forty, fifty, *sixty*? He wanted to have a family some day, just not before he'd set himself up. Before he'd achieved what he'd worked so hard to secure.

Although, he shouldn't forget that Roxy felt the same way. She wasn't after a gold ring. But he also knew, despite her stand the other night, she wanted to spend time with him as much as he wanted to spend time with her.

Ten minutes later, Ivy was saying her goodbyes and Nate was still thinking about Roxy. Maybe he would call. He could pretend to keep busy, pretend he could forget, but the truth was he needed to talk with her again. Talk... and more.

Dammit, he couldn't get away from the fact that he wanted to know Roxy in the most intimate way. He wanted to make love to her—fiercely, then slowly, then all night long. Even now he could feel the satin of her skin beneath his fingers as his hands moulded over her bare limbs, her belly. Her breasts. Awake half the night, staring at the ceiling, he'd imagined the secret taste of her and how she might arch up and grip her legs around his thighs at the same time he lowered and plunged into her damp sweet warmth.

Ivy was right about one thing. He *did* need a hot date. He needed Roxy.

He was saying goodbye to his sister at the door when his phone beeped with a text. Nate checked the ID and near fell over.

I'LL PROBABLY REGRET THIS, the message read, BUT GUESS I'M IN. It was signed ROXY T.

CHAPTER FIVE

Two days later, Roxy and Marla arrived in the red dry plains of Australia's Outback.

From Sydney they'd flown north to Brisbane to board a small aircraft, which had taken just the two of them into the centre of Queensland. Nate had organised a later private flight for himself and Greg. All very clandestine. Another word that came to Roxy's mind was *underhanded*. She was still in two minds as to whether she ought to have given in and agreed.

After their Scrabble game and Marla's admission that she wished those photos and her doubts regarding Greg were somehow a mistake, Roxy had confirmed she'd go along with Nate's plan—but she was far from comfortable. Whether it was sweet-talking her customers or working his way around her and almost into her bed, Nate was a master manipulator. She only had to think of her parents' relationship to know a man's charm—even declarations of love—could be turned on and off to suit. But she wasn't here to dwell on that.

As the four-wheel-drive transfer vehicle pulled up now outside what would be their lodgings for the next few days, she only hoped that Nate's faith in his friend was true and well founded, and a happy ending would justify these deceptive means. She could only pray that her friend would make the right decision for her. And, hey, maybe Marla *would* say 'I do' and wear the gorgeous gown specially created for the occasion…the gown that might make that contest deadline after all.

With a hot breeze blowing in her face and a blazing mid-day sun beating down, Roxy alighted from the vehicle to study the eerily quiet landscape and sprawling, obviously once-grand but presently wholly unglamorous, homestead.

'I appreciate the surprise,' Marla said, 'but when you asked me to push back my plans for California to fit in a girlie escape to a secret location, I expected a tropical island. You know? Lying on some powdery beach, sipping a creamy cocktail.' She swiped at a noisy fly. 'Why this place?'

Roxy took in the homestead's flaky paint then a Frilly lizard scrambling over a bed of dead flowers and tried to make light. Not the Hilton, but didn't the charm of this old homestead make their trip more…interesting?

'Didn't you ever want to experience kangaroos bounding free? The enormous majesty of an Outback sunset?' She recited a couple of lines from a famous poem about a sun-burned country and sweeping plains. 'Who knows how long you'll be in California? This might be your only chance to experience your native country's true character.'

'I don't plan to be gone for ever.' Ducking, Marla waved away another pea-sized fly. 'Just long enough to escape for a while. To forget.'

When Marla's eyes welled and she slid the sunglasses perched atop her head onto her nose to hide the glisten of tears, Roxy tried to swallow the lump swelling in her own throat. Since they'd met in university, she and Marla had been as close as sisters; being an only child from an unstable home, that meant a lot. Too much to lose. And yet here she was jeopardizing that relationship. Then again, this might pay off in the best way possible and make their friendship even stronger.

Roxy held her swooping stomach. God, how she wished everything about this time were over.

At the same time the vehicle pulled away, the homestead's screen door squeaked open and a couple in their fifties moved out onto the wide verandah that surrounded the entire length of the house. The silver-haired man wore pressed jeans, a checkered shirt and a warm smile. In a faded printed dress, his beaming wife held onto his arm until the couple was close enough to extend a hand to greet their city guests.

'I'm Celia Glenrowan,' the woman said, and Roxy shook her weathered hand after Marla. 'Welcome to Glenrowan Station.'

'Celia can show you to your rooms,' Mr Glenrowan said, filing back hair before placing a battered Akubra square on his head. 'Then we can have a bite to eat and maybe take a ride around. You girls know how to handle a horse?'

Roxy spoke for them both. 'I do. I'm sure Marla would love to learn.'

'We got a couple of real ladies that'll suit you both just fine,' Mrs Glenrowan said, heading back to the homestead.

Mr Glenrowan collected the luggage. 'We'll keep the stallions for the other guests. Think the man said they liked to ride hard.'

Marla's brows lifted. 'There's other guests?'

'Due later today,' Mr Glenrowan replied, following his wife.

Marla murmured to Roxy, 'As long as it's not a couple of bad boys on the prowl. Then again, that type usually hit the hot spots—' she plucked at her blouse '—and I don't mean Simpson Desert hot.'

Roxy hid a cringe as her guilt barometer hit an all-time high. While an unsuspecting Marla headed off after the Glenrowans, she took in another sweeping glance over the gum-tree-studded panorama before folding her sleeves up another turn, saying a quick prayer and following.

The last through that screen door, Roxy was apparently the first to hear the churning rumble filtering in from afar. Cupping a hand over her brow, she squinted through the haze and spied a four-wheel-drive hovering on the shimmering horizon. She didn't think she or Marla had left anything behind but had their driver spotted something that he was good enough to want to return? Except the approaching vehicle was red whereas theirs had been white—which meant more visitors?

They four were supposed to be the only guests, but Nate and Greg weren't due for another two hours. Still, as the vehicle rumbled closer Roxy couldn't shake the feeling that one of its occupants was indeed her accomplice in crime. Perspiration beaded across her forehead and her thoughts began to race.

She and Nate had talked over the phone at length about arrangements, including the fact she'd secured the services of her younger cousin, who was in between jobs and grateful for the opportunity to mind the store for some extra cash. But they hadn't discussed a plan B should they land here at the same time. She and Marla were meant to be taking a tour around the property when the boys arrived.

Feeling queasy, Roxy stepped back from the door. Greg was in trouble because of his alleged subterfuge. Roxy could make excuses for herself—for this—but was she really any better?

Soon the vehicle pulled up. The driver let the engine run while Greg jumped down from the back seat, overnighter in hand. Having exited the other side, Nate rounded the tailgate. In such a harsh setting, under such intense circumstances, the sight of him took Roxy's breath away.

Walking into her shop the other day, he'd cut an impressive figure in a dark, tailored suit. In chinos and a more casual white button-down that night, he'd looked so hot, the sight of him had left her parched. But today—*now*—her every thought, every cell, was drawn to the uncompromising masculine sight of him. She wanted to tell herself that she couldn't stand the sight of him. But that would be the biggest lie of all.

When a simple chambray shirt, cuffs folded halfway up two tanned forearms, covered *that* broad chest and shoulders, it was transformed into something extraordinary. Watching those light blue jeans hug his thighs as he sauntered around the vehicle left her feeling giddy. By the time a black Akubra was fitted atop dark hair that ruffled in a rippling breeze, her heart was hammering double time up near her throat. Suddenly she was consumed by thoughts of the sensations he'd so effortlessly brought out in her the other night…feelings that had left her boneless, yearning to have him naked, hard and unapologetically close.

Why did he have to be so screwed up about curses and blessings and drag her into the mix?

She watched as Nate took in the bordering straggly gums and a drunken wire fence that disappeared into a drowsy infinity before shaking hands with the driver through the opened window, then saluting him off. A moment later, the vehicle rolled away, churning plumes of red dust in its wake. Roxy's stomach churned too. Was she meant to stand here, frozen, waiting for Marla to wander out and the bomb to fall? She'd rather dig a hole and disappear for good.

In a deep wry voice, Greg said to Nate, 'Could you have taken us anywhere more remote?'

'The idea was to get away.' Nate moved forward with the gait of a man expecting to step on a landmine any minute. He must feel as anxious as she did.

'Look, I know you're worried about the business,' Greg said, following, 'but you don't need me to make that company of yours a success.'

'That's one man's opinion.' Nate broke into a smile and clapped his buddy on the back. 'Let's get these bags inside and see what's what.'

Roxy shut her eyes as her stomach swooped again. This was the moment. Rather than them run into her here, hiding, better she get her butt out there and face the music now.

At the same time she pushed at the screen door Marla came up behind her and Roxy jumped and swallowed a surprised yelp.

'Our rooms are gorgeous,' Marla said. 'So big and comfy-looking. What's keeping you?' She must have seen the dread in her friend's face and, worried, she lowered her voice. 'Roxy, what's wrong? You look ready to faint.'

Roxy held her friend's shoulders. 'There's something I need to tell you. And before I do, I want you to know that there's nothing I wouldn't do for you. You know that, right?'

At that moment, Marla must have heard the men speaking, recognized the voices, then immediately dismissed it all as imagination because her expression went from worry to alarm to self-reproach in the blink of an eye. But when those voices grew louder, closer, Marla frowned and stepped around Roxy to peer out through the screen door. A heartbeat later, she made a sound as if she'd been kicked in the gut at the same time her knees gave way; Roxy had to dive to hold her friend up before she crumpled to the floor. Together they gazed out as the men strolled nearer, chatting, laughing, although, to someone in the know, Nate's body language seemed guarded.

Marla didn't consult her friend. Rather she straightened and burst through the door. Marla was a deeply feeling person but she could also be steely tough when the situation demanded. It was one of the reasons Roxy respected her so much. And why she was so worried now.

When Greg saw Marla, his smile slipped from his face and his lazy pace ground to a halt at the same time his head slanted to one side, as if looking from a different angle might change what he saw. Carefully he removed his sunglasses and his complexion drained.

Marla spoke first, directly at Greg. 'What on earth are you up to, sneaking around and following us out here like this? Must have taken some doing, Greg Martin, but if you think this is a way to wheedle back into my life, you're mistaken.'

Stunned, Greg was slowly shaking his head. 'Marla? What are you doing here?' He looked to Roxy, who now stood behind her friend, then Nate, and finally his face filled with dark understanding. His jaw jutting forward, he slotted his sunglasses in his shirt's top pocket and glared at his friend.

'You'd better start talking,' Greg said, 'and for both our sakes, it'd better be good.'

Nate wasn't sure how he managed it, but he persuaded everyone to sit calmly around the faded cedar setting, positioned beneath the homestead's corrugated-iron verandah roof, without having his head torn off. Given the tight line of Marla's mouth, she didn't want to share space with Greg, and from the vein pulsing at Greg's temple, he wasn't too comfortable being around Nate right now. But the only alternative was grand theft auto of the Glenrowans' pickup or finding a willing kangaroo to piggyback home, so the pair held their tempers and listened.

Serenaded by bush birds and fortified by tall glasses of Mrs Glenrowan's cool lemonade, Nate explained how this situation had come about, starting with his visit to Roxy's salon. He made clear that Roxy had agreed to this plan only after Marla had announced her trip to California. He also emphasized his belief that to do nothing was sometimes worse than forging ahead with only the best intentions in mind.

He concluded, 'Marla, you're understandably hurt by those photos, and Greg had done all he thought he could to apologize and make that hurt up to you. But maybe if you both sit down and talk about it, face to face, something can be resolved, even if it's only shedding some of these bad feelings before Marla goes to California.'

When Marla quietly groaned and flicked a not entirely repulsed glance Greg's way, Nate's hopes lifted. If she was willing to at least listen, that was a start. But then she pushed to her feet, her slim nostrils flared, and she spoke to Roxy.

'I don't know if I can ever forgive you for putting me in this position.' Her eyes began to glisten. 'After everything we've been through together, you do this.'

While Roxy bowed her head, Marla went to move back inside. But then Greg stood too.

'She only did what she hoped was right,' he said. 'Hell, Marla, if we're talking about friendship, these two are the best. Roxy and Nate have faith in us. Can't you have a little faith too? Just enough to at least hear me out properly.' His heart in his eyes, he stepped forward. 'You're the person I wanted to share the rest of my life with. I still want that, more than anything.'

Nate held that breath while Roxy bit her lip and Marla

glared at her ex. Little by little, the pain in her expression morphed into something less hostile and more yielding.

'I guess I know you didn't do this to hurt me, Roxy,' Marla said. 'It's just so... Well, I never dreamed...' Gathering herself, she drew up tall. 'I suppose, given you and Nate went to all this trouble and we're here, Greg and I could talk.' When Greg sighed out a smile and tipped forward, Marla put up both her palms. 'That in no way means I've changed my mind. Only that I'm willing to hear anything new you have to say.' She looked to Roxy. 'How many days are we here?'

'Four,' Roxy said.

Hugging herself, Marla gazed out over the endless plain of red dirt, tufts of Mitchell grass, drooping eucalypts, and muttered, 'Guess I'd better unpack.'

'I thought we might go for a swim,' Nate pitched in. 'The website shows a great-looking creek nearby.'

'*If* you can believe a photo on a website.'

Marla was being wry about Greg's predicament but she had a point. That website made this place look like an Outback palace. Maybe once—a long time ago. Not that luxury was needed for love to thrive. Heck, just look at his parents.

As Marla headed back inside, Greg picked up his bag. 'I should thank you both for organizing this, but I'll hold off to see how it all pans out. I could as easily end up with a fry pan landing on my head as getting Marla's arms back around me.' He moved off. 'Hope you have something amazing lined up for your next Act.'

Sitting in that flaky timber setting, shards of early afternoon sun slanting in, Roxy had never looked more beautiful or more uncertain. She gripped her chair's arm and waited until Greg was out of earshot before asking, 'I know the overall plan but...what exactly *do* we have lined up?'

Nate leaned closer and, fighting the overwhelming urge to tell her to forget about the other two for a moment and to concentrate working on them, he assured her.

'Our next move can't fail. It involves heating things up at the same time they're both cooling down.'

She nodded slowly. 'The creek.'

'You and I can splash around, share a bit of laughter and lift this mood. When they lower their guard, join in and start talking, we'll leave them to their own devices.'

'I packed a swimsuit.'

'I'm hoping swimsuits won't be needed for long.' When she flashed him a look, he back-pedalled quick. 'For Greg and Marla, I mean.'

Suspicion darkened her face. 'I agreed to help. I'm here. But in case you have something else in mind, I'll be clear. *Not happening.*'

He feigned innocence. 'What's not happening?'

'Us getting too close.'

'How close is too close?'

She deadpanned, 'Kissing-distance close, Nate.'

'Thing is, I think if we show Marla that we've gotten over our differences, she'd be more amenable to getting over theirs.'

'Only we *haven't* gotten over our differences.'

'Right.' His gaze flicked to her full pink lips, then back to her determined gaze and he shrugged. 'I just thought you meant what you said.'

'And just what did I say?'

'That you liked me holding you.' He leaned a smidgeon closer. 'Kissing you.'

Her eyes widened and her mouth quivered before she found a threadbare voice. 'That is *not* the point.'

'What is the point?'

'That you have some crazy idea about curses and, frankly, I don't trust you.'

He remembered the way she'd moved against him, the way she'd sighed in her throat. She'd trusted him then—before she'd frozen up. Now he wondered again. 'You never did tell me why you got distracted that night on your couch.'

A blush stained her cheeks and she gripped that chair arm again. 'None of that matters now.'

'Because you believe in letting bygones be bygones?'

'Because you and me—*us, Nate*—we're done. I agreed to come here only to help Marla, not get all up-close-and-personal with you.'

She stormed inside, a clapped-out screen door slamming behind her, while Nate bit down to stop himself from hauling her back and letting her know just how wrong she was. She thought they were done? Seeing her again, having her near—it only made his reasoning these past days clearer. Stronger. Maybe he wouldn't make love to Roxy the way he'd been dreaming, but one thing was certain.

With four days and four nights, it wouldn't be for lack of trying.

CHAPTER SIX

THE creek turned out to be divine—a wide meandering stream shaded by the far-reaching branches of sleepy coolabahs. The water, babbling over a scattering of polished stones, was clearer than any Roxy had seen. Given the hot afternoon, with neither breeze nor cloud to soften the hard beat of the sun, it also looked wonderfully cool.

Cool was precisely what this scene called for.

Half an hour after Nate's confession on the verandah, Marla sat nearby atop a flat rock overhanging the water, tight-lipped and looking as if she'd rather be chewing ground glass. His face hard, Greg was throwing stones into the water, waiting for the ripples to die before casting another. From the concentrated expression on Nate's face, he was concocting a way to break the deadlock.

Roxy huffed.

Good luck with that.

Suddenly animated, Nate kicked off his shoes, then rubbed his hands together. 'Well, no use standing around. I'm going in. Who's joining me?' The other two ignored him, so he turned to Roxy and asked, 'How about it?'

She forced a smile when inside she was shaking. Not because of Marla and Greg's continuing standoff—although that was discouraging. Not because she was about to peel off this dress and reveal her figure in a bikini, even if her thighs and butt were larger than she'd have liked. What troubled her was what Nate had planned. Some splashing, he'd said. A little laughter. Together in that creek. Perhaps it wasn't too late to back out, go home.

Surveying the water, Nate began removing his shirt, absently unbuttoning, then rolling one big shoulder out of the fabric and the next while Roxy could only stare. Many times, particularly late at night, she'd imagined him sans shirt. She'd expected broad and naturally bronzed, but never this much superbly honed sinew and muscle. That body belonged on a billboard.

Then he started on his jeans.

But, hand on fly, he stilled. She felt him look over and, guilty, her gaze flew up to his. He was smiling, a smouldering knowing grin that lit his eyes and set her face and blood on fire.

Gathering her thoughts, she cleared her throat and angled away. From the corner of her eye, she saw him strolling over…felt him studying her from top to curling toe.

'You're coming in, aren't you?' He eased the jeans down over two long hard thighs. 'Need some help? A zip maybe?'

Sparks rushed through her veins. His remark was meant to remind her of that afternoon in her shop and how he'd drawn her near a heartbeat before his mouth had claimed hers. She'd been lost in his embrace that day—that night too, as well as the evening when he'd dropped her off from Marla and Greg's engagement party six months ago. Each time they'd been fully clothed. The only bare flesh had been their lips, their hands. If he touched her now, given what he *wasn't* wearing, her feet might *never* find the ground.

Jeans kicked aside, he ran a thumb around the inside band of black shorts that hung perfectly on his lean hips. Was it the trail of dark hair, or the hard outline of sculpted abdominal muscles that dipped beneath the band of shorts beside his thumb? Whatever the lure, that span between navel and what those shorts were hiding shouldn't be allowed out in public without a licence.

When she caught his words, 'Maybe I should throw you in,' Roxy was hauled back.

'Don't you dare!'

'What if I do?'

As he prowled closer, those gorgeous shoulders rolling towards her, she backed up and warned him, 'You never know. I might scream.'

'I'll risk it.'

'You don't take those kinds of risks.'

'Maybe I'm on the cusp of a change.'

'And maybe my hair is green.'

Her back met with a massive tree trunk. Boulders rose up either side. Attempt at escape was useless.

Grinning, he kept coming until his chest was so close, if she'd tipped forward a few degrees, she could run her lips over that masterpiece and taste it.

His voice lowered to a deep and private whisper. 'Hey, I think we have their attention.'

She blinked and almost asked, *Whose attention?* But then elements other than the bone-melting effect of his musky scent and body heat filtered through the fog, and she remembered the true situation and slid a surreptitious look the warring couple's way. Although pretending not to, both Marla and Greg were watching, interested, obviously waiting for their next move.

Nate whispered again, a hypnotic sexy drawl.

'Now, take off your clothes.'

Her skin flashing hot, Roxy moistened her lips. But she was overreacting. Of course, he knew she wore a swimsuit underneath. She corrected him.

'You mean take off my *dress*.'

'That's a start.' He cocked his head and summed her up again, his X-ray gaze devouring every inch.

'On second thought,' he said, 'I vote we strip you in the water.'

Knees gone to jelly, she pressed back against the trunk and tried to sound unaffected. 'Who said anything about a vote? This isn't a democracy.'

'You're right.' His brows nudged together. 'It's not.'

He moved so fast, she didn't have time to duck under his arm or try to push him away, not that either move would've made a difference. When Nate scooped her up, she was faced with a testosterone-infused power that both alarmed and, frankly, excited her too. As those muscles locked her effortlessly in and he carried her with sure long strides towards the creek, she felt energized and aroused— a glaring contrast to how she *ought* to feel. She should be outraged, not secretly plagued by the desire to press more into the hard hot feel of him. At least she was genuinely shrieking, kicking her legs and begging that he let her down. If she went swimming, she'd get in at her own pace.

Nate crashed through the water, cool wet soaked up her dress and, laughing, he asked, 'Would you rather fast or slow?'

'What are you talking about?'

'Do you prefer to be dumped or swirled in bit by bit?'

Pushing a palm against his granite chest, she struggled and muttered, 'As if my opinion counts.'

'I like the idea of hearing you scream out my name as I throw you up into the air. But drawing out the experience, taking it slow, appeals even more.'

The fiend. He wasn't talking about the water. He was letting her know how he wanted to take her in a physi- cal, purely sexual sense, even after she'd told him again that wasn't happening. And it *wasn't*. Nothing could make her climb on that hot-cold, curse-on/curse-off, merry-go-round again, no matter how incredibly wonderful his body looked, smelled. *Felt*.

When he swirled around, pebbles crunched beneath his feet and silky water sluiced up her back, over her hips. Loathing to be dropped, she clung on, one arm twined around his strong neck. The hand that had previously pushed at him was now, of necessity, gripping one exceptionally firm pec. He checked out her hold and arched a brow.

'I think you're enjoying this.'

She growled. 'Enjoy *this*.'

Reaching down, she swept up a handful and flung water up at his face.

His every fibre seemed to tense before he shook his head quickly to shift the glistening droplets from his hair. Growling himself now—but with pleasure, not irritation—he pinned her with a devilish look that made her regret she'd tested him. His grin slowly grew, then, without warning, as she'd feared, she was dropped into the drink.

Two seconds later, she came up spluttering—and, damn the man, ready to fight.

She jumped at him—*on* him—and somehow managed to push him over. Or had he simply let her? Either way, she was on top now and intended to take every advantage. Pushing on his shoulders, she forced his smirk under the ripples. The next instant, he was pushing back, jettisoning her over and into the stream.

She battled back and he let her gain ground before he secured her—his hands around and near spanning her waist—while she thrashed and twisted. She'd never been more riled…and he'd never seemed more attractive, particularly with his chest filled with rumbling laughter.

Thing was that she was laughing too—and so hard, she felt *filled* with it.

As the moment stretched out the struggling and laughter eased, but they continued holding and steadying each other. Her hands at the base of his neck, his clasped around her middle, their laboured breathing evened as Roxy grew profoundly aware of those male fingers digging into her flesh, of the way his gaze stroked her lips and how desperately she wanted him to act again without asking permission. This minute. *Now.* She needed him to go ahead and kiss her till the world stopped turning and she couldn't remember who she was, or where, or why…

Without conscious thought, her fingers filed up the cool wet column of his throat, over the hot pulse that beat below his ear, then around the sexy sandpaper-rough of his jaw while his loaded gaze smouldered into hers. As her heartbeat thundered on she drew a line along the bow of his full lower lip and marvelled at how his expression intensified and the muscles in her belly contracted and warmed.

With painstaking care, he lifted her a little higher so that her still-sandalled toes left the creek floor. Falling deeper into the trance, she allowed her eyes to drift shut while she waited for their lips to touch…for his mouth to capture and consume her. Instead she heard her name murmured as if the words had come from afar.

'Roxy, it's over.'

Her eyes dragged open. His face—that mouth—was tantalizingly close and his breath was teasingly warm on her cheek. Wasn't this what he wanted? Why on earth was he waiting?

'What's over?' she asked.

'They've gone. Or at least I'm pretty sure they are.'

Her first thought was to bat those words aside. All she cared about was melding into Nate's caress, knowing more about this sizzle and pull. But as he continued to look down at her, dark brows knitted, her mind shifted and she swam up from the haze. The splashing, joking—*flirting*...

This wasn't for *their* benefit. It was for Marla and Greg's.

If she'd thought her heart had hammered before, this moment her chest—her entire body—felt as if it were booming. Nate's charm never failed to entice her. *Entrap* her. She was as vulnerable this moment as she'd been every other time they'd touched. Her nerve-endings buzzing, she felt aroused to her very core.

But more so she was embarrassed. He'd told her they should let their friends believe they'd got past their differences. But Greg and Marla weren't the only ones fooled. And why shouldn't she be convinced? Nate should give lessons.

Water dripping down her face, she angled to see. Where previously their friends had stood, only dry gum leaves now lay. Lowering her arms, she flicked her wet hands and assumed a resigned mask.

'Maybe they've gone for a trek down the bank.'

Mr Glenrowan had suggested they take his pickup in case, after a big swim, anyone was too tired to walk back. Parking just beyond the bank's skirt of trees, Nate had left the keys in the ignition. Now, they heard that engine splutter to life. Next came a series of distant gear crunches, then the sound of tyres rolling away.

Roxy slouched. 'Well, that was a waste of time.'

'Depends how you look at it.'

The smile and intent was back in his eyes. A pulse popped low in his cheek at the same time his attention dipped to sweep a scorching line across her lips. Then he tipped closer, edged damp hair aside and dropped a light moist kiss on a particularly sensitive part of her neck.

'I don't think they'll come back,' he murmured. 'Doesn't mean we have to leave.' He nuzzled along the line of her jaw, then, at last, his mouth veered towards hers and brushed a single haunting time.

Their lips all but touching, they peered into each other's eyes. When his head drew back an inch, caught again in the tide, she followed and this time her lips did the grazing—once, twice and over again. He might drive her mad but, this minute, she had less than no willpower where he was concerned. If he didn't kiss her in earnest and soon, to hell with it. She'd latch on and drag his head down herself.

Instead, his hot palms slid up over the front of her dress and she began to dissolve as he took his time releasing each button. With drops running down her back, her arms, and her mind and senses racing, she stood before him quivering, waiting, until finally the dress fell into the water that ringed her thighs. Reaching around, he undid her bikini top and caught the scrap of yellow Lycra before it dropped. Then one palm sculpted over the bare-skinned curve of her waist, a hip, at the same time he carefully hunkered down.

While she held her breath, he released her bikini bottom bows then two long fingers slid between her legs and dragged the wet bottoms out. He bunched them in the same hand that held the top, curled his free palm around her back upper thigh and urged her forward when his head slanted and came in.

His mouth touched her just shy of her sex and when the stiff tip of his tongue tickled the spot, her neck rocked back and hands automatically fisted in the damp of his hair. Despite the cool water, she burned all over. Her blood felt on fire and her lungs couldn't grasp enough air. Then he was sucking, so lightly, with such skill, Roxy worried she might begin to shake beneath the thrill of it. He shifted

slightly and, the next she knew, his scratchy chin was rubbing up the sensitive cleft at the apex of her thighs.

Flames shot through her body. She didn't care that they
were out in the open. Hell, she wouldn't have the strength
to stop if they were making love in the centre of Sydney.
And standing here completely naked, enjoying the waves
he so effortlessly whipped up inside her, she only wanted
the sensations—the way he played and moved with her—
to go on and on.

His head came down enough for his lips to nuzzle then
to stroke her with his tongue. She clenched—her thighs,
her stomach, her teeth—and ploughed her fingers over the
back of his scalp, across that broad slick ledge of shoulder.
His hand bracing the back of her thigh, he pressed her in
more and hummed in satisfaction as he drew that small
pulsing part of her into his mouth.

A thousand tingling darts lit and, within minutes, had
joined to hover, ready to rush in and explode all at once.
But then the stroking eased and half of her breathless tension drained away. In another world, she swayed as he
eased to his feet, his chest sliding against her until they
again stood face to face. Before she could focus, his mouth
crashed down, taking hers in a way that had her wondering if this was the same man.

Starving. Single-minded.

Committed.

His mouth covering hers, he collected her in his arms
and moved to the edge of the creek where he laid her
upon the soft grass-covered bank, then straightened to
stand before her. Water rushed down his glistening chest,
packed abs, powerful arms. Then the shorts came off and
she couldn't drag her eyes away. He was tall and built, but
like never before she realized Nate Sparks was a strong
man—and a fully aroused one. As he lowered over her his

hard heat ironed down her front until his mouth found the
sensitive tip of her breast.

Each in turn, he teased her nipples, alternatively twirl-
ing his tongue and nipping the beads while his hand took
over what his mouth had taken such pleasure in only moments before. The spiral of sensation was immediate and so
fierce, she could feel the promise of release a mere breath
away. Being with Nate this way felt so extraordinary, so
altogether new, and yet on a different plane, she wondered
if in another life they'd met like this before.

His jeans had landed nearby. Light-headed, she realized he was wrestling with the belt—no, the pocket—and
drawing something out. A foil wrap. Protection. But when
he shifted up to sheath himself, needing to measure and
pleasure him, she caught him in one hand, squeezed and
led him back. Groaning out a shuddering sigh, he gradually lowered back down and, curving an arm around her
head, tenderly kissed her again.

Lying in the dappled sunshine, she worked his length
from base to tip and down again, revelling in the way he
moved with her while his throat made gravelled, grateful
sounds. When he'd hardened to steel and she sensed his
dam about to break, reluctantly she pulled back and let
him see to the condom.

A heartbeat later, he was hovering above her, reaching
around to find her calf and bring that leg over the back of
his own steely thigh. Her every cell sizzling, Roxy ran her
fingers through the wiry hair on his chest and gazed into
hooded blue eyes that she knew at this minute saw only her.

'I couldn't have spent my life not knowing this,' he
said, 'not know you like this. I wouldn't have let you go.'

When he entered her, she was beyond ready, and yet that
initial nudge caught her breath. As a lit-fuse of sensation
ripped through her his head dropped into her drying hair

and he murmured more words that brought happy tears to
her eyes. Then he began to move, a powerful yet measured
rhythm that matched the deep steady beating of her heart.

Soon the ache of need was everywhere—her *everything*.
While the burn at her core continued to condense and glow,
each second a little stronger, a little brighter, he hitched up
so that his elbows were locked and embedded in the grass
either side of her shoulders. His hands clasped hers where
they'd fallen over her head and as their fingers twined he
closed his eyes and lifted his face, inch by inch, towards
the sun. When he moved again, driving in deeper, thrust-
ing harder, he struck a spot so unstable, so combustible,
she groaned deep in her throat and, on reflex, pressed in
around him.

A barely contained fire began to crackle and leap at the
same instant Roxy found herself suspended high above the
world with only a glimmer of all things perfect to keep her
from falling. As if they'd reached the same plateau at the
exact same moment, Nate took breath and stilled too. A
line of perspiration running from the corner of his brow,
he put strain aside long enough to smile into her eyes, then
slowly, carefully, he moved again.

A moment later, on first a tremor, then a gasp, she was
thrown towards the stars and shattered into a million fiery
pieces.

CHAPTER SEVEN

'You're wondering, aren't you?'

The surrounding eucalypts' minty smell had softened as the day's heat had waned and Nate couldn't remember a time when he'd felt more at peace. But now, hearing Roxy's drowsy question, he slipped from beneath the blanket of his post-coital buzz and absorbed more the amazing reality of what had just transpired. Her cheek resting on his chest, he stroked her hair as they lay twined together among the reeds lining the Glenrowan Homestead creek.

Roxy Trammel was fierce and beautiful and sexy and *fun*. Play-fighting in the water, kissing him near senseless on this bank… Nate only wished he could put life and its complications on hold long enough to enjoy more than four days soaking up this unique kind of joy.

Eyes closing again, he feathered his lips over the damp dome of her crown, breathed in the fresh-water scent clinging to her hair and wound his mind back to her question. She thought he was wondering about something?

In a low gravelled voice, he said, 'Only about having you again.'

When his nether regions jerked at the thought, he mustered his energy, pushed up and slid back into the water, dragging Roxy and her delectable curves along with him. Mid-stream, he wrapped her purposefully in his arms and, while she smiled and ironed herself up against him, he dropped meaningful kisses upon her shoulder, over the honeyed slope of her throat.

'Actually,' she murmured, tracing her nails along his nape and making him groan with want, 'I wondered if you might think I was sorry this happened.'

His heartbeat and nuzzling stopped. 'Are you?'

'Yes.' His head snapped up. 'And no,' she finished and lifted one brow. 'I was determined not to let you get close.'

'Well, you can't get much closer than this. Although I'd like to try.' He drew a lazy circle around that adorable dimple in her cheek. 'Guess this was always going to happen.'

'So, now that it's out of our systems—'

'It's not out of mine.'

That dimple deepened as her eyes darkened. 'It was good, wasn't it?'

'Not good.' His lips skimmed her brow. 'It was great.'

Over the next few minutes, he discovered new places to explore, highly sensitive spots that drove up her breathing and left the skin on her arms covered in tiny bumps. As her fingers fanned over his chest, stopping every so often to circle and pluck a small flat disc, his erection grew and grew. On autopilot, he bent at the knees, got a good grip on her flanks, then hoisted her up. The tips of her breasts tickling his collarbones, she wrapped her legs around his hips, her arms around his neck, and curled in as he manoeuvred her lower half, pleasing and teasing them both. When his tip then entire shaft filled her once again, she sucked back a breath and melted against him.

By the time he remembered protection, Roxy looked to be enjoying the action more than he was, if that was possible. Her fingers digging into his shoulders, her neck rocked back while she drove him on; Nate had to lock his every thought and fibre to maintain control. He was that close to letting go.

Her head coming forward, her lips brushing his, she murmured in a thick creamy voice, 'Shouldn't we see what's happened to our friends?'

He kissed the hollow of her throat, her chin, her swollen parted lips. 'Soon.'

'They might think we drowned.'

'In the most pleasurable way possible.'

Biting down, he pushed in to the hilt and Roxy caught her breath, stilled then, releasing a quivering sigh, began to move again.

After a few more minutes, when his legs had begun to shake from the strain of holding back the tide, she said, 'I thought our mission was to get those two back together, not to—'

Her breathless enunciation of that four-letter word was the most erotic thing he'd ever heard. If he didn't stop now, it would be too late. He disengaged those vital mindless parts even as he kept her close. He needed a second condom and he needed it now.

'They could be off talking somewhere,' he replied, moving with her towards the bank and thinking, *Not that I want to talk at this precise moment*.

'Or they could be organizing separate lifts out of this place.'

Drawing back, he examined her furrowed brow. Roxy might have surrendered to the friction sparking between them, but now her pendulum had swung back to helping her friend. His rational mind said she was right. They should get back. But his sexually activated thought patterns were demanding more time alone. What difference would ten minutes make?

When her chin tucked in and she frowned, Nate realized he'd spoken that last aloud. Determined now, Roxy wiggled away and tramped onto the bank.

'After ignoring her like that, I wouldn't be surprised if Marla refused to talk to me again.'

'You weren't ignoring her. We were setting the mood. But you're right,' he conceded. 'We'll need to work harder if we want to move this forward.'

Her back to him, he let his gaze savour a most tempting rear view as she retied her bikini bottoms then top. Dragging a hand over his chest, already missing her warmth, he waded out too.

She found her dress. 'Moving forward means making sure they spend time together.'

'And that they see firsthand how fences are mended—' coming up behind, he traced his cheek gently up hers '—and how good making up can be.'

She threw an uncertain look over her shoulder. 'As long as we don't get too distracted.'

'I've been nothing *but* distracted.' He edged her around and, setting his forehead to hers, confessed, 'Since that night you kicked me out, I haven't stopped thinking about you.'

She recoiled. 'Please tell me you're not going to mention that curse again.'

'I'm not going to mention that curse again.'

'No more talk about underachieving or not measuring up to all that you can be?'

Casting aside a mental snapshot of Roxy in that white wedding gown, of his business plan going down the gurgler, he nodded. 'Promise.'

And, if he could say that and mean it, couldn't he lighten up more and invite Roxy to his parents' anniversary bash? His folks could conjecture and lean all they pleased. How far a relationship went was up to him. He certainly enjoyed making love to Roxy, more than any woman he'd been with, but he still had all his faculties, didn't he? Hadn't been blinded by a supernova flash of everlasting love and the overwhelming urge to propose and throw his career away. In fact, he felt bolstered. Strong.

Hell, he felt fan-freakin'-*tastic*!

Clearing his throat, Nate got ready to mention that his parents had been married thirty-one years, which would lead to a comment about the party and fact that he'd like her to accompany him, when, looking past his shoulder, Roxy yelped, laughed, then slapped a hand over her mouth as if wanting to take the noise back.

'Did you see that?'

Her finger shook at a place in the creek where ripples had spread out from a central point. Nate glimpsed a shadow wriggling beneath the water's surface…a fur-covered animal with a bill for a beak. She gripped his shoulder with both hands and whispered, 'A platypus. I wonder if she has a nest? They really do look like a cross between a beaver and a duck. So cute!'

'They have spurs on their back paws.' Frowning, he looked around for a stick or a rock. 'I think there might be poison involved.'

Certainly they could have fun, but reality was they were in the wild here, not a suburban backyard.

Roxy only laughed. 'Okay, Worry Wart. We won't disturb her.'

Turning, he slid his palm up her slender waist, over those beautiful buoyant breasts. Memories of the snug feel of her, the fresh feminine taste, filled his mind and, slipping into the zone again, he brought her gorgeous body close.

But, with a grin and shake of her head, she wound away and headed for the path out. Beaten, he slapped his hands against his thighs, then slipped into his shoes, slung his jeans and shirt over one shoulder and, jogging to catch up, followed her out.

'Guess we should leave before a bunyip gets you,' he said, fitting his hat.

'Why me? Why not *us*?'

'They only like the flesh of women.' Securing her hand in his, he helped her through orchid-tipped sprays of emu bush and out onto the open plain. 'Aboriginal folklore says they lurk around creeks and billabongs.'

'I read somewhere they look like gargoyles.'

'Some say they resemble snarling dogs with flippers. Or are covered in feathers with tails like a horse.'

'You really do have an imagination.'

'Says the woman who creates bunny wedding gowns.'

His arm sliding around her waist, still damp and cool from their swim, he inhaled air that dried his throat in two minutes flat. The Glenrowan Homestead was a smudge of grey paint on the horizon. Plenty of time to bring up that other issue.

'My parents are throwing a party this weekend,' he said. 'An annual event.'

'Their anniversary?'

However did she guess? 'I wondered if you'd like to go.' He expected curiosity. Maybe a spark of interest. Instead she nibbled her lip and averted her gaze. His chuckle was hollow. 'Don't act so excited.'

She wound hair behind her ear. 'Are you sure you want me to go?'

'I asked, didn't I?'

'Let's see how you feel when we get home.'

His eyebrows hiked up. 'You think I'll change my mind?'

'I don't think it's a good idea to rush into anything.'

'It's an invitation to a party, not to share the rest of our lives together.' When she nibbled again, he smiled crookedly. 'I'm breaking through my barriers. It's a good thing.'

'I'm not so sure—'

'Well, I am.' He blinked, then cocked his head as a thought struck. 'Or is this hedging about you?'

'Me?'

Walking on, he shrugged. 'Maybe you have more of a hang-up than I do.'

'I doubt that's possible.'

'Did you see your dad much after he left?'

'What has that got to do with—?'

But as her words cut off and the defensive glint in her eyes faded, she let out a breath and started walking again. He wasn't poking fun at her, merely making a point. If he'd had a family background reason for wanting to stay clear of 'trouble', well, so did she.

'After he married again, my mother insisted I visit every other weekend,' she began. 'She said he and I both deserved to know one another. Now I wonder if she sent me to get information more than anything. But his second wife didn't like me much, which was fine because I didn't much like her either. My visits dwindled off to hardly ever. When that marriage broke up too, I began to visit again. Until I found new perfume bottles stashed under the bathroom sink and different nightdresses peeking out from under my father's pillow. He married that third time and I honestly hoped he'd found the one.' Her mouth tightened. 'As far as my father is concerned, one woman was never enough.'

'Do you talk to him now?'

'I guess. I can't forget that he hurt us, but I've tried to, you know…forgive.' With the afternoon sun casting longer shadows over the parched red ground, she grunted. 'I told him once how much he'd hurt me, but he didn't understand. He said he'd never stopped loving me. I don't think he knows what love is.'

'Was he a good dad in other ways?'

'When I was very young, I remember him kissing my forehead every night before I fell asleep. He'd tell me I was his special princess. Growing up, I had these two totally different ideas of him clashing around in my head. There was even a part of me that understood why my mother didn't want to confront him over his extramarital affairs and possibly have him leave.' Her guilty gaze shot across to him. 'I've never admitted that to anyone.'

'You wanted your father. I understand completely.'

A small smile touched her lips, her eyes.

'He could be a whole lot of fun,' she explained. 'A charmer.' She sent a wry look. 'A little like you.'

'Trust me.' He tugged her closer. 'He's nothing like me.'

'My great-aunt Leasie got caught up with a charmer once,' she went on, matching her steps with his. 'Harry Mercer. He made a living selling bogus life assurance in the sixties. She dropped him cold when she found out. He still writes to her from prison, but she never responds. Sometimes I think she'd like to, but she's too smart to bend, even a little.'

'Did your aunt ever marry?'

'She's happy alone.' Roxy corrected herself. 'That's not entirely true. She collects budgerigars. Small. Friendly. Low maintenance.'

'Unlike men.'

'Unlike men like Harry.'

Or like her philandering father. Nate might try to manipulate a situation to get the best outcome for all concerned, but no one could ever accuse him of being disloyal. He might not want to rush down any aisle but when he married, it would be in every sense 'for ever'. Why do something if you didn't intend to do it properly?

As they entered the homestead's yard through the dilapidated picket fence Nate lifted his nose to the air. 'I smell bread baking.'

'This is the bush. Bet it's damper.' Australia's iconic soda bread traditionally baked over the coals of a fire.

Nate sniffed again. 'And some kind of stew.' He held his growling stomach. He hadn't eaten since soggy sandwiches on the plane.

A distant curlew called—a hauntingly lonely sound, Nate thought—and to one side of the homestead's steps, Mr Glenrowan tended a campfire. Suspended over the low-licking flames hung two Bedourie ovens—the Outback's steel-modelled version of the cast-iron Dutch oven. One oven for the stew, Nate guessed. One for the damper.

Looking up, Mr Glenrowan grinned and pushed to his feet. 'I wondered when you two would show up. Your friends've been back a while.'

Roxy's cheeks went pink, and not from the sun. 'Where are they now?'

'Marla's in helping the wife.'

'And I've been collecting wood for the fire.'

Nate searched out that familiar second male voice. Greg was rounding the homestead's corner, a bundle in his arms.

Mr Glenrowan nodded at Greg's stash. 'Good work. Set 'em down there.' He moved towards the steps. 'I'll go see what's keeping those girls.'

Obviously eager to touch base with Marla, Roxy hurried after him. 'I'll go too.'

His expression wry, Greg stopped before his friend. 'All cooled off now?'

Nate removed his hat and pulled on his shirt. 'You should've come in for a swim.'

'Haven't you heard? Three's a crowd.'

'You're forgetting Marla.'

'No. Marla's forgotten me.' Greg set the wood down and stayed crouched beside the fire, watching the flames. 'When you and Roxy got involved, she headed off. I followed. We took the pickup back here. Hell, we even talked.'

'Greg, that's great!'

'About an uncle of hers who owned a property. She explained at length how he'd castrate young bulls. Apparently they'll break through any paddock to get to a cow in heat. She even described the tool used.' Greg visibly shuddered. 'By the time I turned off that rickety old engine, I felt nauseous.'

Nate winced but pointed out, 'She's testing you.'

'Tell my testicles that.'

Nate flicked a look at the verandah. 'She'll be out soon and you'll have another chance. Just follow my lead. Loosen up.'

Greg stopped poking a stick at the flames to peer up. 'What is it with you two anyway? I thought you weren't interested in seeing Roxy again.' One thick brow arched. 'I'm guessing you saw plenty of each other in that creek.'

After that engagement party where he and Roxy had obviously hit it off, Nate had only ever mentioned that he hadn't wanted to see her again. That she seemed highly strung and didn't want to see him again either. He guessed Roxy had told Marla a similar story to suit. No use bringing up kisses and curses. Greg would only laugh and harder than Roxy had. So now Nate told his friend the truth—or a good portion of it.

'Me and Roxy together, here…well, it's an act.'

'An act for what?'

'To show Marla that people deserve a second chance.'

'What I saw happening in that creek between you two was no act.'

'We were mucking around. Hell, I'm a man, she's a woman—'

'And if water hadn't been involved, the flames would've been hotter than these.' He tossed the stick into glowing ashes. 'A crowbar couldn't have pried you two apart.'

'Which only goes to show. If Roxy and I can move forward, imagine how easy it'd be if you got close to Marla for a few minutes.'

Thinking that through, Greg scratched his temple and gradually found his feet. 'Maybe, if I had the right mood, the right opportunity...'

'Roxy and I can help with the first. Then it's up to you.' That screen door squeaked open, slapped shut. He sent Greg a private wink. 'Follow my lead.'

Carrying a bowl of salad, Roxy headed down the stairs. Next came Mr Glenrowan with plates. His wife and Marla followed with napkins, condiments and cutlery.

Mr Glenrowan saw to the damper and laid the bread in the centre of a wobbly outdoor table. 'Butter's there if you want it.'

Nate pulled a piece off the incredibly fresh, steamy loaf and sank his teeth in. Lord, he was famished. But then he remembered Roxy, his manners and the plan. Setting down the bread, he dusted his hands and asked, 'Can I cut you a slice?'

She nodded. 'With a dollop of butter on the side.'

After Nate was finished, Greg came forward, sliced off two pieces and brought one to Marla.

'No butter,' he said. 'Right?'

Marla's eyes widened as if she were taken aback or alarmed by his civility, but then she accepted the plate, even offered a small smile.

Seeing to the second pot, Mr Glenrowan lifted the lid and stirred the contents until a hearty aroma drifted into Nate's lungs and taste buds began to water.

'On a guest's first night,' Mr Glenrowan said, slipping the pot's handle off its rod with the help of a folded tea towel, 'we always eat under the stars.' He surveyed the sky, which had succumbed to a far-reaching dusk, then put the pot on the table. 'Grab some stew and go pull up a log.'

He indicated three log-cum-benches positioned in a U around the fire. After filling their plates with beef and bean stew, Nate and Roxy took the log nearest the homestead. Greg sat on the second of three. Marla took the third.

Roxy set a spoonful of stew to her mouth then, wincing, pulled it quickly away. 'It's hot.'

'Let some steam escape.' Nate took her spoon and wound the utensil back and forth through the stew for a moment or two. Then he lifted a spoonful and asked, 'Mind if I test it?'

Amused, Roxy shrugged. 'Sure. Go ahead.'

Nate set the spoon to his upper lip, smiled and handed it over. 'Should be fine now.'

He wouldn't offer to cool just anyone's dinner but in truth he was only repeating what he'd done many times for the younger kids growing up. Still, it occurred to him now that Greg was eyeing Marla's plate, maybe wondering if her stew was too hot. But she wasn't giving him a chance to help if it was. Dunking her damper, she sopped up stew juice before taking a big, 'I'm fine without you' bite.

Obviously feeling the ripple of unease, Roxy started a conversation. 'Nate and I were talking about bunyips.'

Chuckling, Mr Glenrowan made himself comfortable on Greg's log. 'Noisy beasts.'

Marla swallowed and slanted her head. 'You believe in monsters?'

'Out here,' Mrs Glenrowan said, sitting herself alongside Marla, 'you get to believe in all kinds of things.'

Mr Glenrowan stirred his stew. 'It's actually owls that nest near creeks that make those terrible screeching noises—like a woman's scream.'

Marla lowered her damper slice. 'Are they nesting at the moment?'

'You hear 'em from time to time.'

When Greg crossed to the table to grab a napkin, Mr Glenrowan crooked his finger at his wife and she moved to sit alongside him. More than willing to play musical logs, Greg didn't waste time. He sat down an arm's length away from Marla.

Pleased with the progress, Nate kept the conversation going. 'Bet there's some good ghost stories around these parts.'

'All manner of 'em,' Mr Glenrowan said.

'What's your favourite?' Roxy asked at the same time Nate caught Greg's eye and, in demonstration, sidled a little closer to her. At that moment, Marla dropped her spoon. Greg snatched it up mid-air and edged closer as he handed it back.

'We could tell them about that woman fifty years ago,' Mrs Glenrowan said, looking around the circle while the fire leapt and crackled. 'The daughter of a general on holiday out here from America got hopelessly lost in the bush. The general and his wife spent days searching. They finally found her by a creek.'

'*That* creek?' Roxy asked.

'Yes, but a ways upstream from here.'

Marla sat, riveted. 'Was she…alive?'

'She was breathing but wringing wet and stuck in a trancelike state. She kept saying the water spirit had saved her. She described a handsome man with skin dark as ebony, transparent teeth and eyes like glowing coals set way back in his skull. Every night after that, the girl wandered down to the water to wait for his return.'

In the dancing firelight, Marla's eyes grew wider. 'A ghost.'

'And her lover,' Mrs Glenrowan said. 'Nine months on, she had a baby. Same complexion as hers but the eyes...' As Mrs Glenrowan leaned forward Marla shrank towards Greg. 'The eyes were unusually bright. The same colour as the sun at midday when the sky is filled with wind and dust.'

When Marla shivered, Greg stepped in. 'Can I get you a wrap?'

Marla blinked over and found a weak smile. 'I love ghost stories but...'

'They give you bad dreams,' Greg finished for her a second before a screech echoed through the shadows and Marla jumped, landing even closer to Greg.

'It's an owl,' Mr Glenrowan said, balancing his plate on his lap while he pulled damper apart and, a knowing smile on her lips, his wife kept eating.

Nate sat back. What an intriguing couple.

'How did you two meet?' he asked.

Mrs Glenrowan—'My sister dated his brother.'

Roxy—'Did you have a double wedding?'

Nate threw in, 'Roxy designs wedding gowns,' then spotted Marla's gaze sliding Greg's way. She was thinking about wearing that gown. Thinking about the man she loved being so close. Close enough to forgive.

Mrs Glenrowan lowered her plate. 'Sadly those two didn't marry. They had an argument. A misunderstanding, really. She went off in a huff.'

'And they never made up.' Nate exhaled. For this exercise's sake, he'd hoped for a happy ending.

'Ended up she got hitched to a widower with six kids,' said Mr Glenrowan.

His wife added, 'My sister couldn't have children.'

'So it turned out for the best?' Marla asked.

'My brother never married. Still pines for her to this day.' Mr Glenrowan held his wife's hand, brought her fingers to his lips and murmured, 'I've always been the lucky one.'

'Not that we haven't had disagreements,' Mrs G pointed out.

'But you always forgive me.'

The older pair peered into each other's eyes for a long moment before Mrs Glenrowan brought herself back and let slip a coy laugh. 'Suppose I ought to see to the dishes.'

Marla stood. 'I'll do that.'

Greg stood too. 'I'll help.'

While Marla seemed to hold her breath, Nate also pushed to his feet. 'Roxy and I'll tidy up out here.'

Marla's focus went to Mrs Glenrowan, who was dabbing her napkin against a corner of her husband's mouth before lightly kissing the spot. Marla's lips swung to one side, her brow creased, then she finally nodded. She took Greg's plate first, then, collecting everyone else's in turn, moved inside.

Greg collected the damper and said to Nate, 'See you all later.'

Nate crossed mental fingers.

Hopefully much later.

The Glenrowans went for a long walk, leaving just Roxy and Nate to talk in hushed tones about the progress Greg and Marla seemed to have made this evening. For the first time since agreeing to this plot, Roxy felt truly optimistic. Maybe Nate's plan would work after all.

When the fire died and it became obvious their friends wouldn't be rejoining them, Roxy let Nate take her hand to lead her inside. As they moved up those worn wooden steps a clutch of nerves jumped in Roxy's stomach. She still glowed after their mind-blowing romp in the creek. She couldn't deny she looked forward to enjoying something similar behind closed doors tonight.

But with Greg and Marla's relationship so damaged, she also felt guilty. Hopefully those two had stuck it out during kitchen duties and were on their way to working something longer-term out. So why not enjoy a little more of what Nate had to offer? Roxy thought as they entered the house, which smelled of old wool and fresh billy tea. It wasn't as if this tryst would go on indefinitely, for more reasons than one. Although she did wonder how, and when, it would fold. Not until after that anniversary party...*if* she accepted his invitation. And, frankly, she was curious. Their Glenrowan hosts seemed completely devoted to one another. How would Nate's besotted parents compare?

How would his family welcome her?

Careful to be quiet and not disturb, they padded down a long high-ceilinged hallway walled in faded blue tongue-and-groove. At the hallway's end, they turned left and found their luggage waiting outside two separate bedroom doorways. Nate stuck his nose in one room, the other, then collected both cases and entered the first.

'This room looks like ours.'

Secretly liking the way he took charge, Roxy flicked on the light and crossed to the centre of the room. The bed was big and covered in clean comforters and pillows. An old-fashioned cedar dresser sat bumped up against the far wall. Flimsy curtains floated on the opened window's refreshing evening breeze.

She inhaled and sighed. 'It smells like rose petals in here.'

Nate flicked on a lamp, thumbed off the main light then joined her. As his hot palms curved over her hips she tipped closer, enough for their lips to almost touch. But when his head angled and his grip tightened, she wove her mouth away from his.

'You're being presumptuous.'

A knuckle on her chin turned her gaze back to his. 'Given all that talk about ghosts, I thought you could use some company tonight.'

'I'm not the nail-biting type, remember?'

Irresistibly close, his lazy grin spread. 'Then maybe you should humour me.'

Helpless to resist, she fanned her palms up beneath his shirt, over his flat stomach and relished the way his glittering blue eyes drifted shut. 'What would this humouring involve?'

'I should think lots of petting.'

Petting. 'That's an interesting term.'

'Interspersed with plenty of kissing.'

Holding his jaw with both hands, she brought her mouth to his and kissed him slow and deep and long. Finally she drew away.

'Like that?' she asked.

He growled and pulled her back. '*Just* like that.'

He kissed her even more thoroughly, ironing his palms over her hips, pressing her against him so there could be no misunderstanding about how much he wanted her. Running her fingers up his front, she began unbuttoning his shirt, but not nearly fast enough. He flicked open one button but she held his hand to stop him.

'Hey, cowboy, this is my job.'

His voice was a husky rasp. 'Just thought I'd help.'

She pretended to think it over.

'Well, okay.'

He grabbed the front tails and tore the shirt off over his head. 'There. Done.'

The shorts came off, her dress. Then he threw her over his shoulder and strode to the bed with her yelp of surprise echoing through the room. When he dropped her on the airy mattress and, one knee on the bed, hovered above her, Roxy's every cell flashed hot. With his bright eyes unusually dark, he lowered down. His arm curled possessively around her head then, as a distant curlew cried through the night, he kissed her with more hunger and need than she'd ever dreamed could be possible.

CHAPTER EIGHT

A MASCULINE groan rumbling from beneath the daisy-print covers dragged Roxy from her dreams.

Blinking open her eyes, she smiled at the morning sunshine filling the large room, then smiled all the more as memories of that incredible 'night before' tumbled through her mind. Turning her head, she assessed the rounded shape that spanned the length of the cosy double bed, the handsome face cradled deep in the feather-down pillow. She had to bite her lip to contain the sigh. She'd actually done it…got over her angst and had sex with Nate Sparks, and in several highly orgasmic ways.

The time spent at that creek yesterday afternoon was something for the textbook. Her blood smouldered to even think of the way Nate had used his hands, his voice. His tongue. And then, last night, when they'd made love again, the fireworks had exploded higher. Brighter. She couldn't believe that two people coming together could feel so much like…*magic*.

Although, when she'd curled up into his strong heat in this bed to finally fall asleep, Roxy had had a disturbing thought. If this got any better, she definitely wouldn't be able to see him again. Already he was addictive. She didn't want to get hooked, and neither would he.

She was enjoying the toasty tickly feeling in her tummy

that came from merely being with him when his hawkish nose wrinkled and one long impossibly toned arm stretched high. When that limb dropped over her waist, the impact whooshed air from her lungs. Still asleep, he hauled her near. Naked beneath the covers, Roxy got her breath and slid up against his hard heat. The days might get hot out here in the Outback, but early mornings were perfectly mild.

For a long satisfying time, she studied the planes and angles of his face at the same time her fingers itched to riffle through the crisp hair on his chest then filter over the slow-pulsing hollow at the base of his tanned throat. Pressed up close, Roxy indulged her memories—and fantasies—until she was aching for him to wake so they could make love again.

Maybe a friendly nudge…

Lightly she laid a bent knee over his thigh. When he muttered something, but then drifted off again, she pressed into him more and pinpricks of warmth and desire erupted all over her.

He was hard. So thick and rigid that fighting the temptation to kiss and stroke him awake had become a real challenge. Then he rolled towards her more and his erection poked her belly. He might not know it, but he was begging for her attentions.

With a feathery touch, she trailed a hand down over his hip, across the breadth of that steely thigh then gently—but deftly—she coiled her fingers around him and squeezed just enough.

His engorged length jerked, and again. Leaning in, she dropped a soft teasing kiss on his chest. The wiry black hair tickled her nose at the same time his musky scent drifted deep into her lungs, through her stimulated system. Still, his eyes stayed shut.

She frowned. What would it take to wake him? Maybe she should nibble his ear or trace the tip of her tongue over the seam of his lips or—

A wicked grin curved her mouth.

Or maybe I should really give him something to dream about.

With infinite care, she shifted and began to slow kiss her way down over his chest, the steely ruts of his abdomen. Her tongue wound leisurely around his navel before travelling further south until her lips grazed the hot rounded tip of his erection.

In semi-darkness beneath the covers, she took him inside her mouth and instantly her insides began to pulse. Her grip tightened a fraction as she traced her way further down, while her hold on him dragged slowly up. Her breasts rubbing against his legs, she gave herself over to the heat humming through her veins, and the kindling sparking between her own thighs.

Soon he was moving too—with her, against her. Roxy would have grinned if she'd been able. He was awake, or as awake as he needed to be.

When his movements grew to a pace and thrust she couldn't accommodate, reluctantly she released him and slid up his front, leaving a trail of burning kisses along the way. And as her face met his, she was greeted by the world's sleepiest, sexiest lopsided smile. Easing out a happy growl, he ran a palm over her crown.

'Well, this *is* a good morning.'

'I didn't think you'd ever wake up.'

'Who said I wasn't awake?'

'You were playing possum? That's not fair.'

'Way I see it, it's you who took complete advantage of me. And don't let me stop you.' Offering himself, he lay flat on his back, hands cradling his head. 'Be gentle.'

She was certain her eyes laughed even as her lips pursed to contain the smile. 'And if I'm not in the mood for gentle?'

Without warning, he flung back the covers, scooped her up and swung her over so that she straddled his lap. After a yelp of surprise, her laughter spilled out.

Grinding her hips down while he ground up, he pretended to scold her. '*Shh*. You'll wake up the house.'

'I'm not sure we didn't keep them awake last night.'

His palm fanned over one breast, the ridges of his fingers teasing and rubbing a beaded nipple. And as he moved beneath her and Roxy listened to the visceral tune playing deep inside her she found her eyes drifting shut and the pleasure begin to climb.

With a firm hold on her hips, he manoeuvred his loins and slowly entered her. A hypnotic veil fell and, without conscious thought, she began to move as time wound down to a sweet syrupy slow. Her body was everywhere, exquisite sensations her everything, and as the room grew warmer and his controlled thrusts drove deeper, almost too soon, she found herself balanced on the edge of that wonderful sparkling precipice.

For a pulse-pounding moment, she stilled, arching her spine more, needing to concentrate to maintain the sizzling status quo; this fine line between infinite understanding and heaven was just too good to let go. But as she swayed and clutched his sides her core squeezed more and the world dropped further away.

On a different plane, she recognized a comforting warmth cup her cheek and, buzzing all over, she opened heavy-lidded eyes. The sexiest, most considerate lover ever born was gazing up at her with an expression so focused and pure, it took even more of her breath away.

Perhaps it was that look alone that set the fire free and

ripping through her, or a heady combination of surreal, physical and maybe even spiritual pleasures. All she knew categorically was the power of that blinding-white moment of release when her eyes screwed shut, her head jerked back and a groan was torn from the heart of her.

Moments later, when the rolling waves grew fainter and further apart, finally she withered and lay, spent, on top of him.

She was drifting in some other perfect place when Nate gently eased her over and guided her onto her back. Then he was inside her again, working towards a second crescendo. Kneeling between her thighs, he reached behind, brought her knees up either side of him and continued to love her, hitting a spot that released a brilliant blue flame that tore through and engulfed her again.

She ought to have been mindless. Unable to think. And yet all the while one word swam through her mind. Not *scorching* or *orgasmic*. She couldn't shake it.

This was—*he* was—*magic*.

With Roxy lying worn out beneath him, Nate buried his face in her silken spread of hair, contemplating any likely way they could spend the entire morning wrapped around each other and enjoy more of this, when an odd sound drifted in through the screen covering the open window.

Laughter.

Easy.

Familiar.

A heartbeat after his eyes flew open, he drew up on his elbows, listened harder. At the same time Roxy stiffened then her head whipped towards the sound.

'Am I hearing right?' she asked.

That laughter came again and Nate smiled down into suddenly alert bright green eyes.

'Greg and Marla, chuckling.'

'Talking.' He sprang up, threw his legs over the side of the bed and, elated, smacked the pile of rumpled sheet at his side. 'They're back together.'

'Maybe.'

Frowning, he watched Roxy as she bunched the sheet up under her arms and joined him, sitting on the side of the mattress. 'People who are angry at each other don't laugh like that.'

'A ceasefire doesn't equate to resuming an engagement.'

He nudged her playfully. 'Pessimist.'

'Oh, I forgot. Of course you'd assume that true love conquers all.'

He looked at her sideways and got to his feet. 'No one can deny love is a powerful force.'

'You're the expert.'

She was grinning, that little dimple winking. But she was serious and he wouldn't rise to the bait. He grinned back.

'Well, y'know, maybe I *am* an expert.'

A bath towel, which had been placed at the foot of the bed, had fallen to the floor. He swooped and wrapped it around his hips before heading to the window for a look. Marla and Greg were strolling towards a dilapidated old sheep shed situated a short distance beyond the yard. He couldn't make out their words, but he read the body language. They were walking side by side, *close*, and glancing across at each other for long moments as they talked. Neither looked stressed. In fact, the pair seemed decidedly relaxed.

With the sheet draped around her, Roxy appeared beside him. She studied the scene for a thoughtful moment and finally grunted.

'Just as I thought.'

Squinting at the sunshine bouncing off the shed's tin roof, he asked, 'What do you think?'

'She hasn't forgiven him yet. Or not completely.'

'How could you know that?'

'They're not holding hands.'

His head coming forward, he looked harder and exhaled. Damn. She was right.

'They were the kind of couple who were always touching,' she said. 'His arm slung around her shoulders if they were sitting at home. Her leg sliding up his under the table when they went out to dinner. Always holding hands when they walked.'

'Be that as it may, they've made remarkable progress. By early afternoon, they'll be planning how to let everyone know the wedding is back on.'

Attention still on the couple disappearing around that shed, Roxy brought the sheet up higher under her chin.

'Maybe.' Her gaze dropped. 'I don't think you understand how hurtful a picture can be. It sticks in your brain even when you wish it wouldn't.'

He studied her profile and wondered. 'We're not talking about Greg's pictures from his buck's night, are we?'

She seemed to hold her breath before meeting his gaze again. 'The week after that engagement party, I happened upon a magazine shot of you. You were with a woman. A brunette. Some might consider her attractive. To my mind she looked like a bit of a tart.'

His mind wound back and in a few seconds he had the answer. 'That was no tart. Roxy, that was my sister.'

The sheet clutched higher around her throat but she shook her head. 'No. That's not right. You were *with* her.'

'I assure you, not in that way. Naomi's husband was interstate. I escorted her to an art gallery opening she didn't want to miss. If it makes you feel any better, I haven't dated a woman since that engagement party.'

Her eyes glistened and nose twitched as if she were battling a sudden rush of emotion. 'You haven't?'

'One of my other sisters, Ivy, thinks I'm a boring businessman with no social life.'

A smile lit her eyes. 'She *does*?'

He laughed, then wrapped his arms around her waist, brought her close and murmured against the warm shell of her ear.

'What say we do our bit to help the environment and save water by sharing a shower?'

In case she had any ideas about declining, he dropped his mouth over hers and moments later she was as pliant as warm putty.

'Just remember,' she purred, when he broke the kiss, 'making love for thirty minutes under a shower nozzle doesn't equate to conserving water.'

'I'll remember that if you promise not to work me into a lather.'

'I'll promise if you promise.'

Taking her hand, he led her to the attached bath and assured her.

He wouldn't promise anything.

Despite wanting to stay with her under the jets, Nate only kept Roxy in the shower for ten minutes, enough to froth her up and wash her down. And as he reluctantly turned off the water, in his mind he confirmed that these few days away were the best idea he'd ever hatched. He'd lost count of the times he and Roxy had made love and yet he still couldn't get enough.

Nothing he couldn't handle, of course. This was physical. Fun. He was a long way from falling down on one knee and pledging his heart. Especially now that Marla and Greg were back on track.

After he and Roxy dressed in jeans and tees, they stuck their heads out of the door and smelled breakfast, something salty and greasy, along with eggs and more scrumptious damper.

They ate in a huge old-fashioned kitchen, complete with yellowed vintage oven, scarred hardwood table and the cheerful company of Mr and Mrs Glenrowan. But there was no sign of Marla or Greg, although Mrs G let them know that it seemed some mice had raided the pantry and perhaps the other young couple had preferred a picnic for breakfast rather than sharing their company around the table this morning.

Over a warm cup of tea, Mr Glenrowan suggested a horse ride, so, after the dishes were cleared and Nate and Roxy fitted on suitable footwear, they made their way out front to see about galloping off down a wide-open plain. When they stepped into the sunshine, Mr Glenrowan had four horses saddled and ready. Greg and Marla were there too, chatting to each other while they waited.

Greg spotted them first and he put up a hand in greeting. 'You're joining us for a ride?'

Marla's smile was buoyant and a little contrite. 'Oh. Hi.' She threw a glance around. 'Great day, huh?'

'A beautiful day,' Roxy replied in an overly bright tone.

Mr Glenrowan was checking a gelding's girth strap. 'Who wants this one? He's good 'n' tame.'

Greg stepped up to a fine muscled animal with a glossy black coat and equipment that pronounced him a stallion. His palms smoothed over the horse's flank. 'I'll take this one.'

When all four were mounted, Marla said, 'Greg and I thought we might take a ride on our own, if that's okay.'

While Roxy exclaimed, 'Of course that's okay,' Nate grinned and mentally punched the air at the same time Mr Glenrowan gave instructions to them all.

'You'll find canteens in your saddle bags. Compasses too. It's a big place. Don't stray too far. And, each couple—you keep close together.'

Fifteen minutes later, after a head-clearing stint, cantering over a dusty red flat, he and Roxy brought their horses up to a slight incline.

'Where'd you learn to ride like that?' he asked, resetting his hat on his head.

'Pony club.'

'You'll have to show me your blue ribbon collection some time.'

Swaying in the saddle with the horse's gait, she grinned. 'I wasn't that good, I'm afraid. I only took lessons over a couple of summer breaks.'

'All you need now to really look the part is a pair of breeches and a dressage cap.'

'Don't forget the crop.'

'You'd use a whip to get a horse to move?'

She arched a teasing brow. 'I wasn't thinking about the horse.'

While he laughed, a few clicks of her tongue had Roxy's mount picking up pace and reaching the crest with his own steed close behind. Nate wasn't normally one to gape, but the majestic scene spread out before them was one of the most breathtaking he'd ever seen.

Fields of wild flowers, interspersed with eucalypt woodland, stretched out, covering, it seemed, every square inch of land from east to west. Pinks, golden-yellows, intermingled with patches of snow-white. The carpets of blooms, swaying in a sleepy breeze, looked so soft and smelled so fresh, both he and Roxy could only sit, speechless, and absorb one of nature's most striking canvases.

When Roxy's horse shook its head and blew a noisy breath out of her nostrils, still mesmerized, Roxy walked her mare down the slope and through the wide flowing river of petals. Overhead, Major Mitchell cockatoos squawked. With pink-tinged wings wide, they swooped before settling on tall branches to preen and flaunt their stunning crests.

He and Roxy stopped beneath the shade of a clump of trees. After dismounting, Nate made sure the horses were secure while Roxy roamed around, deep in thought as she ran her palms over a hundred different flower tops.

'I thought the Outback was supposed to be all red dust and dry grass.' Sighing, she surveyed the panorama, then lowered to flop back among the blooms. 'It makes me want to try something different,' she murmured, winding one arm around her head. 'Become a photographer or, better yet, a painter.'

Lowering beside her, he broke the stem of a soft pink flower and drew lines up and down her nearest arm with the petals.

'Or a florist,' he said.

'I do love a pretty bouquet.'

'How about flowers in your hair?'

He threaded the stem behind her ear and, looking into his eyes as if she might see her reflection there, she touched the decoration.

'My grandmother used to press flowers to keep the memories,' she said.

'That's sweet.' He pretended to clear his throat. 'I've, er, never been into flower-pressing myself.'

She laughed. 'Me neither. It seemed silly to try to keep your brightest memories alive by looking back on something all shrivelled and drained of colour. But lying here now, I understand why she did it. It's the connection…an association.' As she gazed up at the sky her expression took on a faraway look. 'Right now, it doesn't seem silly at all.'

She casually lay out her hand for him to take. Holding his breath, Nate took a mental snapshot of her lying among the petals, that flower in her hair, and, with only a flicker of hesitation, he lay down beside her and twined her fingers with his.

CHAPTER NINE

On their way back, Roxy and Nate stopped to check out an old windmill and a run-down shepherd's shack. They even enjoyed some Red Kangaroo spotting, staying well back and quiet while the roos lay sprawled beneath a tree, scratching themselves, or bounding off into a horizon that rippled with heat waves. Roxy had fed kangaroos in sanctuaries but seeing them looking so magnificent and at ease in their natural habitat was something she'd remember for ever.

When the sun blazed down almost perpendicular in the sky, they set their hats firmly on their heads, swung the horses around and cantered back. Later, as they were lashing reins over the homestead's front rail and drinking from their canteens to appease dry throats, Greg and Marla appeared, rounding a verandah corner.

When Marla saw them, a glowing smile lit her face. Leaning in, she spoke quietly to Greg, who acknowledged them too, and together they moved to join their friends, arms slung around one another's backs.

Nate spoke out of the side of his mouth. 'Mission accomplished.'

Roxy's chest tightened with relief and happy tears rose to sting her eyes. Seemed Nate was right. Those two truly *were* meant to be together, no matter what. They'd overcome that social media gaffe—those questionable pictures that had cut Marla to her core—and now they looked set to ride off into the marital sunset. Of course, Marla would need a gown—*the* gown—and Greg would have regained the personal strength needed to get back on board the Sparks Martin Steel train. Roxy released the pent-up air from her lungs. She could hardly believe this crazy scheme had paid off and everyone would find a happy ending.

But then she edged a look Nate's way and she held the spot where her stomach kicked. This short time spent here with him had made her feel so energized, different. Alive. And as he removed his Akubra and Frisbee-ed the black felt hat onto the verandah floorboards—with his strong bristled jaw thrust forward and a smile of victory lighting those incredible blue eyes—Roxy had to hold her jumping stomach again.

She'd gone into this plan reluctantly but also with blinkers removed. She'd known that, even when Nate felt so good pressed up against her, ultimately, succumbing completely to his charm would mean she'd pay a price one day. He'd made clear he wasn't interested in developing their relationship past 'fun' and 'now'. Problem was that being with Nate was *so* much fun, and not purely the sex, although that was stellar.

Riding beside him today—talking about each other's respective businesses, then his sister's plans for the anniversary party and onto how she'd always dreamed of having her own horse—she'd felt as if they *fitted*, like today's dry breeze through those windmill blades, or that surprise field of flowers and their rich red soil.

She might not *want* to think that way—feel that strongly—but there it was. She'd like to believe she wouldn't be upset if he never called again. But in her heart she knew she would be hurt, and deeply.

Dragging her from those thoughts, Nate took her hand and together they mounted the steps to join their friends.

Greg nudged his chin at the horses, drinking their fill from a vintage water trough. 'You really worked them.'

'How did your ride go?' Nate asked.

'Fabulous.' Marla caught Greg's gaze. 'But we've been back a while.'

'Occupying yourselves how?' Nate asked, without a hint of shame.

'Talking.' Greg studied Marla too. 'Making plans.'

'Or, more correctly,' Marla said, 'remaking them.'

Sensing the time was right, unable to hold the emotion back a second longer, Roxy came forward and flung her arms around her friend.

'I'm so relieved you two are all sorted. I've felt sick about the whole thing, particularly bringing you here.' Coming away, sighing, Roxy finished, 'But it's been worth it.'

Nate's grin was ear to ear. 'Hate to say it, but I told you so.' He stuck out his hand for Greg to shake. 'Congratulations—again.'

His brow furrowed, Greg studied Nate's hand while Marla pressed her lips together and shifted her weight to the other leg as if she was uneasy. She said, 'This isn't quite what you think.'

Nate's hand dropped. 'You've made peace, right?'

'Ready to exchange vows?' Roxy asked.

'We are back together—' Greg combed his hair back '—but we've decided to put on the brakes and take things slowly.'

'We've both had time to think,' Marla added.

'And we've talked a lot.' Greg exhaled. 'Thing is,

Marla still wants to go spend time with her brother in Los Angeles.'

'And Greg needs time to take over the family firm.'

At Marla's last remark, Nate's spine straightened and his nostrils flared. 'Take over? When did this happen?'

'My father and I spoke day before yesterday,' Greg said. 'He could see how lethargic I'd been. He told me that I needed direction and that he'd been planning the big handover next year anyway.'

Nate's chin lifted as he muttered, 'Son of a gun.'

'It feels right.' Greg growled at himself. 'I'm sorry I didn't let you know straight out the gate.'

Examining the parched timber near his riding boots, Nate thought a moment before a genuine smile graced his face. 'Like I said—' he held out his hand again '—congratulations.'

While the men shook and clapped each other's backs, Marla explained, 'We figured we'd try a long-distance relationship. If we survive that, we'll survive anything.'

Roxy wanted to be clear. 'So, no wedding?'

Marla squeezed her friend's hand. 'But we do want to stay on here with you two. Have some fun. Build some memories.'

Thinking of the flower Nate had threaded in her hair, the one she'd slipped in her shirt pocket and had pressed against her heart, Roxy found a smile and nodded.

'That'd be nice.'

It wasn't until everyone had hugged that she thought again of that gown, the contest and how now there was no hope. And on the heels of that came another recollection. One that zoomed large in her mind and sent a shower of icicles sailing through her middle.

Her gaze shot to Nate at the same time he blinked, frowned and his gaze shot to her. Without asking, she knew they were remembering the same conversation…his offer if all else failed…her acceptance if it should come to that.

To wear that gown herself and become Nate Sparks's wife.

Visible through their bedroom window, grey clouds laced with black rolled and rumbled in from the east. Glenrowan Homestead was due one heck of an afternoon storm, albeit nothing compared to the one brewing here inside this room.

'Don't be ridiculous.' Roxy dropped her riding boots in a corner, then crossed to enter the attached bathroom. 'Of course I won't marry you.' She closed the door.

Turning away from the sprawling view, he leaned against the window jamb, crossed his arms and spoke loud enough for her to hear.

'We had a deal.'

'I'm certain it wasn't written in blood,' she called back.

'If that gown doesn't make its walk down an aisle by the end of this month, any chance of you winning that contest is blown.'

'I wouldn't have won anyway.' She emerged from the bathroom. 'It wasn't meant to be.'

'You said the same about Greg and Marla.' Moving towards her as she sat on the edge of the bed to remove her socks, he conceded, 'They may not be exchanging rings but clearly they're a couple again.'

'A long-distance couple.'

'Who will phone and visit and, some time down the line, I believe tie that knot.'

'Because of that look they share?' Socks off, she stood and set her hands on her hips. 'That special ingredient.'

'That's right,' he said simply.

'But you and I don't share that-that-that…*thing*, right?

Because if we did, you would never suggest we get married, however good the reason.'

Her beautiful mouth was tight, pressed from pink to almost white. She was upset and he wasn't quite sure why. Their friends were reunited, although, no, not betrothed to be married again. But he'd stepped up to the plate to cover that contest problem with the gown. So why did she have her claws out? Wasn't as if he was doing *himself* a favour, going through with his end of the bargain.

He'd try to be logical. 'Roxy, someone needs to wear that gown in a wedding ceremony.'

She shook her head firmly. 'Wouldn't feel right.'

For Pete's sake. 'Forget about how it *feels*.'

Her jaw shifted a little and she sighed as if she'd never see another Christmas.

'I can't.'

Nate dragged a palm down his exasperated face. If *he* could think of this proposal in a purely pragmatic sense, surely she could. Certainly he didn't want to be a married man, but this was for show, for a limited season only. As she bundled up some delicates he tried again.

'The deal was we say the words and get an annulment.' Then, like a godsend, a light bulb flashed. 'In fact, what happens if we don't sign any papers? Then it won't be legal, binding.' *Genius.* 'Is there anything in the contest about that?'

A little colour returned to her lips. 'I'm not sure. I don't think so.'

'Then it's problem solved.'

'You really are a fix-it man,' she said, but she didn't sound as if she approved.

'All I know is that I don't give up easily.'

He'd seen what could happen if a man threw up his hands too soon. Bottom line, he wasn't his father. He was an achiever and, dammit, he was going to achieve and so was Roxy!

He thrust out his chest. 'So, are you in or out?'

'Out. And before you try to railroad me, just listen. Times are slow everywhere. To be honest, I was almost ready to close my doors, there were so many unpaid bills. But with Ava's deposit I'm almost up to date. And I managed to speak to Cindy briefly before our ride. I didn't want to tell you and jinx it, but she said she has another couple of ladies who are a bee's knee from sliding across some cash.'

He found an impressed face. 'That's sound great.'

She nodded. 'Being in the running was exciting, but the competition was *huge*. I was only ever chasing rainbows. You know that as well as I do.'

'Frankly, I think you have a good chance.'

'Thanks, but you know nothing about the industry.'

'I know how that gown looked on you.'

The image he'd stored in his mind floated up…flowing satin, cinched waist, beading that glittered like diamonds and made her look like a queen. You *bet* he thought she had a good chance.

But her expression was resigned, almost a mask, while her shoulder gave a jerk. 'Guess we'll never know.'

'You're being stubborn.'

'And you're feeling as if you need to pay me back for coming here, doing this for our friends. But you don't.'

He blinked and his arms unravelled. 'You are coming with me to my parents' anniversary do, aren't you?'

He knew this…*affair* wasn't meant to drag on. They weren't on the road to getting anywhere near serious. But he thought they'd settled that question. She was going to the party. Hell, he was looking forward to walking in, having her on his arm.

Before she could answer, her cell perched on the dressing table buzzed. Surprised, Roxy crossed and collected the phone. She inspected the ID and a sunny smile spread across her face.

'It's Cindy. Probably to say she has those other deposits.'

Roxy chirped out a greeting and Nate watched on as she listened more and more intently. Then her face slipped like syrup off a plate and Nate's midsection looped and tied in a double knot. When she turned as white as that china vase on the dresser, he held onto her shoulders for support.

Whatever the news, it wasn't good.

CHAPTER TEN

'WHAT's happened? What's wrong?'

Roxy heard Nate's question. She tried to focus. But she simply couldn't.

A state of total shock. That was it. The world around her was receding. External noise was muffled, far away, unimportant. Her brow was damp and her head felt dangerously light. This couldn't be real. Not when things were beginning to come together for everyone.

Over a desert-dry throat, she rasped, 'I can't believe it.'

'Believe what?'

His grip on her shoulders tightened until the pressure points of each fingertip made her wince and she swam up from her daze.

'It's all gone bad.'

'For God's sake, Roxy, tell me. I'll fix whatever it is.'

A wave of dizziness whirled around her head and she slumped. 'I was too complacent. I should never have left.'

He inhaled slowly. 'Okay. From the beginning, tell me what happened.'

She met his intense gaze at the same time the churning in her stomach grew and crawled up to her throat. Lord, she was going to be sick. 'I need to get back to Sydney.'

'Come again?'

'The shop was burgled last night. They took near all

my accessories and trashed some gowns.' Hearing herself explain out loud made it all somehow real. More frightening. Repercussions were beginning to dawn.

'You don't have security?' he was asking.

'I cancelled when mounting bills got too much.'

'You must have insurance.'

'Some, but the premiums companies charge these days…some ask for more than I earn.'

He scrubbed a hand over his face. 'It's a blow, but you'll get over it. You have to stay strong. Focused.'

Yes. She should. Only one problem. She was numb and couldn't, *couldn't*, feel any other way.

He started to pace the room.

'Surely you still have customers—what about Ava and Violet, for instance?'

'They don't want the gown.'

He stopped dead. 'But they both loved that dress.'

'Violet found another one she loved more. Cindy said she was happy to leave half the deposit to compensate for the inconvenience. When Cindy tried to argue, Violet mentioned her daddy was a litigator.' She dragged her watery gaze up from the worn rug. 'I can't take a lawyer's daughter to court over a deposit, especially now.'

'Half a deposit's better than none,' he reasoned. 'And you have those other two gowns as good as sold, right?'

Nausea made her mouth water. Swallowing, Roxy shook her head. 'Yes. And no. Cindy got the deposits. Unfortunately, those gowns were ruined in the break-in.'

'Roxy, if you need money, I can help. You don't have to pay me back.' She imagined him drawing out a mental cheque book. 'How much do you need?'

'I don't want your money.'

'I can afford it. I've invested well over the years—'

'I'm not a charity case, particularly after…'

Her words trailed off, her gaze dropped and a heartbeat later he coughed out a humourless laugh.

'I'm not offering you money because we *slept* together, if that's what you think.'

'Would you offer if we hadn't?'

He frowned. 'That's…not a fair question.'

Who said anything about being fair?

'I appreciate the sentiment,' she said, bringing her case out from the cupboard, 'but I only want to get home. If you can organize something in a hurry, I'd be grateful.'

CHAPTER ELEVEN

THE next morning, Roxy walked into her shop, feeling as if she'd been away an eternity. The place was a mess. Some rows of gowns remained unsoiled, hanging pristine as she'd left them. One end of the glass counter was still intact, with sparkling accessories adorning clean satin beds. Nearer to the door, however, the glass was smashed and jewellery as well as other trimmings had been removed. To her soul, Roxy felt violated.

Making sure the sign read 'closed', she shut the door and demanded both rubbery legs carry her forward.

Her work. Her life. She dragged her gaze around as her stomach sank and her throat grew thick. How could people do this? She'd worked so hard and now she was as good as ruined. She'd have been better off working for a chain store stacking shelves. No risk involved there. No worry about overhead bills. No need to start again.

The salon's back door swung open and stylish tufts of blonde poked through. Cindy's expression brightened when she saw her company, but the smile wilted as her gaze swept the outside room.

'After the police left, I cleaned up best I could,' Cindy said, edging forward, her hands clasped tight before her.

And beyond her own grief and sense of despair, Roxy noticed her cousin's puffy eyes and realized she'd been crying. She reached for Cindy's hand, squeezed, and the younger woman's dark blue eyes brimmed.

'I'm so sorry,' Cindy said. 'You left me in charge and I let you down.'

'This isn't *your* fault. It's not anyone's,' Roxy grunted, 'except the brainless jerks who broke in.'

A tear slid down Cindy's cheek and Roxy drew her close for a big 'please don't worry' hug. When she was certain her cousin was okay, she patted her back a final time, then crossed to drift around the various racks, trying to piece together what was missing, what had been destroyed.

'I didn't think you'd want to open today,' Cindy said, 'so I kept the closed sign on the door.'

Roxy nodded but refrained from mentioning that, most likely, she wouldn't open again.

'You go home and take your mind off this.' Roxy crossed to the unharmed end of the counter. 'I have some phone calls to make.'

'I can help. Organize dry-cleaning, or put in orders for new jewellery.'

The burn of raw emotion backed up higher, pushing and demanding release. But Roxy bit down, held back. She didn't want to upset Cindy more than she already was. Besides, what good would tears do?

'Thanks.' She ran a hand over the counter. 'But I don't have the money for that.'

'Oh.' Cindy's petite shoulders stooped. 'Then what are you going to do?'

'At this point…' Roxy sighed. 'I don't really know.'

After Cindy reluctantly collected her bag and, with another heartfelt hug, said goodbye—she'd be in touch—Roxy stood behind the battered counter for a torturously long while, hoping that over-exposure might desensitize her pain. Didn't work. It seemed unreal that this time yesterday, she'd been floating on her own private cloud, horse-riding through a vast ancient wonderland. Lying in that field of flowers, she'd felt completely content. Blissfully satisfied.

Now…?

Rounding the counter, she entered the back room. In the far corner, Marla's contest dress hung high and safe, covered in light plastic. Roxy's heart lifted a little and a tiny smile hooked one corner of her mouth. At least she still had her dream dress. Although now, frankly, she had no idea what to do with it.

Give it away? Keep it for posterity?

She came closer and ran her fingertips over the plastic, remembering how divine the satin had felt against her skin that day. She'd never admit it out loud, but she'd thought it had fitted her better than Marla. Nate liked this gown too. He'd seemed certain it would do well in that contest.

She slid the gown off the rack, eased the petal-soft folds out of their cover. The beading seemed to smile up at her, telling her everything would be all right. As much as she wanted to believe, Roxy couldn't see that happening…

But she wasn't about to sit around doing nothing.

Steeling herself, Roxy put on a pot of coffee, got out the vacuum. A bucket and mop too. Needing inspiration, she slipped the contest gown over a mannequin in the main room, then set to work.

An hour later, she was sudsing up the mop when the bell above the door sounded. Curious, Roxy angled around. She was certain the sign on the door had been flipped to 'closed'.

Setting the mop aside, she came forward as a woman in her early twenties, with fire-red hair and several tattoos scaling the length of one arm and shoulder, sauntered in, looked around.

Smiling, Roxy wiped her hands down the sides of her jeans. 'I'm sorry, but we're not open for business.'

'I heard.' The younger woman headed towards the nearest rack and fingered some skirts. 'Your place got trashed.'

Roxy flinched at the word. 'That's right.' She frowned. 'How do you know?'

The woman flashed a wide grin that highlighted two front teeth with a gap you could stick a finger through. 'Police cars were parked outside yesterday. They were asking questions.' She sauntered around and fingered some more. 'I figured you might have a sale to get rid of damaged stock.'

'I really hadn't thought that far ahead. Right now I'm busy cleaning up and—' The woman was wandering towards the contest gown. Roxy sped forward. 'That one's for display only.'

'Wow…it's so beautiful. Teddy's eyes would fall clean out his head if I wore this.'

Roxy didn't want to be rude so she asked, 'Teddy's your boyfriend?'

'Fiancé. He proposed a few weeks ago. His folks live here. Mine'll drive down from Dalby.'

'I'm sure it will be a lovely day.'

'I've left off getting a dress. They're all so expensive.'

Roxy moved to stand a little in front of her gown. 'A lot of work goes into making a wedding dress.' A lot of hard work and affection.

'My sister said I could lend hers at a pinch. You know… something borrowed.' She studied the gown again, up and down and again, three times. 'So, you're not having a sale?'

'Not at this time.'

'You hire out?'

'I can recommend places that do.'

'I only have a week and a bit to get something organized if I don't want to borrow my sister's.'

'I'm sure you'll find something wond-er…' That last word stuttered and trailed as a cog in her brain clicked into place. Roxy cocked her head. 'What date is your wedding?'

'We didn't know whether to book Saturday or Sunday. Teddy's partial to Sunday. His family are religious.'

Sunday. The first of next month.

Roxy let out that breath and swept that crazy thought about slipping into that contest after all aside. 'Sunday weddings are lovely,' she made herself say.

'Except I insisted on Saturday. No sore heads at work the next day.' That gappy smile flashed again. 'So it's set. The thirty-first. The end of this month.'

CHAPTER TWELVE

NATE was pleasantly surprised when Roxy called and wanted to be filled in about arrangements for his parents' anniversary party. He said he could collect her at seven. He arrived at her house five minutes early. When she opened her door, looking incredible the way she always did, to say he was bowled over was a huge understatement.

Her gown was a shimmery silver that hugged rather than clung to her curves. Thin straps, low back, hair thrown up in a messy yet sophisticated style that not only left the elegant column of her neck deliciously available but also took her glamorous look to a whole other level.

She greeted him with a friendly smile and offered her cheek for a kiss. If only she knew how his brain had fogged up at the minute, she might have hidden behind the door for fear he'd carry her away and never bring her back.

Her arm linked through his, he escorted her down the path. The black leather interior of his sports car was a perfect foil for her dress.

'I'm glad you decided to come tonight,' he said, swerving the car from the kerb.

'I'm looking forward to it.' In the shadows, she shot him a glance. 'I was looking forward to seeing you again too.'

His heart beating faster, he changed up gears. 'Have you heard from Marla?'

'Not yet. Any word from Greg?' He shook his head and veered onto a road heading east. 'I'm sure she'll contact me before she heads off to California.'

As he routinely checked the rear-view mirror he nodded. Marla and Greg had made their decisions with regard to relationships as well as to work. He was disappointed Greg had chosen his father's firm over their fledgling enterprise. Then again, he understood. If his father had built a successful company, no doubt he'd be more than happy to take over the legacy, even if it meant compromising a little.

They'd done all they could for their friends. Now Nate was interested to hear what was going down in Roxy's life. Last he'd seen her, saying goodbye at the airport when she'd insisted taking her own cab to her shop, she'd been glassy-eyed. Shell-shocked. Tonight anyone would think she hadn't a care in the world.

'What about you?' he asked, telling himself to keep his eyes on the road, not on the shape of her legs through the skirt of that satin gown. 'How's the shop?'

He heard her sigh. 'I was devastated walking in. Cindy had cleaned up as best she could. I've spoken with the police but they have no leads and, without surveillance cameras, they don't hold much hope of tracking anyone down.'

'It's lucky Cindy wasn't in the shop at the time.' His grip tightened on the wheel. 'Or *you*, if we hadn't been away.'

'I thought the same.'

He waited a few beats. He didn't want to pry or bring down her mood. By the same token, they were only a few minutes away from his parents' house now. They'd have no privacy once they were through the property gates and among the revellers. He needed to know.

'Your gown…was it okay?'

'It was still there.'

'Not destroyed?'

'It was safely hung in the back room. Every bead is in place.'

'You must have been relieved.' He knew he felt relieved for her.

'After I sent Cindy home, I decided to clean up some more. I brought the gown out and fitted it on my favourite mannequin.'

'You have a favourite mannequin?'

'You'd have a favourite car or screwdriver, or whatever. I have a favourite life-size doll.'

He swung the car into his parents' street. A moment later, the estate gates appeared, as well as strings of different-coloured party lights. He could almost feel the vibration from a blaring sound system through the tyres.

He prodded. 'You put the dress on the mannequin, and…'

'I had a visitor—a woman who knew about the break and enter.'

His head snapped around. 'She knew who was behind it?'

'No. She saw the police the day before and enquired. She thought I might have a sale scheduled to shift damaged stock.'

He pressed a remote and the soaring gates opened. The uniformed man at the bottom of the long wide drive tipped his hat and waved them on. A giant marquee had been erected one side of the house. Guests were dancing, drinking, talking. He slowed the car down to a crawl.

'So, this woman,' he said, 'she was after something inexpensive.'

'I'm guessing she wasn't flush with money. She'd have loved to wear any one of the dresses.'

Nate swerved into the covered forecourt and uniformed

help swept up to park the car. When her door was opened, Roxy alighted and surrendered a long low whistle.

'Your mother's relative must have been loaded.' He'd told her the story about the inheritance. She cocked her head to take in the full length and height of the house. 'Nice mansion. Georgian style, yes?'

'A little over the top for my tastes,' he said, having eased out of the low-slung vehicle to stand in the fresh air too. They met at the front of the car where he straightened his black bow tie, then took her hand.

'This woman,' he said as they headed down a path lit either side by lakes of fairy lights, 'did she find a dress?'

'She didn't find a dress. She found *the* dress.'

'Ah. *Your* dress.'

'She fell in love with it. And guess when she's getting married.'

'Before the end of the month?'

'The thirty-first. I thought it had to be a sign.'

'That you should give this woman your gown and re-instate yourself in that contest?'

'With a nip here and there, it would fit her perfectly.'

The marquee entrance was a few strides away. People milling outside were studying the new arrivals. Word would spread like wildfire and any minute his parents would descend.

'Did she pay cash? Leave a deposit?' Enough to get Roxy back on her feet?

'I told her she couldn't have it.'

The sound of crystal flutes tinkling and occasional bursts of laughter seemed to suddenly grow louder. He pulled up so sharply, he jerked her arm. Had he heard right?

'You told her *what*?'

'I said no.'

Somehow he stifled a curse. If Roxy had driven him crazy before, this took the proverbial. She was being sentimental and she couldn't afford that luxury.

'I know you feel attached to that dress,' he said in a remarkably calm tone, 'but can't you put that aside to have a shot at something bigger?'

She laid a hand on his jacket sleeve. 'Can we talk about this later?'

He wanted to say no, he wanted to talk about it now. But she'd had a bad knock, and who was he to say what she ought to do from this point on? He was only the guy who couldn't stop thinking about her. Who'd kissed her, made love to her and wanted to again very much. When she'd phoned, he'd fought the urge not to jump in his car and speed over to see her straight away, but she'd been so distant since receiving news about that break-in. Although he wanted to support her, the bigger issue was not to crowd her. If she'd wanted to see him earlier, she'd have said.

So he'd shown some restraint, even containing himself when her lips had brushed his cheek in greeting tonight. All he asked was to know what she'd decided with regard to that gown, her salon. Whether she was ploughing on or shooting off in another direction.

Like, maybe to California with Marla.

Whatever she decided, he had no control. She wouldn't take a handout, wouldn't take him up on that offer to help get that dress back in its contest. He'd half thought about devising some plan to somehow work his way around one or the other of those options. But she didn't like him being creative where finding solutions was concerned. He'd simply have to put his faith in her choices. It wasn't as if they were a couple. Not a *real* one. Although tonight, he certainly felt proud having her walk alongside him.

In fact, he ought to simply enjoy the evening. Forget about the future. Have some fun as they had out west.

When Roxy changed the subject and said, 'Tell me more about these anniversary nights,' he put aside those other thoughts and concentrated on this evening.

'As you know, my parents' wedding anniversary has always been a big deal,' he said as they moved closer to the marquee, the borders of which were lit by flaming torches. Along the back stone wall, small groups gazed out over a harbour view, which included an illuminated coat-hanger bridge and iconic Opera House shells.

'Even when we were living on a shoestring,' he said, 'at anniversary time my parents managed to find money for a cake and gifts for each of us kids.'

'For the *children*?'

'All five of us.'

Her expression melted. 'That is *such* a beautiful thought.'

He spotted a middle-age pair trundling towards them and shored himself up. 'Here's the happy couple now.'

'Nate!'

His mother sailed up, looking like a diva in a stylish black satin trouser suit. She clenched his face between her bejewelled hands and brought him down to plant a rouged kiss smack on his lips. His father, as usual, was a step behind, looking debonair in a tux with a shimmering gold tie—clearly his mother's touch.

His mother gave her son a 'who's a naughty boy?' look. 'You should introduce us to this gorgeous woman, Nate, dear.'

'Roxanne Trammel, this is my mother, Judith, my father, Lewis.'

True to form, his mother brought Roxy close and gave her one of her famous python hugs.

Looking pleased too, behind his groomed silver beard,

his father smiled his eternally patient smile. 'Great to see you here, Roxanne. I'm glad he finally brought you home to meet us.'

Roxy was still recovering from the hug. 'It's lovely to meet you both too.'

Yes, his parents were sweet and wonderful—cloyingly so. At some point Roxy was bound to hear what a great catch he'd make and how eligible he was. As if he couldn't pick his own wife.

Which wasn't the reason behind bringing Roxy here tonight at all.

Hands laced before him, his father said, 'I believe you design wedding gowns.'

'Do you design other formal gowns?' his mother asked, taking in Roxy's dress. 'The one you're wearing is exquisite. It is your creation?'

'Thank you,' Roxy said. 'Yes, it is.'

'You should get your label on some catwalks,' his mother said.

'Unfortunately,' Roxy said, 'it's not as easy as all that.'

'Well, I'm going to pop down to your shop next week,' his mother went on, 'if you have something that will suit a woman my age, that is.'

'A person your age.' His father chortled. 'You're a classic beauty. Women twenty years younger don't compare.'

His mother cupped her husband's cheek. 'And people wonder why I married him.'

Nate noticed that Roxy didn't endorse his mother's suggestion to drop by the shop. Nor did she reject it, giving no clue as to whether she intended to carry on with The Perfect Dress or walk away.

'Do have some champagne and stay as long as you want,' his mother said a moment before her focus was diverted and she headed off. 'Oh, there's the Davidsons.'

'Have fun, kids.' His father winked and, following his wife, dissolved into the growing crowd of glittering guests.

A brow arched, Nate scratched his temple. 'So, what do you think?'

'I think you're very lucky. And they're lucky to have one another.'

Nate absorbed her sober tone, the sincerity sparkling in her eyes, and for the first time in his life he didn't wise-crack about his parents being joined at the hip or inwardly wish they weren't so damn saccharine and inseparable. Rather he recognized a shift at his deepest level. No one's childhood was perfect but if he had to do it over, he'd choose the same parents. The same memories.

Just as he wouldn't swap any of the memories he'd created with Roxy.

As he found them both a glass of champagne and she glanced around, her hips moving slightly to the music, the tightness in Nate's chest eased. The big introduction had gone well—neither parent had asked when the wedding would be, jokingly or not—and Roxy seemed to be enjoying the atmosphere. Was it that amazing dress or had she grown that much more beautiful these past days? She'd always been attractive in a unique way, but tonight her lips seemed fuller, her hair was shinier. Her subtle powdery scent was nothing short of drugging.

He raised his glass and made a toast.

'To the most beautiful woman here tonight. I second my mother's words. That dress is stunning.' Over the crystal rim, he murmured, 'You're stunning.'

An expression filtered over her face. A combination of pleasant surprise, appreciation…and something else. Something that made him half wish he were ready for 'serious'.

His attention skated to the dance floor and he made an executive decision. 'Let's dance.'

Swallowing a mouthful of champagne hard, she lowered her flute. 'Already?' Her gaze shot to the dance floor and the three couples gyrating to a seventies tune. 'Let's wait till more people are up.'

He removed the glass from her hand, set both on a passing waiter's tray and took her hand. 'I want to dance with you, Roxy.' Coming close, he nuzzled against her ear and a breath of heat blew through his blood. 'Aren't you curious to see how well we move together, swirling around without the water?'

She darted around a culpable look. 'You'll make me blush.'

He laughed. 'I hope so.'

Without giving her a chance to object again, he ushered her through waves of people to the floor, which was set outside beneath a blanket of twinkling stars. As they moved onto the temporary decking the song finished, the previously dancing couples wandered off and a slower, more intimate tune began to play.

Looking around, she nibbled her lower lip. 'Can't we do this later?'

'Like we'll talk more about that dress later?'

Words hovered on the tip of her tongue, but she wasn't ready to broach that subject yet. So she allowed him to curve a palm around her back and let him fold her right hand in his left. At the same time they began to move the main lights faded and a laser show, resembling softly falling confetti, filtered over the scene. Looking so masterful and handsome, Nate brought her deliciously near and soon the crowd seemed to fade as well.

With his gaze glued to hers, Roxy had to concentrate

not to reach up and brush her lips against the sexy half-grin lifting one corner of his mouth. By the time he twined their arms more and hers rested against his lapel, her feet weren't touching the ground.

Wondering if her smile reflected just how dreamy she felt, Roxy admitted, 'This feels good.'

His lips twitched. '*Very* good.' Indulging his natural skill, he danced her around in a tight circle. 'We should do this more often.'

Then something infinitesimal changed in his expression. A slight darkening of his eyes, the faint tightening of his jaw. But then that sexy grin returned and he urged her flush against him while the music wrapped around them and a sea of stars shone down.

With her cheek resting contentedly against his lapel, she was on another plane when the song ended and applause went up. Remembering where she was, Roxy blinked open her eyes and glanced around. An ocean of faces was beaming at them while couples whispered among themselves, Roxy guessed, about how perfect a couple they made. And for a long giddy moment, she had the strangest feeling—a flash—as if this were a rehearsal to a bigger event.

Nate's rumbling voice was at her ear. 'Is something wrong?'

'All those people looking on…' She gathered herself and sent a thin smile. 'For a moment I'd forgotten where we were.'

His frown eased before he brushed away a wave of hair floating against her cheek.

'At least everyone got a good look at your evening dress. You'll get enquiries.'

He was being genuine, but he was also digging for answers. He wanted to know if she intended to continue with the salon. But that would depend on what transpired tonight.

Five minutes later, a woman breezed up to them. Her dress was slimline, high-necked, covered in red sequins. Nate introduced them.

'Janelle, this is Roxy Trammel. Roxy, one of my younger sisters.'

'Roxy, I'm in love with that gown. Everyone's talking about it.' Janelle skated a look Nate's way, then stage-whispered, 'About the two of you too, actually.'

But Nate didn't appear to be listening. He was checking his cell's caller ID. He caught Roxy's gaze. 'Mind if I get this?'

She could tell by his expression it was important. 'Not at all. Go ahead.'

While Nate strode off to find a quiet corner, Janelle spoke to Roxy.

'A friend of mine expects to have the question popped any day now. Would you mind if I passed your name along?'

'Under normal circumstances, I'd love you to. Unfortunately, my salon was burgled recently.'

Janelle gasped. 'Much damage?'

'Quite a bit.'

'When do you think you'll be up and running again?'

'Can't say for sure. I should know more soon.'

'If there's anything I can do to help...' Her shoulders dropped. 'But of course, Nate would've already offered.'

Yes, he *had* offered, Roxy thought. But when push came to shove, would he come through?

Nate's other sisters gravitated over, one of them an effervescent brunette by the name of Naomi. They all five chatted as half a dozen songs played in and out. Each sister made her feel welcome and said she must come to another, less formal family get-together. Roxy longed to say she couldn't wait—she could easily see herself being friends with these women, particularly Janelle, who reminded her of a possum with her large chocolate-brown eyes—but she couldn't be presumptuous.

Only after she'd spotted Nate walking over did Roxy realize how much time had passed. The aroma of a delicious smorgasbord banquet being served inside the marquee teased her nostrils. It seemed dinner was served.

One sister—Ivy—announced they should find their respective partners and grab something to eat. The sisters snatched kisses and hugs from Nate as he moved closer. But on seeing his expression beneath the shadow and glow of party lights, Roxy felt a shiver pass through her. His smile was hollow. His gaze, preoccupied. When he finally joined her again, she felt unease ripple off him.

Rather than start a conversation, ask what she thought of his siblings, Nate swiped two drinks from a tray, passed one to her and skulled three parts of his down. His jaw was clenched, and a muscle beat rapidly and irregularly high in his cheek. What had happened? His face was so dark, she didn't want to ask.

'Guess the phone call wasn't good news.'

He exhaled, then knocked back the remainder of his drink. 'It's Saturday morning in Texas and Mr Nichols is clearing his desk.'

That shiver passed through her again. 'Clearing his desk?'

'His advisors have looked over my proposal, the figures. They're not convinced the investment's viable.'

Roxy didn't know what to say. He'd handled Greg pulling out, but now this? If she felt devastated by this news, how must he feel?

She touched his jacket sleeve. 'Are you okay?' He

blinked, looked down and then directly at her. Earlier he'd looked invigorated. Now suddenly he looked ten years older. 'We can leave, if you want.'

'I'm fine.' Then he raised his chin, rolled back his shoulders. 'I can get another investor.' His eyes narrowed on some imaginary distant spot. 'It's just a matter of pushing forward. Holding on.'

'I wish I could help.'

That seemed to bring him back. His gaze snapped onto hers, then he smiled. 'Like I want to help you with your situation.' He angled more towards her. 'You said we should talk later about your business, that dress. Guess it's later.'

'I don't know this is the right time.'

'Believe me. It's the right time.'

She took in the determined slant of his brows, the glint in his eye and tried not to think about the knot twisting in her stomach.

'There's no easy way to say this, so I'm just going to say it.' She took his hand. 'Nate, will you marry me?'

Nate heard the question. He let the words, the concept, sink in. For an instant he thought she was serious. That she was asking for his hand in marriage, and his heart skipped several beats before thumping back to life.

Then he remembered the dress. That contest that meant so much.

He eased out a breath and laid a palm on his heart. 'This is so sudden.'

Her lovely mouth twitched with a smile.

'That woman who came into the salon looking for a bargain, the one getting married on the thirty-first…I was on the verge of stripping the dress off that mannequin, wrapping it in tissue paper and exchanging it for nothing more than an invitation. After confronting the mess of that break and enter, not knowing whether I'd be able to stay open even another week, I felt I had no choice. At least this way, I had some kind of chance.'

'A *good* chance,' he reminded her, before taking her arm and leading her to a relatively quiet spot around the corner from the marquee and away from the constant thump of music. Climbing the step of an ornate white gazebo, laced with his mother's favourite scarlet-blooming vine, he indicated she sit and finish her story.

'You thought you had to take the risk,' he said as he lowered beside her. 'What changed your mind?'

'After that woman tried the gown on and we both agreed how well it suited, she asked if I could do a quick set of alterations. She wanted the bodice cut lower and the skirt made detachable so the dress could turn into a mini for the party afterwards. I told her the truth. The gown was a finalist in an international contest. If it were to remain in the competition, the gown couldn't be altered to that extent. She could have it free of charge, as long as she was married on the thirty-first and the gown was kept in its original state.'

From the far end of the estate, a stream of colourful lights whistled high into air. Next moment a blast of fireworks covered the previously dark sky. Another and another ignited, turning night into carnival day. Talking over the noise was impossible, so they sat tight and watched until the last celebratory star fell and distant applause and cheers rose up.

Roxy said, 'They'll wonder where we got to.'

'Don't worry about the party. What happened next?'

'The woman explained that her fiancé was in construction and he'd had this great idea. They should say their vows sitting in a bulldozer scoop and travel to the reception the same way.'

Nate's chin tucked in. 'Is that legal?'

'I wasn't thinking about the law. I was horrified for my dress. My jaw must have dropped so she hurried to explain that she'd insisted he have the scoop "cleaned good", that her dress wouldn't get caught on any spiky bits and that his pit bulls could forget about attending the after party. Apparently they go off on heavy metal music. Then she asked if she could light up in the shop. Of course she insisted she wasn't going to smoke in her wedding dress. At least not until after the ceremony.'

When Roxy shut her eyes and withered in the seat, he wrapped one arm around her shoulder and tugged her close. 'Not the sort of photos you want to remember that gown by.' Or to appear in an international magazine.

'I don't care about someone's personal habits or what kind of ceremony they chose. I've seen them all. But I couldn't shake the image of my beautiful gown mutilated by home alterations, grubbied by residual soil fill, mauled by a pack of hyper dogs and littered with crusted burn holes. I thought I could, but I just couldn't.'

Her shoulders felt cool so he tucked her in more against his chest until her cheek lay against his lapel and his fingers were stroking her perfumed nape. 'Which leads us,' he said, 'to this.'

'I reread the rules. I even spoke to an official. There's nothing that says a designer can't wear her own creation in a marriage ceremony as long as it happens by the thirty-first.'

Nate waited for the sweat to break on his brow, anxiety to wreath in his stomach. But he only felt a sense of relief. Both their professional enterprises had suffered a setback. Still he was far from finished, and it seemed Roxy wouldn't give up without a fight either. She was his kind of woman.

'Then it's settled,' he said as she straightened and his focus fell to her mouth, to the lips he'd missed so much. 'We'll be married.'

'What will your parents say?'

'Are you kidding? They'll be ecstatic.'

'Even when it's a scam?'

Grinning, he angled his head closer to hers. '*Scam* is a harsh word.'

'I didn't want to say con.'

'Let's go with temporary merger.' His lips brushed hers and a shower of pleasure that reminded him of the joy and colour of those fireworks shot through his veins. 'Or, maybe, a short-term fusion.'

When his mouth lingered lightly on hers, he felt her dissolve against him. She sighed. 'If you're sure.'

'I have one suggestion. We need a rehearsal.'

'Of our vows?'

'Of the kiss.'

CHAPTER THIRTEEN

AFTER that dynamite kiss, which lasted way into dessert, he and Roxy straightened themselves up, said their goodbyes to the clan and drove to her place, where Nate was invited to stay for the night. He stripped her of her evening gown, got rid of his tux, and that was before they made it to the bedroom. They made love and their coming together this time was different, more honest—at least it was for him.

As dawn spread its fingers up and beyond the horizon he decided he should at last let her sleep. If they were getting married in a week, arrangements would need to be made. Heck, he'd have to see her practically every night.

So he kissed her a final time, a long slow caress neither wanted to end, then he slipped away and drove home with the warm light of the sun rising behind him.

He grabbed a few hours' sleep, showered, then dabbled with the idea of speed-dialling her. Maybe she'd enjoy brunch somewhere nice by the water where they could discuss the arrangements for the coming event. He guessed she'd want to keep it low-key. Small.

As Nate poured a strong black coffee from the pot he scolded himself. Of course it should be discreet.

Still, his parents would be crushed if they weren't invited. His sisters and their partners too. In their minds, this might be the only time they'd get to see him say the words *I do*. He'd need to explain how the situation had come about, that he liked Roxy a great deal. Hell, he *respected* her. But neither of them was desperate for that larger commitment. He'd need to explain that the wedding was purely to help Roxy and her chance with that contest.

And organizing this wedding—whatever a groom was supposed to do—meant he wouldn't have so much time to dwell on Nichols and the fact he needed to find another investor if his plans for Sparks Steel were to go ahead. Lowering into a balcony chair, he sipped the tasty bitter brew—not nearly as good as Mrs Glenrowan's billy tea— and thought he really ought to do some work.

Thirty minutes later, he was still gazing at water taxies whizzing across the blue expanse of the harbour and think- ing about Roxy, when the intercom buzzed. An instant of curiosity turned into hope. Maybe she'd decided to come visit. Then again, he'd never given her his address...

He was surprised when Greg's voice boomed through the speaker. 'Can I come up?'

'You and Marla haven't had another barney?'

'This visit's business.'

As he thumbed the button to allow his friend into the building Nate couldn't help but be optimistic. He'd always thought that once Greg's personal life was in order, his friend's professional happiness would follow. Greg had always felt under-appreciated in his father's firm. Perhaps after further consideration, Greg had decided he wanted back in Sparks Steel after all. Hell, he was welcome any time! As his own father had always said, a heavy load was made so much lighter when two people shared the weight.

When he let his friend in, however, Greg looked as if he'd been trying to cope with way too much.

'You look like crap.'

'I received an email, Nate. From the patent office. It

was stuck in my spam folder. They won't patent our best design.'

Nate waited for the punchline. For Greg to crack up and say he was joking. That he had, in fact, received news that everything had gone through smoothly, as expected, as they'd envisioned it would. But Greg's expression remained stern. And worse—filled with sympathy.

He handed over a printout of the email and Nate scanned the lines, his head growing lighter by the second.

Their steel roof, which incorporated its own unique approach to addressing insulation problems in Australia's harsh climate, had been dismissed on grounds that a similar idea was already in the pipeline.

Son of a bitch.

He'd thought he'd be in his own business within three months, but this, along with Nichols's pass...

'I know you had your hopes pinned on this design,' Greg was saying. 'Mate, I'm sorry.'

Nate wanted to screw the paper up and throw the useless wad—as well as a pile of furniture—against the nearest wall. He felt as if a sledgehammer had belted him in the gut then the head. The cave had fallen in on him. Where to from here?

Greg was still talking.

'I'm glad you have Roxy. Marla and I are so happy you two finally hit it off. When you have someone else to care about, the other stuff doesn't seem half as important. And I want you to know that we're always after great staff at PrimeSteel. If you want to make the move, consider it done. Just until you get this other thing off the ground, of course.'

Nate lifted burning eyes from the floor to meet Greg's commiserating gaze. And for one crazy instant, he wondered if he ought to take up Greg's offer. Maybe he'd be better off bowing to fate, marrying for real the woman who was so obviously right for him, and taking a secure position that would provide a pension and specified vacation time each year.

Greg's arm was twitching by his side. He raised a hand to lie on Nate's shoulder. Instead he rotated away. Greg knew him well. He couldn't abide an overload of pity.

'If you want to go for a beer later,' Greg said, 'give me a call.' He stepped out of the door. 'It'll all turn out in the end, Nate. The way it's meant to. You taught me that.'

As the door clicked shut Nate understood Greg was trying to help. Give him a subtle pep talk about treading water until the lifeboat arrived. But the waves licking his chin were rising and a school of sharks had begun to circle. He hadn't bothered looking into securing another investor. All he'd thought about today was Roxy and their sham wedding. With this latest setback how easy would it be to do as Greg suggested? Meld more with Roxy, opt for a less demanding career path, and surrender to the wider scheme of things. In other words, give up.

He'd rather slit his own throat.

Roxy received the call while flipping through an online catalogue for shoes.

The wedding planned for one week from today was only a means to an end—to see that her gown had its chance in that contest. Roxy was thinking 'garden wedding'. No need to try to book a church, which would be impossible at this late date, in any case. There were a number of celebrants she could contact to see if they were free, didn't matter what time of day. Six a.m. or ten at night, as long as the date requisite was met.

A bunch of wild flowers would make up her bouquet. She'd ask Marla to be her witness. She suspected Nate would ask Greg.

Appropriate lingerie wasn't a problem. What she did need was shoes, something Cinderella would swoon over.

Sitting with her laptop on her living-room couch, she dragged her attention away from a pair of satin pump wedges, with sparkling beads running from the top of the back seam all the way down the heel, to examine the ID on her cell's screen. Her tummy did a back-flip then she went warm all over. She'd hoped Nate would call today. Truth was after the glorious night they'd spent together, she missed him. *Lots.*

And as she thumbed the answer key a thought struck. They would need to get rings. Would he want matching gold bands? Of course there was no need for an engagement ring. Not unless he insisted.

'Are you busy?' he asked and her heart beat faster at the sound of his sexy deep voice.

'Actually, I'm working up a sweat choosing shoes.'

'Shoes?'

'For the wedding. If there's ever an occasion a woman needs a new pair of shoes, her own wedding must be it.'

She laughed, a light breezy sound. But her smile faded when only silence greeted her on the other end of the line. A slither of unease snaked up her spine.

'Nate? You there?'

'Roxy, I can't make it Saturday.'

She tried to decipher the statement. 'You'd rather we did it Friday?'

'What I mean is we need to find someone else to stand in. I'll be truthful. I can't do it. I know it won't be a real wedding, but I can't help thinking that if I watch you walk down any aisle in that dress and I say I do, that'll be it.'

'It?'

'My most important patent didn't go through. Greg kindly let me know I could work for him at his father's firm. Nice offer. I only have to put my tail between my legs and forget everything I've struggled to achieve thus far.'

Her lips felt like two loose rubber bands. She could barely get them to move. 'And going through with this ceremony—the one you suggested in the first place—would seal your fate?'

'I have someone else lined up. A great bloke I work with.'

She felt like crying. Dying. She couldn't believe he was doing this. She'd thought he'd changed. But he'd manipulated her again. Straight-out lied.

She ground out, 'How much did you pay him?'

'Don't worry about that. I just want to make sure this is all taken care of.'

Taken care of. Swept aside. Dismissed.

Last night she'd given herself to him as she never had before. Not only bodily, but with all her heart. All her soul. At one stage, as they'd lain among the moonbeams filtering in through her bedroom window, he'd kissed a loving line down one side of her neck, her shoulder, right down that arm finishing with the tip of each finger. She'd been overcome by the swell of emotion—a powerful awareness she couldn't deny. In real time they hadn't known each other long, but in a way that mattered more she'd known him all her life.

He made her feel happy. Whole. He made her feel *love* like she hadn't believed in. As his lips had grazed hers very early this morning and he'd gently closed the door she'd felt certain about them. She might as well admit it.

She'd fallen in love. And a tiny hopeful part of her had whispered that he might just have fallen in love with her too.

Again and again she'd told herself this wedding wasn't the real deal and yet, the way he'd spoken and behaved last night, she'd thought deep down that maybe Nate wanted it to be. And now he was telling her she needed a replacement?

She wanted to argue. Slap his face. Of course she knew this make-believe marriage was only a means to an end, a way to keep her gown in that contest and her hopes to keep her salon alive. But as the silence stretched and she felt Nate's determination—his fear—the need to object, defend, persuade, disappeared.

Hadn't she told herself one day she'd pay a price? She'd fallen for a man who had vowed never to fall under a woman's spell. No, she wouldn't argue with him. Even feeling as if her insides were being torn out, she wished him well.

As long as he never dared try to see her again. If he did, she swore she'd tear him apart.

But she didn't want to say goodbye looking vulnerable or needy. Because she wasn't. In fact, this episode had made her a thousand times stronger.

'Actually I've had second thoughts too,' she told him, her tone as sincere as she could manage. 'I know rules are rules but when all the other contestants' gowns will be part of a genuine ceremony, where a couple who are committed beyond all else pledge to be there for ever for one another no matter what, I'd feel like a cheat.' And the slam-dunk. 'Guess dishonesty really isn't my deal.'

Another long silence. But she wasn't about to play that game either, batting the ball back and forth, telling herself if she could keep it in the air long enough she just might win.

As a jet of emotion threatened to erupt her grip tightened on the phone and she forced out the words.

'Goodbye, Nate.'

'Roxy, wait. Maybe we should have a drink. Talk about alternatives.'

'I'd rather not.'

'I was only trying to be honest with you.'

She set her jaw, took a breath, cursed her feelings. And cut the line.

Because of lightborn thoughts I've taken infecting international scripture and an other way to
I'd rather stay
I mustn't say it, that to be here with you
She didn't say to be a mask I cursed her tongue
I'd say he knew

CHAPTER FOURTEEN

'I DON'T know why you don't get rid of this clapped-out bucket of rust.'

Standing in his parents' four-car garage, Nate leaned against a pristine workbench and told himself to count to ten. He loved his dad, but, Lord above, the man infuriated him. With the money they'd inherited, he could afford a Porsche and, to be fair, his parents did drive a very nice locally made sedan. But his father insisted on keeping this relic from the past. A bomb. He never drove it, just tinkered as he did now, hunched over the engine, checking and pulling at bits. A waste of time.

Lewis Sparks raised his head from under the hood. 'Rust bucket? This body's as perfect as the day it came off the line. Besides, it was my first car. We've had some good times together.'

Nate wanted to block his ears. 'I've heard the story about the night Grandad caught you necking and banned Mum from seeing you again.'

Through that neat silver beard, his father's grin appeared. 'She sneaked out late at night. We dabbled with the idea of eloping.'

'I don't want to hold you up. I just need that number.' He'd already explained ten minutes ago when he'd first arrived. He wanted the number of the patent lawyer his father occasionally enjoyed eighteen holes with.

'You're having trouble with your idea?'

'I'd rather not go into it.'

His father found a rag, wiped his hands thoroughly, then changed the subject. 'Your mother and I liked your date the other night.'

Pushing off the dusty workbench, Nate held up his hands. 'Before you ask when you'll see her again, she and I have called it quits.'

'Oh.' His father nodded slowly. 'I see. Your mother and I—'

'Dad. Sorry. I really don't have time.'

'Sure. Fine.' His father stuck his head back down near the bomb's engine. 'I'll get Roger's number after I check this battery.'

'I thought you put a new battery in last month.'

'One of the cells was flaky. One flaky cell and the whole caboose is let down. It's not pretty like a flash paint-job or a shiny set of rims, but a good battery's what keeps a car going strong.'

He fiddled with cables, then straightened and rubbed smudged grease off his hands on that rag again; Nate recognized it as a shirt from twenty years ago.

'Mind turning her over, son?'

Grabbing the time on his watch, Nate suppressed a growl. He'd wanted to dash in and out. He'd have got the number over the phone if someone had answered when he'd called. Apparently his mother was out visiting one of the girls. His dad, as usual, had been tucked away in this sanctuary where he kept his toys—this beat-up old Holden and a tin boat he'd had since his youth.

Nate threw open the driver's side door. He would start the car, then they could go inside, get that number and he'd see what could be done about getting another hearing for his patent. He'd already poured a river of money into fees. This was not a little matter.

Dammit, he would *not* roll over now.

Pressed into the smelly vinyl seat, he rotated the key and the V8 roared to life. His father lowered the hood, which snapped into its catch with a crashing boom.

'I'd rather have a dozen of these than one European sports car with a dodgy engine.'

'I have a European sports car, Dad, and the engine runs just fine.'

His father thought that over and tossed the rag aside.

'Guess I'm just easy to please.' The older man's attention shifted, as did Nate's. They both peered out as a car drove up. His mother's. But another car followed and another.

'Hey, your sisters and kids are pulling up too. I'd better warm up the barbie.' His dad started out and hooked an arm. 'Come say hello.'

Nate was about to say again he was rushed. But his father looked so happy to have the family together... Nate mustered a smile and said he'd be out in a minute.

Nate watched as everybody hugged. Didn't matter if they'd seen each other three months ago or yesterday. No one escaped a python squeeze from Mum. Dad must have mentioned his eldest was in the garage. All the women looked his way and various gestures and pleadings called him out. But Nate shook his head, his hands. He wasn't ready yet.

So he sat in that smelly old car watching his family meander up the path, into the house, and as they disappeared through the back door Nate found himself wondering...

Why am I so different?

They always seemed so content. So easily pleased. But he was enquiring. Restless. A weak link.

The flaky cell.

He'd told Roxy he was nothing like her father and yet he'd ignored her feelings, lied to her, let her down.

For as long as Nate could remember, he'd been drawn by the notion of finding his own way, and yet, sitting out here all alone, he'd never felt so lost.

CHAPTER FIFTEEN

'I was told I'd find you here.'

Every fibre in Roxy's body locked and then trembled as that deep sexy voice rumbled down at her.

The day was grey and cold, but she'd needed to get outside and hopefully be productive while she was at it. Rugged up in a red trench coat, she'd found a place in a nearby park to spread out a light blanket and play around with a few sketches for some new dress ideas.

Now she set her pencil aside and, swallowing a calming breath, forced herself to peer up.

Standing with his hands thrust deep into their overcoat pockets, Nate Sparks towered over her. A lock of dark hair fallen on his forehead bobbed with the breeze. His gaze was piercing, holding hers with an intensity that made her quiver. In that moment, it all came rushing back…the way they'd splashed around and made love in that creek. How they'd happily gone without sleep to spend every available minute pleasuring one another in that big soft bed in the bush.

Now, when he moved closer, she instinctively felt her heart lift and reach out to him. But she didn't jump up and into his arms, although, God help her, she wanted to.

'There's a lot happening at your shop today.'

She kept her voice even, her reply short. 'It was time for a big sale.'

His brow pinched. 'How much are you getting rid of?'

'As much as people want to buy.'

'Your cousin seemed to be holding down the fort well enough.'

'I have complete faith.'

Clearly she needed to resize, regroup and, hopefully, start building again. But she didn't have the heart to be there, watching the gowns she'd spent so much time and loving effort on sailing out of the door for a song.

He nudged his chin at the sketchpad. 'What are you doing?'

'Getting inspired.'

'For new gowns.'

'A new life.'

Digesting her words, he nodded slowly, then thought for a long moment before speaking again.

'I want to apologize.'

Her heart jumped but she kept her mask cool. 'Whatever for?'

'I let you down.'

'Yeah. Well.' She shrugged. 'Nothing I haven't coped with before.'

'I'm not like your father.'

'You're certainly not like yours,' she bit back. 'You don't know the meaning of the word *integrity*.'

She was glad he'd called that day and put an end to it all.

'I know I hurt you,' he said. 'I hurt myself too.'

'Let me dig out a tissue.'

'There's still time for that wedding…if you haven't found a replacement.'

Collecting her pencil again, she sketched a few lines.

'I'm over the contest. I did my best. Time to move on.'
Speaking of which...

Grabbing her bag, pad under one arm, she pushed to
her feet and, fighting a cold wind, headed for the car park.

His voice boomed over her head. 'I'm not ready for
this to end.'

Anger and hurt clogging her throat, blurring her vision,
she called back, 'Too bad.'

The determination in his voice hit her again.

'Dammit, Roxy, I love you.'

Her blood stopped pumping as every kind of emotion
funnelled through her centre and then jetted up to fill her
face with scorching heat. Her head was swimming, her
world tilting. He *loved* her. She hadn't expected that. Not
for one moment.

Needing something to hold onto, she angled carefully
around. She swallowed but her words still came out a
hoarse whisper.

'I mustn't have heard right.'

'I'll say it again. *I love you*, in a way I never thought
possible—' he gave a weak lopsided smile '—even with
parents like mine.'

She wanted to ask if he was teasing her. After his
previous stand, whether he truly meant it. But then she
remembered her father declaring his love and her mother's replies... 'Do you, Tom? Do you *really*?' ...and the
merry-go-round would start turning again. Even as a girl
with no experience, Roxy had thought her mother a fool.
She'd vowed never to sound that desperate. Be that gullible.

His brows knitting, Nate stepped closer. 'You don't believe me.'

Her voice, and heart, broke. 'Doesn't matter if I believe
you or not. Nothing in this world could convince me to

get tangled up with you again. So, please—*please*—just leave me alone.'

When she turned again, telling herself to keep walking no matter what, he overtook her and blocked her path. She wasn't about to rant and try to push her way around him. Instead she stood calmly, pinning him with her best death glare even while her very soul begged her to crumple and surrender.

He drew something out of his overcoat pocket. Roxy glanced down. Between his fingers, he held a fine silk thread.

'Could you hold this?'

As his strong tanned hand came forward, her mouth tightened. 'I won't play your games—'

'Roxy, just do this one thing.'

With those gorgeous blue eyes glittering over at her, Roxy remained firm for another five full seconds. Then she huffed out a breath, rearranged her sketchpad and held the damn thread.

From his other pocket Nate retrieved something else. A heartbeat later a shining ring slid down the line and into the palm of her hand. Her eyes wide, she swallowed a gasp and automatically brought the surprise near. It was an engagement ring…a solitaire, clear and bright.

She imagined how it might look on her hand. How her gaze might drift to that finger time and again to make sure it was real and as beautiful as she thought. She thought of how her friends would swoon over the diamond, then envisaged the matching gold band that would slip on in front. Nate stepped into the space separating them and his arms went out to bring her near.

But before he could press her close, she remembered how gutted she'd felt when he'd dumped her cold, and how many apologies she'd heard in her life. A marriage proposal wasn't a cure-all. In fact, given everything he knew about her, it was an insult. Stronger, she dropped the ring back in his pocket and, breaking inside, braced her shoulders and walked away.

She wished he could mend the wound, make her feel differently, but there simply weren't enough words; there was nothing he could do.

Her pace picking up, she saw her sedan appear through her blur of tears at the same time a familiar sound vibrated through the air. She stopped, turned and, sure enough, a horse was nodding its head, pawing the grass. But not just any horse. She was pure white, even the saddle and bridle and reins. But that wasn't all. Walking up to meet it was another horse, black and large, his glossy mane flying in the wind. For a flash of a second Roxy forgot how much her chest was aching. The sight of those beautiful animals brought back so many memories...of her and Nate cantering over Outback planes...of her pony-club days, before she'd become interested in fashion and had only ever wanted her very own horse.

She soaked up the sight for as long as she dared—she didn't want Nate to think she was hanging back waiting for him—but before she had time to hitch up her sketchpad and carry on to the car, something else unusual caught her eye. A well-dressed lady carrying an opened gold-leaf book was walking up to the horses. If this had been any other day, any other time, she'd have stopped to see what happened next.

Of course the first thing to cross her mind was a wedding. A romantic unique ceremony on horseback with that lady, dressed in a pale pink suit, overseeing the exchange of vows. But they were missing the guests and, more particularly, a bride and groom. Perhaps it was a photo shoot or publicity stunt or—

The notion popped in her brain, like a balloon bursting, but as soon as it appeared she shunted the idea aside. She was being ridiculous. That scene had nothing to do with her, with Nate's proposal, or that amazing diamond-and-gold ring.

When a man in a morning suit appeared, collected the horses' reins and began to lead them over, Roxy felt the edge of reality shift and everything but those horses and the memory of Nate's declaration of love faded into the background. But she couldn't believe this was happening. She didn't want to accept that Nate had set this all up. This all might be a coincidence and he'd already left and she was just standing here looking like...

Looking like a fool.

Shoring herself up, she swallowed down ever-rising emotion and prepared to continue on to the car. But a light grip on her arm held her back, and in an instant her entire body turned cold then inexplicably hot. Fighting the giddy spin, she let herself be angled around, then looked up and into Nate's loving eyes.

'The white mare is yours,' he said.

Her voice trembled and tears welled. 'Mine...?'

'To keep. The woman waiting over there—' he tipped his head and Roxy watched the lady nod and smile in greeting '—she'll do the honour of marrying us. I brought your gown with me—it's in my car, if you want to wear it.'

'Nate, no.' She shook her spinning head. 'I haven't said yes.'

His lips twitched. 'You don't think I'd let that stop me.'

He pressed her close and her sketchpad dropped to the ground. 'This is where I'm meant to be, what I'm meant to do. Be with you. Adore and love you every day for the rest of our lives.'

She worked to swallow against the lump growing in

her throat. 'Nate, you wouldn't tease me about something like this. You wouldn't, would you, if this were just some act…if it weren't true?'

Setting his hands on her shoulders, he rested his brow against hers. 'Tell me, Roxy. Say you love me too.'

Tears, built in her eyes, were sitting, ready to spill. She took a shuddering breath, but she couldn't say the words. She wanted to believe so much, and when she thought of his parents, rather than hers, it actually seemed almost possible.

'You've shown me so much, Roxy. Taught me so much. Things I didn't think were important but ends up are the most important of all.' His committed gaze roamed her face. 'I love you. Only and for ever you.'

She felt so weak, helpless and, at the same time, so empowered.

'I want to cherish and protect you,' he went on. 'And I know we'll be happy because I can feel it, Roxy—' he put her hand to his chest '—right here.'

A tear escaped, rolling down her cheek. 'This is what you were most afraid of,' she warned him. Falling in love. 'Aren't you even a little scared?'

'Only in a good way, like when you start a new adventure. One that will last two lifetimes.'

With his eyes glistening into hers and his grip on her upper arm holding her tight, she eased out a breath and gave in to his will. To his faith and their love.

More tears fell, rushing down her face, curling around her chin. She hadn't thought it was possible, but he'd done it. He'd stripped her of her doubt. And she believed, believed with all her heart.

For some there really was a happy ending.

Her mouth wobbling with a smile, she choked out, 'I love you, Nate. You know I do.'

His chest expanded, then he let out a long full breath. 'And I'll never forget it. Never ever take you for granted.'

As her arms threaded around his neck and his head lowered again a collective cheer went up. Roxy's breath caught as she turned her gaze towards the noise. Emerging from behind various trees were Nate's mother and father, his sisters, their husbands and a flock of children. Cindy and Marla were there too, waving, while Greg shook combined victory fists above his head. And there was another person, dressed in chiffon, a gardenia corsage pinned to her bodice. Her throat backed up with her emotion, Roxy croaked out, 'You brought my mother here?'

'All we need now are the bride and groom.'

When, breaking into a bigger, even brighter smile, she nodded, he swept her up in his arms and carried her off to those guests, to their wedding and what was destined to be a blissful new life.

EPILOGUE

LUNGING, Roxy snatched up the hands-free before the phone rang a third time.

Usually at this time of day she turned the volume off rather than down and let whoever it was leave a message. But she was expecting an important call, one she hadn't told a soul about...not even Nate. Thinking of how much their lives might change after this conversation, she felt a little faint. But, God knew, there was no going back.

After she'd answered with, 'Mrs Sparks speaking,' a sophisticated female voice replied.

'I'm glad we're finally able to talk. You're a hard woman to pin down.'

'Well, life's busy, business is booming and...' Roxy paused. She thought she knew who was calling. Now she stopped to ask, 'I'm sorry, who is this?'

'My name is Harper Valance.'

Ms Valance went on to explain that she worked for a well-respected pregnancy and parenting magazine. Her position was managing editor. Butting a shoulder against the nearby jamb, Roxy took it in and gathered her thoughts.

After their wedding day, when she'd worn that special gown, she'd made the contest deadline but had neither won nor come a place. She hadn't been upset. There'd been so much to occupy her mind and her time.

When the required time had passed, she and Nate had signed the appropriate papers, making their marriage legal and binding, and this past year she'd switched from designing bridal wear to having the best time creating her own maternity line. Her shop had been relocated closer to the home she and Nate had purchased together near the harbour, and her affordable outfits were gaining popularity. Clients had suggested opening in other major cities or that she launch an online shop. The Internet certainly made the world a smaller, more convenient place.

Roxy was rapt by the response. She'd begun this new venture with nothing more than a fabulous challenge in mind; she wanted to help mothers-to-be feel and look that much more beautiful. Now, given this phone call, it seemed that word had spread further afield than she'd thought.

Turning, Roxy leaned the other shoulder against the jamb and looked into the adjacent dimly lit room. 'Your magazine wants to do a spread on my line?'

'Actually, we'd like you to consider heading a column for us,' Ms Valance said. 'I've followed your blog "Family Blessings" since your wedding. Congratulations on the new addition, by the way. You and Mr Sparks must be thrilled.'

As her chest warmed and a grateful smile spread across her face Roxy studied the peaceful form bundled up in a cot positioned in the far corner of that quiet darkened room. Her precious baby was sleeping soundly, although Hayley Jane would need to wake soon for her bath and dinner. With Nate's dark hair and startling blue eyes combined with a smile that melted her parents' hearts, their daughter was a delight. Every day was an adventure, filled with emotions so intensely satisfying, Roxy couldn't imagine feeling more content.

Ms Valance was explaining, 'We're interested in your

experiences as a businesswoman, designer, seamstress, wife, mother. Woman. Frankly, I love the energy of your blog posts. Given the healthy number of comments you receive, I'm not alone.'

'That's a wonderful offer, but the truth is I'm rather time poor at the moment.'

'Let me explain.' Ms Valance took an audible breath. 'With your permission, we'd love to use backlist excerpts from "Family Blessings". Of course, we'd also be open to view pieces you might like to create whenever a more, let's say, *exclusive* muse strikes. You have a lot to say and, I'm sure, a lot more to share.'

When Hayley stirred in her cot, Roxy quickly and quietly thanked Ms Valance for the offer. She needed to talk with her husband and would get back to her soon. Setting the phone in its cradle, she had to smile. Once, not long ago, she'd ached for the chance to boost her profile. Make a big career splash!

Now?

Her priorities had changed. *Life* had changed and, in a thousand ways, for the better.

The phone rang again, and this time the caller was the person Roxy had expected. As she ended the call a couple of minutes later the baby stirred again and Nate swept into the room. He stopped to steal a lingering, loving kiss and rub the tip of her nose with his before heading into the nursery.

'I heard the baby squeak,' he said. 'I'll get her.'

Hayley wasn't near fully awake yet, so Roxy held her husband back. His curious look faded into an adoring expression that confirmed every remarkable thing she knew about him and their incredible life together. Reaching on tiptoe, she pressed in close and wound her arms around his neck.

'You're home early.'

'Dalton Majors can look after anything that crops up.'

'The new second-in-charge is working out well, then.'

'Dalton's sharp, decisive.' He cocked his head. 'I didn't think so at the time, but, in hindsight, it was best Greg didn't get on board. This was always far more my project than his.'

She wound herself closer, enjoying her husband's hard heat and divine masculine scent. 'And you didn't need that Mr Nichols or his money either.'

He'd needed to take that leap of faith and do what *Nate Sparks* wanted to do. After that initial hitch, the problem with his patent had been rectified and his company was flourishing, as Roxy had known it would.

As if he'd read her mind, he murmured close to her lips, 'What I need is to make sure you and Hayley are happy, every day, in every way.' He flicked a glance towards the nursery before his palms, hot and steady, slid up her sides. 'I think she'll sleep a while longer.' He leaned in to growl playfully at her ear. 'I could use a lie down too.'

As his mouth slanted over hers Roxy sighed and dissolved.

When they came together—when they made love—the joining was always amazing, and with each passing week, with every passing moment, the love they felt for each other only grew. In her soul Roxy knew this was for ever. Not because of the Sparkses' family 'curse' but because two people could be lucky enough to overcome hurdles from both past and present. Two people could fall and *stay* in love when that unique prize was paramount to them both.

As the kiss slowly broke and Nate's attention turned to savouring the sensitive slope of her neck Roxy fought the sizzle of desire to find the wherewithal to ask, 'Don't you want to know who was on the phone?'

'Mmm...' He found the zip at her back and tugged. 'Later.'

Roxy grinned. He'd want to know now.

'The other day I went to the doctor's to confirm a test I'd taken.'

He stilled. She felt his heart thumping near hers before he pulled back. His expression was anticipation, happiness, disbelief.

'You're pregnant? Again?'

He brought her close, hugged her tight. She knew him well enough to imagine the emotion prickling behind his eyes. Then, as if he'd had a startling thought, he pulled back again.

'Why didn't you tell me sooner?'

She drew down a breath and tried to explain.

'Because something felt...*different.*'

His jaw clenched as he gripped her upper arms. 'Are you all right?'

'I'm great—now that I know the results of the scan and everything's fine.' Her hands cupped his handsome curious face. 'We have *three* babies, Nate. Three little lives growing here, inside of me.'

With an ever-growing look of astonishment, he covered her tummy gently with a big warm palm. She watched his throat work. Saw his chest expand on a deep breath. He blinked, gazing into her eyes, and croaked out a question.

'*Three?*'

Feeling elated, relieved, she laughed. 'That family curse—' *blessing* '—is particularly potent in your case.'

'*Our* case.' Beaming, he gathered her close again. 'This was a group effort. And it'll be a group effort in parenting.'

Her lips twitched. It would *need* to be.

'Maybe we ought to go back to being extra careful about contraception after this delivery,' she said.

'That's up to you. All I know is…' His strong fingers scooped through her hair and held her head firmly so he could look deeply into her brimming eyes. 'God, I love you. I've always loved you.'

He swept her up into his arms and was striding off towards their nearby bedroom when the baby mewed and they both looked back. Hayley was wide awake, kicking and arms out, ready for cuddles.

Carefully, Nate set his wife back on her feet, and as they moved towards their six-month-old daughter he said, 'It's going to be busy around here.'

At the cot, Roxy lifted a giggling Hayley up. 'And noisy.'

Nate screwed up his nose at a suspicious smell. 'And messy.'

Roxy snuggled both of them close. 'Darling, it's going to be heaven.'

Nate's mouth found hers, and as the caress deepened Roxy couldn't help but be struck by an extraordinary, wonderful fact. Every time they kissed, every time he drew her near, the emotion touched a new and beautiful place—a place she hadn't quite known existed until that moment. And each time it happened—every time she was lifted up—the words she now lived by bubbled up in her mind and her heart.

This was the deepest kind of love.
Theirs was the best ever life.

* * * * *

MILLS & BOON®

18 bundles of joy from your favourite authors!

Get 2 books free when you buy the complete collection only at
www.millsandboon.co.uk/greatoffers